CROWS OVER A WHEATFIELD

CROWS OVER A
WHEATFIELD

~

PAULA SHARP

HYPERION

NEW YORK

This book is for Lauren Austin and Diane Lopez,

and once again, for you, E. Sharp.

Portions of the poems, "Leavetaking in New Hampshire," "Versailles, "Lesbos," and "Ver-
klärte Nacht" have been reprinted with permission of Allen P. Grunes. Theodore Roethke's
"Cuttings" has been cited with permission of Doubleday & Company, Inc. James Wright's
"In Fear of Harvests" has been cited with permission of University Press of New England.

Printed in the United States of America. For information address
Hyperion, 114 Fifth Avenue, New York, New York 10011.

DESIGNED BY DOROTHY S. BAKER

Library of Congress Cataloging-in-Publication Data
Sharp, Paula.
Crows over a wheatfield / Paula Sharp.—1st ed.
p.   cm.
ISBN 0-7868-6117-7
1. Abused women—Fiction. 2. Family violence—Fiction.
I. Title.
PS3569.H3435C7   1996
813'.54—dc20   96-11213
CIP

FIRST EDITION

10   9   8   7   6   5   4   3   2   1

ACKNOWLEDGMENTS

I wish to thank Gina Maccoby, for her unwavering encouragement and professionalism; my editor, Rick Kot, for his fine critical sensibility; and Hyperion Publishers, for taking on this book. My father, Rodman Sharp, his wife, Joyce Sharp, and my friends Lauren Austin and Brian Brenneman provided extraordinary friendship and support throughout the period when this book was written. I am thankful to Margaret Diehl for her essential literary advice; to Ross Eatman, Diane Lopez, and Lesley Sharp for reading and criticizing the manuscript; and to Andy Fox and Rosemary Sharp for offering ideas and essential facts. Allen P. Grunes kindly contributed necessary poetry. Jane Miller, Esq., generously consented to review the manuscript and provide advice on Wisconsin law. And one of the devils in this novel paraphrases, with alterations, parts of Michael Taussig's wonderful anthropological works, *The Devil and Commodity Fetishism in South America* (University of North Carolina, 1980) and "The Genesis of Capitalism Amongst South American Peasantry," in *Comparative Studies in Society and History*, Vol. 19 (1977). I am especially indebted to Elizabeth Siskind and Gail Hall, whose considerable experience and skills permitted me the free time necessary to write. Finally, I wish to thank the irreplaceable National Endowment for the Arts for its assistance, and the Writer's Room, where so many essential parts of this work were conceived.

CONTENTS

BOOK ONE

Crows over a Wheatfield

1

BOOK TWO

Muskellunge

55

BOOK THREE

Custody

153

BOOK FOUR

Mirror Universe

277

Much Madness is divinest Sense—
To a discerning Eye—

EMILY DICKINSON

Or is injustice, once suffered, a mirror universe,
with laws of logic and principles of reason the
opposite of civilization's?

E. L. DOCTOROW, *Ragtime*

We are fighting the devil, and the devil is the
law.

MILDRED STECK

BOOK ONE

CROWS OVER A
WHEATFIELD

1

A FEW MONTHS after my mother died, my father brought Ottilie home for the first time. She was twenty-four years old. My father was forty-one. Ottilie was not my father's only surprise: he also brought Matthew, my half-brother. Matthew, like me, was seven. I felt relieved by Ottilie and Matthew's arrival. Shortly before, my father had stood me on a stepladder in front of the stove, telling me that now that my mother had left us, I was "his little woman, Melanie," who would cook and clean for him: I remember feeling baffled as I watched the steam rise from an aluminum pot, spaghetti unfurling in its roiling waters like a mare's tail. Perhaps my mother's death by a long undetected cancer had left my father temporarily addled.

The story of Matt's origins unravelled slowly, in pieces, and never completely. In 1957, the year Ottilie arrived, my father relocated us from Elkhorn, Wisconsin, to the larger town of McCarthy, one hundred miles north, where no one knew any of us. Still, from phrases dropped sparingly by Ottilie, town gossip spooled with skeins of speculation, and the benefit of my own adult hindsight, I am fairly sure that shortly after my parents married, when my mother was pregnant with me, my father initiated an affair with slight, quiet Ottilie, whose pale, luminous beauty must have fascinated him like a candle flame cupped inside the church of his huge hands.

My father had graduated at the top of his class at University of Chicago Law School. Ottilie Crail had not finished eleventh grade. He had become enamored of her when she was sixteen; at seventeen she was pregnant with my half-brother, and forbidden to attend high school. She told us once that she had been a straight A student, and had aspired to attend the local community college and become a teacher. Ostracized by her own family when her pregnancy revealed itself—Ottilie would explain, curtly and elusively, only that the Crails were "churchy"—she had cared for Matt by herself for seven years, utterly dependent on my father for financial assistance. Once, in a rare moment of self-revelation, she told me simply that she and Matt had lived "in plain straightforward poverty" during the time before they joined us. "Your father gave us enough to get by," she said. "But never enough to save. Never enough to run away."

Ottilie seemed, at least then, to accept her family's judgment of her, and to bear no resentment for their decision to cast her out. The Crails lived in Waupaca County, two counties to the north, and were strict Lutherans. For years, when I thought of the word *Lutheran*, I saw Ottilie's muslin coloring, skin translucent as vigil candles, and I pictured the Crails as pale, upright people, living in a serene world where there was no place for men like my father with his chaos of appetites and imprudent choices. I believed Ottilie took solace in the idea of a world like theirs even if it did not include her.

Our father would not allow us to go to church, and so my grasp on religion was vague, pieced together from odds and ends dropped by other children at school. Matt and I knew only that children like us, who were not baptized, would go straight to hell when we died, even if we were good; that if you swore on the Bible and broke the oath, you would choke to death when you next ate bread; that you could sell your soul before you died by signing your name in blood on a document prepared by the devil. For years I had a picture in my head of the devil: he had raven-black hair, a broad beard, and sparkling gray eyes. It was not until I was in my thirties that I realized this vision must have been of my father in the years when my mother still lived. By the time of my mother's death, he was clean-shaven and had fistfuls of curly gray hair.

As far back as I can remember, I feared him. In the days before Ottilie came, my father must have bullied my mother and me; his words to us must have been terrible, because even now, he surfaces in dreams I have about my mother, his face distorted with anger, spewing cruel phrases whose meanings are plain with horror in the nightmare, but nonsensical when recalled after awakening. Awake, I can rarely evoke any memory of a time when he acted in this manner before Ottilie's arrival. What I remember is the atmosphere in our first house in Elkhorn—the suspense and uneasiness and defenselessness that we awoke with and traveled the streets with and lay down with at night.

His ominousness did not arise principally from a threat of physical violence. He was not, primarily, a physically abusive man. Once, he became enraged and threw Ottilie against the kitchen door, knocking her unconscious, but this was only one of two times I ever saw him use such dangerous force against her. (He did not apologize. He never did.) And once, when I was about ten years old, he came at me to strike me as I was setting a table. I cannot recollect what I had done to anger him. But I remember sharply my horror when I raised my hands before my face to defend myself, and his fist came down with such force that the fork I was holding embedded deeply in his forearm. He held up his arm, the fork dangling, and yelled, outraged, "Look what you've done to me!"

With my half-brother, Matt, my father was freer with corporal punishment: once or twice a year he knocked Matt down with a blow to his head; now and then he beat Matt with a belt for offenses I no longer recall; once, he grew so angry, he dragged Matt up the stairs by his hair.

He was a large man, six feet four inches tall, broad-shouldered, wide-handed. He could have killed any one of us easily, if he had chosen to. There was something chronically menacing, threatening, just under the surface, about him. And for all of us, there was never any doubt that he had to have his way, and that he would pursue his way with relentless energy until he got what he wanted, in any situation where we stood in conflict with him.

ONE MONTH after we moved to McCarthy, my father took Ottilie to Chicago, married her, and brought her back home. Our house was mustard-colored and built for the winter, with narrow windows and sloping roofs. It sat on the outskirts of McCarthy, a mile from the nearest other house, and in the eight years we lived there, we never learned the names of our neighbors. Our isolation made me feel that we were a community by itself, governed only by my father's tyranny and beyond the reach of solicitous interference.

The cold of midwestern winters conspired to keep us locked in his world. This is my image of this country's heartland—not the golden oceans of grain charted by John Deere tractors, or the twinkling lights of towns seen from a train window by night. My image of the heartland is a darkening sky descending over impossibly brief winter days, the sun fleeing always, the deeply quilted snowscapes comforting winds so cold they could kill you, driving you indoors to huddle over heating vents in rooms dim and confining.

On the days when my father was home, Matt and I would find any excuse to range outside in subzero weather, while Ottilie worked quietly in the kitchen as my father's voice rose like a spire through the roof and he filled the house with his presence. But we could never stay away for long—numb with cold, our features deadened by wind, we would return, entering through the back door and staying near Ottilie as if she could shield us.

Ottilie was the quietest person I have ever known. She could work without speaking all day in the house, intent on caulking windows, drilling holes for anchors and screws to mount shelves, bleaching the white porcelain plates she washed day after day for years, without ever breaking one, her bleached hands deft and quick. She was small-boned, with translucent eyes the color of strong tea, and pale yellow hair.

Unlike Matt and I, who were dark enough that, in this small town of third-generation Swedes and Poles and Germans, people often thrilled us by suspecting we were foreigners. Matthew looked curiously like me—perhaps we were both throwbacks to an ancestor of my father's who was slight and quick. Matt was taller than me, with more striking features: he had sloe eyes, and long black lashes that seemed almost feminine, and hair the dark brown of wet tree bark. Still, people mistook Matt and me for twins, and often assumed that Ottilie, because of her age and fair coloring, was his stepmother as well as mine.

My father never corrected this misimpression. More remarkably, he would not let Matt call her "Mom" or "Mama" or "Mother"—only "Ottilie." My father claimed, illogically, that he did not want me to feel left out because I was a stepchild, and that he did not want Matt to feel overly special. But we sensed that it was because my father wanted to possess us unsharingly and completely.

When Ottilie first arrived I could not understand why she had agreed to live with my father, but over the course of time I came to believe that her financial dependence on him, her family's abandonment of her, and my father's threats to take Matt from her were the causes. My father reminded her often, in sudden violent non sequiturs during conversations about supper or local news, that if she ever left him, Matt would remain behind—that the courts would prefer a man who stepped forward to care for an illegitimate son to a woman dissolute enough to have had one; that the law would favor keeping half-siblings together over forcing them apart; that no judge would be sympathetic toward a woman who abandoned a husband who did not drink or beat her regularly, or play around ostentatiously, and who was in addition a superlative breadwinner.

The law seemed a terrible monstrosity to me, as far back as I can remember.

In his presence we called her Ottilie or Ottie or Otter, but between ourselves we called her "Mamalie," or "Mama-two," and these were only two words in a private language Matt and I spoke between one another. Alone, we called our father "Mr. Ratleer," and when we were very young, for reasons I no longer recall, "Mr. Three Shoes," and "Buster Brown," and "Honey Bear Number One." His given name was Joel Ratleer.

My father was a respected and influential criminal defense lawyer, much in demand. His work often took him to Chicago, or to small Wisconsin towns where heinous crimes suddenly sprouted after years of peace. Occasionally, during a trial, he would leave us alone for a night or a week, and these were longed-for times of peace and joy for us.

He was powerfully persuasive, and not just to us, his children and captives, but to jurors, also, who ostensibly represented the midwestern community where my father worked. He would take any case, and defended every client with equal passion. He did not believe in absolute right and wrong, but appeared convinced of the sanctity of his vision whatever he argued. Among the clients for whom he secured acquittals were the following: Eldred Fec, who killed his wife when he surprised her with her lover; Loretta Smirke, who forged her husband's signature repeatedly, borrowing against his life insurance, emptying his savings account, and finally selling his family farm without his knowledge; the owner of a vicious dog named, simply, Spot, who had severely injured a child; the president of the Bloodstone cannery, who vandalized the cars of his entire striking workforce during a labor dispute; Shadley Belt, who knifed a scab during a wildcat strike; a man named Harold Paper, who had been arrested for being black and charged with "intending to rob" Heartland Liquors while passing through McCarthy, which had no black residents; and "Walleye," the county's largest dairy farmer and head of the local Order of the Aryan Sons, who, cold sober, mounted a tractor and ran over a Mexican migrant worker in the presence of five witnesses.

Until the famous Lookingbell trial, my father liked to say he had won every case he had ever laid his hands on. I always believed him, but one year when I was visiting Elkhorn during a vacation from law school, I discovered, in the oddest way, that he had lost a case early in his career. While using the women's room in the town bus station, I met the client whom he had failed to defend. We faced each other, applying lipstick in the small mirror over the sinks. When I told her my name, she asked me if I was Joel Ratleer's daughter. Her name was Cecilia Sparks, and she had once been arrested for stealing $1,500 worth of welcome mats from the Woolworth's where she worked as a cashier. She told me without rancor that my father had completely bungled her defense, trying to throw suspicion on the store's manager. She explained that following her incarceration, she had been sent, almost immediately, to the women's ward of the state hospital for the criminally insane. It had taken her three years to steal all the welcome mats. She had used them to carpet her front yard, and had been surprised throughout her trial that my father had never thought to argue that she was not responsible for her actions because she was crazy.

2

MY FATHER'S EXPLOITS as a lawyer often appeared in Chicago,
Milwaukee, and local papers, and in 1964, after Ottilie and Matt had
been with us for seven years, a front-page article ran in the *McCarthy
Courier* regarding the first homicide in half a century to occur within
the county limits:

> Prominent attorney Joel Ratleer has announced that
> he will be taking Mrs. Lookingbell's case on a pro
> bono basis. "I believe," Mr. Ratleer said, "in the right
> of every accused, no matter how wretched or misera-
> ble, to a fair defense. Mrs. Lookingbell's case is a
> professional challenge, and her plight has moved me
> personally, as I'm sure it will many members of the
> public."

Mrs. Lookingbell was a live-in babysitter who had murdered the three
children of a widowed farmer, Frank Czepeski. She had drowned them,
one by one, in the bathtub. My father basked in the notoriety of the case.
It meant that he would be the focus of everyone's attention, the eye at
the center of the hurricane, and of course, it would drum up business
from paying clients. For years afterward, despite the unusual outcome
of the case, every wealthy farmer and town merchant within driving
distance arrested for petty fraud, drunk driving, or domestic violence
would be on backslapping terms with my father.

Mrs. Lookingbell had been released without bail, a fact generally attributed to Joel Ratleer's genius as a lawyer, since murder suspects were virtually never freed on their own recognizance. My father was said to have argued that "Mrs. Lookingbell would never abscond because she was born in McCarthy, has never been more than fifty miles from McCarthy, and has already paid for a cemetery plot in McCarthy. She poses a danger to no one, since the only people she has ever been accused of expressing animosity toward are the Czepeski children, who are now all dead."

Mrs. Lookingbell dropped by our house shortly after her release. I could see there was something not quite right about her, although I did not yet know who she was; she simply identified herself as Joel Ratleer's client. My father never divulged the specific facts of any trial he was working on until it was over. After he had won a case, he would call Matt into his office, reveal the intricacies of the defense's strategies, and quiz Matt for hours on them, as if instructing him on the cabala. My father wanted Matthew to be a lawyer like himself, and often kept him awake late at night when Matt was in grade school, indoctrinating him on fine points of the rules of evidence, and the trial tactics of renowned lawyers such as Clarence Darrow. Joel Ratleer believed his son was a prodigy, and that Matt would grow up to be a famous jurist, perhaps a Supreme Court justice, a credit to the Ratleer name.

Ottilie invited our guest into the living room, and Mrs. Lookingbell followed, carrying her head too high, like a horse in need of a martingale, and tossed her hair self-consciously. She was in her late thirties, and would have been beautiful, if her mannerisms had not been so eccentric. She had long chestnut hair pulled back in a ponytail, was slender with slender ankles, and wore red high heels and a close-fitting white dress too cool for the weather. She waited on our sofa, nervously lighting one cigarette after another, while Matt and I spied on her from the hallway. She took out a poppy red lipstick and applied it extravagantly between puffs. At one point she stared at our ancient mustard wallpaper and said aloud to no one in particular, "Doesn't he give his wife any money for redecoration?" She waited an hour, increasingly jittery with impatience, and left abruptly, telling Ottilie that my father "had better learn to be where he should be." After she left we found a pile of Virginia Slims, half-smoked and rimmed with red lipstick at the tips, as if they had been used for spearing game.

She had dropped by while my father was down south on business unrelated to her case, traveling with a group of lawyers who had entered the limelight defending protesters arrested during freedom rides. He had accompanied two civil rights workers in a van en route to a sit-in, and only minutes after my father exited the vehicle in order to make a phone call, an unidentified assailant had driven by and fire-bombed the van, killing the men inside. Ottilie and Matt and I had gathered around our television the night before when my father suddenly appeared on the national news to passionately decry the terrible event. He looked leonine and outraged and powerful.

Mrs. Lookingbell came to our house again the next day, before my father returned. When Ottilie explained that she did not know what time my father might be back, Mrs. Lookingbell still invited herself in, and perched on the edge of the couch, as if the repetition of her futile visit of the day before would serve to communicate to my father the urgency of her case. Ottilie asked her to stay as long as she wished, and brought her a dish of butter cookies and a pot of dark tea.

Matt and I found the presence of an eccentric adult both entertaining and disturbing. We watched her again from the hallway.

"What are you staring at?" she asked, looking not at both of us, but only at Matt. "If you're so fascinated, why don't you come in here and socialize?"

Matt entered the living room, and sat on the edge of the sofa, across from Mrs. Lookingbell.

"You stay there," she told me. "One of you is enough."

Matt gave me an embarrassed smile.

"How old are you? Fourteen?" she asked, with the tone of an adult who knows children as part of her daily business. We both, in fact, were fourteen. "Where is your father?" Mrs. Lookingbell asked. "He should have been here yesterday."

Matthew explained, in a voice meant to be consoling, that our father had been unable to return home because of the tragic turn of events involving the civil rights workers who had been on the news.

Mrs. Lookingbell listened to Matt unimpressed, lit a cigarette, and stared toward the ceiling. "Oh, yes, I saw him," she said. "It's no surprise he was the one who survived. He looks as if he thinks he could never die." She ignored the tea and butter cookies.

"I guess you want to know why I'm here," she said. "I'm here because I've committed a terrible crime, and I'm told that if your father's my lawyer it won't matter whether I'm guilty or not."

The front door slammed, and my father loomed in the living room doorway, all anger and energy. I wondered when he had arrived: Had he been there from the beginning of the visit, and stood in hiding, eavesdropping?

"I see you've met my son, Matt," he said. "He's brilliant. A genius." He glared at Matt until he withdrew into the living room hallway. My father sat on the couch and took Mrs. Lookingbell's small hand between his two enormous ones. He told her reassuringly, "So you thought I had forgotten about you. Never! All through the last three days, my mind's been half on your case." He shot us both a look, brows furrowed, meant to hurry us out of the hallway and into the kitchen. We retreated from his view.

"I hope," said Mrs. Lookingbell, "that your mind will be *all* on my case from now on."

We listened to my father's low murmurs as he spoke with his client, his voice alternately cajoling and forceful. After fifteen minutes we heard him escort Mrs. Lookingbell to the front door; we heard his laughter as he helped her on with her coat and her responding titter; we heard the door slam.

"Matt! Matthew!" my father called.

We entered the living room together as he sat down on the sofa.

"Come here a minute, Matt," my father ordered. He pulled Matt toward him, affectionately ruffling his hair, and chided, "So, you've been entertaining my clients, have you? Making sure I don't lose business while I'm gone?"

Matt looked at him uncertainly.

"That's very considerate of you, Matt." He ruffled Matt's hair again. "It's nice to have a boy who helps his father out like that."

Now Matt smiled in spite of himself. He said, "She came here twice, and she didn't want to leave."

"So you thought you'd take it on yourself to chat with her a little about her case?" My father tightened his grip on Matt's hair, and we both knew, suddenly, that something was wrong. "Don't ever," my father began, bringing his face up close to Matt's, so that his crooked bottom teeth were only an inch from Matt's chin. "DON'T TALK TO MY CLIENTS!" he shouted. My father had done this before to me, screamed with his mouth agape only inches from my ear; the effect was disorienting and even terrifying. Matt tried to pull away, but was unable to. He reached for the back of his head where my father twisted his hair. "Don't you understand that you've just heard an *admission*? That if you were called into court to testify, you'd have to say Mrs. Looking-bell told you she was guilty?" He released Matt's hair. Matt lost his balance, and fell backward onto the sofa.

"Don't ever talk to one of my clients without my permission, Matt."

Matt uprighted himself, but my father grabbed him by the wrist to detain him a moment longer. "You didn't hear anything she said today, do you understand me?" he asked Matt. "Or maybe I should make you co-counsel, now that you know so much. As my co-counsel, you are not under any circumstances to discuss the Lookingbell case with anyone except me. Is that clear? This case is likely to be in the news for some time, and I expect you to keep your thoughts to yourself during that period."

In fact, the case dragged on for almost nine months. My father created one delay after another while Mrs. Lookingbell went to work at the Bloodstone canning factory and improved her reputation as a gainfully employed, trustworthy woman. During this period my father would call Matt into his study to discuss various strategies for Mrs. Lookingbell's case, each time swearing Matt to secrecy, each time implying that Matt should feel special for being taken into my father's confidence. Matt would listen compliantly, and try to give my father the answers he required.

WHEN MATT AND I were in grade school, we were inseparable. On the weekends when weather turned warm, we would wander along the shoulders of the highway into town, playing a game where we singled out targets and threw rocks at them. We both had perfect aim. At the height of the game, we would throw in unison, and try to hit the target at the same time, so that our rocks clacked together. Or we would go to a local lake and design fishing lures, then cast our lines in tandem, so that they cut the same mystical arabic letters in the air. (We loved the names of fish lures: the Daredevil, Johnson's Sprite, Fred Arborgast's Hulla Popper.) As we walked home together, Matt planned fantastic journeys for us—when we were adults, we would live far away, in New York City, Buenos Aires, and Peking. We would explore the equatorial selva and coral islands near Fiji, journey underwater in a bathyscaphe, be the first civilians to homestead Mars once interplanetary travel was established. Matt had a gift for devising whole worlds, and at times the histories he spun from our imagined travels preoccupied me more than the hard facts of our day-to-day lives.

Although my father always proclaimed that Matt was a genius, I am still not sure whether my half-brother really was, or whether my father simply wanted him to be. I knew, however, that I was not a genius and I savored the realization that my lesser brilliance would save me from my father's scrutiny. He also was not inclined to have the same ambitions for a daughter that he harbored for his son. As a result, I had privacy and space to move in. Matthew had neither of these.

Two years before the Lookingbell case, in seventh grade, Matt had decided to take up chess, and by midwinter he was promoted to the high school chess team and had won a state championship held in Madison. My father studied famous chess matches, and hovered behind the judges at tournaments, moving his hand slightly as Matt lifted a piece in play. My father also kept a green notebook, in which he wrote down Matt's moves in every high school match, annotating each with descriptions of "the negative or positive impact of Matt's unconscious use of physical posture and gestures on his opponent." My father became infuriated when Matt finally lost his first game in eighth grade, at the regional level, in an inexplicably stupid move even a novice would not have made. My father drove Matt home after the contest, refusing to speak to him, while Matt sat in the back seat, throwing his chess pieces one by one out the car window onto the highway.

The following year Matt found and repaired an old box camera, and carried it everywhere, shooting portraits of us and his schoolmates. As a joke, he sent a picture he had taken of a McCarthy High girl, Aletta Knorr, to the Miss High School Beauty of Wisconsin contest, and four months later, a team of urbane men carrying clipboards, their faces orange with QT tanning dye, knocked on her door and announced that she was a finalist. At the state pageant, when they asked her what she felt a woman's most important quality was, she answered, coached by my brother, "To be demure"—they gave her the title, and sent her to Atlanta for the national beauty competition. She and two other girls from midwestern states climbed out their hotel window the midnight before the contest, in defiance of its strict curfews and chaperoning rules. The girls found themselves in Atlanta's red light district, rounded a corner, saw a policeman shoot a fleeing man in the back, and then returned to their hotel rooms without telling a soul what they had witnessed.

Matt's photograph of Aletta Knorr appeared in the Milwaukee and local papers. With depthless curiosity, my father raided the spaces under Matt's bureau and bed and confiscated his photographs. My father had the ones he liked best framed. (Several self-portraits of Matt simply disappeared.) When looking for the pictures Matt had taken of Aletta Knorr, my father also found Matt's diaries. My father not only read the diaries: He brought them to work and had his secretary type up pages he thought demonstrated conclusively that Matt was a child prodigy. He also took poems Matt had written and hidden between the pages of the encyclopedias he kept on his shelves. I remember one poem, titled "Learning to Kill Deer," began:

> *Father, let me turn*
> *back toward the bridge:*
> *Pity, like a doe, listens*
> *below the ridge, terrified.*

My father declaimed it to us over breakfast. I don't know how Matt survived these invasions as long as he did. My father's intrusions became a problem for me only in my second year of high school, when they took the form of periodic searches of my room to insure that I was not dating boys without his knowledge.

I think that withdrawal into my imagination saved me from my father's omnipresence. To this day I am a compulsive daydreamer. In any uncomfortable situation, I find my mind wandering, taking me somewhere, anywhere else. I can easily imagine a character more real than any person in the room with me, reconstruct a man before me easily into someone more reserved, more passionate, gentler, more companionable. This is a trait ill befitted to a judicial career, and at times has embarrassed me in the middle of a dull case, when I have looked down from the bench and wondered what an arguing attorney has recounted.

DURING THE YEAR of the Lookingbell case, my father's obsession with educating Matthew took on a remarkable intensity. There was a period when it seemed that every evening, he would corner Matt in the study, and speak at him until long past bedtime. Ottilie would sit outside in the living room, frowning over the afghan she was crocheting, and looking up every now and then to shake her head.

"He just won't back off," she told me once, in despair, after Matthew had been in the study for hours. "If he doesn't let up, he's going to kill Matthew."

She rose and knocked on the study door: She rapped lightly, almost too softly to be heard. The voice inside stopped, but no one answered her. "Matt needs to go to bed," Ottilie said.

"Leave us!" My father commanded.

"Matt? I want you to come out here a minute."

Before my father could restrain him, Matt slipped through the door and fled up the stairs. Afterward, we heard my father ranting at Ottilie long after we got in bed.

We knew how futile it was for Ottilie to intervene on our behalf, and we felt terrible when she did. I remember one time two years before, when she had demanded an audience with my father because she believed he should allow me to visit my mother's family, the Kloneckis. It was the first time I had ever heard Ottilie insist on anything. She and my father fought behind their closed bedroom door, and his words to her were harsh, persuasive, seductive, daunting, crooning, charming, and cutting.

"You've never been able to love Melanie, because she's not your child. And now you want to send her away. You intend to orphan her!"

I heard Ottilie crying. I wanted to run into the room and tell her what I knew: that he was wrong, that I believed she cared for me. That he was jealous of his ownership of me, that I preferred her love. I did not say these things, because I did not have the words for them yet—I had only the feelings, but the feelings were certain and definite.

Afterward, my father never mentioned the subject of my mother's family to me, but a few weeks later, Ottilie brought me a box, covered with blue velveteen, containing a few scraps of crocheting, my mother's engagement ring, a silver band with "Katie Klonecki" engraved on it, and two photographs of me at ages one and four. Ottilie had been unable to find pictures of my mother anywhere. (After we relocated to McCarthy, my father never mentioned my mother, ever.) Ottilie told me that my mother's family came from Tampico, Illinois, and that they were "Horse People," from which I later understood she meant people who dealt in horses for a living. However, for years after she gave me the box, before I was able to visit with my mother's family, I imagined them as centaurs, but smaller, men connected to the bodies of Shetland ponies, galloping under a bright sky through hot piney woods.

Ottilie's confrontation with my father over his increasing involvement of my brother in the Lookingbell case met a similar end. My father
simply overrode her protests. The following evening he called Matt to
his office after dinner, and kept him there for hours, reading legal reports aloud to him until long past midnight, praising or scolding him
according to his answers. Whether my father loved Matt or any of us is
a question that I am unable to answer to this day: I cannot imagine the
quality of feeling my father experienced when he looked at a person
whose will and separateness were unrecognizable to him. I sensed only
that he would find it intolerable if any of us got away from him. And
when I asked myself whether I loved him, I could not find the feeling:
Uneasiness or wariness or fear blocked the way to my heart.

3

BY THE TIME Matt and I turned fifteen, the Lookingbell case and
Joel Ratleer were in the local news almost every day. A Bloodstone cannery worker, Maureen Huffey, reported that she had heard Mrs. Lookingbell say she had drowned the Czepeski children, "just like kittens,"
holding them down by "the scruffs of their necks." My father told the
McCarthy Courier, "People in this town are too intelligent to be swayed
by morbid rumors. Obviously, Mrs. Huffey is fabricating. Human children do not have neck scruffs, and Mrs. Lookingbell is too fond of cats
to have thought of such a comparison." A newspaper photograph of her
appeared over the caption, "Imelda Lookingbell holding one of her four
cats, Rainer." A complacent silver tabby gazed up at Mrs. Lookingbell.
She smiled back at him, her pretty profile turned toward the camera,
her smile remarkably similar to the cat's.

Matt had taken the photograph, at my father's request, although at
the time Matt did not know the picture's intended purpose. When Ottilie showed Matt the newspaper, he was angry. Ottilie teased him to
make him laugh, saying, "She looks as if she's planning to eat the cat."

During this period, when the Lookingbell case was at the height of
pretrial publicity, Matt and I would leave home together as soon as we
returned from school, and take a road through the snowed-over cornfield behind our house to the only section of woods within miles of
McCarthy. The Midwest of central Wisconsin does not communicate a
sense of frontier or suggest the possibility of adventure. There are no
forests, no oceans, no mountains, no craggy gorges. The land's flat vastness threatens that the world will go on endlessly the same, no matter

how far you journey, that there is no escaping where you are. The woods were one of the few deviations in the farmland around McCarthy, which was planted almost unvaryingly with hay and corn.

In the woods was an abandoned cabin where Matt and I spent whole days hanging out together. We would build fires in the cabin's crumbling fireplace, and sit on the floor warming ourselves, talking or not talking, and sometimes smoking marijuana we purchased from Vernon Peek. Vernon was a hippie from Madison with a blond John Brown beard and a two-foot ponytail, whom Aletta Knorr had met before dropping out of the University of Wisconsin in her first semester. Aletta now ran a little store in town called God and Things, below the apartment where she and Vernon lived. The air in God and Things was so thick with incense that your lungs ached when you entered. The store specialized in scented candles, handmade soaps, incense, leather handbags and hats, India print dresses, and blue jeans. Sometimes Matt spent Saturdays in the little room in the back of the store, smoking dope and talking with Vernon about Eastern religion and Wittgenstein. (Vernon was a graduate student in philosophy, and had been working on his dissertation for six years.)

Matt liked the way the marijuana "freed his head," he told me, but I was never able to enjoy it the way he did. It made me feel groggy and stupid, and I only smoked it occasionally. I had been told that some people were unable to get high from smoking grass, and I feared that I was one of them, a person even a drug would not enliven. I knew that the drug affected Matt more strongly: He would describe for me turquoise strobe lights darting around the fireplace and dark blossoms of light in the windows, and once he stepped outside and watched pink Scottie dogs hanging from a tree like Christmas ornaments, and barking.

Sometimes Matt would go to the cabin alone. I would see chimney smoke uncoiling over the woods and know he was there. On such occasions, I usually left him to himself, wanting to respect his privacy—I had secret places where I also hid, sometimes for hours, such as the abandoned quarry pit west of McCarthy. I would walk down there with fresh baked potatoes in my pockets to keep my hands warm, and lie in the pit, hidden from view, listening to the stillness around me, and plotting travels that would take me far from home and McCarthy. On other days, I marked as mine one of the ice fishing huts abandoned by itinerant fishermen: I would walk across McCarthy Lake, drop a line, and catch panfish on a Russian hook baited with rubber perch eyes. I could sit for hours, as the lake gathered strength under me like a live and chimerical animal, darkening into black ice and then thawing and pocketing dangerously as the winter progressed. Bundled in wool, poised over schools of gregarious yellow perch, a small handwarmer stove next to me, I would read Jack London stories, savoring the solitude of the characters adventuring in the Klondike, and imagining myself to be either a dog or human impervious to wolves and avalanches. Sometimes the solitude seemed so heavy I could touch it: On such occasions, I would leave the lake, longing for warm-weather fishing or Matt's company in the cabin.

One day during the Lookingbell trial, Ottilie surprised me by asking if I would accompany her to the cabin, where she had seen Matt head a few hours before. "I'm going stir crazy," she told me, her hands folded placidly in front of her on the kitchen table. It was so unlike Ottilie to ask for anything, that I felt something like excitement as we plodded across the field to the woods. Our boots strayed adventurously from the driveway; they broke through the crust on the snow, so that walking was difficult: At times, we found ourselves waist-high in a snow drift, and had to backtrack and zig-zag in order to reach the trees. Our toes froze in our boots and we looked longingly at the smoke unravelling over the cabin.

When we arrived, Ottilie called inside to Matt. He opened the door and looked surprised to see us. The air was redolent with the smell of grass, and Matt's eyes were pink, the way they got after he had smoked not two or three joints, but a dozen. He grinned at Ottilie, who would not have known the smell for what it was, and she entered.

Ottilie smiled as she crossed the threshold. Matt had jokingly furnished and decorated the shack. An armchair and a couch from a junk heap faced the fireplace. An old bookshelf held Time/Life volumes from a science series, with titles such as *The Mind*, *Growth*, and *The Sea*. He had torn a few pages out of *The Mind*, framed them, and hung them on the walls. They showed paintings by Van Gogh, which chronicled his progression toward final madness: The last was of a gold-and-red wheatfield rustling around a grassy road, with jagged crows flying unsteadily overhead through a jittery sky. The painting's title had been translated as *Crows over a Wheatfield*.

"That picture," Matt told Ottilie, "is like Jimi Hendrix in paint. When I look at it, it feels like hard rock played too loud to hear."

"Why *do* you turn your music up so high?" Ottilie asked.

"Because then it feels like I do inside. It understands me." Matt laughed.

Above the mantel Matt had hung a framed picture of Ottilie, his favorite photograph of her. It showed her paused in a doorway, holding a tower of cups, her eyes and the contents of one of the cups the only dark areas in the photograph. Behind her, the kitchen window revealed a snowscape that reached forward to claim her, tucking and wrinkling itself into her hair and shirtsleeves. Her eyes focussed inquiringly on the camera, as if the photographer had something important to tell her.

Ottilie looked at the portrait and said simply, "I always liked this. I wondered what happened to it."

"Sit down, Mamalie," Matt told her, pushing the armchair toward her. There was a shyness in the affection between Ottilie and Matt, as if both were aware that her youth made it difficult for her to hold the full authority of motherhood—when she came to pick us up at school on occasion, strangers still mistook her for a high school student. Matt took Ottilie tenderly by her arm, and pulled her around before the fireplace.

Ottilie sat silently in the armchair, gazing into the fire, out the window, at the mounted Van Goghs. She looked happier than I had ever seen her.

After that she would bring us things for the cabin: braided throw rugs, curtains she sewed from burlap sacks, cinnamon rolls hot from the oven, cadmium blue bottles salvaged from the antique trash heaps that littered the woods. She came only when my father was not at home. I think she feared he would follow her otherwise, and that our hideout would be discovered.

When she came, she would read, or crochet, or we would listen to Matt's cassettes on his tape player: the Grateful Dead and Jimi Hendrix and Frank Zappa or (Ottilie's preference) the Mamas and the Papas. Or we would play endless rounds of a variation on checkers invented by Matt, with complicated rules that allowed a player to invade the other side and change colors, or to assume both colors for several moves, before returning control to the other player.

It embarrasses me now to describe our times spent in the cabin, because thinking back on them, I wonder if we hadn't all been driven a little crazy by then. Although we never spoke about it, the three of us pretended to ourselves that this was our home and that we were all one another knew of family.

I ALMOST NEVER confronted my father, because I believed I could not prevail against him. But the year of the Lookingbell case, I clashed with him, once. That year Harper Lee's *To Kill a Mockingbird* was required reading in the schools. Gregory Peck, as Atticus, the benevolent lawyer-father of the child telling his story, made my teacher's heart flutter, and even my father went to a movie theater in Chicago with a pack of defense attorneys to see the film. It was a movie that everyone talked about, and that lawyers loved. And perhaps because of some comment made by Joel Ratleer to reporters, the *Chicago Tribune* described my father in reference to the Lookingbell case as "a figure with a presence, as formidable and arresting as a Harper Lee character."

When the movie came to our local theater, my father exhorted us to go see it. He wanted to watch it a second time. But I did not wish to go. I had found reading the book painful: The father's special bond with his daughter, who had the enviable name of Scout, bewildered me and made me uncomfortable, and I could not reconcile the image of Atticus with anything I knew—it was a picture that felt dangerous. What I liked were the gloomy and monstrous characters of *Wuthering Heights*, the book the ninth grade had been assigned to read in the fall— although the passion between Heathcliff and Catherine seemed nothing in comparison to the love that Matt and I felt for each other, unified against the turbulent background of the Ratleer house.

I was troubled also by the fate of Atticus's client, whose conviction and eventual murder on the way to prison added a thrill to the tragedy that illuminated the lawyer's blind heroism. I wanted Harper Lee's book to end differently, with the defendant free and the law exposed as the evil thing it was, finally vanquished. When I handed in the book report about *To Kill a Mockingbird* required for English class, I received the only D I ever earned in school, and a note to rewrite my paper.

My father grounded me, and for the single time that I recall, he took an interest in my education. He summoned me into his study, sat me down at his desk, and departed for his office in town after telling me that I was not allowed to leave my seat until I wrote an "A" report. But the words would not come to me, and I stared out the window, toying with my pencil. That Saturday I sat at my father's desk from seven-thirty in the morning until seven-thirty in the evening, fiddling with the same handful of sentences, reading and rereading titles on the shelves of law books towering over me. (He owned three copies of Clarence Darrow's selected writings, *Attorney for the Damned,* and the single work of fiction he possessed was Rand's *The Fountainhead,* which he reread repeatedly after proclaiming it "an homage to the genius of Frank Lloyd Wright and genius itself.") When my father returned home, he bristled with irritation at the inarticulate half-page I had written. Overcome with the absurdity of being disciplined like a wayward child at the age of fifteen, I laughed while he read my words.

He was furious. He grabbed me from behind by the shoulders and lifted me halfway from my chair. Crushing me to his chest, he whispered in my ear that I would sit in his study all night and into the morning, if necessary, until the report was done.

"No," I told him.

But he overcame me. He forced me back into the chair, and leaning all his weight on my shoulders until I felt a sharp pain in my spine and thought my collarbone would snap, he said, "Yes, oh yes."

He left me there, but at midnight, he returned. When he saw the untouched page in front of me, he told me that he expected the full report by morning. His daughter, he said, was not going to be a high school dropout. He didn't want to catch me asleep, or see the light turned off in the study, or there would be hell to pay.

His threat made it impossible for me to sleep: I stared at the book's cover, and its green-and-red lettering wobbled nonsensically on the gold background. When I did allow my eyes to close, I was spooked by the image of Boo Radley, the children characters' ally, pale as a worm and driven to idiocy after decades of being imprisoned by his family in his own home. I heard my father prowling in his room above me, the creak of him climbing into bed, and then the house fell into silence, weighted by his presence overhead.

At two o'clock, the stairs spoke under someone's footstep, and fearing he was returning, I opened the book and pretended to read. But it was Matt, wearing maroon pajama bottoms, his hair tousled into a dark flame. At fifteen he was lean and long-waisted and beautiful.

"Melanie," he whispered. He pulled a straight-backed chair toward my father's desk, sat down next to me, and took my pen. His hands were olive-skinned and long-fingered, and he wrote quickly on the paper in front of me, laughing to himself: "The killing of mockingbirds is a necessary evil, because they are actually miniature hawks that lie in wait in trees, ready to attack us. Alfred Hitchcock would have made a better horror movie if he'd used mockingbirds instead of seagulls."

I felt a laugh rise in me, cracking open my sense of despair. I had not realized how bad I felt until Matt sparked me back to life.

"You have to just give him what he wants, without really giving him what he wants," Matt told me with a wry expression, although his tone was serious. "You'll never believe what Mr. Ratleer plans to do in Mrs. Lookingbell's trial. Christ." My brother looked suddenly sad and confused. He buried his face in his hands. "Do you want me to stay down here with you until you're done?"

At that moment love for Matt overpowered me; I touched his sleeve. He looked exhausted, more tired even than I felt.

"No, I write fast when I want to," I said. "I'll be done soon."

"You're not afraid of being left alone in his lair with all the law books?" Matt stood and gestured at the walls of legal tomes rising over us. "I can't stand this place."

"Thanks, Matt," I said. "Go to bed."

After Matt stepped into the hallway, I wrote my report on Boo Radley, finishing around four o'clock in the morning. I so avoided any reference to Atticus or the legal struggle at the heart of the book that my report was strained, distorted, almost delirious.

In the morning I copied what I had written in a neat, round script. My father looked over my shoulder and said, "Let's see if this one makes the grade." I got my usual A, and a notation from the teacher that read, "curious and imaginative." After school my father demanded to see the graded paper. "Now, Melanie," he said, "that wasn't so painful, was it?" He frowned at the title, *Boo*, and handed it back.

He never read it, and Matt and I, after consuming a plate of hash brownies baked by Aletta Knorr, burned the report ceremoniously in the cabin fireplace, giggling manically. The pages turned into red-and-black-striped snakes that soared upward through the chimney, wingless but somehow adept at flight.

4

ONE SATURDAY my father left to spend the weekend in Waushara County in order to unearth information on the Czepeskis, who were from there. Matt had risen early, to elude him, and lay low in the cabin. When I found Matt, he told me that he "did not want to accompany Mr. Ratleer on one of his infernal missions." Ottilie and I decided to drive into McCarthy, do some shopping, and have lunch in town, and Matt came along with us. Something happened then that made an indelible impression on me, because it was the first time I had seen Ottilie lose her composure.

We arrived downtown before noon, and stopped in Sears to buy new jeans for Matt. (He had grown four inches in the last year). When we entered the men's department, we saw Mr. Czepeski standing at the counter. He looked overwhelmed by grief, pared down to nothing by his losses. His clothes hung loosely on him; he had clearly been heavier-set at one time. He paid for the new pants before him without speaking, as if the slightest effort would be unbearable, added to the burden of suffering he already carried.

When Matt saw him, he grabbed Ottilie and me by our arms and led us out of the store. "Don't make him have to look at us," Matt said. "He might know who we are."

My brother steered us toward The Plow, the only eating establishment on Main Street. He was visibly upset after seeing Mr. Czepeski. Once inside The Plow, Matt said that he wasn't hungry enough to eat anything, and talked in a quick, nervous voice. He told us he was going to stop by Aletta's store to see Vernon Peek's wolverine. Matt explained that there was now a caged wolverine in the back of God and Things. Vernon had found the animal caught in a trap, and brought it home to nurse it back to health. He believed that kindness to animals was the root of all good, despite the fact that he admitted the wolverine was "a nasty little beast" who had nearly "chomped his hand off at the wrist" before he managed to cage it. The wolverine was a kind of lure; people would come to the store and head down to look in the cage until the animal raised its nose and growled at them. Aletta both liked and disliked the wolverine. She felt it attracted some customers and scared away others, and that its smell competed with the odors from the store's incense.

Matt left Ottilie and me at the table, saying that he would get a lift home with Vernon Peek. Ottilie and I both ordered sole the way we liked it, plain, without lemon or butter. She told me that she had gone to school in Waupaca County with some Czepeskis, who she believed might be Mr. Czepeski's cousins. She said they had been good students like her, and that they had kept to themselves and never spoken up in class. I nodded when she told me this: I, too, was a hardworking and unassuming honors student, quiet as Ottilie. (Years later, in law school, it was the same. Everyone seemed astonished to learn that I had tied for first in my class. "I was never aware," one of my professors told me when I asked him for a recommendation, "that you were in my seminar.")

After we finished eating, as we exited the restaurant, Ottilie stopped so suddenly in front of me that I ran into her. She stood frozen, facing a group of people coming toward us on the sidewalk: a man dressed in a khaki, fur-lined parka, flanked by two women. I thought it must be Mr. Czepeski again, walking among the group, but I was mistaken.

"Crails," Ottilie said. At first I did not understand her. "It's my father, and his sister, and sister-in-law."

The Crails came nearer, and when they were only thirty feet away, the older woman in the group faltered, her eyes resting on Ottilie. Then the Crails, as if by invisible agreement, turned around and headed in the opposite direction. Ottilie ran after them, crying, "Stop! Stop!" but they quickened their pace.

Ottilie halted. Her arms clenched at her sides, she yelled, "It's me! Ottilie! Ottilie! It's me! Come back for me! It's me!" She called after them until she was hoarse. Several blocks away the Crails climbed into a pickup truck, and vanished.

As she drove home, Ottilie stared fixedly at the road, saying nothing. She looked numb. When we arrived at the house, Ottilie crawled into bed, although it was still afternoon. Smoke curled from the woods above the cabin, but she refused my invitation to go there.

I walked toward the woods, feeling an unnameable terror. I did not want to know that Ottilie longed for a life that by necessity would exclude me, that would abandon me to deal with my father by myself. By the time I approached the field's edge, I was crying. I could not remember the last time I had cried. Perhaps it had been years; I prided myself, in those days, on my stoical reserve. I ran into the woods, my vision blurred by tears. I imagined that I was one of the Kloneckis, half-horse, wild with feeling, racing dangerously along the narrow path that snaked between the trees. I did not stop until I reached the cabin. Then I wiped my face on my sleeve, and waited until my heartbeat quieted before entering.

I found Matt lying on the braided rug before the fire. He showed me a jar of mushrooms soaking in plum-colored water, and told me Vernon Peek had given him some peyote. I was afraid that if I tried it, my sense of isolation would desolate me, and I shook my head when Matt offered me the jar.

In the corner of the cabin was a wooden crate, with straw bedding inside and wire mesh stretched across the front.

"What's this?" I asked.

"It's Vernon's wolverine," Matt said. "Aletta won't let him keep it in the store anymore. He's going to stash it here until it gets better, and then we're going to let it loose in the woods." The straw inside the crate moved, and the wolverine raised its head: It stared at me with beautiful, ferocious eyes, and lay back down.

"I feel like the top of my head just came off," Matt told me.

I sat next to him and watched the fire. He described to me what he saw: He said there was a plant growing in the flames, invulnerable to them; and an animal made of fire, what he called "the physical manifestation of emotion"; and he understood that it was true: You could step in the same river twice in exactly the same way each time, because everything could and would be repeated. He saw his soul leave his body and swim back into it.

After dark fell I led Matt by his sleeve to the house. He was too confused to find his way back himself. As we walked toward the square of light in the kitchen window, he told me that it looked like "an enormous friendly bug" and that he wished that he, too, were a yellow bug. I took him to his room, and he fell asleep in his clothes, murmuring ecstatically to himself.

Before I went to my room, I checked on Ottilie. She was still in bed, turned toward the wall. Her bedside lamp was on, but she was motionless, except for the movement of her breathing under the covers.

"Mama-two?" I asked. When she didn't answer, I approached her and touched her shoulder. I told her in a hoarse whisper, "Please don't ever go off and desert me."

She stirred under my hand. She had been crying; her pillow was damp.

Without turning around, she said, "Don't worry, Melanie. I wouldn't leave you or Matt here. I'm just tired. Try to get some sleep."

I wished that she would say more, that I could linger a while. "I'm sorry about the Crails," I told her.

"Is Matt all right?" she answered.

"Yes. I guess. No. He'll be OK in the morning."

I stumbled down the hall to my room and, exhausted, fell asleep almost immediately. I had terrible nightmares. I had the first in what would become a recurrent dream, the dream I still have, of our house in Elkhorn. My mother is seated next to me on our sofa, her face buried in her hands. The roof of our house is gone, and my father's head bends over us, gigantic and enormous under the stars: It looks distorted, gaseous; it pulls apart and swells and rejoins itself. He is screaming at us. I cover my ears and hide my face to keep from seeing him, and suddenly, my mother is gone and I am my mother, seated alone on the couch.

That first night I had the dream, it was longer and more complicated than it has become, honed down with its endless repetitions through the years: Matt and Ottilie appeared, hovering above my father like figures from a Chagall, and I once again became myself, sitting on the sofa. Vernon Peek was also there, and Mrs. Lookingbell. She strode into the living room in her red high heels and seated herself so close to me that we blended together, and for a moment I was her: haughty and sarcastic, wearing bright red lipstick and smoking like a chimney.

I slept late in the morning. Ottilie was up with Matt in the kitchen, making pancakes. We carried them in steaming towels to the cabin, and spent the day playing Matt's private version of checkers, listening to his tapes and heaping the fire so high with dead wood that it roared.

Ottilie showed me an envelope: a pale blue square addressed to

Tampico, Illinois. She told me that she had written the Kloneckis that morning, before I awoke. I felt such love for Ottilie that I could barely hold the letter. This was the culmination of what had happened to her, the day before, with the Crails: She determined that I would not be kept from my own family. I sensed she had discussed the letter with Matt and told him what had happened in town, because he looked at the envelope and said, "Oh, Crails, Crails, Crails," in an ironic, exasperated tone, as if he had been aware for a long time of what they were like.

I asked Ottilie what she had heard about my mother's family, but she said she knew next to nothing. I confessed to Matt and Ottilie that I thought of the Kloneckis as people who were half-horse and half-human, because of what Ottilie had told me years before about them being "Horse People." Matt speculated about the Horse People, keeping us laughing for almost half an hour. He invented names for them, and described their daily activities: Their favorite dish was blood sausage with oats; they had such names as Black Gold Klonecki and Sparky Klonecki and Uncle Paint; they slept standing up in their feather beds.

All Sunday we held each other together. You will think that in my womanhood since leaving that life, I have never recovered from it: that numbness deadened my heart, that passion fills me with terror, that I ran to embrace those things that destroy in the very act of promising intimacy. But I have not always. The miracle, devastating to despair, that lies at the heart of this account may be the only reason for telling it—that despite my father's unrelenting coercion, and Ottilie's speechlessness and the unbearable pain of what followed, the three of us knew how to love and kept that knowledge alive in us, day after day. This fact to me is not proof of any genius on our parts: It evidences the brilliant durability of compassion, the routine, dependable force of our love for each other, the unquenchable urge in human beings to give and seek solace.

MRS. LOOKINGBELL delivered the Kloneckis' reply to Ottilie's letter. On Mrs. Lookingbell's third and last visit to our house, she arrived at our back door with a message for my father, who was away in Waushara County, this time having taken my brother with him.

"I'm sorry," Ottilie told her. "You seem to have trouble pinning him down."

"Mr. Ratleer seems to have trouble being pinned down," Mrs. Lookingbell answered. "I hardly expected to find him. I've brought him a note. I intended to drop it in your mailbox, but after doing so, I decided delivering it in person would be safer." She handed Ottilie a pile of letters from our mailbox and cried, "Saturday mail!"

Ottilie invited Mrs. Lookingbell in, and helped her off with her coat. She was dressed outlandishly, in kelly green patent leather boots and a tartan kilt. A red tam teetered on the back of her head.

As soon as she sat down, she snapped open her handbag and lit a cigarette. Ottilie carried a dish of blueberry muffins to the table, and poured Mrs. Lookingbell a cup of coffee. I wondered if Mrs. Looking-bell was lonely for company. It must be hard, I realized, to be the sole murderess in a small town; everyone must avoid her.

"I don't touch coffee or sweets," Mrs. Lookingbell said. "They make me fidgety. God knows I'm fidgety enough already." As if to convince us, she jiggled her knee under the table, causing the coffee to leap nervously in its cup and spill onto the saucer. Mrs. Lookingbell lit a second cigarette, blew smoke through her nose, and grew still.

Ottilie sorted through the mail: There were a dozen letters for my father from charitable organizations; a cream-colored paper, folded into fourths with LOOKINGBELL printed in block capitals on it; and a manila envelope bearing the Kloneckis' return address. Ottilie handed it to me, saying, "It's from your mother's family!"

Mrs. Lookingbell narrowed her eyes and stared at Ottilie. "Who are *you*?" she asked. "Mr. Ratleer's oldest daughter?"

Ottilie blushed. "I'm his wife," she answered.

Mrs. Lookingbell raised her eyebrows. "Who's the boy Mr. Ratleer's always dragging around with him?" It was the first time anyone in McCarthy had been bold enough to ask such direct questions about our family. I knew that people talked about us, but their speculations, however accurate, were based primarily on deduction and invention.

"That's Matthew, our son."

Mrs. Lookingbell raised her eyebrows, gave a little bark of a laugh, and said, "Oh, that Joel Ratleer is a world unto himself, isn't he?"

Ottilie smiled, but did not answer.

"What I need," Mrs. Lookingbell said next, "is a ticket to freedom. It has become very uncomfortable to live in this town with Mr. Ratleer sticking his nose in front of a reporter every two minutes." She stood up abruptly, and said, "I would love to stay and socialize, but I really have too much on my mind right now."

She picked up her coat, and rushed out the back door. We watched her stride down our road to the intersection where the local bus stopped. She waited there for forty minutes, rather than remain inside with us.

Ottilie left me alone in the kitchen. I opened all the mail, even Mrs. Lookingbell's letter. Inside the manila envelope was a note written in a shaky hand, and signed "Roscoe Klonecki, your loving grandfather":

We were all so excited to hear news of you. You had become a mystery to us through the years, as we lost contact with your father after your mother's death and his departure from Elkhorn. He never wrote. I have grieved to see you. We hope you will send us your picture and come here to visit us. I have collected here a photograph of your mother and some other items.

The contents of the envelope included a family tree, showing that I had four aunts and three uncles and over a dozen cousins; a copy of my mother's birth certificate; her college diploma from the University of Michigan, indicating that she had majored in "Paleontology and Surveying" (I had not even known she went to college); and a picture of my mother. It was the first photograph I remembered having seen of her. Had she not been dressed in saddle shoes, I would have mistaken it for a picture of me: she had the same broad cheekbones and full mouth that I had never noticed before in myself, the same dark hair falling straight as water from a rock.

Mr. Klonecki's large envelope also contained a smaller one, yellowed with age, on which was scribbled, "As this was not addressed to me, I did not open it—Katie sent it to her mother before Mrs. Klonecki died. My poor wife never read it." The idea that someone had respected the privacy of a letter for fifteen years amazed me. For a moment after reading my grandfather's message, I hesitated, but I was able to overcome my compunctions and opened my mother's letter. It contained an oversized postcard of Elkhorn, bearing uncancelled stamps; perhaps my mother had thought better of mailing it for all the world to read, and so concealed the postcard in its envelope:

Joel's mother came here again for one of her interminable stays. She seated herself like a queen on the sofa, leaning back on three pillows! From there, she orders me around like a servant. She's a strange woman—she lost a son when he was six months old, and she still carries his picture around in her pocketbook. She talks about him as if he had died yesterday, and believes he would have grown up to be a president, if not an American saint. She told

*me her husband had been a "monster and a brute." When I tried to confide
in her about Joel, do you know what she said? "My son would never hurt
anyone! I refuse to believe you!" And then, "You know how men are—you
let them do exactly what they want, and then when they're busy doing it,
you find time for yourself, to do what you want." No wonder! Mama, I
have made a terrible error in judgment. I should not have married so
quickly. I want to come home.*

The letter was dated Christmas 1949. I had been conceived less than
three weeks before; my mother must not have known yet of her pregnancy.

I felt hungry to discover more. Perhaps if Roscoe Klonecki's manila
envelope had contained other letters, I would have refrained from un-
folding Mrs. Lookingbell's message. But I read it, as well. It said, curtly:

Mr. Ratleer—
*I am not willing to be electrocuted. To save myself the risk of such an
eventuality, I would prefer to throw myself at the court's feet and offer a
plea of guilty in exchange for a little mercy and compassion.*
—Imelda

I do not know how my father answered this letter, how he persuaded
Mrs. Lookingbell to let her case go to trial. Perhaps he told her that
Wisconsin did not have capital punishment, or perhaps he simply ig-
nored her statement of intent.

5

SPRING IN MCCARTHY begins and ends in May; the snows thaw, and the roads sink knee-deep in mud; shrews and weasels rush from ·their flooded holes; crows descend, seemingly from nowhere, and perch on the lone fir tree planted outside the McCarthy County courthouse, screaming "Law! Law!"

On the Friday morning of May 15, 1965, Joel Ratleer led his client, Mrs. Lookingbell, into the courtroom of Judge Oren Tainter. "Mrs. Lookingbell wore a beige linen suit, and crossed her legs at the ankles," the *McCarthy Courier* reported.

> Mrs. Lookingbell's attorney, Joel Ratleer, offered her a cigarette, but she demurred with an imperious gesture, and retrieved a cigarette from her purse. Mr. Ratleer's 15-year-old son, Matthew, sat at his right hand, taking notes as his father whispered to him. The prosecutor, Nels Verken, looked emotional as he rose to give his opening speech. He characterized Mrs. Lookingbell's crime as "the most sorrowful act ever committed in McCarthy County," and cautioned the jury not to allow his famous and clever adversary, Mr. Ratleer, to befuddle them. Murmurs arose among the spectators when Mr. Ratleer informed the court that he would waive his opening speech.

Extra folding chairs had been brought into the courtroom and set up along the back walls to accommodate the trial watchers; over a hundred members of the public were turned away. Ottilie and I sat in the rear, near the door, looking over an expanse of blond and brown heads. It would be the first time I had ever seen my father try a case.

Two men seated themselves beside me, and I overheard them reveal that they were lawyers, old law school classmates and colleagues of my father's from his early days in Chicago. One of the men said that my father had told him about Matt many times. "Joel thinks the boy's as intelligent as Joel always proclaimed himself to be." The other lawyer laughed, and said, "No one's that smart," apparently unaware that I was Melanie Ratleer.

Matt turned around and gave me a little ironic salute. The day before, he had unfolded a piece of yellow legal paper to reveal to me a dozen tiny cellophane squares—he told me that they were "window-pane acid," a kind of LSD I had never heard of. He had explained that if the trial got too bad, he'd pop one in the middle, "just for the pleasure of leaving my body and flying around the courtroom." He had apparently done the acid several times before with Vernon Peek. I was glad he did not ask me if I wanted to try it—Aletta Knorr had told me once that LSD could "fry your brains." She had heard that some people had bad acid trips from which they never returned, and that afterward they acted like crazy people. She had added that it was hard to tell if this was just "the usual antidrug bullshit propaganda." Our local radio station broadcast religious announcements telling us that marijuana was a devil weed that drove people to suicide or lives of depravity, which we laughed at, and which led us to distrust anything adults told us about narcotics. I wondered now, as I watched Matt, whether he was facing the trial high or sober.

Judge Tainter, ponderous, with a head that seemed too large for his body, rustled his black robes and turned toward the spectators when delivering his opening charge, as though they, and not the jurors alone, were determining the verdict. The spectators stirred and rippled with excitement and self-importance. The judge quoted Brandeis and Cardozo and reminded all present of the role of the "legal process as the single guardian of the morals of the community," and concluded by saying, "During the attorneys' ever courteous questioning of the witnesses, you must remain in your seats and keep your mouths closed."

The prosecutor, Nels Verken, looked impatiently at the wall clock. He had a lanky, scarecrow build, and had dressed like an undertaker in a somber black suit. As if, in a murder trial, life should be inverted and death take precedence, Verken called the coroner as his first witness. The coroner, a small, quick man with a lively stride and yellow socks, bolted up the aisle and bounded into the witness seat. He attested that the victims' cause of death had been "asphyxiation by drowning."

Police Officer Oren Gilmore followed, wearing his dress uniform. He related that he had received a call from a "hysterical female voice," and that upon arriving at the Czepeski house, he had found all three children "not breathing, sopping wet, and fully clothed in their beds." He noted that the Czepeski farm was by itself in a solitary wheatfield, and that no one else was nearby except the defendant. He added that he had always found the wheatfield an odd sight, since everyone else in McCarthy County grew either hay or corn, and Mr. Czepeski never seemed to harvest the wheat. Officer Gilmore reported that Mr. Czepeski had later told him that he grew mostly corn, but that every year he planted a field of wheat too small to harvest by machine, because he liked to look out the window and "see it rippling there," and that he, Officer Gilmore, had thought this strange, but did not consider it his business.

Officer Gilmore had then taken Mrs. Lookingbell to the police station, where she told him frankly that she had "decided to put herself out of her misery by putting the Czepeski children out of their misery." When Officer Gilmore was done testifying, Maureen Huffey of the canning factory, in Sunday clothes and with her hair newly done, took the stand to repeat the facts reported by the *Courier* earlier that year: that she had heard Mrs. Lookingbell say she had held the Czepeski children by "the scruffs of their necks" and "drowned them like kittens."

Mr. Czepeski was the final prosecution witness: He looked hollow-eyed, even thinner than he had that day in Sears. He testified that after his wife's death two years before, he had found himself unable to care for his three children, ages six months to three years, and to keep up his farm. He accordingly had placed an ad in the *Courier* two weeks after the funeral, asking for a live-in babysitter, "good with children, cleaning, and cooking." Mrs. Lookingbell had been the first person to respond.

Mr. Czepeski said that he had been "a little taken aback by her prettiness," and worried that it might not look right for him to have her living at his farm, now that he was widowed. However, as she was older than him by "at least ten or fifteen years," he thought this might discourage people from drawing the wrong conclusions. Mrs. Lookingbell, her profile turned toward the courtroom, arched an eyebrow when he said this, and smiled wryly.

No one else had responded to his ad, Mr. Czepeski continued, and so he had hired Mrs. Lookingbell. She seemed experienced with children, he noted—she told him she had four grown daughters of her own. (He had learned only recently that this was not true; she was childless.) The Czepeski children liked her well enough, and she had kept the house in the kind of order it had not known since his wife's death. He never had any cause to think that Mrs. Lookingbell was mistreating the children, and the only thing that had bothered him about her was that "she seemed a little high-strung, that was all, and she smoked more than most people like to."

Mr. Czepeski seemed hesitant to malign her in any way: he praised Mrs. Lookingbell's budgeting skills, and claimed that she baked knockwurst with sauerkraut and raisins, the way he liked it, which he had considered thoughtful of her, and that she had sometimes "borrowed his pants or a shirt and patched them or sewed on a button without his asking." It was clear, the more he talked, that Mr. Czepeski was a singular man—that he possessed an unusual kindness and delicacy that prevented him from speaking harshly even of the person who had murdered his children. Although he never looked at Mrs. Lookingbell as he spoke, there was no tone of rancor or vengefulness in his voice. He seemed merely sad and bewildered by how his life had unfolded. As he spoke of the day, barely a year after his wife's death, that he had come home to find the police in his house, his children already borne away in an ambulance, everyone in the court felt a mixture of sorrow and horror: Here was a life that was a testament to the meaningless redundancy of human suffering.

Mr. Czepeski stated that on the day of the crime, he had left his house at 5:00 A.M., with Mrs. Lookingbell in charge of the children. He could see his house from where he worked in the field, and would have noticed if a car, or even a person on foot, had approached his front or back door. He noted that "other than religious people carrying their magazines," he had few visitors. Mr. Czepeski concluded by saying that, to his knowledge, no one had been near the children that day except for Mrs. Lookingbell. He looked away from the defense table when he said this, as if, while he wished to speak the truth, he was sorry to have to lay blame on anyone.

Now that I am a judge, I know that anything can happen in a court of law: Juries can send a man away for life after viewing the plainest evidence of his innocence, or acquit a man whose guilt could not be more manifest. But I remember wondering at the close of the prosecution's case why my father had taken on Mrs. Lookingbell's defense when the evidence against her was so overwhelming.

My father stood, allowing himself to tower, for a moment, over his own client, the stenographer, and the row of spectators behind him. Then he approached Mr. Czepeski and in a hushed voice said: "It must have been terrible for you after your wife died. I myself am a widower, and I remember well the terrible loneliness of that first long year. I felt the sky had fallen in—" My father paused, bowing his head. He stood before the spectators not as a defense lawyer with dubious morals, but as deeply human, a man bereaved.

Mrs. Lookingbell uncrossed her ankles and stirred peevishly in her seat, as if to discredit my father's statement. (I listened aghast, since my father had brought Ottilie home mere months after my mother's death. And then I wondered if it was true that, at least briefly, the loss of my mother had unhinged him.)

"I imagine it must have been a tremendous relief to you when Mrs. Lookingbell arrived."

"She helped out," Mr. Czepeski answered.

"Imelda Lookingbell had every womanly virtue, didn't she, Mr. Czepeski? She was hardworking, conscientious, frugal, loyal and self-sacrificing?"

Mr. Czepeski nodded.

"A lawyer's life is like a mountainous stone country," my father said next. "There are peaks, periods in which the advocate climbs to the heights and gains a commanding view of the flatlands below. But most of the time, he remains on the plains."

Mr. Czepeski looked puzzled. I recognized what my father was doing: it was a way he had, in the middle of a dialogue with Matt or Ottilie or me, of suddenly speaking nonsense, that did not at first sound like nonsense, with the intent of unbalancing and demeaning the listener. I wondered then how many of the ways he dealt with us at home were the practiced techniques of legal advocacy.

"Today, Mr. Czepeski, I stand on the plains. I have a humble confession to make. I confess that when I look at Mrs. Lookingbell, and think of your circumstances, I wonder if you weren't a little fond of her."

Mrs. Lookingbell tossed her ponytail, turned toward the spectators, and rolled her eyes.

"Was there something between you and the defendant?" Before Mr. Czepeski could answer, my father reached forward and made a snatching gesture, as if retrieving his own question from the air. "You don't have to answer, Mr. Czepeski. We'll let it go for now."

Mr. Czepeski frowned.

"Mr. Czepeski. Frank. You're from Waushara County, aren't you?"

"I was raised there."

"You must know just about everyone in Waushara County. Do you know Martin Flock?"

Mr. Czepeski nodded.

"And Luke Schoonover?"

He nodded again.

"And Molly Felt?"

Mr. Czepeski flushed.

"How well do you know Molly Felt?"

"Nothing happened," Mr. Czepeski said.

"What?"

"Nothing happened."

"When did nothing happen? A few days before you hired Mrs. Lookingbell?" My father lowered his voice. "Do you mean nothing happened at the Badger Motor Inn?"

"No. We just backed out on it. I felt all dead inside, and we just backed out on it."

"No?"

"No. I just went all dead inside."

Without pausing, my father asked, "Would you say you're a man who likes women?"

"Women?"

"Did you like Imelda Lookingbell? Did 'nothing' also happen between you and Imelda Lookingbell?"

Mr. Czepeski looked confused. "No," he said, finally. "Not in the way you mean."

"She's nice-looking, isn't she?" my father asked, gesturing at his client.

Mr. Czepeski looked away, to his left.

"You yourself said that she was pretty, didn't you?"

"Yes."

"Frank, before I rest, is there anything you'd like to tell this court?"

Mr. Czepeski looked blankly at my father.

The audience shifted uncomfortably. I wondered if anyone could believe that Mr. Czepeski had been romantically involved with Mrs. Lookingbell. I thought that my father, guessing other men to be like himself, and blind to the grief printed on Mr. Czepeski's face, had finally stumbled on a poorly chosen strategy.

"This is ridiculous!" Mrs. Lookingbell said.

Now the spectators turned toward the defense table. Mrs. Lookingbell was slouched back in her chair, her ankles crossed and a long ash gathered at the end of her cigarette.

My father looked over his shoulder at his client, smiled, and told her, "I fully expected that you would come to his defense."

Beside me I heard one of my father's legal colleagues say, laughing cynically, "He's a diabolical Atticus."

My father told Judge Tainter, "I'm finished with Mr. Czepeski. I'd like to begin my examination of Mrs. Lookingbell and the other defense witnesses on Monday." My father handed the prosecutor a witness list containing three names: Martin Flock, Luke Schoonover, and Molly Felt.

Judge Tainter stirred above Mr. Czepeski on the bench. "Cardozo," said the judge, clearing his throat. "Cardozo once counseled that 'We do not pick our rules of law full-blossomed from the trees. The standards or patterns of utility and morals will be found by the judge in the life of the community.' You, ladies and gentlemen of the jury, are the representatives of this community, and I expect you to hear and consider the evidence with open minds. Do not let your imaginations run wild this weekend."

6

A CRIMINAL LAWYER'S summation is, for him, the dramatic climax of a case. In it, he reorganizes the evidence to fabricate a story that will convince the jurors of the defendant's innocence. My father spent all weekend in his study, talking bombastically to himself, rehearsing his summation, while the prosecutor drove to Waushara County to interview Molly Felt and Martin Flock and Luke Schoonover, wondering what they had to do with Mrs. Lookingbell's case.

In fact, Martin Flock and Luke Schoonover had no connection whatsoever with the case, and Molly Felt would only confirm what Frank Czepeski had attested. What no one knew was that my father had never planned to call any of these people as witnesses; he did not even intend to let Mrs. Lookingbell take the stand. Since in criminal cases the law presumes innocence and places the burden of proving guilt on the prosecution, the defense is under no obligation to present evidence. My father had indicated that Mrs. Lookingbell and three others would testify on Monday for a sole purpose: He intended to embarrass the prosecutor, Nels Verken, who would naturally wait to hear all the defense testimony before preparing his summation. Thus, when my father arrived in court on Monday, with a carefully wrought speech, the prosecutor, caught off guard without a summation prepared, would be left to stammer extemporaneously.

By Saturday evening my father still could be heard in his study, chuckling and repeating lines out loud as he scribbled them down. At about five he emerged from the study, holding a stack of paper, and said,

"Where's Matt? I want Matt to come in here." He reread something on the top page and laughed admiringly.

"Matt's not home," Ottilie said quietly.

"Well, where is he, then?" my father demanded.

I said, "He went to the movie theater." Matt was at the cabin: Ottilie and I both knew that he had left for there early in the morning.

My father growled. "This is no time to be watching movies. As soon as he gets in, send him to my study." He returned to his office.

My father emerged several times in the next two hours to inquire whether Matt had returned. Each time my father growled and shook the papers in his hand, progressively more impatient, until I grew edgy and fearful. There are things that carry with them a threat of violence more potent than violence itself: The bite of a vicious dog would never chill my blood like a copperhead crossing my path in the woods.

Before dinner I slipped out of the house and ran down to the cabin to get Matthew. I found him there with Aletta Knorr. They were seated cross-legged in front of the wooden crate containing Vernon's wolverine. The wolverine stared back at them, chary and cunning.

Aletta said, "He's beginning to smell amazingly bad. It's almost like he's a skunk." She was dressed in a sari and wore several bracelets, which clanged against one another on her arm. She looked like a beautiful exotic deity: After the Miss High School Beauty of Wisconsin contest, she had pierced her nose, grown her red hair long, and started wearing it in three braids.

Matt didn't say anything. He stared at the wolverine, wide-eyed.

"Windowpane," Aletta told me. "I told him not to take so many."

Matt looked at me, but did not see me.

"Mr. Ratleer's ranting and raving because Matt's not home," I told Aletta. "He wants Matt to come admire something he wrote."

"I wouldn't count on it," Aletta said. "You better go back and hold him off at the pass. I'll bring Matt home later."

I left them there. When Matt did not appear at the table for dinner, my father was outraged. "Matt should be home!" he proclaimed. "Ottilie, don't you know where your son is? Tell me where he is, Ottilie."

I answered him, and the sarcasm and rebelliousness in my voice surprised me. I said, "Maybe he's reading law books over at the courthouse library."

My father struck me on the side of my head, and I went reeling. My chair toppled, and I grabbed the table to keep from falling.

"Don't think I don't know where to find him," my father said. My head throbbed where he had hit me. "He's at that little shack in the woods you like to waste time in." It filled me with horror that my father knew about the cabin.

"In this house," he said, "we all eat dinner together." He headed for the front door.

"I'll get him," Ottilie said, following my father, laying a hand on his arm as he reached for the doorknob. He must have seen the flicker of fear in her eyes, because he said, "What are you trying to hide? Do you think Matt can hide anything from me?"

He left, slamming the door behind him.

I ran out the back door and raced along the muddy right edge of the field to warn Matt. When I reached the woods, I could hear my father in the distance behind me, twigs snapping beneath him as if under the prowl of a lumbering animal.

I opened the cabin door and whispered, "Matt! Aletta! Get out of here. He's coming." Aletta and Matt, lying on their backs on the braided rug, stared at me dreamily.

I grabbed Matt's hand and said, "Please come on! Stand up!" He let me pull him half to his feet, then collapsed and giggled.

My father filled the doorway. "What's going on here? A *girl?*"

Aletta climbed slowly to her feet.

"Get up, Matt! Get up!" My father jerked Matt upward by his arm. He flopped back onto the floor, and then sat up, looking bewildered.

My father kicked him.

"Get up! Get up!" he shouted. He kicked Matt again, hard, two or three times. Then he yanked him to his feet.

Matt looked at him with wide eyes. "What?" he asked in a brittle voice.

"Stand up when I tell you to stand up!"

My father propelled Matt by his shoulders out the door, and half-dragged him, half-pushed him into the woods.

"Jesus," Aletta said. The wolverine rustled in his cage, making a noise between a purr and a snarl.

We heard my father's voice receding in the woods: "Out here lolling around with a girl when the most important work is being done on a trial! That's not what I taught you!"

"I better go home," Aletta said. "Tell Matt I'll get hold of him as soon as I can. I hope he doesn't catch too much hell."

She fled from the cabin and left me standing alone, shaking. The door was wide open, crooked on its hinges, and the cabin seemed vulnerable and violated. I was careful to close the door gently, to check that it still held shut when I moved my hand away. I realized my father did not have any idea that Matt was high. I imagined Matt, startled and uncomprehending, his mind snapping with each of my father's shouts and curses and shoves.

When I reached the house, all the lights were on. Matt had broken away from my father and locked himself in the downstairs bathroom. My father was in the kitchen, beside himself with fury, rattling the drawers under the counters, looking for a screwdriver so that he could take the bathroom door off its hinges.

Ottilie came up behind him and said, "I think Matt must be drunk."

My father turned around. "Intoxicated?"

I almost cried with relief: I seized on this alternative, which seemed so much more wholesome than the truth. "I guess Matt and Aletta just wanted to see what it was like to get drunk," I volunteered.

Suddenly, my father threw up his hands and laughed: it was a loud, roaring laugh. "My boy's drunk! I got drunk with a girl when I was just his age!" He shut the drawer and said, "Well, there's nothing to do but let him sleep it off."

Perhaps he reacted this way because he preferred to believe that liquor, and not Matt's willfulness, explained Matt's resistance to him. Whatever my father's motives, he left Matt alone, and all the next morning he joked about Matt's staying so long in bed, how he must have one hell of a hangover, how we should all be careful to tiptoe by his bedroom and speak softly, so as not to wake him. At noon my father drove to his office in town, and told us to let Matt know that he was expected to be "up and dressed in a suit, ready for trial on Monday morning, and prepared for a wonderful surprise."

Matt did not emerge from his room until evening. As he passed me in the hallway on the way to the bathroom, he stopped, took my arm, and told me in a frightened voice, "I had nightmares and nightmares all night, only it seemed that the night had no end to it, that time wasn't setting limits on anything anymore?" He looked at me questioningly, as if unsure that he had communicated what he wished. "I thought I was in the study, and bats were flapping off the shelves. The Czepeskis were sitting in the middle on chairs, and the bats were biting them. They were eating them." The expression of horror on Matt's face frightened me more than his words. I hardly recognized him; he seemed transformed into someone else by his fear.

On Monday Matt appeared in the courtroom, looking ashen and frail. He seated himself in a middle row, behind the prosecutor, and when my father signalled my brother to move to the defense table, Matt, withdrawn, hunching his shoulders, looked away as if he had not noticed.

ON THAT SECOND DAY of the trial, Luke Schoonover and Martin Flock were there, subpoenaed by my father, and so was Molly Felt, indignant and fully prepared to testify that nothing had happened between her and Frank Czepeski. She sat down right next to Mr. Czepeski in the courtroom, a blazing proclamation of their innocence. She had been furious to learn upon her arrival in court that she would not be called, no less furious than Nels Verken, who sat motionless with rage before his oak prosecutor's desk, his arms folded and his mouth set in a bitter, lipless grimace. Luke Schoonover and Martin Flock looked straight ahead with puzzled expressions, their hands idle in their laps.

Nels Verken stumbled though a disorganized recapitulation of the evidence, backtracking several times to remind jurors of facts he initially bypassed. My father then delivered a summation which was reported in its entirety by the *Courier*, and later anthologized in two University of Chicago law school textbooks on trial advocacy. The textbooks, unlike the *Courier*, omitted any reference to the prosecutor's outcry regarding my father's unethical tactics; nor did they mention any of the objections to my father's summation voiced by his own client.

Judge Tainter flapped his robes and ordered the courtroom, which was alive with commentary, to die down.

"Gentlemen of the jury," Joel Ratleer began, standing to his full, impossible height. He walked within a few feet of the jury box and let his gaze linger just above their upraised heads, and then he turned toward the courtroom spectators. "Friday, you heard the judge counsel you not to let your imaginations run wild. But I tell you: Neither should you close your minds to the unthinkable, because there is no limit to human possibility.

"A man's wife dies, abandoning him and his children. He's not a steady kind of person: although he's a farmer, and we expect him to be stolid, conservative, not given to flamboyance or laziness, he doesn't fit the mold. Every year he plants a field with wheat, which he never harvests. Do you understand what I am saying? That he toils in the sweat of his brow to sow, but never reaps. Strange, isn't it? Who knows why? Mr. Czepeski is not an easy man to understand.

"But he is a man.

"There enters into his life an attractive woman—so pretty, he can't bring himself to look at her, now that a rift has risen between them. As Molly Felt might agree—"

Molly Felt gave my father a black look.

"—Mr. Czepeski likes women. And Mrs. Lookingbell is eminently likeable: As Mr. Czepeski himself told us, she's pretty enough to start mouths flapping. But she's more than that. She's solid, dependable, conservative. She's hardworking. She knows how to budget. She eliminated the disarray that Mr. Czepeski had allowed to claim his household. She sews on buttons he doesn't notice are missing, and patches holes he didn't know were there.

"Which one of these two people is more likely to commit a deranged act, an act that the people of McCarthy could not even have imagined? Weigh them in your minds. Which is more likely?

"Mr. Czepeski testified that no one else came to his house that day. It was just him and Mrs. Lookingbell.

"What happened that day? Imagine you are in Frank Czepeski's wheatfield, lying low, watching. Imagine that you witness what happened. What do you see? You see the house, all quiet inside. The children, like angels, asleep in their beds. And Mrs. Lookingbell, too, is asleep.

"A man, up early as only a farmer would be, peers out at his wheatfield from a downstairs window. He climbs the stairs. What happens next? Close your eyes, because what happens next is unthinkable and unimaginable.

"Why would a man kill his own children? Should you, sane and regular people, know the answer to such a question? Why would a man spend days of hard labor sowing an entire field of wheat, and never harvest it?

"The man leaves the house through its back door. In a few hours, the police receive a call—not from the man—of course not from the man, but from a *woman*. She's hysterical. She has seen what cannot be imagined.

"The police arrive at the house with an ambulance, sirens blazing, but Mr. Czepeski doesn't hear them. He's so busy in his field that he doesn't hear the clamoring call of sirens, doesn't run home to see his children carried to the ambulance and taken away.

"Who faces the police? The woman. She is a woman accustomed to protecting others. Almost reflexively, she moves to protect the man. The man she loved. The man she thought she understood, but now cannot understand."

Mrs. Lookingbell made an indignant gasping noise at the defense table. Molly Felt placed her hand protectively on Mr. Czepeski's forearm.

"There's one thing that really troubles you about the prosecutor's case. Out trot two witnesses who allege the defendant confessed her guilt. Does this make sense to you? Do criminals run to the police saying, 'Oh, take me in, I'm the one who did it?' Of course not. What man, capable of a heinous crime incurring the most horrendous penalties, would run to embrace his punishment? What motive could Imelda Lookingbell possibly have for confessing? Why does she call attention to herself? She shouts out, 'I confess! Arrest *me*. I did it.' "

Mrs. Lookingbell's voice arose behind my father: "And make no mistake about it."

The judge directed Mrs. Lookingbell to be quiet.

"The defendant, even now," my father continued, "would like to convince you that she is the guilty one. Is she? Is she guilty? Yes, but not of the unimaginable. She is guilty of the most understandable of acts: love. The defendant has placed herself in that chair in order to save the man she loves.

"And he's going to let her!"

Mr. Czepeski's mouth dropped open slightly. Behind him, Matt buried his face in his hands.

Mrs. Lookingbell rose to her feet.

Spreading her arms at her sides like a great bird, she fastened a look of mortal hatred on my father and cried, "And just what kind of man are you, Mr. Ratleer? You're a threat to society! A threat to society!"

The spectator's heads turned first toward Mrs. Lookingbell and then toward my father.

Judge Tainter rustled his robes and shouted, "The defendant will be seated!"

Instead, a hideous and homicidal expression crept onto Mrs. Lookingbell's face. Her arms still outstretched, she screamed, "I HAVE TALONS AND I WILL USE THEM!"

The bailiff approached her from behind and grabbed her arms, and the judge ordered the courtroom cleared.

IN HIS CHAMBERS Judge Tainter insisted that a psychiatric examination be ordered for Mrs. Lookingbell, to determine whether she was competent to continue to stand trial. My father argued vehemently against this: His client was not going to spend her life condemned to an insane asylum, and the judge had no right to deprive her of a fair trial simply because she had cracked under the nervous strain of a criminal prosecution. At the very least, she had the right to hear the verdict. Judge Tainter reluctantly agreed, but held that in the event of a guilty verdict, a psychiatric examination would be conducted before sentencing.

Nels Verken delivered his rebuttal arguments to an empty courtroom: only the judge, the lawyer, and the jurors were there. My father waived his client's presence and agreed to keep the courtroom doors closed. He did this, he later said, so that if Mrs. Lookingbell was convicted, he could appeal and demand a reversal and retrial on the grounds that her constitutional rights to be present at her trial and to have a public hearing had been violated.

The jury deliberated overnight and into the next day, and then hung itself. No one really believed, however, that Frank Czepeski was guilty of murdering his own children, and he was never prosecuted or even called in by the police for further questioning. In attempting to explain to the *Courier* why the jurors had not reached a verdict, the foreman said, "We just got lost."

The trial's culminating event, however, was that during the last day of deliberations, Mrs. Lookingbell absconded. Judge Tainter issued a bench warrant, but the dragnet of the law failed to capture her.

7

MATT ALSO DISAPPEARED, for two days. He did not come home the night after my father's summation, and was absent from the courtroom the next morning. Despite my father's delight at the outcome of the case, he was furious with Matt for not appearing at the last hour of trial, when the jury reentered the jury box to proclaim its defeat. Local and Chicago news teams flocked outside the courthouse, and my father stood alone before the cameras, answering reporters' questions with witty rejoinders, while he wondered where both his client and his son had gone.

The night before, when my brother failed to appear at home by eleven, my father strode through the woods, calling Matt's name angrily before him, but the cabin proved empty. When my father returned to the house, he shouted at Ottilie and me, "You're conspiring with Matt to sabotage my joy at the hour of victory!"

Early in the morning, after my father left for court, Aletta Knorr called Ottilie and me. Aletta told us that Matt had spent the evening with her and Vernon, and then headed south of town. Matt had claimed he was walking to the Czepeski farm, "to see Mr. Czepeski's wheatfield with his own eyes." Vernon had followed Matt in a pickup because, according to Aletta, Matt had "really lost it." He had whispered to Aletta that he had taken seven hits of windowpane.

Vernon later told me that he had convinced Matt to climb into the pickup, and that Matt had told him to "get us the hell out of wherever we are." Matt directed them south along back roads until he said they had reached the Czepeskis'. According to Vernon, Matt climbed from the pickup and stood in front of a giant field of mud.

Matt told him that the field was "crawling all over itself," and that, despite the darkness, he could see "the green-and-yellow snakes of wheat" with "black flowers flitting over them and red stars all over the ground." Then he started to shriek: a high, childish sound, crazy with fear. Nothing Vernon did would calm him.

After what seemed like an hour, a light went on at the end of the field, and two men carrying rifles came out, thinking someone was being robbed or killed. The men were Ole and Bill Calio, and Vernon and Matt turned out to be nowhere near the Czepeskis' farm. They had driven all the way to Fond du Lac County. The Calios helped Vernon wrestle Matt to the ground—he fought them with his feet and fists and bit Vernon. It took all three men to load Matt into the truck, tie him down in the back, and transport him to the Fond du Lac hospital.

While my father drove to the courthouse to hear the verdict, the doctors at the hospital were vainly pumping Matt's stomach, and when the jury entered the jury box, Matt's chest convulsed, his breath sputtered suddenly, and the doctors thought they had lost him. By the time Vernon finally pulled away from them to call us, he said that "the doctors were half-dead and Matt was half-alive."

They saved his body, but not his soul: When Ottilie and I drove to Fond du Lac, we found Matt curled up like a spring fern in his hospital bed, his eyes wide open with fear, his thumb in his mouth. They kept him in the hospital for three weeks, and during that time my father refused to visit him. Ottilie and I sat together in Matt's room each day, stunned by sorrow and horror. We felt as if we were inhabiting a nightmare: we could not reach him through the fog of voices haunting him. He would scream, or argue unintelligibly with people only he saw, or he would cry loudly and bitterly for hours at a time.

One evening, a doctor from the Fond du Lac hospital came to our house personally. He was an old doctor, with a halo of fine white hair and a Slavic accent, and he described for my father Matt's condition: He was psychotic. He saw things; he believed the devil was after him; he spoke incoherently or not at all. The doctor felt that arrangements should be made to transfer Matt to a private hospital where good long-term psychiatric services were available. When the doctor left, my father retreated into his study and slammed the door.

Ottilie and I, dazed and crying, walked down to the cabin. It was a damp night, the air soft and thick, paused on the brink of rain. We built a fire and studied it, played checkers listlessly, thought of nothing to say. After a while, the purrs of the wolverine spooked us. We decided to let him go. We pushed the crate outside, and unlatched the grate. The wolverine threw himself instantly toward freedom, twisting ground-ward, snarling with joy at the sight of the woods, and rushing into the furry blackness of the night air.

But even after we released the wolverine, we felt uneasy. We waited. And then my father arrived, in one of his rages.

He burst through the door, and he was on us. His voice preceded him. He shouted, "Why didn't you look after Matt? Why didn't you watch him?" He grabbed Ottilie by the neck and shook her. He banged her head against the mantle, repeating his accusations, until I thought he would kill her.

I jumped on my father's back to pull him off. When he turned on me, Ottilie and I both ran. We ran crazily, bumping each other like a pair of flighty deer, scrambling for the door but missing it, and backing into the corner, sobbing.

By then my father no longer saw us: His wrath had blinded him. He knocked the photograph of Ottilie from over the mantel, and threw it in the fire. "This drug den!" he shouted. "The only place where I'm not keeping my eye on you, and you drive yourselves to ruin in it!" He tore down the other photographs and pictures decorating the walls. He also threw them into the fire, and then our checkerboard, the books we kept in the cabin, the afghan Ottilie had been crocheting for months, and my manila envelope from the Kloneckis, which I had hidden there. He broke the cabin windows and kicked the door off the hinges. And then he left.

Ottilie and I spent the next week sleeping in her car in Fond du Lac. We washed at the bathroom in an Esso station, and wore the same clothes every day: Ottilie turned her collar up high to hide the bruises on her neck. We passed our days at the hospital, moving slowly and not thinking clearly, our lives unravelling with every movement we made, and every word we spoke. What I felt then most was a suspension of feeling, and then a sense, a numb fear, that I would never be able to feel anything again easily. One morning, when we accompanied each other to the hospital, Matt was gone: My father had arranged by telephone to have him transferred to a private hospital in Chicago.

Ottilie called the Kloneckis collect. In a quiet voice, she told them what had happened to Matt, and recommended that I spend the summer with them in Illinois. The Kloneckis agreed to take me in. They called Greyhound and paid for my ticket, and Ottilie drove me to the Fond du Lac terminal.

As I approached the bus with her, Ottilie leaned toward me and said, "You don't have to come back, Melanie. Roscoe Klonecki says that you're welcome to stay on in the fall." I was startled by her suggestion— that she would be willing to remain behind, alone and eternally, with my father. But after the bus doors gasped closed behind me, I realized that she was going to leave him.

8

OTTILIE DID NOT abandon my father until both Matt and I were gone. She stayed with my father until the hospital staff wrote, saying that they anticipated a prolonged stay for Matthew, and advising against visitors from the family for the first several weeks. After the letter arrived, Ottilie slipped through my father's hands like flour through a sieve. She departed one afternoon, ostensibly to the grocery store, and took nothing with her but her purse and an album full of family pictures. She travelled east to a town called Muskellunge, near Sheboygan, to stay with the divorced wife of an uncle my father had not even known she had.

That summer my father wrote me long, self-pitying letters. He did not understand my brother's illness as a tragedy that befell Matt. The tragedy was all my father's—how could the universe have suffered him to have a son who was not whole? He complained that he was overburdened, dealing with the Chicago hospital, undertaking a divorce, and holding a private practice together, and suggested that I stay in Tampico. "No one in my family has ever been psychotic," he wrote me. "Perhaps the Crails may be able to shed some light for you on the origin of Matt's sickness." My father never mentioned Ottilie. He remarried within a year.

I remained with the Kloneckis until I entered the university, and afterward, I stayed in Tampico for most of my school vacations. My mother's people were unlike anyone I remembered knowing, but I liked the sense of kinship I felt with them. They had a way of keeping practi-

cal things in focus at all times, of living without a thought for the troubles that entangled and disentangled themselves in my other life. I told
them about the name Horse People and Matthew's stories about them,
and the Kloneckis thought these funny and began, among themselves,
to call one another the Horse People. They were mostly farmers and
teachers, and my grandfather was in fact a horse dealer; they scorned
and laughed at lawyers, and years later when I told them of my decision
to go to law school, they chided me good-humoredly. They mistrusted
criminals and police to an equal degree and saw neither glamour nor
distinction in my presidential appointment years ago as one of the
youngest district court justices in our federal circuit.

Since my childhood ended when I was fifteen, and Ottilie came to
live with us when I was seven, I think of her as being there always, but
in fact it was only eight years. She was thirty-two when she escaped.
With the assistance of her aunt, she returned to school and became a
hospital technician. Matt never went to college, or married or had children. After a decade of living on and off in hospitals, he moved into a
halfway house in Muskellunge near Ottilie.

But that was almost a lifetime later—that summer the Kloneckis let
me take the bus to Chicago to see Matthew on weekends, once he was
allowed visitors. In the hospital I would sometimes hear nurses whisper
the words "schizophrenic" and "LSD" and "paranoid." The doctors
could not tell us whether his psychosis resulted purely from the drug,
or whether it had lain there dormant like a seed, year after year, waiting
the right conditions to make it take root and emerge. In those early days
Matt stared at me forlornly and did not seem to know who I was. On
one visit he summoned me to a hospital room's mirror, and asked me
to assure him of what I saw there. He was terrified: He said that when
he peered into it, he saw a beard spread over his face, across his chin
and cheeks and eyes and forehead, until it concealed him. I stood before
the mirror with him, and I had to look away—I was afraid I would see
what he did. I left the hospital, dizzy with pain, feeling as if half of
myself had been torn away.

As I walked across the grounds to the bus stop, I passed other patients—dazed-looking women, and men talking to themselves. I saw a
man wandering on a hill overgrown with stubby sumac trees, their poisonous vegetation bright red with early fall. He walked without direction amid the velvety branches, and at first I thought he must be one of

the patients, caught in a labyrinth of his own misperceptions. I was startled when he turned and I saw he was my father, his face contorted almost beyond recognition with grief, and his utter aloneness in coping with his loss, and I almost approached him.

BOOK TWO

MUSKELLUNGE

1

TO EXPLAIN the story of Mildred Steck, how she brought us down into the dark reaches and later buoyed us above our own lives, I will have to take you back to what was a second end and beginning for us, for Ottilie and Matt and me. You will have to approach Mildred's story by setting aside the world as you have come to know it, by accepting what Mildred told me in 1977, when she was still a young woman. She said then that she believed some people lead half a life, but that other people lead several: Whole stories and histories crest in a moment, and some human beings are lost in the turbulence, and some buoy up, intact, above water, and swim to shore. Mildred also told me then that the daily sorrow of adjusting to Matt's loss of his mind had left Ottilie half a person. And Mildred said that it had left me less than half a person: that I had opened the coffin lid of the law and walked in, and that's what it would mean to be Judge Ratleer, to be admired and even feared in the halls of justice.

Unlike Mildred, I am not religious. I have striven more than once to wrestle faith into existence, to feel its muscles straining against my arm, its breath in my face, but I have never succeeded. Some inner restraint has prevented me from seeing God in a grain of sand or a turbulent sky or even in the raw power of a tornado. However, I believe in the devilish inclinations of human beings as they walk and breathe and kick up the earth. The devil reappears in each generation in myriad forms, but those overcome by him often perceive too late that his modus operandi in every case is the same—he waits for that moment when you believe or wish to believe that he is not as bad as he appears; you look for goodness in him, give him the benefit of the doubt, feel for him. And then he arises, monstrous and terrible and devoid of mercy, and takes you to hell.

In late 1976 while I was clerking for the Second Circuit Court of Appeals, I received a call at work, from Ottilie. She told me that Matt was in jail, and had been charged with resisting arrest and battery of a Chicago police officer. Ottilie insisted that the charge was libelous: that, having used excessive force to subdue him, the police exaggerated their story of the assault. In the reports that I read later, the police asserted that Matt "raised hell as soon as Officers Caputo and Rivak attempted to subdue him, and thereafter the perpetrator attacked one of the officers with his own nightstick."

Mildred's assertion—that some people lead half a life or several lives—is especially true for the insane, and helps explain how Matt had found himself in such circumstances. Matt's madness had twisted him into a different person more than once. Anyone who has ever loved a child or sibling or spouse afflicted with psychosis will bear witness to the terrible and confusing nature of that loss—will attest that madness both takes away a person with the finality of death, and leaves him behind to struggle on as himself and to face all the usual tragedy he might have unbearably borne had he been allowed to really be himself.

In the dozen years following his first hospitalization, schizophrenia altered Matt beyond recognition. He had been a teenager and still growing when he stood in the Calios' mud field. Within a few years his body lost its graceful slightness, and he gained a foot in height. In 1976 Matt was six feet four, and the drugs they used to dull his anguish and paranoia slowed him and made him put on weight until he had almost doubled in bulk, and at other times, robbed his appetite with jittery fervor, leaving him gaunt and hollow-eyed. Haldol and Thorazine caused his hands to shake as if he had the d.t.'s; they unfocused his vision so that he developed a narrow-eyed stare. When he forgot to care for his appearance, neglecting to shave as if not perceiving the onset of adulthood, his beard sprang thickly and his dark hair grew long and wild. To someone who did not know him, Matt was frightening: an enormous, unkempt man who resembled Charles Manson.

A month before Matt's twenty-seventh birthday, the Chicago police initially detained him simply for his appearance: Two people in a neighborhood where Matt fell asleep on a bus-stop bench had called the local precinct. One woman reported that he "looked like Frankenstein," and that he had "glared at her with a menacing, devilish stare," and a store owner had complained there was a derelict outside his entrance, scaring away business.

After the police brought him to the station, Matt gave them Joel Ratleer's telephone number in McCarthy, perhaps out of a sardonic sense of despair. My father hung up when he learned the nature of the call. Following the first year of Matt's illness, my father had divorced himself entirely from Matt; to Joel Ratleer, Ottilie and her son no longer existed.

Nine years before Matt's arrest, the week I had entered the University of Chicago at age seventeen, my father had called me to tell me of his frustrated hopes that Matt would distinguish himself in college. I answered that he needed to visit Matt in order to see the depth and breadth of Matt's illness, and my father did not respond. He viewed my persistence in allying myself with Ottilie and Matt as a betrayal. When I told him that I could not accept his terms—that I reject Ottilie and Matt, as he had, if I wished to continue to relate to my father—he threatened to withhold money for my tuition. When I entered my third year of college, he made good on his threat, and I took out loans, doubled my course load in order to graduate early, and worked long hours as a research assistant on weekends and holidays. Upon his death my father would leave all of his money to the University of Chicago.

In college and law school, I took a dark pride in my independence from him, but as I grew older I learned that by cutting himself off from our family after Matt became psychotic, my father had robbed me of all adult opportunity to understand his lack of sympathy for Matt. Occasionally I would meet other people my age who had a sibling afflicted with schizophrenia, and they would tell stories of fathers who sold their houses and incurred unpayable debts to fund a child's psychiatric care; or forgiving tales of fathers who retreated from psychotic children after years of painful, failed attempts to help them; or bitterly sad accounts of fathers who believed a child's psychosis was a cruel prank, a form of vicious self-indulgence intended to undermine parental expectations. I never answered with stories about my father; I did not even have the satisfaction of knowing with certainty that egotism had led him to reject a son who was psychotic. I suspected, however, and still believe, that my father left us behind and moved on to a new life simply because it was possible for him to do so. And when I imagined what the opposite might have been—Matt contending, as a schizophrenic, with Joel Ratleer, I thought my father's choice might, inadvertently, have been the kindest for us all.

After my brother reached age eighteen, my father's health insurance no longer covered him, and Matt was transferred from the private asylum, where he had resided for three years, to the state hospital system. He often fled state psychiatric facilities to visit with Ottilie, or to roam the streets and sleep in fields or parks. When the police found him asleep on a Chicago park bench in 1976, they did not know at first that Matt was psychotic; they assumed that he was a drunk.

After my father refused Matt's call, the police interrogated him during booking, and he answered irrationally. The police reports stated, "In response to the officers' questions regarding where he lived, the perpetrator answered, 'Doesn't it bother you that when Jesus cast the demons from that man, they jumped into pigs? And then the innocent pigs ran into the water and drowned?'" Apparently, during the arrest, Matt had been silent. It was not until he spoke that the police realized he was insane, and transferred him to a Chicago psychiatric hospital.

Ottilie confided in a local minister, Reverend Steck, whose church, the Park and Pray, had opened a halfway house in Muskellunge, Wisconsin. It was Ottilie's greatest fear that Matt would end up in prison, either because his mental illness led him to do something he did not understand, or because it invited the false accusations of others. She drove to Chicago to fetch Matt, and Reverend Steck sent his daughter, Mildred, to accompany Ottilie. They found Matt dazed by an overdose of Haldol and badly beaten, and thinner than Ottilie had ever seen him. Ottilie believed that he was starving to death, that he was too disoriented to find his way to the downstairs asylum cafeteria and that no one among the staff had troubled to notice.

After Ottilie visited Matt, I received another call at work. This time Ottilie told me that Matt had escaped from the Chicago psychiatric hospital, and that he had done so with the assistance of Reverend Steck's daughter. Ottilie related this story with breathless disbelief and a kind of unbridled hilarity I had rarely seen in her. She stated that while she had argued with the hospital staff about Matt's condition, Mildred Steck had led him into the women's bathroom, pried open a high window, and coaxed him through it into the bracing Chicago winter. After escorting Matt to her car, Mildred brazenly returned to the asylum entrance, had herself readmitted as a visitor through the hospital's locked electronic doors, and then pulled Ottilie away from the head nurse, whispering in her ear, "I grabbed the guy. You drive the getaway car."

Ottilie concluded her phone call: "Mildred is really not like anyone I've ever known before. You'll have to meet her to decide what you think of her."

Ottilie was worried about Mildred's actions, but justified them when speaking to me by saying that Matt might have stayed in the hospital interminably if we had sought to release him by legal means. Eventually, Reverend Steck visited the Chicago police and State's Attorney's office, and the charges against Matt were reduced to a disorderly person violation without jail time, on the condition that Matt reside in the halfway house associated with Reverend Steck's church, or a similar psychiatric facility.

Some time later Ottilie wrote me that Matt seemed less psychotic than he had once been, and no longer suffered frequent hallucinations. The greatest change in him, she added, was "in every other part of him. The bitterness of his life has made him someone else." She asked if I could take time away from my work to stay the following summer in Muskellunge and visit with Matt, because he had withdrawn so far into himself that she was afraid "he might get lost there and never return."

Matt did not write me. In the early years of his illness, he had sent me letters that were half-intelligible, laced with delusions about the imminent coming of the world's end. During college, when I still visited him regularly, he often did not recognize me. He would refuse my calls to the hospital, answering the phone and pretending to be someone else, advising me that Matthew Ratleer could not be found and was unavailable, would I like to leave a message? If I brought him clothes to supplement the tattered ones that he wore in the hospital, I would return a week later to see another inmate wearing them. I once discovered all the letters I sent to Matt over a two-year period stacked unopened in the metal footlocker he kept underneath his bed.

On other days he spoke with clarity and welcomed me, and then we would play chess. Matt never lost his command of the game and continued to beat anyone who played him. I brought Matt books on chess, and subscribed to the *New York Times* for him so that he could read the daily chess page. He would call me late in the evening while I was studying, and launch into lucid analyses of famous matches. Then his mind would zig-zag suddenly, and he would speak crazily, incoherently, as if the words came from a deeper part of him. He said that the FBI had planted transistors in his chess rooks, that it was sending him unsettling messages, that its agents sang hymns in a code spelled out in the moves of the *New York Times*'s bishops.

A hospital psychiatrist had discovered Matt wrote poetry, and loaned him a book by Hölderlin, with the original German poems on the left-hand pages, and their English translations on the right—and although Matt had never studied German, he found that he could read the originals fluently. He mailed me a page torn from the book, on which he had scribbled:

> *Melanie, have you ever found that you can read a foreign language without having seen it before? This would prove, probably, that the things we see and what people see from the perspective of other languages are the same. A Hund and a dog really are one animal.*

More troubling to him was that the German poetry translations had nothing to do with the originals. Instead they contained psychiatric literature meant to tamper with his mind. Matt also confided frequently that the president of the United States was psychotic and plotting to destroy the government. If Matt watched television without the sound, he could read conspiracy and madness in the president's gestures and mannerisms. If he turned the television off, the president continued to try to communicate with him through electrical appliances such as air conditioners. When news of Watergate first broke, Matthew was overwhelmed with relief that others had finally grasped what he had known all along.

A hospital chaplain gave Matt a Bible, and afterward, religion provided him with a language that could communicate the horrors of his madness to the sane. Once, I sent Matt two hundred dollars when he pressed me desperately for spending money, and he later told me he had left the cash stacked neatly behind a picket fence to assuage the anger of "the bad man" who was pursuing him. When I asked him who the bad man was, he clicked his tongue and shook his head at my naivete and answered that of course he had meant Lucifer.

In those days the grief I felt from losing Matt, from looking for him but not always finding him, accompanied me everywhere until it drove me far from home. He was the point of departure and return in a journey in which I wandered without seeing or feeling. After I finished college at the University of Chicago, I fled the Midwest to attend law school in New York. The law's dull cadences reverberated comfortably within the numbness that surrounded me like a house through most of my young womanhood. When I returned to the Kloneckis for school vacations, I visited Matt on weekends at the Chicago hospital where he resided. After my grandfather died in my earlier twenties, I no longer returned to Wisconsin, except at Christmas. Each Christmas Ottilie and I would meet at the hospital, and open presents with Matt in a family room redolent of cigarettes, while outside in the hallways, inmates yelled gibberish or screamed with terror at phantoms.

Matt called me two or three times each week during the first years after I moved away. On his better days, he talked of escaping the Midwest and traveling, as we had when were young—he had plans to visit Crete and Venice and Buenos Aires, to take an ocean voyage around the earth. (I never knew how to answer him; the immigration laws of many countries, our own included, denied visas to the mentally ill.) And he wanted to take a ferry to Beaver Island in the center of Lake Michigan, cross to the other side, and then hitch a ride to New York City to visit me. The idea of Matt traveling was more frightening to me than to him—I envisioned him wandering away and disappearing within the paths of his mind, unable to return, fallen to predatory criminals or police in some distant city where we would never find him. And I feared him showing up at my doorstep, huge and disheveled and confused; the explanations I would have to make to my landlord, neighbors, friends; the grief I would have to bare to the world if I was forced to explain that my brother whom I loved was insane.

When I tried to discourage Matt from adventuring, he would become angry, and refuse to speak to me for weeks afterward. I knew he sensed that, out of bewilderment or cowardice, I feared him trying to visit me. With time he called me less and less frequently, and eventually sent me only envelopes enclosing fragments of his poems. These seemed at once articulate and full of meaning, eerily beautiful and purposely inaccessible:

But always there is a darker love
passing over the Midwest;
so natural as to be unearthly
the body you are tempted into.

. . .

The lesson of history is lonely
and I am lonely, too
I cannot stand
that damn fool of a stepbrother of mine
Who hurries on. France is eternally France
But where are you? Seven hours west
The sun is rising.

In the early days of Matt's illness, I had dreams in which I stared into a deep well, and saw Matt's face there, shattering and composing itself on the dark surface of the water below.

I buried myself in my lawyer's life in the Northeast, in the studious silence of appellate cases and hundred-hour work weeks, until I became unrecognizable to myself. I haunted bar libraries until late in the evening and lost myself in the endless intricacies of the jurisprudence of federal practice and the conflict of laws. The law multiplied in my blood like a voracious virus until it filled the hollow places. It took an irresistible hold on my life and soul and imagination: winters, springs, and summers passed, and I never watched the trees leafing and blossoming or dying, so deeply was I engrossed in the pursuit of my occupation. Before the occurrence of those events that, if made known, would have led to the termination of my judgeship and my eventual disbarment, I rose quickly through my profession with a quietness that bordered on secrecy. (It is easy for those who have power to impute their own thoughts to the taciturn. Over and over, my career was championed by influential law partners, judges, presidents of the bar association, each imagining that I was what he wanted me to be.) Once, I worked for two years without taking a single vacation day, and after that period, there were mornings when I was unable to call up any image of Matt's face.

IN MUSKELLUNGE, after Ottilie first brought Matt back there, people crossed the street when he approached them on the sidewalk. They backed off, startled by his appearance. Ottilie wrote me that small children wailed and became frantic if Matt looked at them, because their mothers pulled them too close and clutched them too tightly when he passed. He was too large, too disordered, monstrous. And although on his best days he seemed as sane as you or I, on his worst, he muttered to himself and held conversations with people who were not there.

With time, however, in the way of small towns, people grew accustomed to Matt's presence, and began to accept that he posed no threat. After a few months he had never been observed in an act of violence, or exposed himself in public, or even appeared drunk on a back street. Mostly, it was the sight of him with Ottilie, her frail arm looped around his elbow, her quiet assuredness as she walked beside him, that led to the community's circumspect tolerance, if not acceptance, of his presence.

On Sundays Ottilie accompanied Matt five blocks down from her house to the Park and Pray. Within the community of that church, Matt's ominous presence became dependable and expected, part of the fabric of things. Many members of the congregation felt holier if they could engage in a conversation with Matt without averting their eyes from his startling appearance or revealing that they found his dialogue incoherent.

Matt's life had not always been without attachments and romance. Occasionally he introduced Ottilie or me to a girl from the state hospital, someone stricken like him with schizophrenia, who shared his peculiar blend of despairing humor, his horror at the hand that life dealt the psychotic, his sense of confusion and isolation and difference. When he was younger, there was a woman named Clover who would ride to Chicago from Winnetka when the mental health center where she stayed granted her permission to travel. He dated a girl on his ward, Caroline, until her parents sent her to a private hospital in Milwaukee, fearing that Matt would get her pregnant. When he was in his late twenties, Matt was passionately, deeply grateful to any woman—among the social workers and psychology students who drifted in and out of mental health centers on six-month internships—who showed any concern for him at all.

After Matt moved into the Park and Pray's halfway house, Ottilie wrote me that Mildred Steck seemed to be the only person who could tempt him into socializing. Ottilie's letters were as full of information about Mildred as if Ottilie herself had fallen in love with her. I knew before meeting Mildred that she had a two-year-old son, to whom Matt was attached, that she spoke several languages, and that she had taught a Spanish class at her father's church on Thursday nights, which Matt attended unfailingly. She was, according to Ottilie, "religious in an unusual way." Mildred was married to a man with "ideas as radical as her own," who Ottilie believed was somewhere in South America doing research. Mildred was willing to discuss religion or poetry or languages with Matt, and the conversations they had, Ottilie noted, "almost sounded sane."

Mildred's father, Reverend Steck, was a former Lutheran minister evicted from his pulpit during the fifties for his heretical views and opposition to Joe McCarthy. He later headed a Unitarian church in Madison and became a midwestern William Sloane Coffin: He was a passionate man respected for his sincerity and willingness to set himself at risk for his political convictions. Under his sly directorship, his church in Madison had harbored war resisters and Mexican migrant laborers and political refugees from Central America, supplying them with false identities and helping them set up homes in big cities like Chicago and Detroit where such people could live in anonymity.

Reverend Steck had moved to Muskellunge, the town of his youth, to head a smaller church, whose main project now consisted of running the halfway house. A Madison psychiatrist, armed with the latest unorthodox theories on nutrition and vitamin therapy, as well as Haldol and Thorazine, visited the house weekly. Reverend Steck had been kind to Matt when he first arrived in Muskellunge, allowing him to work mornings in the Park and Pray as a handyman and caretaker, and encouraging him to participate in an organic gardening project behind the church. Ottilie told me that Reverend Steck's own wife had been hospitalized on and off for manic depression during the decade preceding her death, and perhaps that was why he, like Mildred, had a soft spot for Matthew.

IN 1976, I was engaged in my second federal clerkship and had been promised a position as an appellate lawyer in a respected civil rights firm, to begin the following year in June. (At twenty-seven, I would be the youngest attorney and the only woman the firm had ever hired as an associate.) It was my driving ambition to become a federal judge, to write opinions that reverberated with the compassionate wisdom of Thurgood Marshall, that turned the law against itself in order to negate the wrongs wrought by the treacherous and neglectful Gods of earlier courts. I had no desire ever to enter a state court as a trial lawyer, to rub elbows with scurrilous defense attorneys like my father.

One morning, early in my last year of clerking, I noticed a plum-sized bruise under my rib cage. I could not imagine where it came from: I had not fallen, had not been punched or kicked, had not been in any accident that I remembered. And when, after a month, the bruise did not fade, I finally consulted a doctor who told me that I would need chemotherapy: The same cancer that had killed my mother now had descended to test its charms on me.

The doctor had discovered a tumor the breadth of a fist under my rib cage, and he told me in a curious voice, leaning forward as if looking for symptoms of emotion on my face, that the cancer would kill me if it was not treated aggressively. Each Friday evening I withstood the treatments, drove home sick with nausea, and spent all weekend in bed. By Monday I would be steady enough on my feet to take a taxi to my job. During this period I never missed a day of work, although I grew distant from the man I had been seeing for two years, and our relationship evaporated. (He told me that the passion that had brought us together had twisted into an inward battle in which he had no role, that I had replaced my love for him and everything in life with a greater fury to battle death. He was a writer; he talked this way.)

By the end of 1976, the tumor had shrunken and then disappeared, as mysteriously as it had come. I felt a strange commingling of satisfaction that the cancer had been vanquished, and resentment that it had intruded into my life at all. And within the resentment, I harbored a deeper anger that death, which had cheated me of a mother, would now rob me of my sense of ease—that even as a young woman, I would sense death leaning over my left shoulder, reminding me that the beauty and glitter of life could be taken away as easily as they were offered.

I did not tell Ottilie about the illness until my treatments ended. I felt almost superstitious, that speaking of the cancer would imbue it with power, and that my silence would suffocate it. When I let slip the information that my treatments were over and had been successful, Ottilie became angry with me, and followed my phone call with a letter:

> *Do you think your suffering is so special that you can't bring yourself to speak of it? How can you forget we love you? If your mother had told her family sooner, they might have helped her. It amazes me that you would think of dying without even visiting. What would Matt have done? You need to find time to see your brother.*

The closing words of Ottilie's letter stung me. I did not want to return home to Wisconsin with its bitter winds and opaque gray skies, to compare my life's trajectory with Matt's world of hardship. I steadfastly had resisted Ottilie's invitation to spend an entire summer in Muskellunge: I could not even picture life in Wisconsin in the summer. When I tried to conjure up the image from my memory, I thought only of icy winds that froze our tears, and crows swooping through the delicate black branches of leafless trees, throwing lavender shadows on blinding snow-scapes.

In the weeks after my treatments ended, I daydreamed of taking off six months between jobs, of doing something extravagant, as people who have been liberated from the immediate threat of death are said to do. I thought of visiting places that had always struck me as full of adventure: Tierra del Fuego or Tasmania or the Antarctic. I arranged to start my new job six months late, the following January, but afterward I was unable to settle on a travel itinerary. I felt aimless and rose late in the mornings, wrapped in daydreams, and at night I slept badly, my sleep interrupted by nightmares so vivid they seemed more real than my waking life.

In one nightmare I awoke in a tunnel, soft and snug as a sleeping bag, and crawled wormlike to the light, struggling free only after what seemed like days of labor. When I emerged, I believed I would be a swallowtail, iridescent and weightless, but instead I was a hideous bird with oily, dark wings, joyful at my preposterous ugliness and freedom. In another dream I attended my own wake. My coffin lay stretched on a bench in a courthouse, and the nine justices of the Supreme Court stood around me weeping. In another I dreamed that I had returned to the doctor for a follow-up examination, and he informed me that I no longer had to worry about the cancer returning, because the X rays showed that I had died already.

In the worst nightmare of that period, I dreamed about Matt. In the dream Matt was not as he was then, disheveled and psychotic, or as he had been when we were young, a beautiful, lean dark-haired teenager. He was a middle-aged man with the flat yellow eyes of a goat, who smiled sardonically and asked me to accompany him into a cornfield, its rows dark as the alleys between tenements, where he promised to kill me swiftly and painlessly if I cooperated. "You have too much already, and I have so little," he told me. "You're helpless anyway." The sound of my own protesting voice awoke me, and for hours afterward I was unable to shake the terror of the dream. I called Matt the following day.

When Matt first picked up the phone, he gave no greeting to indicate that he was on the other end: All of my questions fell into an answerless silence. Finally, when I told Matt that Ottilie had written me about his Spanish lessons, he answered, "Have they told you not to speak any foreign languages there if you want to get a job?" He paused, waiting for a response. "Do you know this movement of some guy somewhere, either it's New York or New Mexico, who wants English made the national language? They say you have to be careful to speak only English or no one will hire you, and you can go to jail. Do you know about this?"

I answered that I had decided to spend the summer and fall in Muskellunge. Then our conversation terminated abruptly, because Matt hung up on me. But I had committed myself, and I could no longer stay away.

2

THE GREYHOUND from O'Hare to northern Wisconsin drove haltingly, discharging passengers at every windblown lakeshore town between Zion and Fredonia. June wheat and corn gilded the fields, far from harvest. To the east Lake Michigan glittered like a false ocean. Landmarks I must have seen in my childhood tugged at me, portentous as the images of dreams: a leafless oak forking like inverted black lightning in the vastness separating two farms; an oblong barnyard trampled hard by wide-hipped womanly cattle; a golden field racing away from the road toward an infinitely thin gray wire of horizon.

I recognized a pier where I had once gone fishing as a child. I remembered a stream rushing into the lake near the pier, multitudes of inedible suckerfish clattering landward over the gravelly streambeds. They swam so thickly you could almost catch them with your hands. My father stood on the stream bank, goddamning the fish as they paraded below, his voice manic with dark humor. He bent toward the water with a snow shovel from his car's trunk and pitched the fish onto the banks. They lay everywhere around us, u-mouthed and gasping. But there were so many that they lacked individual fear: Those that escaped rioted by us, the water smashing like store windows. Afterward, Matt and Ottilie and I wandered down to the pier and stared into brown water while my father fished off the end, quiet as a man pretending to pray. I imagined fish smirking below in the deep shadows, silent as churches, their mouths closed on their names: mackinaw, tongue, rainbow, splake, cutthroat.

The bus's air conditioning made goose bumps rise on my arms, while the midwestern summer's stifling heat rippled over the highway like a mirage. I changed in the Greyhound's cramped bathroom: I shed the lawyer's suit I had traveled in from LaGuardia and pulled on a windbreaker jacket, jeans stiff with newness, a T-shirt rough with sizing. I slipped the jacket's hood over my hair and examined myself in the bathroom mirror: My features looked masklike, numb. I felt a jolt of fear, an overwhelming impulse to return to Chicago and fly home.

When I arrived in Manitowoc, neither Ottilie nor Matt was at the bus station. The smell of pigs thickened the damp air. My windbreaker trapped the humidity, and I pulled it off and waited outside the station door where the heat was slightly less stifling. A radio blared pork prices, bank foreclosures on farms, advertisements for chemical fertilizer and pesticides. A teenage couple cried bitterly as a girl boarded the bus, dressed in army fatigues. A man helped his drunk friend through the station's doorway, and eased him into an orange plastic chair before he slid, boneless, to the floor. A young woman wearing a tie-dyed sundress and a derby hat leaned dreamily against the outside wall.

I imagined how different a person I would have to be to wear a derby, or even to contemplate buying one. I pictured myself walking the narrow path of my one-hundred-hour work week, dressed in my navy blue suit and white blouse, briefcase in hand, my hair tied back, and the derby hat tilted over one eye. I flashed a gangsterish smile at a Southern District Court judge, and the image folded in on itself.

A dozen Canada geese gathered at the edge of the bus station's parking lot, honking and shoveling up spilled grass seed. When they saw me, they strode forward boldly, their snake necks raised, black masks slanting over malicious eyes. A toddler circled the building behind them. He wore a tie-dyed shirt that matched the young woman's and, despite the heat, one of those wool ski masks that would become so popular later as disguises for muggers and terrorists.

A goose swivelled its neck, and brought its masked head up to his, hissing. The boy drew back, startled, and yelled, "Kill it! Mommy, kill it!"

His mother laughed and stooped next to him, circling his shoulders with one arm, and waving her derby at the goose with the other. "You have to honk at them before they honk at you," she told him. "HONK! HONK!" The bird lifted a foot and stepped backward.

"HONK! HONK!" the boy repeated.

When I smiled at him, he turned away and hugged his mother's legs lovingly, pushing his face into her dress's crinkled cotton. Then he leaned forward and stared at me through his mask's eyeholes.

"I'm Spider Man!" he said. His eyes were a startling silvery gray, narrow as minnows. His mother had the same eyes, and a face I had often seen in Wisconsin in my childhood—wide, with a pointed chin and high, Slavic cheekbones. She was of medium height, large-boned, long-waisted.

She stepped toward me and caught my arm. I pulled away reflexively; I can't stand to be touched by strangers.

"You must be a Ratleer," she said. She smelled faintly of incense and sandalwood soap. "I'm Mildred Steck." Her silver eyes disappeared in shadow when she smiled. "You look exactly like Matt, except he's bigger. Matt freaked out and ran off, so Ottilie sent me to get you." Mildred said this all matter-of-factly, as if Matt's flight were to be expected.

"Ran off?"

"Ottilie was driving here to pick you up, and Matt jumped out of the car when she stopped at an intersection. Then he took off across an alfalfa field. Ottilie parked and went looking for him. She called and asked me to drive you home."

Mildred's familiarity with Matt made me uneasy. I realized with chagrin that I felt both jealous and relieved that someone, anyone else, was close to my brother.

I retrieved a large cardboard box from the Greyhound's underbelly. I had packed the box with a Hermes Baby typewriter and copies of legal cases, statutes, and law journal articles. I intended to spend my time in Muskellunge resourcefully, writing a review of unconstitutional forms of discrimination engendered by the insurance industry.

"The car's this way," Mildred said, picking up my suitcase in her free hand. As she strode ahead of me, her braid—honey-colored, thick as a boa constrictor—swung behind her.

"Oh, Lord," she sang, "won't you buy me a Mercedes Benz?" Her own car was the centerpiece of the parking lot: an ancient turquoise Cadillac with MILDRED written in flowery gold script on the driver's door, and a metal ornament, shaped like a pig, fastened to the hood in place of the Cadillac insignia.

When I caught up with her, her profile astonished me—from the front, she was pretty and ordinary, but from the side, she was captivating. Only once or twice in my life have I seen a woman whose profile was more arresting than her full face. When Mildred turned her head,

her high hairline and wide mouth made me think of Renaissance paintings of martyred women saints of uncanny beauty. The effect was dis-
quieting, almost as if she were two people. (Years later, when I would
see Mildred Steck's face displayed among post office wanted posters, I
would feel an odd pleasure from the deception the FBI portrait perpe-
trated by showing her only from the front, looking indistinguishable
from a thousand other midwestern women.)

Mildred opened her car trunk and heaved in my suitcase. Beside the
spare tire were a dog-eared copy of *The Marx Anthology,* a poetry book
called *Monster,* and several paperbacks including *Soul on Ice* and *The
Wretched of the Earth.* Beside these were a child's orange life preserver,
a disassembled rod and reel, and two tackle boxes, one of which lay
half-open with a black revolver poking from it. I must have looked
surprised because Mildred said, "Don't worry. It's not real—it's just a
starter's pistol my dad uses for this boy's track team he coaches in Sheboygan. It takes blanks."

She pulled off her son's ski mask. "That's Ben," she introduced us.
Ben flashed me a mischievous smile, revealing a face like his mother's—
heart-shaped, with high cheekbones and a wide mouth. "Ben, this is
Matt's lady-lawyer sister."

He snuggled against his mother's neck, and peered at me over her
shoulder. "I have a penis," he told me.

Mildred laughed, and helped Ben into the car.

"I would please, please like—" Ben said.

"The crackers are in the back," Mildred told him.

"I would please like a cracker," Ben finished, as he crawled onto his
seat. Mildred buckled him in, and placed a lunch box on his lap.

I sat in front and watched the farms race by as Mildred drove: A
grassy field fidgeted along the road; a hawk hurled down his shadow,
and it glided translucently, a cross made of water, over a blue roof; red
poppies flared between the rusted ribs of a corn thrasher.

When we were a few miles north of Manitowoc, Mildred turned
inland onto a narrow highway. "You and Ottilie, quiet as the grave,"
she said.

I grinned amiably.

"I once drove all the way to Chicago with Ottilie," Mildred said,
"and Ottilie never once said a thing except, 'I like those snowy owls.
That's the first time I've seen one in years.' I craned my neck around to
see the snowy owl, but I guessed we'd already passed it because I

couldn't see anything. I wondered how many miles we'd driven past the owl since Ottilie spotted it and thought to comment on it. She never pointed it out to me, no, just soaked it up quietly all by herself. At least you don't look like a lawyer."

"I would please, please like an owl," Ben said.

I told Mildred I'd changed out of a suit on the bus.

"No, I mean *you* don't look like a lawyer. You don't have that look, that snaky look."

"I would please like a snake," Ben said.

"My father's working on Ben to make him say please," Mildred told me, "so Ben's been's torturing me with it all day."

I turned around. Ben sat tenderly and affectionately lining up rows of crackers on top of his lunch box. His hands were square, wider than they were long, with short fingers. His hair was cinnamon-brown, and he gave off a spicy boy smell that made me think of burning leaves—the way Matt had smelled when we were children. Ben began a winding tune that sounded like "Puff the Magic Dragon."

"Matt's teaching Ben to sing," Mildred said.

Ben immediately stopped singing. He pressed his face against the car window and left a foggy mask on the glass, with large skull holes and a shrunken mouth.

"Really? Matt is?" I asked.

"Yeah, Ben's crazy about Matt."

I thought my brother must not be too bad off if he had been able to befriend a child. Perhaps his illness had become more subdued, or he could control it better.

"This is where I always stop to thank the Lord that I was born in Muskellunge, because I could have been condemned to life here instead," Mildred announced. The car approached a dilapidated town consisting of a single store, a gas station, a barn with a pigsty behind it and in an adjacent lot, a small, pale blue house. "This place has six inhabitants," Mildred said. "A man who sells gas and hamburgers, named Mr. Eklund, and his pigs." A road sign identified the intersection as an unincorporated town named "Eklundville."

"A while back, Ottilie told me you were dying," Mildred said next. "Still dying?"

I smiled and answered dryly, "No."

"You look pretty good." Mildred adjusted her rearview mirror. She had slender wrists, and wore a Spiro Agnew watch.

I asked Mildred about herself to deflect her examination of me. She talked obligingly, with surprising candor, most of the ride. She had an unusual style of speaking, earnest and self-mocking, like a raconteur delivering a sermon whose primary purpose was to outrage his audience and secondary one to convince them of the underlying truth of his words. She told me that she was twenty-five years old, and had been born and raised in Muskellunge, where her family, she said, "had been made famous the day her mother walked down Main Street with her skirt over her head, accusing passersby of being agents of the Kremlin." After her mother's death, Mildred's father had relocated to Madison, where she attended part of high school and then college. She had obtained a B.A. in Romance languages, despite the fact that the university suspended her for a semester for her "participation, half-naked, in a demonstration." She had worked after graduating as a freelance writer for *The Progressive*, but "was forced to resign," she said, because she was "more progressive than *The Progressive*." Then an old Brazilian friend of her father's who headed an office at the World Council of Churches hired her as his assistant. She had met her husband, Daniel, while traveling in Brazil on World Council work. He was there doing research for a Fulbright. Now she earned a partial living translating documents from Spanish and Portuguese for Amnesty International.

Mildred rolled down her window and tilted her head toward the wind. Precipitously, the outside air snatched her derby—it sailed up into the sky in front of us and then dipped under the car's wheels.

"Whoooah!" Ben said.

Mildred slowed, looking in the rearview mirror, and said, "Squashed flat as hell." She got out of the car and walked back along the road.

"It flew," Ben told me.

Mildred returned with the hat and handed it to Ben. "It was old," Mildred said wistfully. "Dad used to wear it when I was in high school." I wondered what kind of minister would wear a derby hat.

"It looks like a cow pie," Ben said.

"And before that, my mother used to wear it all over Muskellunge, just to bother people. She was once forced to leave an American Legion assembly because she refused to take it off. It's sort of an heirloom. I got married to my husband Daniel in it."

Mildred drove on and told me that her father had not yet met Daniel but was sure to like him, because they both shared "the same innocent politics and will to save the world." Mildred said that her father was "so pure of heart it made you want to cry," that after he had been blackballed by his first church's board, he continued to believe that Mc-Carthyism was an aberration in the hearts and minds of Americans, "even in our country's heartland where John Birchers are more plentiful than knockwurst," and "right through the election of McCarthy's kiss-butt, Nixon." Mildred said she sometimes feared she would inherit Reverend Steck's idealism and openness along with his genes, which she held to be her greatest potential flaw as a political activist. "I hope to God that something happens fast to harden me," she concluded ironically. She then continued to talk unguardedly about herself.

Mildred explained that she was attracted by the World Council and liberation theology because of her father's work, and because of the way politics and religion mixed to produce views that riled everybody. She said that the purest pleasure for her in life was to irk people, and that her favorite political figures were John Brown, because he was so outrageous that no one could decide if he was brilliant or crazy, and Malcolm X, because he "made no bones about provoking everyone." She liked the way he called white people "blue-eyed devils." Although like her father she admired King, her heart would always be with people who had no sense of diplomacy. This sometimes bothered her husband, Mildred said, but she didn't mind bothering him. He had written a thesis on the importance of resolving all conflicts through dialogue.

"He despises lawyers," she said. "Daniel doesn't believe in the adversarial process."

Daniel was ten years older than Mildred, and came from a small Wisconsin town called Ripon. His family had been wealthy and left him a large trust fund, but "you would never know it," Mildred said. Like her, he was committed to liberation theology. He had graduated from Yale Divinity School, and was working on a doctorate in comparative religion at the University of Wisconsin. She believed him to be brilliant. Mildred had married Daniel in Brasilia, after what she called "not just a whirlwind but a tornado romance," and then she had resigned from her work and lived with Daniel in the Amazonian interior, while he gathered research on evangelism among itinerant farmers and miners. Mildred noted with pride that she had had Ben by natural childbirth, with only the assistance of a midwife, in a frontier town where there were no doctors. She had remained in Brazil until her husband's work took him to a mining town within a malarial area. She and Ben had then returned to the States while her husband finished up his research.

"Daniel wanted us to stay, but I had to put my foot down for once. I told him it was just too risky for Ben. But you know how men are; they don't have any sense."

I did not answer what I thought, that most men would have more sense than to drag a two-year-old into a malarial area and to expect a wife to have her first child in the middle of the Amazon without medical care nearby. But I was enjoying Mildred's outrageous and intelligent banter. The longer I listened to her, the more pleasantly off-balance I felt.

"Here we are, at the Pissville city limits," Mildred announced. "I'm glad my father and Ben are getting to spend some time together. But Jesus, sometimes I think I'll lose my mind if I live another week here."

Muskellunge in 1977 was a town of 12,000 people, drained of commerce and activity by the neighboring larger city of Manitowoc. Inside Muskellunge is a brewery that makes Pferd beer. As we entered the town, we passed a thirty-foot billboard shaped like a frothing beer stein. All around the stein were small signs, set in the ground like tombstones, representing the Masons, Lions, Shriners, Kiwanis Club, and John Birch Society, seemingly attesting to these groups' willingness to drink Pferd. Pferd has an undefinable aftertaste, and the air that wafted from the brewery over the town smelled sour, a cross between cod liver oil and manure and hops.

"We're supposed to meet Matt and Ottilie at this seafood place called Musky's," Mildred said.

I thought suddenly of the expression "butterflies in your stomach," and then understood that I was feeling them. I had not realized how nervous I was about seeing Matt. For a moment I imagined him sane and beautiful and strong: He would rush forward, take me by the hand, ask me about my work, talk about chess, and show me his poetry. We would sit on the porch together, watching fireflies appear and vanish like falling stars. Then I pushed from my mind the image of Matt as he might have been, feeling that I had betrayed him by my thoughts.

Ben's warm breath tickled the back of my neck. "I eat fish," he said. "I *eat* them."

Musky's was apparently on the other side of Pissville, because Mildred sped through the town as quickly as possible. We passed a five-block strip of bars and assorted stores on the main avenue, called Walleye Street: a Piggly-Wiggly supermarket; a theater advertising long-forgotten movies; a store called Shove's with an overhead sign reading LIQUOR—BEER—CHEESE—BAKERY—LIVE BAIT"; an Armed Forces Recruiting Center; a gray stone courthouse, many-storied and imposing for so small a town; a curious yellow brick building with red brick swastikas set above the door under a sign that said VEIL AND GOWN, evidently a bridal apparel shop; a Woolworth's; and several stores with signs that said simply FOOD, CLOTHING, DRUGS; and a Sears outlet destroyed by fire.

We exited onto the highway that led north from Muskellunge County to Kewaunee County. On the far side of Muskellunge was a farm equipment dealer. The gaudy yellows and reds and emeralds of John Deere tractors, harvesters, and threshers spread below a twenty-foot billboard that cautioned:

STOP ABORTION!
(YOU KNOW IN YOUR HEART)
IT IS MURDER!

Under this was a picture of the human embryo from the movie *2001: A Space Odyssey*, floating through a starry sky. Muskellunge was ahead of its time in this one respect—it was the first Wisconsin town to generate a concerted protest against *Roe* v. *Wade*.

"That guy from *2001* is the most famous fetus in the world," Mildred said. "And he fits right in here. There's weird politics crawling all over Muskellunge." Mildred told me that although she considered herself psychologically incapable of having an abortion, she was against the proposed Hyde Amendment, which would cut Medicaid funding for abortions. She called it the "Dr. Jekyll and Mr. Hyde" Amendment, and then she volunteered a slogan for local right-to-lifers: "If I'd had to choose between being born in Muskellunge and being aborted, I wouldn't be here today."

I laughed.

"The Baptist preacher who raises money for those billboards, Reverend Hatch, considers my father his rival, and once accused him of stealing the Baptist church's parishioners. Hatch thinks they changed over because of some voodoo power my father has, mesmerizing people with his communist sermons—his private *Invasion of the Body Snatchers*—but the truth is, half the ladies left Reverend Hatch's church because they

like to work in my father's organic gardening project. Reverend Hatch
just doesn't know what power the Feed and Seed store holds over the
souls of his flock, how far they are willing to stray in order to discover
my father's secrets for growing the biggest tomatoes in Muskellunge.
And then, my father's single—nothing like a handsome widowed minister to attract pious ladies. He's cult material. Reverend Hatch acts like
he tied his pecker to his leg with a shoelace ten years ago, and hasn't
touched it since."

Mildred pulled up outside a restaurant with a giant yellow neon
fish on its roof and a sign that spelled MUSKY's. "Musky" is the local
affectionate term for a muskellunge, the voracious and predatory member of the pike family that spawns in Wisconsin in April. The neon fish
had the elongated body and forked tail of a musky, and its eyes were
large and slightly skewed, giving it a demented look.

"That sign is Muskellunge's claim to fame," Mildred said. "You can
watch it watch you from anywhere in town."

The restaurant's other salient feature was just inside the entryway,
a thirty-foot aquarium full of silty green water, in which Musky, the
restaurant's hungry mascot, lived out his days. Musky was a five-foot
muskellunge caught in the nearby waters of Lake Michigan. He had a
proprietary smile and a long, mossy gray body that rested with the taut
stillness of a predator on the tank's bottom.

A second, smaller aquarium, set at a right angle to Musky's, contained other famous fish of Wisconsin: walleye pikes and smallmouth
bass, slimy sculpins and suckers and alewives. Labelled drawings on the
outside of their tanks identified the various fish and described them as
"food fish," "bait fish," or "of no commercial value." On the outside of
Musky's larger aquarium was a sign that read:

> This Great Lakes dweller grows as large
> as eight feet, and eats anything from water bugs
> to valuable food fish to muskrats.

The implication was clear: the inhabitants of the smaller tank were
Musky's supper. Ben raced to the larger tank and placed his face at
eye level with Musky's. The fish turned imperceptibly, its duck-billed
mouth locked in an ominous grin, as if he were considering Ben for
dinner.

The restaurant was dark, lit murkily by the aquariums. Single candles illuminated the faces of diners eerily from below. At the back of the restaurant Ottilie's pale hair flickered, and she waved at me. Beside her was a man in a minister's collar. At least four men were seated around her at the table, and the air above them was thick with smoke. As I approached, Matt looked down, refusing to acknowledge my arrival.

"Melanie!" Ottilie called. She rushed around the table, and she hugged me, delicately, as if afraid that I bruised easily. Although she was in her mid-forties, she still had a girl's slender gracefulness, and had hardly aged, except that crows' feet appeared beside her eyes when she smiled. I felt awkward hugging her: I had grown angular and thin and looked even taller than usual. (I thought of what I had told the man I had been seeing, when the chemotherapy was halfway done—that I had become so gaunt and morose I looked like a female Boris Karloff. He had not disagreed; he had nodded and said, "Just like the Mummy.")

Behind Ottilie, Matt glanced at us and turned away. He had thick, wild hair and a tangled beard.

"Matt's just anxious about seeing you after so long," Ottilie whispered.

"Hey, Matt," I said, but he did not answer.

"We were all looking forward to meeting you," the minister told me, rising and extending his hand. It was calloused and sandpapery, square with broad fingers that made me think of cigar stubs. "I'm John Steck, and these men are my buddies from the Park and Pray." He spread his arms wide, and rocked on his heels as he talked, radiating a quiet, charismatic energy. He was my height, with plow yoke shoulders and a chest so large that I literally could not have encircled it with my arms. Nothing about Mildred's father other than his white collar worn over a plain gray flannel shirt, suggested a man of religion. He had a round, jocular face, silver eyes, and wiry hair the pale brown of pilsner, tied back in a short ponytail.

As I shook the reverend's hand, I saw that the tables immediately surrounding ours were all unoccupied. Five yards away, a family sat, their forks half-raised, watching us.

At our table the man nearest to me, dressed in a navy blue sweatshirt, black tie, and tweed jacket, sucked with furious energy on a cigarette, as if he were drawing oxygen from it. The man beside him, diminutive as a twelve-year-old and dressed in a boy's jeans and sweater, muttered under his breath, "The sky is falling, the sky is falling." He also smoked; although his cigarette still burned far from the filter, he lit it against a new one, which he held in his hand while finishing the first. Next to him a reedy man with a Clark Gable pencil moustache sat staring at nothing, a loose smile on his face, a faint smell of cologne or cognac emanating from him. I realized then that these men were from the halfway house where Matt resided, and I sat down among them.

Their names were Stretch Rockefeller and Adolf Dmytryk and Dr. Stanley Eatman, and over the next few months I would get to know them all fairly well. No one in this thrown-together society of men was dangerous, or even unpredictable. Stretch Rockefeller never said any phrase longer than "the sky is falling" in the entire six months I stayed in Muskellunge, but he was able to cook breakfast each morning at the halfway house, standing on a stepladder that allowed him to reach the back burners. Adolf Dmytryk carried a Coca-Cola bottle with him everywhere he went, filled with a honey-colored liquid, too pale to be cola, which turned out to be one-hundred-proof dandelion wine he fermented himself; he only acted crazy when he wasn't drinking. He read the Bible or watched television, and sometimes would play a half-game of chess with Matt before losing focus and wandering away. Dr. Eatman was an entomologist who had been fired from an Illinois university after a nervous breakdown that led him to paint his colleagues' office doors with descriptive terms derived from the names of insects: Skunk Beetle and Snipe Fly, Blood-sucking Conenose Bug and Toe-Biter. He woke people in the halfway house with his screaming nightmares and his sleepwalking, and had gloomy periods when he would perch alone on the couch in the living room, arguing loudly with himself.

That evening Matt seemed the worst off of any of these men, although he was the youngest. He sat hunched in his chair, withdrawn and brooding. He looked in my direction only once, early in the meal: He narrowed his eyes and gazed at me flatly. His stare seemed intentionally threatening, and I thought that if I had not known him, if he had not been my brother, I would have wondered if he was dangerous: I would not have entered an elevator alone with him, and surely would have crossed the street if I had seen him approaching me on my block after dark.

Ben pulled himself up in his seat, grabbing Matt's shoulder for balance. Beside his grandfather, Ben seemed like a parody of Reverend

Steck, a smaller version whose chestiness was exaggerated by the stalwart shape natural to toddlers.

"Ben," Reverend Steck said, beaming affectionately at his grandson. "if you stand in your chair like that, you'll fall and break your head, and all the hay will come out."

"No it won't," Ben answered. He half sat down, kneeling on one leg and keeping the shoe of his other foot on the chair. Then he chattered to his grandfather, seemingly inured to the presence of the halfway house's residents.

"SAVE THE BUTTER!" Dr. Eatman shouted.

Rockefeller took eight or nine butter squares from a dish at the table's center and began slathering them on a half-slice of bread. Dr. Eatman stood up and grabbed Rockefeller's wrist, and lifted him out of his seat. A child's beaded leather belt circled Rockefeller's slender waist.

"He eats too much!" Dr. Eatman told me. "We have to chain the refrigerator at night to keep him from eating us out of house and home."

"There's plenty of butter," Reverend Steck said, passing Dr. Eatman a plate from his end of the table. Dr. Eatman and Rockefeller sat back down. Dr. Eatman stacked four squares of butter on his bread plate and curled his hand protectively in front of them.

"At first they blamed me; can you believe it?" Dr. Eatman said, looking at me. "When all the food started disappearing at night from the icebox. It took a while for us all to catch on, he's so small. It was a mystery! Does he think a prodigious appetite will make him grow?"

"Who are *you*?" the man with the Clark Gable moustache asked me. Without waiting for my answer, he presented himself as Dmytryk, and then he introduced all of the other members of the table, including Ottilie and my brother.

"That's Matt's sister, for Chrissake," Dr. Eatman said. "It's his goddamn sister, for Chrissake." He stubbed out his cigarette on his plate.

"Don't curse, you dumb fuck," Dmytryk answered. "There's a preacher present."

Mildred laughed, and Dmytryk flashed her a charming smile.

"The sky is falling!" Rockefeller muttered.

Ben looked around at the adults and said, "Fuck!"

The family at the occupied table nearest to ours stopped talking and stared at us.

"Fuck!" Ben shouted. "Fuck! Fuck! Fuck!"

"Simmer down, Ben," Reverend Steck said.

"The sky is falling!" Rockefeller repeated.

"What would happen if the sky did fall?" Mildred turned to Rocke-feller, speaking with ease and familiarity. "Would we have stars in our soup?"

He smiled back at her as if he found this funny, and answered, "Probably."

"Fuck!" Ben said again.

"Just don't say 'Oshkosh,'" Reverend Steck told his grandson.

"Oshkosh," Ben answered. "Oshkosh, Oshkosh."

"You devil!" Reverend Steck replied.

Mildred told me, "Dad couldn't get Ben to stop repeating curse words—he has this radar for knowing when he's overheard something he shouldn't say. So Matt convinced him that 'Oshkosh!' is the worst swearword. All you have to do is to tell Ben not to say it, and then he'll say it, and he won't bother with the other ones."

"It works like a charm," Reverend Steck interjected. "It taps right in to a two-year-old's delight in being bad, and it keeps him from using the f-word and the like when he wants to rile the adults. Well, usually it does. Whatever you do, Ben," Reverend Steck said in demonstration, facing his grandson, "*Don't* say 'Oshkosh.'"

"Oshkosh," Ben complied.

I looked at Matt, but he sat unresponsively, staring at his own hands as if surprised by them; they were large hands, almost tremendous, like Joel Ratleer's. I wondered if Matt exaggerated his antisocial qualities to shield himself from examination. Surely he couldn't be completely out of things if he thought of something that clever for waylaying a two-year-old.

Dr. Eatman leaned toward me and announced in a loud, wheedling tone, pointing at Dmytryk, "His Christian name is Adolf."

"I never use that name!" Dmytryk said emphatically. "My parents couldn't have known any better," he explained. "I was born before the first war."

Reverend Steck steered the conversation away from an argument, by focussing on me and asking about my legal career. His questions made me uncomfortable, and so I asked Reverend Steck about himself. He related that he had resettled in Muskellunge because fishing was his passion. Matt and he went fishing at Lake Muskellunge or Lake Michigan every Saturday. Reverend Steck spread his short-fingered hands on the table before him, and told me other things I did not know: that Matt had proven invaluable to the church as a handyman, repairing cars and refrigerators, and even electrical wiring.

"Matt fixed Ben's electric Godzilla," Mildred volunteered. "And he mounted the pig hood ornament on my car and painted it."

"I need a used car," I said, looking at Matt. "I haven't had one for years, living in New York. Can you help me find a car and fix it up?"

Matt did not answer. He looked over my shoulder, half smiling, as if sharing a private joke with someone there.

When the waitress brought the rolls, she hovered indecisively over Dr. Eatman's plate, black at the center from his cigarette, and then snatched it from him. He looked startled, and acted disgruntled until Mildred handed him her plate.

Everyone ordered fish. When the waitress came with the meal, Ben refused to touch his. He would only eat food off Matt's dish, sneaking away french fries teasingly and flirtatiously. Matt seemed to find this funny; he finally smiled. I saw him cut up a piece of fish, and push it to Ben's side of the plate, then pretend not to notice when Ben ate it.

"My name is Benjamin," Ben began a litany someone had taught him. "I'm almost three years old, I live in Musselunge, my mommy's name is Mildred Steck, 22 Lincoln Road, telephone four five four—"

"The sky is falling!" Stretch Rockefeller interjected. Behind him the fish tank bubbled and roiled, and the muskellunge lunged toward the glass and then sank into shadows.

"Ben talks really well for his age," Ottilie told me. "Matt was just like that."

Reverend Steck turned toward Ottilie, his gaze lighting on her hair and hands, and I saw that he was taken with her: her girl's figure, that pale hair that wouldn't gray, hands like delicate miniatures of Matt's, long and slender with almond nails. If I had been Reverend Steck, I would have longed to press my lips to her hand. I imagined myself as him, isolated in my religious role, restricted by my office from leaning forward and nuzzling that fine hair and rubbing my whiskers against that skin, smooth and translucent as eggshell.

"Ben speaks so well," Reverend Steck said, "because he talks nonstop. He won't be three until October, but he's put in more mouth mileage than most four-year-olds, so he better speak well." Reverend Steck smiled proudly, and rumpled his grandson's hair. "It's because his Mom loves him so much and talks about everything with him."

Ben leaned back in his seat with a look of utter satisfaction. He smiled, banged his fork on the table, and sighed.

Ottilie gave Reverend Steck an abstracted smile; her thoughts were clearly elsewhere. I wondered if Ottilie ever returned his interest, but, gauging her mild reaction, I decided against it. I believed that Ottilie did not want to be swept away by love, that she wanted only the freedom to live without the invasions of others, that she thirsted for safety and privacy with passionate intensity. Ottilie had told me once over the phone, several years before, that a doctor at the hospital where she worked as a hospital technician had been courting her and finally proposed to her. I asked her how she had responded, and she answered enigmatically, "I don't have to marry again." When I pressed her for clarification, she said, "I feel like I've passed through that stage—that I've been a wife already so I don't have to prove myself to anyone again by getting married."

Dmytryk lifted a Coke bottle from beside his chair and poured himself a glass of honey-colored liquid. No one seemed to notice, except Dr. Eatman, who looked up at me, shook his head, and said, "He doesn't have any vowels in his name. 'D-M-Y-T-R-Y-K.' Can you believe it?"

Dmytryk smiled modestly and said, "It's true, not one vowel. It's Polish."

" 'Steck' used to be a long name ending in 'owski,' " Mildred said.

"Does it mean anything?" Dmytryk asked.

" 'Steck' doesn't mean a thing, as far as I know," Mildred told him. Dmytryk nodded his head earnestly, and I realized in that moment that Mildred had been conversing fluently with all three of the halfway house's residents seated around me, as if her linguistic talents encompassed not just foreign languages, but the ability to charm through any means of communication. I wondered if her experience growing up with a mother who was crazy had given Mildred an intuitive ability to engage in off-kilter conversation. If Matt had lost his mind when I was younger, would we be closer now? But I banished the thought—the notion of my childhood without Matt to talk to, without his articulate and sensitive conversation, was unbearable.

"I see," Dr. Eatman answered in a stentorian voice. "The meaning of your name has been lost to the mixed-up taxonomies of immigration authorities."

"Maybe I'll make the name Steck infamous," Mildred said. "And then it will come to mean whatever I make it mean."

"Well, that's just like Mildred," Reverend Steck told Ottilie, "reinventing the world as she goes along."

Ottilie smiled. "I always liked that expression, 'reinventing the world.'"

Mildred said to me, "My husband's last name is Munk." The unearthly handsomeness of her profile caught me off guard again. "I couldn't even consider changing my name when I got married. 'Mildred Munk' sounds like someone Little Miss Muffet fed to the spider."

"I can't wait to meet this famous son-in-law of mine," Reverend Steck said. "By the way Mildred describes him, he can walk on water."

The words seemed sarcastic and pointed, but he smiled, and I saw that he had meant them good-naturedly.

"Daniel will be back any day now," Mildred told me. "He's going to stay here while he applies for teaching jobs and pulls a book together from his research."

Matt looked up from his plate with a stunned expression. I wondered if he had such a crush on Mildred that her husband's imminent arrival distressed him.

"The sky is falling!" Rockefeller said again, this time with a humorous expression, as if even he did not believe it.

"Yah, yah," Dr. Eatman said. "If you say that one more time, I'll personally pull down the sky."

Rockefeller looked distressed. He emptied a Pferd beer bottle into his glass and tilted his nose into the foam. On the bottle's label a red horse's head arched, bodiless as a chess knight.

"What's Pferd like?" I asked Rockefeller.

"Horse piss," Matt answered. It was the first time he had spoken all evening. But when I looked up, Matt had already turned his head away from me, and it did not seem possible that that familiar voice, clear and ironic, could have come from the brooding, bearded man who sat across from me, his dead silence maintaining itself at the center of the cacophony around him.

"Pferd is undrinkable!" Dmytryk said emphatically. "It's worse than Old Milwaukee and Blatz! Worse even than Minnesota beers! Meisterbrau! Schmidt's! Hamm's!"

Dr. Eatman leaned forward and said in a confidential tone, "It is a source of pride among many of Muskellunge's inhabitants that they have never raised a can of Pferd to their lips, although many local Pferd factory workers admit to having relieved themselves into the brewery vats in the hope of improving the product."

"Have some of my stuff," Dmytryk ventured. He lifted his Coke bottle and poured two fingers into my empty water glass.

When I sipped it, the liquor seared my throat and left a taste like rusted iron in my mouth.

"Now *that's* horse piss!" Dr. Eatman said. He laughed.

I smiled idiotically, and to be friendly, took a second swallow. "Christ," I said. "Doesn't this kill your stomach?"

"Don't say 'Christ.' There's a reverend present!" Dmytryk said.

The liquor had an almost instantaneous effect: It melted the gloominess that usually nestled in my heart. I drank rarely. I had always felt too sharply the allure of alcohol, that startling moment of chaos and buoyancy when liquor enters the bloodstream. Dmytryk's wine coursed through my veins with a sumptuous, exhilarating destructiveness.

"Melanie," Ottilie said teasingly, "you look like you just bit something alive!" She laughed, and I put down my glass.

The waitress returned to our table with the check, although no one had asked for it. Reverend Steck settled the bill for everyone and refused my offer to contribute to the dinner. When he walked to the front counter to pay the bill, the entire table fell silent: Dr. Eatman, Stretch Rockefeller, Dmytryk, and Matt stared after him, as if the reverend's absence left them feeling lost and confused. When Reverend Steck returned, everyone rose to go. He deposited a generous tip on the table.

As I stood to leave, I saw Matt lean against the table and pocket the tip money.

I felt a hand take mine, and looked down. It was Ben's. He peered up at me with that endearing, heart-shaped face, and then looked startled. He clearly had intended to take someone else's hand. He let go, and ran off. When I looked up, Matt was already at the restaurant's entrance, close behind Ottilie and Reverend Steck.

I took a five from my coat pocket and dropped it on the table. Then, thinking of the task faced by the waitress who served our group, I laid down an extra dollar. I felt a stab of sorrow: I wondered if wherever Matt went, people kept away from him and watched him covertly, uneasy at his presence. I followed the crowd through the restaurant's exit.

Outside, Ben lay slumped on Mildred's shoulder, suddenly asleep. Matt climbed into Reverend Steck's van with the other men from the halfway house. Reverend Steck helped Mildred take my luggage from

Mildred's trunk and carried it to Ottilie's car. She had offered me my own room in the house where she lived.

"Good night, Ottilie," Reverend Steck said, his voice sensual, sinking into the darkness. She smiled but did not answer him: She murmured, "Hmmm." A yard away, behind the van's window glass, Stretch Rockefeller's diminutive face peered at me and then receded. Overhead, the neon musky flashed on and off, making my long shadow loom before me and vanish.

Ottilie and I climbed into her car. "I'm glad you've come," she said. "It'll do Matt so much good."

"Christ, Ottilie," I answered. "Matt pretended I wasn't there all evening. He must be angry I've been away so long."

"Maybe he just doesn't want you to see him like this," Ottilie said.

"Like what?"

"Poor and unshaved and crazy and hopeless."

"Is he really hopeless?" I asked.

Ottilie drove for a while in silence, as if measuring her words. Then she said, "Yes, yes, he is. I think he doesn't hope for things anymore, because there's nothing left in the world that he wants and can still have. I think he lives from day to day." Ottilie spoke these words with the quiet, reasoned honesty she had always had. I wanted to ask her how she felt, as a mother, saying these things about her son, but I didn't. An old pain, familiar and endless, welled up inside me.

Matt's absence seemed to fill the car seat, the intentional quiet he had nursed all night nestling between us. Before us, the lights of Muskellunge flickered like fallen stars, and the purple sky spread above the town, impassive and starless.

3

DURING MY FIRST three weeks in Muskellunge, Matt avoided me as if he found my very existence unbearable. If I entered the garden behind the Park and Pray because I saw my brother there, he would lay down his hoe and rush off. If I neared Matt and Mildred as they sat with their heads bent together over Ben, snickering at an intimate joke, the scene would dissolve as swiftly as a Forty-second Street three-card-monte game responding to a policeman's approach. Once I saw my brother and Mildred perched on the hood of Mildred's car, taking turns kissing the top of Ben's head while he squirmed and giggled between them. When Matt saw me, he stopped, Ben grew quiet, and I felt as if my presence had quelled all feelings of mirth around me. I began to wonder whether, in his psychosis, Matt had assigned me some symbolic meaning that represented his fears. I knew it was not unusual for people afflicted with psychoses to ostracize most vehemently the very people with whom they shared the strongest attachments.

Matt's behavior added greatly to the estrangement I was feeling from everyone and everything at that time. Perhaps this is why, when I met Daniel Munk, I was so drawn to him. Ottilie worked late shifts at the hospital, from noon until midnight, and I was left to myself most of every day and all evening. I filled my first weeks in Muskellunge poring over my photocopies of legal articles. When my studies exhausted me, I visited the halfway house or Reverend Steck's garden and engaged in unusual conversations with Dmytryk or Stretch Rockefeller or Dr. Eatman. ("There are over 300,000 species of beetles in the world, and if certain ones were to disappear," Dr. Eatman warned me in a portentous tone, "the entire ecosystem would fall into disarray. It would be more catastrophic than a moon-sized meteor striking the earth.")

Or I killed time wandering up and down the town: East-west streets were named after fish, and the north-south ones after Republican presidents. Muskellunge was small enough that a monarch butterfly picking its way through fields of milkweed north of town would fly directly down the main avenue to reach farmland to the south, instead of circumventing the business section. I inspected the local library, loitered in every store, and visited the local courthouse. (The presiding justice, Judge Bracken, had held sway there since the fifties: Educated at the University of Michigan, he still had all his hair, and his own portrait hovered behind him over the bench.) I saw every matinee at the local theater, and I memorized the aisles of Shove's, the cheese, ammunition, and bait store: Cereal boxes shouldered Ax House Rat Traps; beer bottles teetered over buckets containing guppies; baby bottles snuggled against bullet boxes.

Shove's had a small sit-down counter and a few tables where Mrs. Shove served breakfast and sandwiches. She was a short woman with swollen ankles, and sat on a high stool behind a cash register she never used—she liked to tally up purchases on a paper pad. She wore a starched apron over an auburn polyester dress that matched her hair. She told customers she had lost both sons to faraway cities, Atlanta and Los Angeles, and she kept their pictures in frames behind the cash register. They looked like Mr. Shove, with square shoulders and square jaws and crewcuts, except for their eyes, which were Mrs. Shove's, green and almond-shaped. Mrs. Shove told me that her eyes looked wrong on the boys—"too girly." She talked indiscriminately to customers and carried on shouting conversations with her husband across the store.

While eating breakfast there during my second week in Muskellunge, I learned that Mrs. Shove had tried for almost a year to persuade Mr. Shove to attend the Park and Pray. He had ended up accompanying her to church on the Sunday Reverend Steck had invited a guest minister from Madison. The minister had played "Kurt Weil sing-alongs" on the organ, and then delivered a sermon that began, "The bread is Christ. Christ has risen! The bread is revolution! The bread is rising. The revolution is rising!" Since then Reverend Steck evidently had become one of Mr. Shove's favorite topics of conversation. Mr. Shove called him "Red Reverend Steck," and had even made up a song about him to the tune of "Mr. Johnny LeBec," the famous butcher who had ground his customers' dogs and cats into sausages:

> O Red, O Red, O Red Reverend Steck
> I told them they would pay!
> They've all been ground to sausages
> Behind the Park and Pray.
> Now all those churchy ladies
> have disappeared, they're dead!
> All mailed off to Russia
> to feed the starving reds.

I heard Mr. Shove singing this in the back, as he lifted boxes and opened new inventory shipments, dressed in electric orange overalls. He referred to the halfway house as the Unitarian Funny Farm.

"Don't pay him any mind," Mrs. Shove told me. "He repeats that song every Sunday after I come home from church. And he sings it on every occasion after Reverend Steck has visited the store, or even passes by on the street."

It was Mrs. Shove who told me about the Pferd Beer Factory tours, and urged me to "take advantage of Muskellunge" by attending one. On a restless Wednesday I climbed the only hill in Muskellunge to the factory—an inferno of monstrous vats, the sickening odor of fermenting hops, and men huddled around the diamond glitter and clinking of bottling machines. Behind the Pferd factory was an incongruous structure, an enormous gutted barn housing a herd of a dozen Percherons and annexed to a large paddock of beaten dirt. The manure smell from the giant draft animals commingled with the fumes from the factory to produce the sulfurous aroma that I learned most Muskellunge inhabitants associated with Pferd. The tour guide explained that the horses pulled the central float of the Pferd Beer Parade, held each September in commemoration of the factory's founding date. He showed us a post-card of a Miss Muskellunge of bygone years settled in the midst of a foamy yellow dress, drawn by the Pferd team in somber imitation of the Budweiser Clydesdales.

Behind the factory the Pferd Percherons schooled together around the paddock, biting and crowding one another, unruly as Shetland ponies. They loped lazily in the heat, their coats ragged, tangled white manes foaming over their withers, their massive bloated stomachs like beer bellies swaying under them. I liked watching the horses. On a second Wednesday I considered making another trip to the Pferd factory: it was advertising special evening tours to celebrate Pferd's once-a-year beer. But late in the afternoon I became engrossed in designing a cross-referenced chart of the insurance statutes of fifty states, which definitively set forth their idiosyncrasies and commonalities. (I had learned the key to perfect legal scholarship: to be comprehensive and diligent, to capture and order every detail of the law—in short, to know everything, and to know its place.)

Mildred interrupted my work at four-thirty with a phone call. She wanted me to come to her house to help her stuff envelopes for a pro-choice group. "What else are you going to do?" she demanded. "Lock yourself in your room all night, breathing lawdust?" I hesitated until she told me that her father was taking Ben and the residents of the halfway house on an outing. I then agreed to visit with her, without fear of encountering Matt and scaring him away.

When I arrived at Mildred's house I found her upstairs, putting the last stamps on a thousand envelopes. They lay scattered on the waterbed where she sat cross-legged in electric orange overalls like Mr. Shove's. A bracelet adorned with small bells tinkled when the bed undulated beneath her. A woodcut poster of Harriet Tubman, "The Black Moses leading her people on the Underground Railroad to the Promised Land," covered one wall, and above it was a photograph of John Brown, his beard and hair blown backward like fire in a wind. Mildred told me, "Horace Greeley said that the Harper's Ferry Raid led by John Brown was the work of a madman, for which he had nothing but the highest admiration." I sat down on a rocking chair appliquéd with photographs of Che, Angela Davis, John Brown, and Mighty Mouse.

Mildred pulled out a stack of twenty one-dollar bills, balanced them on the bed frame, and wrote ABORT REPUBLICANS! in bright red ink across the masonic eye above each dollar's Egyptian pyramid.

When I looked questioningly at a sample bill she passed me, Mildred said, "It's a perfect means of dispensing information. Imagine the tens of thousands of hands through which a dollar bill circulates. It's the best political flier there is."

Twice during that summer, those bills would come back to me: once from the cashier at the movie theater, and another time when I stopped at a local bar for a cold Pferd—a bartender slid my change over the counter, and a crisp bill beckoned to me in red letters.

On the last dollar in her stack, Mildred added a subscript and showed it to me: IF ONLY REVEREND HATCH'S MOTHER HAD ENJOYED THE RIGHT TO CHOOSE—SUPPORT STATE FUNDING OF ABORTIONS. Afterward, Mildred persuaded me to attend one of Reverend Hatch's Wednesday evening sermons at Walleye Baptist Church. (The name made me think of a congregation that was somehow skewed, its pews arranged with purposeful crookedness, its minister elected for his singular ecstatic vision.) She wanted to invite me, she said, "for a night on the town."

When we left the Stecks', we saw Mildred's father and the men from the halfway house walking by the burned-out Sears store on Walleye Street. Ben rode on Matt's shoulders, swinging at overhanging trees with a wooden sword. Dr. Eatman talked animatedly to Dmytryk, and Rockefeller pulled up the rear, exclaiming to himself. They paraded by Shove's, Reverend Steck's blond ponytail bobbing, and I imagined Mr. Shove singing "Red Reverend Steck" after them.

"Wednesday night bingo," Mildred said. "My Dad takes the men to the Catholic church every week for their bingo games. Sort of an interfaith gesture. Hatch's church doesn't permit gambling, so this is my father's way of letting the Catholics know not all Protestants are wet blankets." As the men moved down the sidewalk, heads turned and passersby furtively watched Reverend Steck's procession.

For the five-block trip between the Stecks' house and Hatch's church, Mildred insisted on taking her car. She gunned the motor, honked at every crosswalk, hooted at men. When we stopped at the only traffic light, it seemed that every person on the street was looking at us, at the Cadillac's pig hood ornament and the car door with its gold script spelling MILDRED.

"Since they're going to stare anyway, we might as well give them something to stare at," Mildred said. She waved to a group of women in front of the hardware store, who looked away, pretending not to notice us.

"Can you imagine growing up here," Mildred asked me, "with a father who was a card-carrying commie and a mother who used to sit at Woolworth's soda counter, wearing a leopard skin hat with a veil and smoking through a cigarette holder? When my mother got really manic, she would pretend to be from Paris and speak with a French accent to the Woolworth's cashier."

Mildred turned left off Main Street. The early evening sun nosed the clouds like a fish caught in a net. A police car pulled in front of us, and Mildred drove an uncomfortably close distance behind it.

"That's Chief Komar. He's been the police chief here since before I was an embryo. He's just as likely to lock you up for drinking on your own front porch as he is to send you home after you shoot at a man in the middle of the street. My mother used to call him 'Minnie Musso-lini.'" Mildred accelerated and passed the police car.

"Christ," she asked, "don't you ever talk?"

I asked Mildred what Matt spoke about with her when they were together.

Mildred apparently found this funny: She half suppressed a laugh and answered, "Well, when Ben's awake, we just sort of tool around outside, mostly in the garden. It's not like there's tons to do in Muskel-lunge."

"I almost took the Pferd Beer tour for the second time this evening," I volunteered.

Mildred snorted. "Good idea. They run late. We'll go see the Pferd ponies after church." She turned abruptly down a side street and into an alley, and stopped in front of a boarded-up bar with Budweiser and Pferd signs in the window.

"Let's get stoned before we go over to Reverend Hatch's," she said. "It'll be an education to see him that way."

"I can't. I had to give up smoking."

"This is hardly tobacco," Mildred answered. She pulled out a joint and lit it. "I almost never get to smoke reefer anymore now that I'm a mama. You have to be on your toes all the time around a toddler—I've only been able to sneak about five joints in all on the afternoons when my dad's been babysitting. It's grueling to face Muskellunge without an altered mind."

"I took an oath not to break the law," I said. I contemplated, for a moment, the professional consequences of Chief Komar catching me in Mildred's car with marijuana. I saw myself at the booking desk of a small-town police office, smirking like a wayward teenager, refusing to answer the sheriff's questions, my black hair long again, and sprouting from a red bandanna. "I could have my license to practice suspended," I told Mildred. "Or worse. And besides, that stuff never works on me."

"This will," Mildred said. "It's Wisconsin Gold. Homegrown."

After she took a few puffs, she closed her eyes and said, "Smell! It's organic."

I had never taken drugs of any kind since Matt had become psychotic. But when I breathed in the Wisconsin Gold, its odor was delicious. It reminded me of Aletta Knorr and Vernon Peek, and my brother listening to Jimi Hendrix in the cabin. I felt sad thinking of them, and the sadness drew me closer to Matt.

"This stuff really lets you let go of the controls," Mildred told me.

I took Mildred's reefer.

"Sometimes it's nice to watch things go all helter-skelter," she said.

I breathed in some smoke, held it in my lungs and leaned forward, waiting to see if the drug would make me feel like my brother must feel most of the time.

"Talk!" Mildred told me.

I sat quietly for a minute, drawing several times on the joint and letting the smoke linger in my lungs before returning the joint to Mildred.

"I'm sort of amazed Ben is—well, that he's not put off by Matt," I answered.

"Why? Because of all that hair and how big he is? Matt gives Ben toys and plays silly games with him. They share little jokes. Matt sticks to himself on his bad days." Then Mildred told me her theory that psychotic men have more hair than other men. "It's not scientifically verifiable yet," Mildred said, "but it'll be proven some day—all the crazy guys walking around with thick, wild hair. Try to think of one sane middle-aged man with hair like Matt's. Insanity is the cure for baldness."

I couldn't. She passed the joint back, and I inhaled it for a while. I realized that I had never talked about Matt with anyone other than Ottilie. "Do you leave Matt and Ben alone together?"

"You think I shouldn't?" Mildred asked, but then she said, "Ben won't usually let me leave him alone. He'll hang around with other people, but only if I stay within eyeshot. Even when I deposit Ben with my dad, just for a few hours to get a night off, Ben grabs hold of me and tries to drag me back in the door. He's always been that way, shy with strangers, especially men. When he first learned to walk, he wouldn't go anywhere unless he had his hand on my leg. Not for balance, but more as if he was keeping tabs on me. Matt's the first man other then my father who Ben's warmed up to—it's because Matt's patient and funny with him. I've never been apart from Ben overnight since he was born. When I drive to Chicago to pick up Daniel at the airport, I'm going to stay there two days for a short second honeymoon, and that'll be the longest Ben's been away from me."

"It's nice of you to keep Matt around," I said.

"I like Matt. I don't do it to be nice," Mildred answered. But I did not really believe her. One of the things I remember most clearly about Mildred Steck before the course of her life turned suddenly and changed her was her essential kindness. Her patience with and affection for her son and my brother. I looked at Mildred's profile, and its beauty seemed to lift an inch from her face, hover in the air, and remain poised there. I felt a rush of goodwill toward her and everything else. I understood that my disorientation had joined hands with Matt and his disorientation, and I lay back, resting against the soft skin of the world, feeling all of a piece.

"It's not as if your brother's dangerous, Melanie," Mildred said. "He's not even unpredictable—not like my mother, who used to fly into these states where she'd go after the kitchen chairs with a crowbar. Matt's style of craziness is different—it's as if a part of his mind is broken, or his wires are crossed. He just gets mixed up in the way he looks at things."

The silence inside me became palpable, a shadow with weight to it, sloshing inside the container of my being. "How does Matt look at things?" I asked Mildred, but she did not respond. I realized that I had not spoken aloud; I only thought I had.

Then Mildred said, "My dad's in love with Ottilie. John Steck finally gets the nerve to go after somebody, and it ends up being someone just like you who never says what's on her mind. Christ, women have been throwing themselves at Dad ever since my mother died, and he's never noticed. Has Ottilie ever been crazy in love with anyone? Really out of her mind in love?"

I thought about this, wondered for a moment about what the quality of Ottilie's relationship with my father must have been when, as a sixteen-year-old girl, she first met him. "I don't know," I said.

"I mean crazy enough in love to feel off-balance, kind of a loss of perspective. Like the way I feel around Daniel. Or this passionate thing between you and Matt."

"Me and Matt."

"Yeah, you guys are intense. I wondered if Ottilie is like you, quiet but intense. Maybe she just hides her feelings, and really likes my dad but you just can't tell."

Before I could think of an answer, Mildred said, "That's how I feel about Daniel. I swear to God that man melts my bones." I sensed this was where she had been leading all along. "If I just look at Daniel, I can't think about anything except the next time we're going to be naked together. We can get so close I feel like he's wearing my skin."

Mildred lit a new joint, took a puff, and passed it to me. She talked, and I listened and forgot to pass the joint back. I smoked it until I felt it burn my fingers.

"When I was a kid," Mildred said, "I used to have this bed next to a bay window, and I'd watch the stars at night, and slowly, they would dim out, and I'd get scared because the stars had disappeared—but really what was happening was that I was sleepy and my eyes were closing and I didn't realize it. There was this sort of—loss of perspective. It's like that when I'm around Daniel: I can't see anything around me; I lose my bearings. It's scary, it's great. Before I knew him, I didn't think there was a man on earth that could do that to me. The first time we met, I felt this sense of kinship, like he'd known me all my life. 'It's because you married your father,' my friend Fatima in Brazil used to say. 'Well, that's obvious,' I'd say. 'He's older than me; he's pure of heart, just like Dad.' But that doesn't explain it. When he takes off his clothes, I feel like my pussy is going to jump out of my soul. It's more like we're connected spirits."

I, too, had once liked to plummet into passion, to feel myself racing downward to a place where there was no bottom, and no edge, where I could not even sense the limits of my own skin. But it wasn't closeness with another person I had coveted. It was the shedding of myself, the sense of escape, of intoxicating flight.

I thought again about Mildred's question, had Ottilie ever been crazy in love? I had felt that way with the man I'd left the year before, but I could not bring myself to dwell on it now. (Sometimes that year I had imagined the cancer personified—a man with a hawking cough and menthol smell, dressed in a dark suit with an oily sheen, slipping his hand around my waist, prodding the fertile places, the wildly reproducing cells.) I believed the cancer had killed the possibility of such feelings in me: After it went into remission, I felt only physical terror and then just a formality of feeling. I thought about how this state of insensibility was to some extent natural to me, and wondered if the cancer had affected me more than other people, because of this. And then I saw how the cancer insidiously linked everything: me, the soggy clouds washing over the humped back of the setting sun, the grain fields lapping against Muskellunge, the corn rows sailing in perfect perspective toward a meeting place on the horizon, logical and precise as the language of legal statutes, as orderly and invulnerable.

"This is the first time in my life I've smoked this stuff where it altered my brain chemistry," I said. But when Mildred did not respond, I again saw that I had failed to speak what I was thinking.

"Can you hear me?" I asked her.

Mildred laughed. "You must be really buzzed."

"I don't usually buzz," I said.

"If you concentrate on your mouth when you talk, it helps."

I tried this, and said, "Mouth." We both laughed giddily. I concentrated harder. "I used to see some guy in New York," I said. "But I broke it off."

"How come?"

Words reeled away from me, and I had trouble winding them back into sentences. "I got too sick to fuck. I fell in love with him for his prickle."

Mildred laughed, and I slid to the floor, giggling without emitting any noise. I banged against the Cadillac's door handle, and the door sprang open. I found myself on my feet, half standing, half lying on the car seat. I straightened up.

"When I perpendiculate, it clears my head." The cornfield behind the Cadillac folded like a sweater and then unravelled. "Does Matt ever do this anymore?" I asked Mildred. "Smoke dope?"

"He once told me he can't because it makes him feel more paranoid than he already is. And then he thinks it's against his religion." A church bell sounded, mystical and serendipitous. The bell's noise spangled and dropped through the air like lead sinkers.

"We should get going," Mildred said. "You won't believe this Hatch guy. He acts like he stepped right out of the Salem witch trials." She opened her car door. "I better not drive over to Walleye Baptist with us in our altered mental states. Can you walk?"

I took Mildred's arm. Our elbows joined like wings, veered away in flight, and returned to us. We waded through currents of periwinkle air shimmering up the streets of Muskellunge and eddying in the yard of a white church that bobbed on its foundations. A red window waved like a handkerchief, beckoning us. A large sign anchored in the green sea of the church's lawn proclaimed:

HOW MUCH DOES AN ABORTION COST?
ONE HUMAN LIFE!

In the early evening sky, behind the Walleye Baptist Church and over the road to the beer factory, the Pferd Percherons swirled amid stars twinkling like bottle caps.

"Smoking makes me hungry, but all I have is hashish brownies," Mildred said, extending a paper sack toward me, opened. I looked at several brown squares; they were small and dense as iron ingots. I popped one whole into my mouth. Then I took the entire bag, and walked quietly into the church, chewing and thinking.

Reverend Hatch stood behind a podium at the back of the church aisle, a wispy man with feathery black hair and a high-pitched voice. When he saw us, he turned away with a superhuman swiftness. Throughout his sermon he avoided looking toward the corner where Mildred and I sat.

"I'm provoking him just by breathing the air in his church," Mildred said. "He recognizes me as the wicked offspring of his adversary. He probably thinks I'm here as a spy." She snickered, lifted a Bible from the back of the pew ahead of us, and thumbed its pages.

Reverend Hatch's sermon began, "Who is the devil?" And I began to feel angelic as he answered his own question. I imagined I was a joyful spirit, perfumed with a sweet alfalfa smell I thought of as "mari-human." I felt myself grow warm, and knew that as I sat there, I glowed redly, my skin the color of a hand held against the bulb of a flashlight. I admired Reverend Hatch for being able to continue speaking without being distracted by my luminous presence.

I found it difficult to follow his sermon: It ran amok from one topic to another, from the white horse of Revelations to the evils of abortion and organic gardening to the dangers of Catholicism. Reverend Hatch spoke with such a frenzied energy that even I was tempted to throw coins into the collection dish. I felt something strange in my pocket, retrieved it, and stared at the remaining brownies. I ate two and did not offer Mildred the remaining ones. I realized I had not shared any with her, but when I tried to give her back the bag, my hand would not obey me—it returned the bag to my pocket and then fluttered emptily to my lap.

Reverend Hatch's choir rose, singing, "Oh the way is long, and

Satan is a-waitin'." Mildred joined in lustily, with a loud, croaking contralto. The song enveloped me, threaded through the needle eye of my ear and pulled tight over my mouth. When the collection plate reached us, Mildred dropped in a dollar bill: REVEREND HATCH'S MOTHER flared toward me in bright red.

We slipped together from the pew toward the purple-blue door of the twilight. "So as I go, I say," the choir sang after us, "get behind me Satan!"

I joined in, although I did not know the words, and to this day, I am uncertain whether I only imagined singing them, or actually filled the night with a kind of singing-in-tongues, a melodious gibberish.

AS SOON as we reached the road outside, Mildred said, "Let's head up the hill and look at the Pferd ponies."

On the walk to the beer factory it became clear to me that I had smoked and eaten vastly more than Mildred. Because under my feet the road undulated and glistened like the back of a weasel, but under Mildred's it was quiet and subdued, dark brown and roadlike, and above her the moon was as calm as a polished tooth.

She asked in a ruminating tone, "Do you believe in Satan?" Before I could answer, she said, "I don't. My feeling is, if God is God, he wouldn't want to make a hell to put people in. If he does, he's not God."

My voice climbed a dark ladder of air, and leapt away. "I don't believe in God, but I believe in hell," I said. At that moment, I saw it in front of me, expansive and golden, a field of fur, leonine. Then I made my mind veer away, back into a comforting, blanketing darkness.

"You're such a Gloomy Gus," Mildred said, laughing.

"I don't see how heaven could be heaven if there's a God around to rule it," I answered.

The Pferd Beer factory sparkled in front of us. Lights glittered over the front door, and a bright banner commanded, DRINK OUR ONCE-A-YEAR BEER. Inside on a table stood a row of sample bottles emblazoned with red chess knights and the words PFERD'S STRAWBERRY BEER. I laughed, wondering what the writing really would have said if I had not been high.

Mildred poured two samples from a keg, and handed me a four-ounce Dixie Cup. She sipped her Pferd, said, "Pigshit!" and spat on the ground.

A grim and stately tour guide looked up sharply from where he stood in front of a small group. His suit was cranberry-colored, his tie a maze of plaids. I thought I saw one of the crowd of tourgoers lean forward and sniff the air beside Mildred.

"Samples are for the end of the tour," the guide said, but I was unsure whether he was talking to us. His words roped the air, swirled backward, and lassoed him.

"Don't drink it, Melanie!" Mildred warned. "It'll make you gag."

I took a small sip: The once-a-year beer tasted just as if someone had poured strawberry cough syrup into cheap ale. The shock of the taste almost sobered me: It wobbled like a red rag on my tongue, and I put down my cup. I ate the last two or three brownies to expunge the medicinal taste from my mouth.

"They started this a few years ago: fruit-flavored beer," Mildred said. "Last year it was peach."

We followed the guide at a lurking distance. He glared at us throughout the tour, because Mildred kept up her own private tour a few yards behind the last sightseers, her words shadowing his.

"Pferd is a pale lager," the tour guide said brightly, and then Mildred's words clung to his in a furry whisper: "A lager so thin and tasteless, it can be consumed only by the six-pack or case, and is preferred by teenagers and by men who drank Pferd as teenagers."

"Founded fifty years ago"—the tour guide's voice darted into silence like the tail of a snake under a door, and Mildred's chased after it— "Pferd has struggled for two quarters of a century against Manitowoc's Budweiser plant, but our brewery has maintained its edge by watering down our beer with workers' urine and then fixing prices at 80 percent of Bud's."

We followed the guide into a room where workers, plugs in their ears, bent over the great jeweled clinking of the bottling machine's conveyor belt, beside which even Mildred's voice vanished into tarry blackness, and then we emerged into an enormous dark room, as skywardly deep, I thought, as a steeple. I realized we were outside. The ammonia smell of manure brightened my perceptions.

The tour guide talked about the Pferd Beer Parade float and gestured inside a paddock where shadowy Pferd horses foraged amid dusky hay bales. My voice disconnected itself from the herd, galloped forward to meet the tour guide, reared into a question. But I could not call up the words for things that needed urgent retelling. Other words offered themselves, pale as the print on a legal notice: "Isn't there some kind of copyright or logo infringement lurking somewhere here?"

Mildred snorted. The guide looked at me quizzically. My mind took on a terrible clarity: "Weren't the Budweiser Clydesdales first?"

The guide dismissed my curiosity peevishly, explaining that the competitor Clydesdales really did not fit in with the name Budweiser. *Pferd,* after all, was German for horse. He slipped away before I could corner him to ask more questions: I had many questions, only partly formulated, not yet in the word or idea stage. He led the tourgoers into the factory to sample the once-a-year beers. Mildred and I remained outside.

"What's this?" I heard Mildred ask. She was some distance away, under a blue floodlight behind the factory, where it adjoined the fence. She took a step forward and disappeared.

I circled the paddock and found her in a large storeroom with walls of galvanized iron, and wide double doors. An overhead fan blew sweltering stinking air around the room, so thick with heat that it resisted my legs like a whirlpool of mud. Mildred leaned over a long aluminum tank.

"Christ!" she exclaimed. "This smell could murder! It must be the stuff they throw out. Maybe it's old, rotten fermented hops. Or maybe this is their secret ingredient, who knows?"

I leaned over the tank: the smell was both noxious and pleasing, but overpowering. It threatened to grab me and not let go, and I stepped back through the doorway.

Mildred ambled to the paddock, and I followed her, stepping inside the luminous outlines of her sandal prints.

The horses were gathered in a clump under a dim light, indistinct as fish schooling under water. As I leaned on the gate, I believed I could see them clearly, their beautiful watery manes and eyes like black fish-within-fish.

They made me think of the Kloneckis. "I used to want to be a horse when I grew up," I told Mildred. "Instead I'm a lawyer aspiring to be a judge."

"What a loss," Mildred said. "You've opened the coffin lid of the law and walked in."

"I have these relations, the Kloneckis, who used to raise horses," I said wistfully. "I used to visit them in the summer, instead of Matt."

One of the horses detached himself from the rest and swam up to us. He raised his muscular jaw and moved his nose delicately over the fence.

Mildred unlatched the gate to the paddock.

"He wants out," she said.

The horse glided through the gate as joyously as a hat blown upward by the wind.

"I've returned him to the wilds," Mildred pronounced.

The Percheron nuzzled the grass and walked slowly forward, kissing the ground. He bumped the far wall, and his muzzle extended into the wide doorway under the floodlight. He stepped forward into the noxious air of the storeroom until his nose touched the cold aluminum of the tank we had bent over earlier. His lips moved upward, kissing the metal until he reached the rim. His ears darted forward. He whinnied. Then he plunged his neck into the tank, and sank his muzzle into its foamy waters.

The other Percherons answered his whinny. They trotted around the paddock, and nosed the gate with curiosity. They broke loose, and herded into the storeroom to join the first Percheron. They shouldered one another near the tank and sucked up the fermenting contents, making a long, loud noise like a backward waterfall or a shout traveling inward.

"Time to go," Mildred said.

We wandered down the hill toward the car. Behind us I thought I heard the neighing of horses, their ebullient footclops.

As Mildred drove us home, Muskellunge spread before us like a luminous garden: Pink streetlights blossomed in rows, the peacock blue eye of a police siren opened and shut, windows rippled like yellow grain in the Park and Pray. And in that moment, I saw it: The great vast universe set in motion by an uninterfering God, its breathtaking goodness and glittering desirable evils all spectacular and miraculous, and I did not want anything, ever, to change.

"Matt always works late at night in the church," Mildred said. "He likes to turn on all the lights. He cleans up and fixes things." She pulled into her driveway. "That's the problem with Ottilie my dad doesn't get," Mildred mused. "She's like you—she's half a person and the other half is the part of Matt she misses. She's like a half-lost soul." And that's when Mildred told me her theory that some people lead half-lives but other people lead several—she described it all as an ocean that pushed you under and then tossed you up, and she said that no one would ever hold her under for long, and that Matt was "fine and whole, in his own way," and that I should let go of my sorrow over him and just take him as he was, that he was lonely for me, probably even at the very minute he was working in the church. But I did not really believe Mildred and I had difficulty following her because my thoughts began to rock, boat-like, and then they tipped over, swirled in my head and roared like white water.

"You're in no condition to sleep," Mildred said, pulling me out of the car. She led me into the Stecks' house and upstairs to a spare room, and pushed me into bed.

I heard Ben say down the hall, "Mommy? Mommy, I'm right here!" Mildred answered, "Coming, Sugarbeet." And then the darkness folded over me, a woolly song, and I rose upward on its textures, into sleep.

IN THE MORNING Mildred woke me up. When I opened my eyes, she stood over me, Ben riding on her hip, grinning and watching me with his minnow eyes.

"The horses are mostly down in the cemetery," Mildred said. She smelled like alfalfa. "The whole volunteer fire department and police force are out trying to round them up."

We walked outside, Mildred swinging a bag of carrots, Ben still glued to her hip. It was true. The Percherons had come down into the town looking for the tender places, the mushrooms softer than horses' muzzles, the pink clover of newly watered yards, the gentle cemetery lawns. As we walked down Main Street, we spotted one Percheron in a dandelion field beside the burned-out Sears store, and another grazing in the large plot in front of the Muskellunge County Courthouse. When we reached the cemetery, we saw that most of the Percherons had collected there, proud and statuesque as monuments.

Ottilie was patting a horse and laughing, looking like a schoolgirl, her hair down and unbrushed. Matt stood beside her, smiling. When he saw me, he turned away.

The fire department rounded up the Percherons slowly, coaxing them with quart buckets of oats, slipping nooses around their necks. One or two horses proved difficult to catch. They looked hungover, untempted by food.

In the end only one was left. Every now and then, Chief Komar or a fireman would approach him, and he would back off, as if the noise made by footsteps on grass was too loud for him to bear. He would shy at nothing, and skitter away to a low headstone, or a veteran's flag. Finally, the Percheron leaned against a cool monument, resting his cheek against the marble forehead of a bas-relief angel.

Mildred walked toward him with her bag of carrots, Ben still on her hip. The horse lifted his head and stared at her with the dim recognition of a carousing buddy. Mildred tucked a carrot in Ben's hand, and then wrapped her hand around his, saying, "Don't let him eat your fingers by mistake!"

The horse took a step closer, wiggled a prehensile lip, and bit the carrot's tip. Ben patted his nose and said, "Just eat the carrot!"

A *Muskellunge Eagle* photographer snapped their picture, and it appeared the following morning on the front page of the town newspaper, under the headline, "Citizens Help Fire Department Round Up Prize Draft Horses." The early light caught Mildred's profile, so that her hair haloed around her face. She smiled at the photographer ironically, her son cradled happily in her arms, the Percheron holding his box head high above them, self-consciously regal, like a horse of the Magi. Behind them all, Matt, tall and wild-haired, loped away in a gangly run, up the road to the Park and Pray.

4

OTTILIE'S HOME in Muskellunge was magnificent. It was owned by the divorced aunt with whom Ottilie had lived after she left my father. The aunt was independently wealthy and spent her days traveling around the world: Every three weeks a postcard from the Southern Hemisphere would arrive in our mailbox, or a package wrapped in foreign-looking yellow paper and smelling like nutmeg, or a letter bearing a stamp portraying a marsupial or monstrous reptile. The aunt, whom Ottilie affectionately called Mimi (her real name, oddly, was Violet), encouraged Ottilie to stay in the Muskellunge house, which Mimi's family had kept as a summer residence. Ottilie looked after the house well, and saved Mimi the cost of a caretaker.

The house sat near Muskellunge Lake, behind a windbreak of fir trees. It had oak floors and stained-glass windows, sumptuous tapestried couches, and fireplaces in each of the five bedrooms and living room. On weekends Ottilie liked to sit in an overstuffed peacock-blue armchair near the living room's high stained-glass window, basking luxuriously in royal blue and garnet red sunlight. She enjoyed the house's extravagance in that way special to people who have suffered long periods of hardship and denial. She often wandered slowly through the rooms, touching and admiring the objects around her. She especially liked a glass case in the den that held curios from the travels of Aunt Mimi's past family members: a jaguar tooth, a large geode containing amethyst crystals, the gigantic quills of an African porcupine, fossil ferns pressed into shale, arrowheads, brown honeycombed Petoski stones from Lake Michigan, a beaver's skull, and an Australian bull roarer attached to a string made from human hair. Aunt Mimi's father and brothers had been famous anthropologists and naturalists. According to Ottilie, Mimi had married into the Crail family hoping for a conventional life, but had panicked after a few years and fled her husband. The Crails considered Mimi eccentric: She listened to opera records on Christmas Eve, she wore a silk gown when she walked through the cow yard, and she corresponded by shortwave radio with a Russian named Mr. Shekailo.

Bookcases made up the walls of Aunt Mimi's den and living room, as if her family had spent its Muskellunge days bent over the thumbed pages of *Travels with Charley*, *The Voyage of the Snark*, and *The Voyage of the H.M.S. Beagle*. When Ottilie was home on weekends, I would sit with her in the den, reviewing my law articles while she read John Steinbeck and Jack London, and the sun streamed through the windows. Red and blue light bathed our arms and hands and ankles, and we took solace in each other's company. I conversed quietly, or not at all—Ottilie and Matt were the two people in the world who had never expected me to fill in my silences. Still, Ottilie talked more than she had when I was young. She spoke of her former life in McCarthy as if it were just that—another life, distant from the one she had found. She was more assured than she had been then, and happier.

Once as we sat together, a smile played across Ottilie's face, and she paused in reading Steinbeck's *The Pastures of Heaven*, and said, "Listen to this: A man in California named Junius Maltby lets his farm go to rack and ruin, while he and his little boy walk around barefoot, and sit by a stream all day with his hired man talking about nothing at all!" I remembered that the Crails had been farmers, and that Ottilie had never been out of Wisconsin except on her trips to Chicago to get married, to visit Matt in the hospital there, and to bail him out of jail, and I wondered at the mystery of who Ottilie was: she never talked about her upbringing. Moreover, as a child I had never surprised her bent over a book. (It would have been impossible for her to read while my father was home, because he would not have tolerated such a distraction from him.)

The Sunday evening in mid-July when Daniel was scheduled to arrive from Brazil, everyone gathered at Ottilie's. Mildred had left Ben in her father's care for two days, and travelled to Madison to meet her husband and enjoy their second honeymoon. As Ottilie built a fire in the living room's hearth, I saw Matt through the screen door leading to the porch. He lingered on the back steps but would not come in. When Reverend Steck arrived, Ben ran out to the porch to join Matt. Matt pulled a Matchbox truck out of his pocket, Ben shrieked with delight, and Matt's face lit up also. He whispered something to Ben, and Ben answered by tucking his chin and singing in a high, mosquito voice:

> *Oh you can't get to heaven*
> *On a pair of skates.*

Matt sang with him at the end in a melancholy baritone that made Ben laugh: *You'll roll right past those pearly gates.* After this Matt said, "Whatever you do, don't get on my shoulders," and Ben cackled and immediately climbed the steps and scaled Matt's shoulders. When Matt stood, Ben yelled, "I'm high in the sky!" and Matt strode into the back yard's darkness.

Ottilie sat in her peacock-blue armchair, rather than beside Reverend Steck on the couch. Mildred's father talked about his organic garden until he seemed to become self-conscious about the fact that he was doing all the talking. Then he stared at the fire, crossing first his left ankle over his right and then his right ankle over his left. Finally, he suggested that we pass the time by exchanging ghost stories.

"That's an idea," Ottilie answered.

At Reverend Steck's prompting, I spoke first: I told my ghost story succinctly, in three or four sentences. It was the one about the man with a golden hook for a hand who is out on the loose killing young couples. "He creeps up behind the car where the girl is necking with her boyfriend," I said. "They have a lovers' quarrel over whether they should go home because of radio reports about the killer. The boy steps on the gas pedal, and the couple streaks away, only to find the golden hook dangling from the car door's handle the next morning."

Matt's low laugh and Ben's high giggle joined each other in the back yard.

"Firefly! Firefly!" Ben yelled.

"This way!" Matt's voice rose under him.

Ottilie said, "I was never good at stories. Matt used to tell them to Melanie when they were little. He had one with a refrain that went, 'And there were five holes in the dead person's heart, and the china doll's fingers were dripping with blood.' I can't remember the whole thing now. It ended with the china doll melting when a man held a lit match before her, and with Matt saying, 'And you never know where she'll appear again.' Melanie used to beg for it, and then she'd spend all night in a slumber bag on Matt's floor because she was afraid to sleep alone in her own room."

"I don't remember that," I said.

Reverend Steck told the best story, about a snake that would swallow other animals and then slink off to its cave in a jungle to digest them. Certain animals, such as people, proved too large to digest. After three years, they would emerge, only a little dissolved by the enzymes of the snake's bowels, and almost intact except for small details. They had lost their memories, and no longer knew that they were human. They emerged left-handed, even though they had been right-handed before. They had no sense of right and wrong, and no sense of smell. "And then a few of these people, three to be exact, migrated to Wisconsin. One became a Baptist minister, one became a sailor in the Great Lakes merchant marine, and one became a senator—"

He never finished the story. Daniel and Mildred burst through the front door, their faces flushed, their eyes shining like new lovers'.

"Ben, your daddy's here!" Mildred called out.

Matthew and Ben entered from the back porch, holding a jar of fireflies. Ben raced ahead and shouted, "Mommy, you came back! You came back!" as if Mildred had been gone for weeks. But when Ben saw his father and mother standing together, their arms entangled, he stopped beside my chair and looked doubtfully at them.

Mildred stepped forward and knelt down. Ben rushed to her then, crying "Mommy!" and threw his arms around her passionately.

"Oh, I missed you!" Mildred said.

"Benjamin! Benjy!" Daniel cried, kneeling beside Mildred and holding out his arms.

Ben clung to his mother. When Daniel reached for his son, Ben shrieked, and ran back to Matt, clutching his leg and hiding behind him. My brother stood just inside the back door, his hair a black mane, his shirt half tucked in.

Daniel looked embarrassed and said, "Well, who can blame him? It's been six months—a lifetime to a two-year-old." If he was startled by Matt's appearance, Daniel didn't show it.

Mildred coaxed, "Ben, don't be scared, Honey. It's Daddy." But Ben stayed where he was.

"Well, he'll come around on his own time," Daniel said. He turned to Reverend Steck and shook hands.

"Son," Reverend Steck said. "I feel as if I've already met you."

"I feel the same," Daniel replied. "It's an honor to be married to the daughter of such a well-regarded man of religion. And the man who raised Mildred."

"She's one of a kind," Reverend Steck said.

"She's a gold mine," Daniel answered.

Matt lowered himself into a rocking chair near the back entrance of the living room, and Ben crawled into his lap. The jar of fireflies flickered between Matt's long hands like a miniature galaxy. Ben watched Daniel warily from a distance until the rocking chair's motions lulled him to sleep.

Daniel was tall and graceful, with that rare shade of dark red hair that is almost wine-colored: If he had been a woman, I would have assumed Daniel used henna. He had brown eyes flecked with gold, and his face was angular and handsome. The tug of attraction I felt surprised me; I could not remember the last time I had noticed a man's looks. Daniel had a diffident air at first, and when Ottilie addressed him, he spoke especially softly, as if in deference to her quietness.

Daniel sat with Mildred on the couch across from Reverend Steck, and listened and answered respectfully as Mildred's father engaged him in a discussion of politics: Daniel agreed it had been a remarkable year, with Carter in the White House, Vietnam draft evaders pardoned, Chávez and the Teamsters signing a pact, and Agnew sentenced to three months in jail. Daniel shared Reverend Steck's view that the conviction of Joanne Chesimard was a crime, as was the success of the movie *Rocky*, which Daniel heartily concurred was "racism at its most brilliant— idiotic." Reverend Steck and Daniel disagreed slightly when discussing Carter's tying of U.S. arms aid for Brazil to an increased observance of human rights in that country.

"They have a right to self-determination," Daniel said.

"But not to use violence to suppress the self-determination of others?" John answered.

Daniel quickly backed away from the discussion with an apologetic smile and said, "Jimmy Carter and the Pope were out in a boat on the Mediterranean, and a gust of wind came along and blew off the Pope's miter. Carter said, 'Wait a sec. Let me get it for you.' He stepped out of the boat, and walked across the water, about twenty yards, snatched up the miter, returned to the boat and gave the Pope back his hat. The Pope was impressed, and thanked him effusively. The next day, the newspapers reported: 'Carter and Pope in boating accident. Carter can't swim.' "

Reverend Steck laughed, and said, "Nothing could be truer. That's a first-rate joke." He asked Daniel about his research.

Daniel answered shyly. When Mildred drew him out, Daniel's face lit up and he gazed at her with such tenderness that I filled with yearning. His eyes glittered as he spoke, and he had a wry, funny delivery that made us all laugh. Only Matt did not seem to like him. He eyed Daniel sullenly and jealously.

Mildred goaded Daniel to relate the dangers of life in the Amazon. He told us that he had swum in lakes filled with piranhas, but they paid him "no more attention than cows grazing in a field." A swarm of killer bees had maintained a hive only fifty yards from his house, but he had drugged them with smoke by building five small bonfires in a pentagram around their rotted tree, and so secured their honey "without a single bee sting, and their honey was as sweet as they are vicious—it made American Tupelo seem like cheap corn syrup by comparison." He had once been caught in a flood during the rainy season, and had sailed down the main street of a city in a small skiff. And although I looked at Mildred to say that Daniel was exaggerating, she confirmed the truth of each story, saying that she had stood by as a witness, shouting at Daniel to stop his foolishness, but that he had ignored her. She laughed indulgently in retrospect, and said, "He makes me so mad when he acts like that."

To all of us except perhaps Matt, there was something magical about Daniel. Perhaps it was just the happiness that he and Mildred shared. Or perhaps, for me, it was different: he had defied the laws of nature and come out unscathed, and this was a triumph for those of us who feared the danger of frostbite and the destructive power of tornadoes. That he could brave natural disaster and deceive it empowered us all, made us fear our mortality less, and for an evening, his words filled me with a pleasant sense of undirected rebelliousness.

AFTER DANIEL'S ARRIVAL, whenever I sought Mildred's company, she would be with him in their bedroom at the Stecks' house. Ben passed the time following his grandfather and Matt everywhere. Rever-

end Steck told Ottilie that Ben had been acting out since Daniel's return.
Ben was territorial around his mother and jealous of his father's presence, and Reverend Steck wanted to encourage Ben to branch out, to
get closer to other people, and to give Mildred a little rest. During that
time I would see Ben riding on Matt's or Reverend Steck's shoulders,
or eating red rocket Popsicles with Matt and Reverend Steck outside
Shove's, or passing tools to Matt as he lay under Mildred's car in the
Stecks' yard, the top half of his body hidden. Matt and Ben's closeness,
and Mildred and Daniel's intimacy, contrasted uncomfortably with my
own lack of connection to anyone.

The first week after Daniel's arrival, I found working in my room
impossible. Aunt Mimi's presence could be felt everywhere in the house,
but most of all in the room I occupied, which had once been her boudoir. The top drawer of my desk held a dozen silk scarves, a pair of
topaz earrings lying in an abalone shell, and several bottles of ancient,
expensive perfume. Beside the bed was a standing oval mirror and a
peacock-blue armchair that matched the one in the living room. A
leather-bound book on the boudoir called *Passion in Burma* contained
letters written from three different lovers pressed between its pages, all
addressed to Mimi.

Two weeks after Daniel's arrival, I spread out my photocopies of
case law from fifty states, intending to annotate my cross-referenced
digest of insurance legislation. But I was unable to think: Actuarial tables spilled randomly through my head, and I pushed my papers away
impatiently. I imagined the rustle of Mimi's nightgown, and pictured
her stretched out languidly on the bed behind me. And then I saw
myself as Mimi—I would wear persimmon-colored silk, smoke Indone-
sian clove cigarettes, and lie in bed watching the smoke's slow whirl-
winds spiral over me until just the right feeling pricked me, a tickle of
passion that made me smile and rearrange my pillow.

I decided to take a walk outside, to clear out my thoughts. As soon
as I left the house, I headed for the Park and Pray, hoping, perhaps, to
see Matt. At the end of the road, the setting sun grazed in a fiery field
of wheat. The Pferd horses whinnied at the top of the hill. Their voices
were high and musical, like a chorus of women.

I lingered at the Park and Pray's entrance. The church had a high
domed ceiling, painted oddly, blue with brown speckles, so that I felt as
if I were standing inside a robin's egg. Through the back door I spied
Reverend Steck in a tangle of vines and broad leaves. When I entered

his garden, he held up an enormous green squash, large as a water-melon, and said, "How do you like this? It would surely win 'The Largest Zucchini That Wasn't There Yesterday Contest.' Come walk around with me and admire my horticulture."

Reverend Steck strolled through the organic garden behind the church with a joyous, proprietary energy. His wiry ponytail lay askew, and he had unfastened his minister's collar so that it curved upward from his neck like an ox horn. As I walked beside him, he explained his theories of religion and organic gardening: he believed that people should treat God's green earth with tenderness, that rue was a natural insecticide for protecting boysenberries, that mint and pennyroyal would chase away slugs, that one kitchen match and a banana peel would provide enough phosphorous and potassium to double a tomato plant's yield.

He laughed at himself and said, "I guess I consider kitchen matches to be organic because of their commonplace, everyday use in our lives." Behind Reverend Steck, members of his church flock moved through the garden, plucking pests from branches or yanking weeds from the ground. Rockefeller's small shoulders, narrow as a child's, bobbed into view behind a row of raspberry plants. He grazed slowly along the thicket, picking and eating berries, and then ducked into a bush's shadow. Behind him, Matt and Ben and Mildred appeared alongside a stand of tomatoes. Dr. Eatman stood nearby, stomping on a can with its top and bottom cut out, embedding it around a small tomato stalk. He waved at me. Daniel was nowhere in sight.

Reverend Steck continued in a self-mocking tone, so that I could not tell when he was serious, and when he wanted to pull my leg. He said he believed that the sane and insane should live side by side in harmony, and that no insect that man could not outwit deserved to be killed. As a child he had loved insects, particularly beetles. He and his brother had kept two iridescent green dung beetles as pets for five months in a Cortez cigar box; his father had done missionary work in Honduras, where insects were spectacular.

"They looked like jewels with legs, like living emeralds," Reverend Steck said. "Beetles are miracles of beauty. Who could not admire a scarab like the rose chafer? A creature evolved as a distillation of the pleasure of smelling and eating roses?" Reverend Steck confessed that his weakness for entomology had led him to seek out Dr. Eatman after learning from an entomology newsletter of his collapse. (Stretch Rockefeller and Dmytryk had been sent by the Unitarian Church, straight from the state hospital.) "So that if Dr. Eatman lends an overdetermined quality to my organic gardening project for the sane and insane, this is because the project is a creation and a dream, and so it's overdetermined in the way dreams are." I laughed. I could see why Reverend Steck's congregation liked him; he seemed to take delight in everything.

"My son-in-law tells me that beetles in Brazil are magnificent. He claims that Charles Darwin named a Brazilian beetle after himself." Reverend Steck frowned, smiled, and then said, "My son-in-law is quite an impressive young man, isn't he? When Mildred wrote me about him, I thought her descriptions were too colored by young love to be trust-worthy. But he's everything I might have hoped for in a son-in-law—intelligent and compassionate."

After this Reverend Steck showed me his sunny Lemon Boy toma-toes, the stars of cucumber flowers, constellations of blueberries. He told me that his favorite poem was Roethke's "Cuttings" and declaimed it like a sermon:

> *This urge, wrestle, resurrection of dry sticks,*
> *Cut stems struggling to put down feet,*
> *What saint strained so much,*
> *Rose on such lopped limbs to a new life?*

He told me with enthusiasm that he loved Roethke, and the German lyrical poets and the midwestern writers who imitated them. He had given Matt several poetry books after he saw that my brother had a copy of Hölderlin's works. Reverend Steck said he found it remarkable that Matt could write poetry even in the depths of psychosis.

I answered that the amazing thing was not that a psychotic could write poetry, but that psychosis had gone so far in compromising Matt's gifts.

Reverend Steck paused, and for the first time during the walk, his face grew serious. "Melanie," he said, "maybe that's why Matt's been avoiding you; he sees his life reflected in your face with such bitterness."

I frowned.

"Or maybe it's that Matt sees all you've accomplished—you've be-come everything your father wanted him to be. You know, I think there's no contact between Matt and his dad right now."

The mention of Joel Ratleer took me off guard. Uncertain what to answer, I said, "I haven't spoken to my father in over ten years, since he first gave up on Matt. I don't think he's been in touch with Matt during that time."

"Ten years?" Reverend Steck seemed astonished. "Ottilie never told me that it had been ten years! But then, she never tells anyone anything, does she? In all the time I've known her, she's only once come to me for help—when Matt was in jail. I'm a minister. I like to solve problems." His smile was Mildred's, warm and ironic. "In all this time, Ottilie never once said she had no help from your father—"

"I like to think of Joel Ratleer as being in remission."

"Remission."

Reverend Steck's innocence left me at a loss. I did not want to begin to describe Joel Ratleer to this minister, who loved his daughter and grandson with such obvious devotion, to explain how there were men who picked up and cast off lives, surfacing and resurfacing as the new husband of one woman after another, like the devil himself putting on and taking off disguises.

"Well," Reverend Steck said. "I see I'm treading on your toes. I'll stick to my own territory and mind my own business."

A woman appeared at the end of the road in a brown A-line dress, and a scarf the faded red of a chicken wattle. As she approached the Park and Pray, Reverend Steck turned to watch her. It was Mrs. Shove. She slowed in front of the church, as if deliberating, and read the announcement of Sunday's sermon. Then she continued on, rounding the corner and hurrying on her way toward downtown Muskellunge.

"Maureen," Reverend Steck said. "Maureen Shove. Her husband pressured her to leave the church, because he's uncomfortable about the halfway house. Many people are. But that's the Park and Pray's mission, to embolden people to embrace with compassion the very things they fear, and so to enter the community of God—" Reverend Steck caught himself in midsentence, and said, "At what point did I stop talking to you and start preaching?" Then he squared his shoulders and sang:

> O Red, O Red, O Red Reverend Steck
> I told them they would pay!
> They've all been ground to sausages
> behind the Park and Pray—

"Have you heard that one?" Reverend Steck asked me.

I nodded.

He smiled, narrowed his eyes, shifted his expression and said, "This is what Mr. Shove told me when he came to visit our church: '*Never* look a weirdo in the eye.'" Reverend Steck let his voice rise an octave, charged it with a note of hysteria, leaned toward me as he spoke, and suddenly I could see Mr. Shove, an edgy, uncomfortable man bursting with his own opinions. "'That's my life's motto, now and always; never let your eyes meet with a weirdo's or he'll latch on to you and there'll be hell to pay!'" He waggled his finger. The impersonation was very funny; I laughed out loud. I wondered if the Park and Pray's members knew of Reverend Steck's talent for mimicking his parishioners.

Reverend Steck looked over my shoulder: I turned, and there was Dr. Eatman, waving to me to come join him. "Dr. Eatman likes you; he thinks you're amusing," Reverend Steck said. "Because you act so grave all the time. Well, I'm going to leave you two alone. I don't want to hinder your association."

Abruptly, Reverend Steck strode into his squash patch and recommenced harvesting zucchinis. As I lingered to watch him bend over an orange trumpeting blossom, I saw that the garden was a work of genius, a dreamed patch of creation on the edge of that desolate Wisconsin town. Gratitude that my brother was part of Reverend Steck's concocted world soared inside me: squash flowers gleamed everywhere under broad leaves; beyond them eggplants shone in their green chalices; purple martins somersaulted overhead, and cicadas racketed in the high branches of a willow.

I headed toward Dr. Eatman amid the tomatoes. He pressed a Contadina can into the dirt around a tomato plant and said, "Do you know what these are? Barriers against cutworms. Pretty diabolical, isn't it—protecting young tomatoes by planting tomato puree cans around their stems?"

He stooped and unearthed a handful of white turbans, twisting as if from their own inner wisdom. He raised them closer to me, and I saw they were grubs, grotesque, each the size of a man's thumb, but with tiny brown claws and hideous umber heads.

"Cutworms," Dr. Eatman said joyously, and beside him I felt joyous and manic. Dr. Eatman pulled on a pair of gardening gloves, solemnly explaining that the nicotine stains on his hands left from smoking could spread disease to the tomatoes and peppers. "They're all in the same family," he said. "*Solanaceae*. Most plants related to the tomato are deadly poisonous: jimpson weed, henbane, belladonna, tobacco. Imagine if everyone in your family was deadly poisonous."

Daniel appeared suddenly, without warning.

Dr. Eatman started, and said, "Where did *you* come from?"

"I was reading a book on the wall over there," Daniel said. He was wearing cutoff shorts and a T-shirt, a leather cowboy hat, and leather boots with strange, pointed toes.

"These are called *sapatões*," he told me, lifting up one of his boots. "All the Brazilian cowboys wear them. A Brazilian friend of mine gave them to me, and this hat, too. The equatorial sun was turning me into a redneck." He lifted his hat, showing me a slight sunburn amid the moss of his nape hair.

"What have we here?" Dr. Eatman said, taking Daniel's book from his hand. "*The Uses of Enchantment* by Bruno Bettelheim? Who would ever have thought that old Dr. Brutalheim would climb onto the best-seller list in 1977?" He made a face at the book and, returning it to Daniel, told him, "Psychiatry is not a science!"

Behind him, Daniel raised his eyebrows and held back a smile.

"Entomology is a science," Dr. Eatman pronounced. "Oceanography is a science. Psychiatry is just alchemy by another name. Witchcraft. Hypnotism. Shady dabblings into the inexplicable." He widened his eyes, lifted his fingers in a ridiculous undulating motion before Daniel's face, and in a voice mocking the popular image of a hypnotist, said, "Look into my eyes! Your eyelids are getting heavy; you are light as a feather and stiff as a board. You will go into a deep, deep sleep, and I will stare into your soul and reveal the mysterious mysteries of the universe!" Dr. Eatman laughed loudly, and Daniel stepped backward, looking bewildered.

Dr. Eatman plucked a bug from a tomato vine. Fastening an eye on me and wiggling his eyebrows comically, he said, "Who knows what weevils lurk in the hearts of men?" Then he laughed again, uproariously, at his own joke. I thought he probably had been an entertaining professor before he lost his marbles.

Daniel and I stood by watching as Dr. Eatman stomped the rest of the tomato cans into the earth.

"How are you and Ben doing?" I asked Daniel.

"Oh, he's coming along," Daniel said. "I think he's afraid I'm going to steal Mildred from him."

Daniel regaled me with tales about gardening in Brazil, describing homesteaders there as if they were pioneer settlers of a mythical land. He said that the unfarmed soil of the Amazon was so fertile it defied imagination. If you just spilled a bag of beans on the ground in the morning, "they would sprout before nightfall, and grow so fast the naked eye could see them move." Cherry tomatoes appeared in such abundance that the farmers there uprooted them, calling them a *praga*, plague. Even after Daniel consumed a salad of cherry tomatoes to demonstrate their edibility, the farmers who watched him plowed the vines under, insisting they were poisonous. In Brazil Daniel had discovered that plants we considered annuals, such as peppers and eggplant, which grew to be only two or three feet in the midwest, reached gigantic proportions where unimpeded by winter. On Amazonian farms collards looked like palm trees, okra grew to twelve feet, bell pepper bushes bore a hundred fruits at a time.

Daniel's words created such a longing in me: It was as if he had looked into my heart and seen the things I wanted most and tried to pull them into the open air. As he talked, I imagined myself in Brazil, stealing the honey of killer bees, harvesting plagues of cherry tomatoes with indifference, swimming with piranhas.

Behind the last row of tomato plants, Mildred's voice rose, and she and Matt and Ben came into view all at once, moving in a tight group. "*My* favorite book," she told Matt, "is *The Martian Chronicles*. I love the story where all the black people leave the United States for Mars because they've had it, they're fed up, and the white people freak out. What will they do? Who will clean their houses? Who will they call stupid so that they can feel smart? How will they be lords of the land with no one to lord it over? It's my greatest regret that I was born before space travel."

My brother nodded, as if he understood implicitly. Then he saw Daniel. Matt's face froze, and took on a malevolent expression. Abruptly, he walked away in the direction of the church. Mildred watched him go.

"Ben!" Daniel said. "Come to Daddy!"

Ben wrapped himself in Mildred's skirt. Mildred stroked his cheek.

Daniel stepped toward him. Ben held out his hand as if to shield himself and shouted, "Oshkosh! Oshkosh!"

"It's OK," Daniel said from where he stood, but he looked a little hurt.

I saw they needed to be alone, and so I followed Matt's path back to the halfway house. Below me an ant walked her head-of-a-pin trail, silently. On the edge of the garden Dmytryk lay asleep or unconscious, his head propped on a rock, his pencil moustache curling above a serene half-smile, his arm crooked tenderly around the shoulder of his Coca-Cola bottle.

When I entered the halfway house an overpowering smell of bacon filled the back hallway; I felt as if I could taste the air. I found Rockefeller in the kitchen, hovering over three boxes of bacon sizzling in three separate pans. I told him good morning, but he didn't answer. He dismounted his stepladder, poured a cup of coffee from a percolator, lifted my arm, and placed the cup in my hand. Then Rockefeller returned to his ladder, drained the bacon over paper towels, and carried it all upstairs on a platter, running ahead of me as if afraid I would ask for a bite. When he heard my steps on the landing, he slammed his door.

The house was nicely kept inside, with oak floors and a wide stairway with polished oak banisters. Upstairs was an office for the Madison psychiatrist who visited the residents weekly; inside was a desk for the nurse who dispensed their medications, and an alcove where a caretaker slept at night to assure no trouble arose among the inmates. (On the man's nights off, Reverend Steck slept on the cot. He had once told Ottilie he felt at home there.) Each resident had his own bedroom, with a wooden sign bearing his name on the door—the result, I guessed, of a woodworking project at the halfway house. The signs said A. DMYTRYK, STRETCH ROCKEFELLER, and DOCTOR E. Matt's read simply, RATLEER.

Matt was not upstairs. His bedroom was tidy to the point of asceticism. His top sheet was folded with geometrical exactitude over the blanket, and the lines of his pillow ran perfectly parallel to the bed's hospital corners. A row of poetry books, ordered not alphabetically by author but by size, sat by his bed. They must have come mostly from Reverend Steck: they were by Trakl and Hölderlin, Roethke and James Wright, Richard Hugo and Rilke. There were two Spanish grammar books, and bilingual translations by Robert Bly of Spanish and Latin American poets. Chess books, ordered according to the colors of their covers (yellows on the right; whites to the left; blues and blacks in the middle), ran across the lower shelf. Beside the books was a stack of one-dollar bills, piled as neatly as playing cards.

An ancient manual typewriter, a battered chessboard, and a leather-bound Bible sat on Matt's desk. Beside these were travel guides to Peru and Greenland and Crete, and a handwritten list of distant cities with musical names: Adelaide and Mitylene, Oslo and Tegucigalpa. Next to these were a magenta felt-tip pen, a book of poetry translations titled *Fragments by Hölderlin,* and an anthology of German poetry, fallen open to a dog-eared page where Matt had underlined in magenta: *"O hoher Baum im Ohr!"* whose meaning escaped me. In the margin Matt had scribbled, "Oh tall tree in my ear!" but I doubted the words could mean this. Matt also had written, in the margin of a second book by Hölderlin, a series of verb conjugations that appeared to be hybrids of Spanish and English and German: *Ich conozco, du conocist, he kennt, wir coknowcemos, ellos kennen.* Under these he had penciled:

> *Near the borders of the world I wait*
> *The delirium shows me its darker edge.*

Beside the books were paper scraps, some as small as postage stamps. They bore nonsensical phrases, fragments of sentences and even single words: "A wind amid the ragged nets," "cold," "O cold mountain above the harbor," "in a jagged wind," "flaxen light," "Mitylene," "Wind."

Matt stood poised in the doorway. There was a fraction of a moment when I registered the expression on his face—a look of disbelief and horror.

Before I could say anything, Matt came toward me, shouting, "What are you doing? Are you crazy? You're crazy!"

Matt pulled me away from his desk, and then pushed me again, violently, toward the door. He roared—he threw back his head and let out a noise that seemed half-animal and half-human, pronouncing the word *roar* distinctly, but shouting it in a harsh, rasping way.

And then he yelled, "Out! Out! Get out! Get out! Out! Out!" He grabbed me, wrenching my arm, and shoved me hard, so that my head hit the door jamb.

I tried to pull away from him, crying, "Let go, Matt! Let go! That hurts!"

Reverend Steck and Daniel ran up the stairs. The footsteps of others sounded behind them. Reverend Steck entered the room and grabbed Matt's forearm.

"Matt, take your hands off her," Reverend Steck said.

"Get her out of here!" Matt told him.

"She can't leave if you don't let go of her."

Matt released me.

"It was my fault," I said. "I came in without asking." But I was shaken. "I was just trying to find you, Matt."

Matt fixed a venomous look on me, and then he roared again. The noise he made was so loud that afterward my ears rang. Behind Reverend Steck the three other men of the house stood, peering inside the room. Stretch Rockefeller looked frightened. He repeated, "Oh no, oh no, oh no, oh no." Dr. Eatman told him, "Close it up, Stretch," and Dmytryk offered him a bottle, but Rockefeller turned and ran down the stairs.

"Get her out of my room," Matt said.

"She's going," Reverend Steck answered. "But we'll have to talk about this, Matt. You know that the first rule of this halfway house is no violence of any kind whatsoever."

"He wasn't violent," I intervened. "He didn't mean to hurt me."

Matt smirked when I said this.

I felt dazed as I left the room. I heard Matt tell Reverend Steck behind me, "She was trying to steal my soul!" I walked slowly down the stairs. Before I reached the bottom, Daniel took me by the elbow and steered me toward the back steps.

"Are you OK?" he asked, sitting down next to me.

"Yes," I said. "I'm just shocked a little." I held back tears.

"I don't care if you cry," Daniel told me.

I felt overwhelmed with pity for myself. It wasn't enough, I thought, that I'd fought off death for a year; now I had to fend off life's sorrows and hardships. At that moment I longed to be back at work in New York, burying myself in the impenetrable language of Justice Rehnquist, scoffing at the ponderous illogic of his sentences.

Daniel offered me a cigarette. I thought longingly of Mildred's homegrown marijuana.

"Thanks, but I had to give up smoking," I said. I didn't tell him why, or that since doing so I had been both irresistibly attracted to and repelled by the smell of tobacco. I thought of how, since the cancer, I had felt overly fragile, as if I did not trust my own body to support and defend me. Perhaps this is why I had felt so shocked when Matt grabbed me.

"Matt and I used to be so close," I said.

"And now he won't let you anywhere near him."

"No."

"I know the feeling," Daniel said, smiling a little. "I guess we're sort of in the same boat. My own kid acts like I'm Count Dracula."

I laughed softly.

"Benjamin, 'son of my right hand.' That's what his name means. That why I liked that name."

I heard a clattering on the stairs, and then, "The sky is falling! The sky is falling!" "Aw, drink some Pferd," Dr. Eatman directed. "It'll calm your nerves." "It always does," Dmytryk remarked. The three men's steps receded toward the kitchen.

"Those guys were pretty upset," Daniel said.

"Yeah." I felt embarrassed that I had caused such a commotion. Evening was slipping over the town, and at the end of the road Aunt Mimi's house rose in brightness, its colored windows mirroring the brilliant purple sky. I alone had disrupted the harmony of this world. I wished I were anyone else; I recalled Reverend Steck's impersonation of Mr. Shove, and I wondered how it would feel to be such a man, to say, "*Never* look a weirdo in the eye!" A temptation to utter the words choked me, and then let me go.

Instead, I said, "I love the twilight when the sky turns that purple color."

"Changing the subject," Daniel answered. But he didn't press me, and I was grateful he was there. I felt the bond between our two predicaments.

"Once, when I was visiting this farmer in Brazil," Daniel said, "I told him that in the States, the sun sets at a different time each day, depending on whether it's winter or summer. The farmer just wouldn't believe me—since the sun always sets at exactly the same time near the equator. I tried to explain that twilight comes as early as four in the winter, as late as eight-thirty in the summer, but he just laughed, thinking I was spoofing him. He asked me, 'How could they trust the light enough to farm there, if that's true?'"

It was odd to think that a foreigner would find our lives too fantastic to be credible.

"We just have to keep plugging away with Ben and Matt," Daniel said. "Mildred's dad pulled me over last night, and we got to talking about Matt and Ben and Mildred and he suggested that we all go together on a fishing trip. He thought if we gathered outside, with less pressure to socialize, Matt might feel less cornered, less anxious about being around you, and you could approach him more easily. And he thought it might give me a chance to get Ben to warm up to me. He said he'd lure Ben away from Matt and Mildred with the promise that I'd show Ben how to fish."

I hadn't been aware that Reverend Steck was watching over everything so closely. It made me feel uneasy to know that someone was trying to divine thoughts I kept to myself.

"It's worth a try," Daniel said. "Mildred's dad asked me to collect some nightcrawlers one of these nights so that we have enough bait for the men in the halfway house, too. Want to help me look for worms?"

"That's really inviting," I answered. "I can hardly turn it down, even with all there is to do in Muskellunge." But anything seemed better than being left alone with myself. We agreed to get up one day that week before dawn, when the nightcrawlers come out to lick the dew off the ground. Daniel suggested that we look near the creek bed behind Ottilie's house. And so, we made a tentative date.

We heard footsteps behind us. It was Dmytryk. He circled me quietly, and standing on the bottom step in front of us, he offered a Coca-Cola bottle, corked shut.

"This is for Matt's sister," he said, setting it down on the step. Then he stood there, waiting for me to respond.

Daniel picked up the bottle, uncorked it, and sniffed it. "Whew," he said. He took a sip.

"Cheers!" Dmytryk told us.

"Cheers!" Daniel answered. He passed me the bottle. "Here, drink it, Melanie. This is a very good night to get drunk."

Dmytryk grinned devilishly.

I took three large swallows of his liquor. It felt like fire in my throat and made my thoughts swirl.

"Only a little while ago, Mildred and I got stoned on marijuana," I said. "And now you're getting me drunk."

Daniel took several sips of Dmytryk's wine, without flinching. "Marijuana?" he asked. He seemed surprised. "I used to try to get Mildred to smoke grass with me in Brazil." There was an edge I couldn't define in his voice, jealousy or longing or wistfulness. "She always said she couldn't smoke with Ben around. But that Brazilian grass—maconha—it makes you feel like you're flying." He drank more dandelion wine, and gave me back the bottle.

I also drank more, and I began to think of dandelions, and to wonder how such sunny, commonplace flowers had conspired to become wine. I waited for that moment when I would feel myself unhinge from my own skin and emerge a butterfly with edgeless wings, but it never came. The liquor lacked the delicacy of Mildred's marijuana; it closed over my thoughts like a shovelful of earth. I passed the bottle to Daniel, and he passed it back to me, and at some point, the twilight slipped away. Daniel and I sat talking about everything and nothing, amid the shrieking of crickets and glitter of fireflies.

I forgot about Matt, and I never asked myself what he felt, sitting alone in his dark room, reviewing the night's events. I don't remember a word of anything else Daniel said. When I awoke in the morning, I was lying on the couch downstairs in the halfway house, and Rockefeller was in the kitchen, frying four rations of bacon.

5

ALL WEEK Daniel labored to restore harmony among us all. I would see him and Mildred sitting on the halfway house's porch, gazing at each other, their arms intertwined, as if they had fallen in love only the day before. Or I would come upon Daniel clowning boyishly in the garden with his father-in-law, tossing a zucchini back and forth like a football. Or I would find Daniel playing chess with Dmytryk while Rockefeller hovered anxiously over them and Dr. Eatman cheered from the sidelines, "ruthless!" "viciously competitive!" and advised Dmytryk how to move. Ottilie told me that Daniel had even tried to make peace with Matthew by bringing a book on chess to his room, but that Matt had thrown the book down the stairs, and slammed the door in Daniel's face. I also tried to visit Matt, but when I knocked, he refused to open his door.

A week after the incident at the halfway house, it rained in the morning, and Daniel came by Ottilie's and gave her a card that I thought was very funny:

> *Please tell Melanie that she is cordially invited to a nightcrawler hunt in the creek behind Ottilie's house at 3:30 A.M. tomorrow. Nightcrawlers are said to be especially abundant after a gentle rain.*

"Why *my* house?" Ottilie said, handing me the note. When I reached for it, she said, "Melanie, he's married."

"It's not like that," I answered.

Daniel and I met beside the stream that ran near the edge of the

Stecks' property, carrying heavy flashlights and buckets half-filled with dirt. The night was cloudless and moonless, black, except for Musky's neon fish on the north horizon: Its yellow eyes flickered, watching all of Muskellunge. Daniel wore his cowboy hat and *sapatões*, and when I saw him, I felt as if I were about to embark on a dangerous quest in a strange land. The beams from our flashlights crossed like antennae, soared into the trees, rested on the ground. Daniel's *sapatões* left deep, pointed impressions in the mud.

"A shooting star," I said.

Daniel turned around, and another fell. During August every year, belts of meteorites position themselves in their orbits above Wisconsin, and fall in predictable showers. Within the next ten minutes, as we stood watching, another three or four fell, and then they stopped.

When we came to a log laid across a gully's stream ten feet below us, Daniel said, "Look what I can do." He pulled his hat in front of his face, and blinded by it, walked across the log, balancing perfectly and hardly testing the surface in front of him. Crossing sightless there seemed impossible, like playing a violin with gloves on.

"I practiced this for hours when I was a kid," Daniel said. Then he turned around and walked back.

"And what's more, you lived to tell about it," I answered.

"It's not as hard as it looks," Daniel said. "It's all in your feet. You don't realize until you try that balance comes from your sense of touch rather than what you can see."

"Ah, it's all sleight-of-foot."

"Ho, ho. Want to try it?"

"No."

Daniel jumped down from the log. "It's nice and muddy here," he said. We shone our lights onto the wet ground. The long bodies of earthworms lay everywhere, half in earth and half in air. They shied from our lights. I turned mine away, squatted, and grabbed a night-crawler.

"Come on, you little crawly," Daniel crooned in the darkness behind me. "You struggly buggly, you earth eel."

I laughed, joined to him by the awareness that we were both experiencing the same groping blindness and the feel of the nightcrawlers. The darkness heightened our sense of touch and intensified the extraordinary sensation of pulling on those slippery, elastic bodies. The nightcrawlers clung to the earth without claws, battling our grips with nothing but the muscles of their fear. We gathered them for two hours, until even when empty-handed, I could feel them twisting inside my palms.

"It's like mining for worms," I said.

As we filled our buckets, Daniel talked about his work in the Amazonian mines. "Gold mines in Brazil aren't dark," he began. "They're wide pits, a hundred yards across, and the men scale them like ants. What interested me when I was doing my research was this practice they had there that was supposed to enhance the luck of an individual miner. The miner would engineer himself into a position of trust with a young couple, until he was honored by being called upon to be the godparent of a newborn child. Then, as the godparent, he would attend the infant's baptism in the local church. As the priest pronounced the baby's Christian name, the miner would touch a piece of gold in his pocket, and the child's soul would go into the gold instead of the child.

"After that whatever the child's baptismal name had been would become the name of the gold nugget. So, if the child was going to be João, or Clara, or Nelson, that would be the gold nugget's name. Later, when the miner walked into a mine, he would drop the nugget, and say to it three times:

> *Nelson, will you come back to your father?*
> *Will you come back to your father?*
> *Will you come back to your father?*

Then the man would pick up the nugget, and put it in his pocket, and after that all the gold in the mine would be attracted to him, and he would find a hundred times more than his fellow miners. Of course, the church condemned the practice, because it leaves the child who should have been baptized without a soul, spiritually cut off and eviscerated, and condemned to limbo or purgatory forever after death."

I thought it strange that the church would condemn the practice, for the condemnation itself implied a belief in its efficacy. A worm slipped from my grasp and I shivered, considering how easily a child's soul could be lost.

I daydreamed of traveling the Amazon with Daniel, of descending into the wet malarial pits of gold mines and traversing rivers. In the daydream, this was no betrayal of Mildred—it was just an imagined story, and so I could people it with whatever characters I wanted. And as Daniel talked, I imagined that it was me telling his stories instead of him. This is a habit I have—that sometimes in the very act of reading or listening, I will appropriate the ideas of the speaker or writer. I forget in the imaginings that my thoughts are not mine, but instead vicarious.

"And there are people who do this with dollar bills also, with cruzeiro notes," Daniel continued. "They touch the money just when the priest says the child's name, and the note is baptized instead. It is believed that when such money is given in commercial exchange to, say, a store, that all the money in the store will flee to the hands of the godparent who baptized the bill. Once, the owner of a local bar said that he heard rattling in his cash register when he turned to fill someone's glass, and when he came back, the register was empty, and he saw that a baptized bill had made off with all his money. Another time a woman went into a local supermarket, and a policeman standing on line behind her heard her say, 'Nilda, will you come back to your mother? Will you come back to your mother? Will you come back to your mother?' He arrested the woman immediately, and she's probably still serving time for attempted robbery. On another occasion a mine owner heard clattering in his cash box. When he opened it, he saw two cruzeiro notes fighting it out, and realized that he had been spared the spiriting away of all his cash only by the strange coincidence that two people must have passed him baptized notes on the same morning."

I was so enchanted by Daniel's words that the stars disappeared in the light of morning without my noticing. When I looked up from my pail of worms, Daniel stood only a foot from me, the dew wetting his socks, the fox-colored hairs on his arms glistening, distinct in the dawn light.

I told him, "You're eyeing me as if I'm an especially desirable night-crawler."

"You look so otherworldly standing there, like a wood nymph. You're so tall and willowy."

The dawn's coolness made a chill run down my spine. A feeling opened in me, took flight: I suddenly missed the writer I had been seeing the year before, the tobacco smell of his smoker's hands, the long wings of his shoulder blades, the place where his neck nape slipped into his collar.

"A penny for your thoughts," Daniel said.

I was thankful for Daniel's tenderness, for the awakening of feeling in me, even if it had nowhere to go. His words seemed like no more than a half-pass, innocent, an expression of kindness. I felt lightheaded and happy for the first time in a long while.

"I was thinking that I must be the first wood nymph to graduate from law school."

Daniel laughed, held up his bucket. "I think we've got enough worms to harvest the whole lake dry." He offered to take both pails back to the Stecks' house, and after that we parted.

As I headed home toward Ottilie's, the hair on the back of my neck stood up, and I imagined I heard steps behind me. I thought of the soul of an infant slipping into the thumbed picture of a dollar bill. I turned and looked behind me, but of course no one was following. As I walked home, I could still feel the nightcrawlers muscling against my palms.

ON SATURDAY MORNING Reverend Steck roused the men early, and I joined him outside the Park and Pray to help load supplies into the van. His own rod was beautiful and complicated, polished like driftwood at the handle from long use. It made me like Reverend Steck that he, an expert angler, would take the men fishing with bamboo poles and two buckets of worms.

Dr. Eatman stood beside the van, staring spellbound at Reverend Steck's box of fishing lures and flies. I leaned over him. Every fly is modeled after a specific insect, and I could see why Reverend Steck's flies would captivate an entomologist. They were idiosyncratic and spectacular, as if a Dr. Frankenstein of the fisherman's world had imbued them with diabolical life: Bits of fur and feathers, suggestive of insect pincers or stingers or biting mouths, were grafted onto hooks with minute threads. On one I saw a long iridescent feather the exact shimmery hue of a bluebottle fly, and wondered if Mildred had brought it back from Brazil. It looked lethal, as if it could strike a fish dead.

Ben refused to sit in the van with his father and insisted on riding with his mother in Ottilie's car. I was embarrassed when I saw Matt crawl into the car's back seat. I knew that he was crazy and not strictly accountable for his actions, but I felt he was making himself a wedge between Ben and Daniel.

Daniel frowned when he saw Matt enter the car. He no longer looked at ease about Matt and Ben being together. Daniel approached

Ben, laid his hand on his shoulder from behind, and whispered something to him.

Ben became hysterical. He looked at me frantically and wrested his shoulder from his father's grip. Then Ben screamed, "He's a bad guy! Cut off his arm! Shoot him in the asshole!" He ran toward me and clutched my legs, almost knocking me off balance.

"Hey, hey," I said, stepping back and patting him on the head.

"Ben!" Mildred said. She stooped down in front of him and he threw his arms around her. She smoothed his hair and kissed his forehead.

Reverend Steck looked on with concern. "Where would Ben learn to say something like that?" he asked.

Mildred answered: "Maybe the shooting stuff is from watching cartoons."

Daniel said quickly, "He could have learned those words from other kids, I guess. Or from anywhere, really. They're just in the air that little boys breathe." He sighed and got into the van.

During the ride Daniel set aside his feelings, determined to be in a good humor for the outing. He joked with Reverend Steck, who chided him like a son. They talked about liberation theology and the World Council of Churches, and then swapped fish stories.

Reverend Steck stopped at Shove's to pick up extra hooks. As he parked, I saw Mr. and Mrs. Shove arguing beside the cash register. Mr. Shove's square, stocky face turned toward Reverend Steck as he entered the store, and Mrs. Shove scuttled to the back and began arranging shelves. I thought it must be uncomfortable for a minister to have to rely on the general store of a parishioner who had left the fold.

Steck returned to the van and said, "Those electric orange overalls he's wearing are just like Mildred's." He laughed and added, "Mr. Shove might take comfort in the fact that my daughter has styled her dress after his."

On the way to the western side of Lake Muskellunge, where fishing was apparently best, Reverend Steck told us that the "Musky" of Musky's restaurant was really Musky Junior. Musky Senior lived amid the shadows under an old dock in Lake Muskellunge, and he would emerge periodically in order to torture fishermen. He was an alligator-sized fish, over six feet long, who watched all bait with indifference, sometimes nosing it in a tantalizing manner but never biting. Reverend Steck had designed elaborate lures and strategies to hook him, and

Musky Senior had watched his antics in mocking silence. Reverend Steck said that on the occasions he had seen Musky Senior, he felt that the fish was lying in wait, fishing for him.

"In 1939, efforts were initiated to adopt the muskellunge as the Wisconsin state fish," Reverend Steck told Daniel. He concluded dryly, "Sixteen years later, in 1955, the legislature passed the proposal without a single dissenting vote."

We passed a state park entrance gate, and the van lurched over a speed barrier in the road.

Daniel told me, "In Brazil, those bumps are called 'sleeping policemen,' *policias durmientes*." He added under his breath, as if quoting someone, "'There's a sleeping policeman in every one of us; he must be killed.'"

"We called them 'Thank you Ma'ams,' when I was a kid," Reverend Steck said.

When we arrived in the van, Matt and Mildred were already out on the lake with their rods. Ben, a child's bright orange life preserver strapped to his chest, wandered down the beach with Ottilie. He turned toward his mother and waved to her; she waved back; he repeated this ritual several times. Matt stood on a sandbar, casting his line expertly into the radiant water. The western sky brightened behind him, gilding the lake, and the shadows of trees fell like cut timber over the water, lengthened and disappeared. Standing by himself, Matt could have been anyone, any whole and sane, fairly young man reading the water's surface for the lively signs of fish. Mildred leaned against a rail in the middle of a long dock, looking lithe and unworldly, contemplating the glittering water. At the pier's end, two men were fishing, and as the sun rose, the men's hats and Mildred's hair seemed to glow like embers and catch fire. If Wisconsin had not been associated in my own inner landscapes with a violent, freezing darkness, with self-devouring fears, with looming madness and lingering dread, I would have been moved by the beauty of this early morning vision.

Reverend Steck walked to the waterline, said something to Ottilie, and then picked up Ben and put him on his shoulders.

"I'm high in the sky!" Ben cried.

Reverend Steck returned with Ben, and Daniel and I pulled the gear out of the van. Ben eyed Daniel from on high with a poker face. Daniel and Reverend Steck guided Dr. Eatman, Dmytryk, and Stretch Rockefeller around the bend to a small pier in an inlet south of the larger pier. Ottilie and I hung back, watching Matt and Mildred.

One of the men at the end of the dock gestured at Mildred's tackle box and called something to her in a low tone. He approached her, pointed at her rod, and then, half-circling her waist with his arm, wound her reel a turn. Mildred stepped away, and her voice rang distinctly in the dawn light.

"Fuck off!"

Matt looked up from where he stood fishing.

"Yeah, fuck off," the other man called to his friend. They were both young and shirtless, drinking from Pferd beer cans. "Hey, hey there, no offense," the first man said to Mildred, raising his hands as if defending himself from an assault. Ottilie and I walked out on the pier to join her.

"Christ, those jackass he-men sportsmen get on my nerves," Mildred said when we reached her. "If there's one thing I can't stand, it's these *Deliverance* types with their fancy rods and reels acting as if they've come to tame the wilderness. You know: Man against Fish. If I didn't like to fish so much, I'd never fish."

I asked Mildred what the man had said to her, and she answered that he had wanted to give her "some pointers on what kind of bait to use and how to cast it while a strange man feels up your rib bones." She added, "I'm sure I know a lot more about fish than he knows about women. I used to come out here almost every morning in the summers when I was a kid and catch trout with red hots and canned corn." She reeled in her line. "They don't even need those fancy rods if they're staying on the pier. The big fish like the shallows, where it's cool and murky. All those guys are going to get is a basket filled with teeny yellow perch."

She grinned conspiratorially at me. Grabbing the sinker in her right hand, she pitched it, baseball style, forty feet over the water, the hook and line chasing after it as the reel spun out of control.

The men watched. One of them whistled.

Matt also watched; he turned toward Mildred and smiled, and then his chuckle sounded across the water, low as a skipped stone.

"That's how you do it, you poor fast-handed fishless bastard," Mildred said.

Ottilie had a laughing fit. She held her stomach and bent over, and between laughs said, "You-tickle-me-Mildred, you-tickle-me-Mildred." I slapped her on the back. I had never seen Ottilie lose control like that.

Everything Mildred did from then on seemed calculated to puzzle and torment the men, and to tempt Ottilie into another laughing fit. Mildred reeled in her line several times, took the sinker in her hand, and threw it again. She jiggled the line crazily in the water, whipped it back and forth like a snake, let it go still. After twenty minutes, she picked up the sinker and attached a long lure to it—a yellow feather with black bands and a stinger, and tossed this, overhand, one last time into some shallows near the bank. She sang what she called "Reverend Steck's favorite hymn" in a low, ironic voice:

> *Love is strong as Death,*
> *Jealousy cru-el as the grave.*

A green arc leapt skyward and twisted in the air. Mildred shouted, "There he is! Got him!" Then she whispered to me and Ottilie, "This is ridiculous. You never catch anything over there. This fish is just doing me a favor."

The fish leapt again, only fifteen feet from Matt. He whooped as it crashed back into the water: It was a three-foot muskellunge. It surfaced, heading straight for the open lake, then it leapt out of the water near the men's lines, doubled back, and dove under the pier. We heard something strike the pier's wooden supports beneath us, and then the line slackened and became still.

Mildred reeled in the line, and at the end of it, the stunned fish. She dipped a net into the water and lifted the muskellunge onto the dock.

"Someone do CPR, quick!" Mildred shouted. But, as if to reassure us, the fish opened its mouth and gasped, then flopped its forked tail. Mildred said then, loud enough for the men to hear, "We'll have to put him out of his misery." She reached into her tackle box, I thought for something to club it with. Instead she pulled out the starter's pistol. It looked dense and black and unnatural. She pointed it at the fish's head.

Ottilie gasped and raised her hands to her face. The men at the end of the dock watched, motionless.

Then Ottilie bent over again, clutching her sides and laughing. "Oh," she said. "Oh, oh, oh!"

Mildred dropped the gun back into the tackle box. She waved at the men and said, "You really thought I was going to shoot that old fish, didn't you?"

One man stood transfixed; the other shook his head, snickered, and turned back to his fishing.

Ottilie sat down saying, "Oh Mildred, oh Mildred, I have to stop, I'm going to—" Ottilie looked up at me. "Melanie! Melanie!" she repeated until she became breathless with laughter. Matt watched her and smiled. Our eyes met, but Matt looked away.

Mildred worked the hook from the muskellunge's mouth. The fish's muddy green eyes watched her coldly. When the hook came free, she picked up the muskellunge with both hands, held him over the water, and let go. He fell straight down, like a lead sinker. Then he came to life, flipped slightly as if testing his surroundings, darted forward, and became a shadow's shadow.

"Melanie," Ottilie said. "You looked so surprised!"

I realized there had been a moment when, forgetting that the gun was only a starter's pistol, I had fully expected Mildred to fire.

AFTER MILDRED let the muskellunge go, she and Ottilie sat on the dock with their ankles in the water. But I felt too restless to stay with them and walked along the water's edge, looking for polished stones. I waded in the lake toward Matt's sandbar. A rainbow arced in the mist over his fishing rod; as I approached, he waded farther from me, receding with the rainbow. I desisted and returned to walking along the shore. As I rounded a sandy area I saw Reverend Steck standing on a stream bank about thirty yards away, his line in the water. Several fish heads already poked from his basket. Daniel sat cross-legged on the small boat dock nearby, a pole resting beside him.

Ben lay on top of his life preserver, a few feet away. Daniel's voice sounded quietly over the water: "And *then* the Giant said: 'Fe Fi Fo Fum. I smell the blood of Benjamin! Be he alive or be he dead, I'll grind his bones to make my bread.'" I left them alone where they were. I knew that I should circle back and try to talk to Matt, but I did not have the courage, so I headed off in search of the men from the halfway house.

I located them in a small marshy area. Dmytryk and Dr. Eatman had tangled their lines and were bickering so loudly that every fish for miles must have heard them. Stretch Rockefeller refused to fish; he sat on a high rock, with billows of cigarette smoke rising behind him, and watched Dmytryk and Dr. Eatman. Finally, Dmytryk threw up his hands and walked off, sulking and sipping from his Coca-Cola bottle. Then Rockefeller climbed from his rock, picked up the tangled poles, and held them both over the water, standing absolutely still except for the violent puffing of his cigarette.

Dr. Eatman took a drop line from the tackle box, stalked off to a stone ledge, let the line fall in the water, and struck a serious fishing pose. He exclaimed loudly every few minutes over insect life: "Eureka, a whirligig!" "Watch your toes, it's an eastern toe-biter!" "Hail to Doubleday's bluet and the slender damselfly."

At one point he motioned to me solemnly, holding his finger before his lips to command me into silence. When I neared him, Dr. Eatman pointed to something on the rock—a hideous gray insect shaped like a tank.

"Don't move!" he whispered. And there on the rock, I witnessed the most miraculous transformation I have ever seen in nature. A slit appeared in the back of what I saw was the carapace of some hard-shelled larva that had crawled from the water. Out of the shell emerged an albino body with a pinpoint of white on its back. The white speck expanded to a miniature triangle of lace, and after that, slowly, imperceptibly, it unfolded until it stretched impossibly wide into the gossamer wings of a colorless dragonfly. And then, tiny ghosts of color appeared on the animal's abdomen: a mint green that darkened into emerald, a sky blue that deepened to sapphire, sightless eyes that shadowed into the violet-black eyes of a horse. This entire metamorphosis took twenty minutes, and passed so gradually that the naked eye could not detect the changes from one moment to the next. In the end the dragonfly lay absolutely still in front of us, utterly complete and resplendent, and a second later it upended and whirred with incredible speed into the air and vanished.

"Hah!" Dr. Eatman exclaimed, rubbing his hands gloatingly, as if he had been responsible for the miracle. "Let that be our unutterable secret." Then he asked, pressing his face too close to mine, "Why does Mr. Munk persist in coming to the halfway house every five minutes to babble on and on to your brother?" I hadn't known that Daniel had been trying so hard. Before I could think of an answer, Dr. Eatman picked up the drop line, and shaking his head, wandered away.

I walked toward the lake and saw Mildred standing between Daniel and Ben on the dock. As I approached her, I realized that she and Daniel were arguing.

Mildred's voice rose over the water: "Damn it, Daniel! What's Ben doing down here on the dock with his life preserver off?" She was angry, close to tears. "It's the first time I've left him alone with you and—"

"Mildred honey, please calm down. You can see Ben's fine."

"I've told you, it's not safe to bring a child around boat docks without a life preserver. What did you do, take it off?" She held the orange vest up before Daniel.

"Nothing can happen to him as long as he's here with me."

"Who are you?" Mildred answered. "God?" She lifted Ben, who buried his face against her shoulder, and she carried him off the dock. I wished she had chosen another time to confront Daniel, instead of the very moment when Ben first seemed to be warming up to him. But I thought the strain of things was probably just telling on her.

Daniel stayed where he was on the dock. He picked up a pole, baited it with a multiworm tangle, and dropped the line into the lake.

When I approached, Daniel handed the pole to me and said, "I've never had the patience for fishing."

I held the pole compliantly and watched small yellow fish dart around the knot of worms at the end of the line. I wondered if Daniel knew I had overheard his argument with Mildred. I stared down into the water, looking for Musky Senior. I could see farthest in the water darkened by my shadow. I imagined that if I were a fish, I would be something stony and lurking, like a gar.

Daniel made no allusion to what had just happened. He pulled off his T-shirt and stretched out on the dock. He was lean and well built; the sight of him caused a somersaulting in my stomach.

As I held the line, Daniel told me that Brazilian farmers could not believe that in America, fishermen sometimes sat for hours on a lake or by a stream, hoping to catch only one or two fish and perfectly content to catch none at all. He said that in the Amazon's tributaries, all you had to do was to drop a baited string into the water, and fish fought with each other to hook themselves. He had once asked a farmer how big the biggest fish he had caught behind his field was and the farmer had said, "*Mais o menos o tamanho dum bezerro*"—about the size of a calf.

Daniel stopped talking. He sat up and said, "Melanie. There's something I have to tell you."

I didn't move or speak; I just wanted to hear him.

"It's about Matt."

"Matt?"

"I don't know how to say this, but I think Matt may have hurt Ben."

I drew myself inward. "Hurt Ben? What do you mean?"

"I was just talking to Ben here on the dock. It's the first real conversation we've had since I came back from Brazil. Ben told me that Matt threw him across his room and kicked him. I asked him if Matt had ever done anything like that to him before, anything scary, and Ben told me that Matt sometimes pulls his hair, and that Matt has punched him."

A sense of horror filled me: I could not, would not believe what Daniel was telling me about Matt. Even if I had seen with my own eyes what Daniel described, I could not have accepted the truth of it.

"But Ben's crazy about Matt! He doesn't act scared when he's around my brother. Ben climbs on Matt's lap, and jokes with him and practically flirts with him—"

Daniel grimaced. "I'm sorry, Melanie. I know this is hard for you to hear. I didn't mention anything to Mildred yet. I didn't want to with Ben standing there. But Melanie, I feel you should know. Ben told me that Matt's been saying some frightening things to him. You know how Ben's been avoiding me? At first I tried to convince myself it was normal; I knew Ben needed to get used to my being around again. But it's been weeks now, and he still acts terrified. So I asked Ben if Matt had said anything to him about me. He said Matt told him that I was going to sneak up to his bed at night and carry him into the woods and kill him."

I struggled to put words together. "Ben's not even three. Kids that age say anything. They don't really know the difference between what's real and what they imagine."

"I don't think a little kid could have made up the things Ben was saying." He searched my face, as if hoping for understanding. "Melanie, I want Matt to stay away from Ben until we can check this out. I might need your help."

"Help."

"I need you to watch Matt carefully, to keep an eye on him to make sure he isn't left alone with Ben. And if you can, see if Matt will talk to you, if you can learn anything from him."

"But Matt doesn't let me near him."

"You're his sister! If you can't help Matt, who's going to?"

"But you know I—"

"I'm not going to let Mildred handle this. I don't want her caught in the middle. I'm going to ask her to stay away from Matt, because it's impossible for her to go anywhere without Ben following."

I felt stunned and could not think of the words to answer Daniel. The sun shimmered overhead, and the water twinkled mockingly, and there seemed no bottom to sorrow in the world.

6

OTTILIE WAS FURIOUS. Reverend Steck came to the house on Sunday to speak with her about Matthew and Ben, and she refused to believe any of it.

"Who is this Daniel? Who is this Daniel?" she asked me when I returned home after visiting the halfway house. I had been looking for Matt, but had not found him.

"Is Daniel so jealous of an insane man's affection for his son that he would make up such a story about him? Matt wouldn't hurt a fly!"

Ottilie was so unlike herself, so angry, I was almost afraid to confront her.

"Ottilie, Matt sort of got violent with me at the halfway house two weeks ago," I said, although I remembered having denied his violence at the time.

"He didn't mean to hurt you!" Ottilie shouted, and her words came out of her strangely, hoarse, the cry of someone unaccustomed to raising her voice. "You frightened him! You went into his room and were looking through it like—"

"But he did shove me." I sat down on the living room couch. Ottilie remained standing before me, rigid, her hands clenched.

"What Daniel is talking about is different," Ottilie said. "It's deliberate. Deliberately hurting a child! Impossible."

I both knew Ottilie was right and did not know. I found myself formulating the arguments that Daniel had used against me. "But a child wouldn't make up such specific facts."

"We don't know that Ben did. We only know Daniel says he did. Matt loves Ben! Really loves him. And Ben loves Matt. Ben is not afraid of Matt!"

"That's what I said to Daniel when he first told me."

Now Ottilie's voice quieted and returned to her.

"I don't like Daniel," she said. She paused, studying my face. "I tried to like him, but I had a bad feeling about him from the first night he came here. It's because of Mildred—Mildred has not been the same since Daniel arrived." I hadn't noticed this. "She keeps to herself too much."

"But she's his wife. It's natural she'd want to keep so close with him when they've been apart so long."

Ottilie looked at me without replying. Then she sat down beside me and said, "I don't think the way Ben acts around Daniel is natural. Ben's telling the kind of stories that—that Matt used to say about Joel."

Was it possible, I wondered, that Matt was engineering Ben to repeat the experience of his own childhood? That by telling him stories Matt was teaching Ben to fear his father? The idea appalled me.

"No," Ottilie said quietly. "It's not what you're afraid of. Melanie, I know what I'm seeing. I saw it with Matt when he was little, but I didn't know what it meant until we came to live with Joel." She groaned. "Oh, Melanie!"

I was not sure what Ottilie wanted to say. I took her hand, and we sat there for a long time, without speaking.

Finally, Ottilie told me, "I'm going to talk to John again. He says if Matt is a danger to Ben, Matt may not be able to live at the halfway house anymore. Melanie, Matt's here. He's upstairs in your room. He's upset. Please try to talk to him. John told Matt that he can live in the halfway house for now, but that he has to stay away from Ben until we get this sorted out."

She took a silk scarf from the closet and tied it around her hair—one of Mimi's, a sea-green interwoven with blue—and left me alone in the house with my brother.

I CLIMBED the stairs to my room but I did not find Matt there. A note had been left on my bed. I unfolded it, and read:

A wind amid the ragged nets
        Mitylene
in a jagged wind
        cold
Oh cold mountain above the harbor
blue as the sea is blue
At dawn
            women gather up the flaxen
world
            singing in the gradual light.

When I read Matt's poem a stillness took my heart, threatening to let me into a lovely dark water. I did not know what the words intended, but I wanted to believe they contained a deep meaning I could not grasp, and I held the paper as if it could give me the answers to all my questions.

And then I saw Matt. He was sitting on the floor, leaning against the bedstead. He had shaved, and I almost did not recognize him. His face looked pale and vulnerable, worn by experience. It was so different from the face of his youth—it was longer, and lines curved around the corners of his mouth, and he had my father's jaw line. Matt's eyes were almost black, intelligent, full of pain. His agony was so multifaceted, I could not consider, in that one moment, all it encompassed: his cruel severing from Ben, his separation from his only woman friend, who was also his closest friend, the threatened loss of his home and freedom, his life without love or companionship, the fright of his own mind.

I sat down on Aunt Mimi's peacock-blue armchair, facing him. He didn't roar and command me to leave. He watched me, still and obedient. And this made me saddest of all, that Matt's fear had forced him to turn back to me, that it had robbed him even of the small luxury of choosing whom he would spurn.

"I love this," I said, lifting up Matt's poem.

He stared at the floor, his long hands clamped between his knees. I noticed how beautiful his hands still were, how long and shapely and expressive.

He jumped up, suddenly agitated, and lurched toward the door. "Melanie," he said. It was the first time he had spoken my name since I'd arrived in Muskellunge. He lingered for a moment, shifting his weight from one foot to the other, anxiety possessing his features. His voice rose and broke on the last note like a boy's. "Mildred's husband is the devil!" Matt clamped his hands in his armpits, looked at me imploringly, and ran from the room. His steps clattered down the stairs, the front door slammed, and I heard Matt's hoarse cry as he fled across the front yard, and silence dropped on the house.

OTTILIE RETURNED several hours later, her eyes red from crying. Reverend Steck had taken her into his grandson's room, pulled down Ben's pajamas, and shown Ottilie marks on him: the imprints of a man's hands—purple crescent moons of fingernails, bruises circling each thigh in wide bands. "Mildred discovered them last night when she bathed Ben. That's when Daniel told her what Ben had said about Matt. Oh, Melanie, it was awful! Ben cried when we touched his legs."

"But Ben wasn't alone with Matt yesterday," I said, and suddenly I had changed roles with Ottilie as we faced each other in my room, testing our doubts and fears.

"Yes, yes he was, for a short while before the van arrived"—Ottilie's voice rose into a question and quavered—"Matt took Ben behind a rock to show him the tadpoles in the pool there?"

"What does Ben say?"

"He won't answer us. We asked him how he got the bruises, and he said he didn't know. He's not even three years old! Do you know how hard it is to get a child that age to talk when he doesn't want to?"

She stopped, looking confused. She held her hands to the sides of her face as if trying to steady her thoughts. Then she said, "John is going to Chicago this weekend, to check out some halfway houses there. He's promised me he won't just send Matt off to a hospital, but he doesn't think he should stay here without supervision, because a condition of Matt's release after his arrest in Chicago was that he has to live under supervision in a halfway house or hospital. Mildred and Daniel will be leaving next week, to take a trip with Ben in Door County, in order to get him away from here and sort things out. Oh, Melanie, I can't believe this is happening. Things were going so well for Matt here. He had friends, he had a home, it seemed too good to believe."

TWO DAYS LATER Reverend Steck returned from Chicago and came to the house at breakfast time, asking for Ottilie. From my room I heard him say, "I spoke to an old colleague at the World Council of Churches who administers some soup kitchens." He and Ottilie entered the den. "He has to inquire whether they can accept more inmates." As I listened to Ottilie's quiet murmur and Reverend Steck's low voice rise, my heart pounded, and panic rose in me. I did not want to know what was being planned for Matt, how the decisions of sane adults like ourselves would determine his fate. I fled out the kitchen door.

Across the road Daniel was walking with Ben in the Park and Pray's garden. I thought it cruel of Daniel to bring Ben so near the windows of the church and halfway house, where Matt might see him. Ben and Daniel held hands and crossed together into the neighboring field. Then Daniel let go of Ben, and headed toward a giant green tractor left on the edge of the field. He climbed into the tractor seat, and waved at Ben, beckoning him to join him. Ben came nearer, and Daniel climbed down. He lifted Ben into the seat, seven feet in the air. Ben called out a few words, snatched away by the wind so that I could not hear them; I thought of him perched on Matt's and Reverend Steck's shoulders, crying, "I'm high in the sky!" Something about the scene bothered me, but I was too distracted by my thoughts to dwell on it, too unsettled by recent events to watch Daniel and Ben more carefully. Daniel had not spoken to me since the fishing trip, and I had avoided both him and Mildred while Reverend Steck was away. Ben looked lucky, seated up there, way over the precarious world.

AFTER THAT Daniel, Mildred, and Ben left to go camping and traveling in Door County for ten days. I imagined them there, sleeping in Wisconsin's eerily beautiful northern woodlands, with otters slithering in the reedy currents around them, the spooky cries of loons flitting toward them across dark water. While Mildred and Ben were gone, Matthew stayed in his bed at the halfway house all day, facing the wall of his room, and came out only for meals. His beard would grow back for a few days, and then he would remember to cut it. When I joined him for lunch or dinner, he did not chase me away. He sat across from me in his chair, his elbows on the table, his face a mask of despair, sunken in silence. Even the effort of eating seemed too much for him.

Sometimes, in the middle of a bite, he would simply stop chewing and stare at nothing.

After Mildred and Daniel returned from their trip, I saw them, from a distance, several times over the next two weeks, as they walked together on Main Street, or behind the garden, looking like a happy family. Except that once, when I turned a corner so quickly I almost ran into them, Mildred gazed up at me, startled, and her face looked sad and careworn. Even from the side, she seemed less than radiant, her profile that of a saint who has lost faith. I was glad to know that she did not take Matt's excommunication from her world so lightly.

Daniel seemed animated and joyous with Ben. I would see him out in the garden, throwing his son into the air, or letting Ben cling to his back while Daniel crawled and pounced on all fours like a bear. When I watched them, I felt distanced from Daniel. His accusations against Matthew stood between us, and I no longer saw Daniel without the distortion of some undefined resentment that made his very gestures around his son bother me: His actions seemed exaggerated and ostentatious, as if he felt he were being watched, and was trying to convince every onlooker that he was a dedicated father. But I was honest enough with myself to acknowledge that my annoyance was rooted in the sadness I felt comparing Daniel's happiness with Matthew's loss.

Reverend Steck visited Ottilie's frequently after Ben returned to Muskellunge with his parents. In late August Mildred's father made two more trips to Chicago, and each time he came to the house afterward to speak with her. On the second occasion, he knocked at the door early in the morning, when Ottilie was asleep, and looked more worried than after the other times. When I answered the door, he said, "I need to talk to Ottilie as soon as possible," and although he must have known that she slept late because of her work schedule, he seated himself in the living room to wait for her, tugging at his minister's collar. When she came out, dressed in her nightgown and bathrobe, he said, "I returned from Chicago last night. But I'm here about something else—" After I walked upstairs, I heard John tell Ottilie, "One of my former parishioners, Mrs. Shove, came to the Park and Pray this morning with a bad story. It seems that people here in Muskellunge have noticed—" They entered the den, and before he closed the door, I heard John say, "The last thing Mildred needs is to deal with this town's gossip. I don't know if it's true, or even how to tell Mildred."

THE LAST DAY of August, I ran into Daniel and Ben at the Kmart. I was turning into the aisle for household supplies when I saw Ben. He was standing in front of a mirror on sale, making faces. I heard him say, "I'm a monster!" and then he stuck out his bottom teeth and lifted his hands like claws.

"Ben! Son of my right hand!" I drew away from Daniel's voice, into the next aisle. I did not want to have to talk to him.

After I finished in the cashier's aisle, I again saw them. Ben was goose-stepping across the parking lot. Daniel grabbed his hand, and Ben sat down on the pavement. Daniel, whose left arm encircled a large bag, tried to lift Ben with his right, but Ben resisted, bending forward and tucking his hands under his chin.

"All right, Ben!" Daniel shouted irritably. "You're really trying my patience, but don't think I'm going to lose my patience! You can stay here, and I'll come back for you tomorrow." Daniel spun around and walked to Mildred's car. Ben lifted his head to watch from where he sat in the parking lot.

Daniel opened the Cadillac's door, slid into the driver's seat, then shut the door behind him. He turned on the ignition and the wheels rolled slowly backward. Ben sprang up and ran frantically toward the car.

I chased after Ben, repeating his name until he turned around. Then I gathered him up from behind, concerned that he would not have the sense to avoid the wheels of the moving vehicle. Ben collapsed against me sobbing.

When Daniel saw me, he cut off the ignition and opened the car door. Then he rested his head on the steering wheel.

"Boy, that was really stupid," he said.

I didn't say anything.

"I can't believe I just did that. Ben's been crying and screaming all afternoon. He made me carry him all over the Kmart, and every time I set him down, he threw himself on the floor and started hollering." He sighed. "That was a really, really stupid thing I did, really stupid."

"Yeah," I said. Ben clung tightly to me.

Daniel sighed again. "I just got fed up. But that's no excuse. It's inexcusable. You have every right to judge me. I've been trying to get

Mildred to leave me alone more with Ben. I guess I'm just not that great with little kids."

The words TONKA FIRE ENGINE blazed in bright red on an over-sized toy truck poking from the package on the seat next to Daniel. I felt sanctimonious and judgmental, and softened when I saw his face. He looked overcome with remorse and embarrassment.

"A parking lot is kind of dangerous for a two-year-old," I said. My words sounded hollow, so obviously and ridiculously true that I couldn't think of anything more to say.

"Yeah, it is. Melanie, you know I would never do anything to endanger my own son. Things aren't—," Daniel began, but his voice thinned and he stopped; he looked worried and confused. "Things aren't going that great between me and Mildred. I guess it's just the strain of our separation, after she came back here so early from Brazil, and then we're living at her dad's, and there's everything with Ben and Matt." Daniel looked miserable.

I felt myself relent.

"Christ, when we were in Brazil, Mildred worshipped me," Daniel said next, and then retreated into his thoughts. After a few moments, he added, "Melanie, Mildred's jealous. I never thought of her as being that type. She even thinks there's an attraction between you and me."

I must have frowned.

Daniel reached for Ben, but Ben gripped me harder, as if he wanted to burrow into me.

"You know what I would like?" Daniel said. "Just a little time to myself. Could you deliver Ben home? Mildred works with this abortion rights group in Sheboygan on Wednesday nights, but her dad's at the house."

"Sure," I said. "Sure. Things will work out. Don't take it all so hard and fast." I felt sorry for Daniel and Mildred.

Ben kept a stranglehold on me as I carried him toward the bus. I was surprised at the density of him. He could not have weighed much more than thirty pounds, but by the time the bus arrived, my arms ached with the strain of holding him. He fell asleep moments after I sat down in the bus. His warm breath rustled against my ear, his hair had that cinnamon smell. I had never longed for children, but as I sat there, I felt that I was clinging to Ben as tightly as he was to me, and I understood how much more precious he was than anything else my arms had held in a long time. A sense shifted somewhere in me, not yet a thought, and I felt tired.

When the bus let me off in Muskellunge, I carried Ben to the Stecks'. Ottilie was there when I arrived, carrying Ben in my arms. She and Reverend Steck were sitting on the couch, their voices low. Ottilie held the reverend's hand in hers, and they both sounded worried. I was afraid to hear what they had been discussing—I knew it was the fact that Matt would be sent back to a hospital. Ottilie and Reverend Steck looked up at me. Strain showed plainly in both their faces.

"Ben!" Reverend Steck cried, as if he had not seen his grandson in years. He pulled Ben from my arms.

"He fell asleep," I said. "I ran into Daniel at the Kmart, and he asked me to take Ben home."

"Melanie, we need to speak with you," Reverend Steck said. But Ben stirred and cried mournfully into his grandfather's shoulder, "I want apple juice!" Then Ben began sobbing hysterically and kicked and bent backward so that his grandfather almost dropped him.

"Later?" I answered. I slipped away while Reverend Steck and Ottilie occupied themselves with Ben.

I headed to the halfway house, looking for Matt. I bumped into Stretch Rockefeller in the hallway, and he scuttled by me. Almost as an afterthought, he said, "The sky is falling!" and hurried on. I walked by Dmytryk's door; he lay on his bed, passed out. Matt's room was empty.

Dr. Eatman poked his head from his doorway, looking irascible. "Your brother is *not* here," he said. He drew his head back in the room, and slammed his door. Behind the closed door, I heard him arguing with himself. I wondered how much Matt's predicament had upset the balance of life at the halfway house.

Afterward I looked for Matt in the church, but it was dark and empty. I strayed down Walleye Street. The shops were all closed, and a delicious gloominess wrapped me as I walked past them, staring in. I saw Mr. Shove in his electric orange overalls, unpacking vegetable crates in the back of his store. He frowned at the cabbage heads he was arranging in the vegetable section; he lifted his face and frowned at me, and I turned away. I saw a thin man with his nose pressed against the window of the bridal apparel store. As I neared him, I thought I recognized him as Reverend Hatch. When he heard my footstep, he hurried on. I caught my reflection in the bridal apparel store's window: I looked ghoulish, too tall for a woman, with sunken shadowy pools below my cheekbones, and overlarge hands, like claws. My image was draped in the gaudy ghost dress of a Muskellunge bride glimmering on a hanger. A store clerk startled me, a pale girl with a ponytail. She ducked from behind the gown and peered at me like a double. I walked on.

I strolled around town twice and drank three Pferds at Tikalsky's, a local bar with a forest of deer and elk antlers on every wall. Pferd bottles lined two shelves along two facing mirrors. The reflections of the labels' red horse heads formed a cavalry whose forces seemed legion, infinite.

I read my placemat menu, which promised "knockwurst 'n' kraut," potato soup, or a cheese plate, and which was bordered by the duplicated business cards of local enterprises, as well as a rectangle representing Reverend Hatch's church, which said only, "Are you a pregnant teen with nowhere to turn? Call our Pregnancy Information Center." I bought a fourth Pferd, opened it, and took it outside in a brown bag. I carried the beer bottle with me to the local theater, tucked it under my shirt, and drank it slowly while watching the movie. It was *All the President's Men*, and I fell asleep in the middle. I awoke over an hour later, at the beginning of the next run. The effect of awakening in that dark theater to scenes I believed I had just viewed was disorienting. I left before the movie was over, as Deep Throat was telling the journalist Woodward that his life would be in peril if he pursued the Watergate conspiracy's trail further. As I walked out into the night air, I felt edgy and off-kilter. I was uncertain what time it was, and whether I should go home to sleep, or keep myself awake.

The clock on the Walleye Baptist Church said 11:30, and its bells played a half-melody. The eye of half-moon above it seemed skewed; it listed westward toward the gaudier flashing eyes of Musky's neon fish. At the end of the street, a light was on in the Park and Pray, and I oriented myself toward it, hoping Matt might be there.

As I threaded along the Park and Pray's walkway, I saw that the front door was propped open. At night the church's high-domed ceiling receded into shadow, and the Park and Pray looked drab and uninteresting. It had an institutional appearance, with its linoleum floors and pale walls. Matt was mopping the floor around the organ in the front of the church, his back to me. Protruding from the first pew were a pair of pointed leather boots attached to the legs of a reclining figure.

Daniel said, "The place looks real nice, Matt. Real clean." I stepped back, thinking I had intruded on something important. I hoped without reason that Daniel might be trying to make some sort of reconciliation with Matt, to resolve the dilemma that ensnared us all. I felt grateful to Daniel for trying.

"Cleanliness is next to godliness," Daniel said next. At first his tone seemed wry and joking. Then he added, "But you're still just a janitor." Matt went on mopping as if he hadn't heard anything. "I said, 'a janitor.' A goddamned janitor."

Matt stopped for just a moment. He stood his full height, leaned on the mop. Then he returned to his work. I stepped back from the doorway.

Daniel continued: "You think Reverend Steck values you, don't you? That he loves you like a son? It never occurred to you that he just likes free labor like any old penny pincher out to save a dime? You're nothing more than cheap labor to him. An ornamental testimony to his religious beneficence toward the maimed."

Matt paused again, his back to us both. I could read in my brother's stillness, his tense grip on the mop, depthless anger.

"Stay away from me!" Matt said in a tight voice. Then, louder, he added, "Stay away from everyone! You aren't here!"

"Cheap labor. No, that's wrong. You're the hunchback, the church hunchback."

Matt turned, the mop pole in his hand, and swung once, wildly, in Daniel's direction.

Daniel screamed, and when he sat up, I saw him rubbing his shoulder. The mop clattered to the floor, and Matt ran past the church organ through the back exit.

"YOU GODDAMNED PSYCHO! YOU PSYCHOPATH!" Daniel screamed. "The police are going to know about this!"

I froze.

I saw Daniel stand casually and stretch. I saw him strike a match and cup his hands around his cigarette. The flame lit up his face: his gold-rimmed spectacles sparkled, and a smile stretched under them. He leaned against the side of a pew. I stepped onto the front path that led to the church.

Daniel's footsteps sounded in the aisle. As he turned into the church entryway and stepped into the night, he almost walked into me: our faces were within an inch of each other.

"Melanie!" he said. He turned around and stared down the church aisle, and then up at the domed ceiling. "It's such a pretty church. It's a nice place to sit and think." The wretched look I'd seen in the Kmart parking lot passed over Daniel's face again, but now his words sounded hollow. "Thinking is something I really need to do right now."

He seemed to search my face for something. But I don't have an expressive face.

"Or maybe what I really need is someone to talk to. Would you mind just talking with me?"

I thought of the hundred things I could say at that moment, but I did not tell him any of them. Even if I had been inclined to speak, I wasn't sure yet of what I believed. What I felt then was a suspension of belief. I could not assemble what I knew about Daniel into the image of any person I could recognize.

We passed down the road together into the darkness. Once, as we walked under the street lamp, I looked into Daniel's face; he struck me as handsome even then, despite what I was beginning to know. I allowed myself to feel drawn to him; I imagined that if I had not just witnessed what I had, my blood would have quickened, I would have longed to know what it felt like to melt into his fiery embrace. And then I looked away.

"Let's go out to the garden and search for shooting stars again," Daniel said. "That was nice."

I accompanied him toward the garden, although I felt I was being led into danger—that he was now doing literally what he had done when he enticed me into joining in his vision of Matt. I wanted to hear what Daniel would say next, how he would orchestrate his words and actions.

"This is a good place," Daniel said. He stretched out on the ground, gazing into the starry heavens. He drew on his cigarette, and its ash blossomed and shrank. Beyond him the land lay in blue shadow under the half-moon. The garden seemed to balance on Daniel's bent knee, tilted, ready to slip into a denser darkness.

I lay down near him, but not right beside him. It was a little past the season for falling stars. Still, after ten minutes, two or three meteorites shot through the air. The last was brilliant and long-tailed and astonishing, and vanished in an instant.

"A lot of shooting stars always fall when I'm here," Daniel said.

As I stared at the night sky, I wondered what exactly Daniel intended by his words—whether he meant that he was always lucky to catch the moments when the shooting stars fell, or whether, with some outlandish egomania, he believed that he caused them to fall.

"Melanie," he said, "I wanted to tell you how sorry I am about this business with Matt and Ben. It's awful to think how your brother must feel, how you must feel—" He stopped, as if the violence of his sympathy kept him from speaking further. He sounded so sincere that, listening to him, I could have believed he believed himself.

And I had a passing understanding then of what Daniel's words meant to him: he thought that simply by saying something, he made it so. He was as elusive to himself as the truth must have been: as alive in each moment as a cresting wave, with no thought of the future and no recollection of the past. I thought of how, around Reverend Steck, Daniel acted like a like-minded son, and how he reflected back Mildred's shining love, and how with Ottilie he was soft-spoken and reserved. I thought of how he seduced me with stories, spoke the words I would have if I had known my own desires better.

My intuition told me to handle Daniel cautiously, although I underestimated his skill and intelligence, and did not fully comprehend that revealing what I knew would only give him the chance to change shape, to present himself differently to others sooner than he might have, before I could anticipate and prevent his actions. I would later regret that I turned to Daniel as we lay there, and addressed him directly, that someone like me, who so seldom spoke, would choose that time to speak.

"Daniel," I told him. "I'm onto you. Stay the fuck away from Matt."

He did not move when I stood. He lay quietly without answering, listening to the rustle of the grasses.

I WALKED to the halfway house and climbed the stairs to Matt's room. His desk light was on, a chess book open beneath it. In the dimmer light on the far side of the room, Matt lay in bed facing the wall, the covers pulled over his head so that a single tuft of hair protruded.

"Matt," I said. "I saw what happened in the church tonight. You were right about Daniel. I don't really know what he wants, but I think he may be dangerous."

A sob wrenched from Matt. He sat up, gave me an agonized look, buried his head in his hands, and lay back down.

Matt cried and cried.

I listened to him, overwhelmed with regret for the smallness of my heart, for my willful blindness, for having lacked the generosity of spirit to make the leap between what my brother had once been to me and the person he had become.

"I'm sorry, Matt. I'm so sorry. I was afraid Daniel was telling the truth, and I just ran from it." And then it took me: love. It welled upward and soaked me like a dark scented tea, pervasive, unendurable, held back so long that I had to struggle for its name.

"Stay here," Matt said. "I'm scared. I'm scared. Just stay with me until I fall asleep." I sat on the floor in the corner. Matt lifted his head to make sure I was still there. Then he turned back to the wall, and in twenty minutes, his breath flowed quietly and evenly. But I knew I would not sleep that night. The news that had come to my brother as a release jangled in my veins like an electrifying blood.

I watched the single street lamp outside Matt's windows, moths blazing in the light's circle, hard-shelled beetles diving harshly against its bright glass. And waiting there with my brother, I knew with certainty that he had never injured Ben and never would, and that, for some reason beyond my grasp, Daniel had hurt Ben. I wondered what kind of person would find pleasure in tormenting an insane man, and I could not fathom Daniel's motives. It is said that those who look on the face of God are never the same, but surely this also must be true for those who see the devil, his disguises shed and his veils withdrawn, in all his starkness. I felt a tug in my mind, a moment of semi-recognition, and I sensed that once I understood Daniel, I would not be the same. And then I remembered that Ben and Matt already knew him, situated as they were in the eye of the hurricane of Daniel's lie. I recalled Mildred's face the day we had run into each other on the corner, and I questioned whether I had misread the sadness in her demeanor, whether she had already begun to divine what I had not. I thought of Ottilie and Reverend Steck, their heads lowered over their murmuring voices, and I wondered how much they knew, and whether I had been the last to figure out what everyone else already saw clearly. Finally, I pictured Ben poised on the lofty seat of the tractor, and in the parking lot, and at the lake, and in the garden, and on the very day Daniel had arrived. I realized that in each instance, Ben had not simply looked frightened; he had been terrified.

BOOK THREE

Custody

1

THE LAW is a miraculous water that flows upward, that seeks the high places, the craggy pools where power collects, the source of the spring. Energetic, shamelessly swift, or suddenly slow, stagnant, and deadening, it destroys with indifference, like an act of nature, or an act of God: a blizzard or flood. It is wonderful to say: *Law.* The word swirls in your throat and holds your mouth still. Say *law, law, law,* and you will feel like a bird of monotonous song, or the heartbeat of an insistent alarm, or a relentless sawing away.

On the night Daniel first showed himself to me, I sat in my brother's room until the last cricket shrilled like a police whistle. I thought of the imminent exposure of Daniel's violence toward his son, and weighed Daniel's threats to have Matt arrested, and I sensed that whatever happened, Daniel would ensnare us all in legal proceedings. But even then I did not know how easily Daniel would use the law to add depth and complexity to our nightmares, to shape our actions and thoughts to meet his.

When I left Matt sleeping, the horizon was already pinkening over Ottilie's house, and dew clung to my pants. The Pferd horses whinnied at the end of the road. Two headlights gleamed through the morning fog in front of me, and I stopped abruptly, almost running into a vehicle. But it was only the town's police chief, Komar, idling his engine. He leaned out the window, his face shrewd and belligerent, and said, "We're handing out summonses to people who don't smile." I passed him before the meaning of his words sank in. I felt compelled to find Ottilie and talk to her immediately, and I hurried on.

All the downstairs windows in Ottilie's house were on. It looked ablaze. Reverend Steck's van was parked in the driveway. I thought of circling the house and entering through the back door, but I did not want to deliver my message with Mildred's father there: Ottilie's relief would be met with an equal share of his horror. I climbed the steps and peered through the front window into the living room. Reverend Steck sat next to Ottilie on the couch. The fireplace lit their faces, and their heads bowed intimately together over the coffee table. I entered without knocking.

"Melanie!" Ottilie said, rising from the couch. "Sit down with us." Reverend Steck's face rested on his hands, his elbows on his knees.

"There's something I have to tell you," I said.

"No! Just sit down, Melanie!" Ottilie said. She sounded exasperated.

"It's about Daniel."

Reverend Steck raised his head and asked, "What do you know about my son-in-law?"

"We've received some news, Melanie," Ottilie said. "Some news affecting Matt."

My heart sank: I had been mistaken in my hope that Ottilie and Reverend Steck already suspected Daniel.

"Matt's not the one who's been hurting Ben," I said. "It's Daniel."

Ottilie and Reverend Steck looked at each other.

"What makes you think so?" Reverend Steck asked.

I groped for the words to explain what I knew, but they ran from me, turned on me, snarling. I realized that my knowledge was a jumble of painful intuitions and distasteful perceptions. "I saw Daniel in the church with Matt. He was torturing Matt. Mocking him and belittling him. Daniel goaded him until Matt lost his temper and struck out. And then Daniel threatened to go to the police. Daniel didn't know I was there. When he saw me, he acted as if nothing had happened. He even told me he was worried about Matt." I stopped, wondering if I was making sense. "Daniel left Ben sitting in the middle of a parking lot at Kmart today, while he got in a car and turned on the ignition. He did it on purpose. He placed Ben in danger on purpose. He wanted to frighten him. He left Ben sitting on the asphalt in the driving lane of a parking lot." I halted again. "What Daniel was doing to Matt—it was weird. Sadistic. Daniel is not what he seems. He's hiding something. Everything. There's something not right about him." I looked around helplessly. "I can't explain it. But I know I'm not wrong. Daniel is dangerous. Mean."

"Capable of intentionally hurting his own son?" Reverend Steck asked. His words were measured, cautious.

"Where's Ben?" I answered suddenly. Perhaps the fear in my voice finally moved her, because Ottilie stepped forward, took my arm, and steered me to the armchair.

"Ben and Mildred are upstairs," Ottilie said. "They're asleep."

"Upstairs with Daniel?"

"Daniel took Mildred's car a few hours ago, and left a message on my door saying that he's gone to Chicago for the week," Reverend Steck said. "So we're not worried about him coming home right away. Mildred and Ben are sleeping here, just as an extra precaution."

At first Reverend Steck's words made no sense to me. But then I asked, "You know?"

Ottilie nodded. Her pale hands tugged at the brown fabric of her dress.

"How long have you known? Does Mildred know?"

Reverend Steck answered, "A former parishioner of mine, Maureen Shove, came to me last week with a story. Maureen said she had seen Daniel acting—strangely—with Ben." Reverend Steck's silver eyes slipped into shadow. He gripped his knees with his hands. "Now Mildred has told me that Daniel's conduct with Ben has been—inappropriate. She believes he's been hurting Ben."

"Daniel's been violent with Mildred," Ottilie said. "And—"

Reverend Steck asked imploringly, "Why didn't she say anything sooner? To think she would have walked around holding this in. Why did she wait so long?"

"She didn't wait that long," Ottilie said.

Reverend Steck buried his face in his hands, and a sob, ragged and astonished, tore from him. Ottilie placed her arm around his shoulders. I watched from the armchair, feeling uncomfortable and not knowing whether I should speak.

Ottilie said, "Melanie, why don't you get some sleep?"

"I doubt I'll be able to," I said. But I started for the stairs. Halfway up I stopped and asked, "What did Mrs. Shove tell you?"

Reverend Steck raised his hand halfway to his mouth, muffling his words. "She said that she saw Daniel carry Ben across part of a field by his hair."

"Christ!"

Ottilie told me, "Please speak with Mildred when she wakes up in the morning."

My legs felt wobbly. "Talk to Matt. Everyone should talk to Matt. He feels scared." I climbed to the top of the stairs and peeked into the room where Ben and Mildred were staying. Ben lay asleep on a blue chenille bedspread, his arms and legs thrown wide in abandon. The bedside lamp was on, and Mildred was awake. She sat beside Ben, studying his face. I had not meant to bother her. I intended only to look in and pass by, but as I stole away, Mildred called to me, and then followed me into my room.

Mildred sat on my bed. She looked exhausted. She had not dressed in a nightgown; she wore jeans, and a man's short-sleeved shirt—Daniel's. "Melanie, did my dad and Ottilie tell you?" she asked. Mildred looked away when I nodded yes, and then she asked, "Have you ever wondered what happens to the people you dream up? The ones you picture when someone tells you about relatives or friends you've never met? You imagine their faces and hands and how they talk, and then you meet them, and they don't look or act like the picture in your mind. What happens to the person in your head? Does he just get thrown away, or go off to some limbo for people you've thought up? What do I do with the Daniel Munk I was in love with?"

What happens to the Matthew I had imagined? I wondered then. Matthew, the threat to children. The hunchback. I felt lucky that this vision that sprang from my fears could now be relegated to the same oblivion where forgotten nightmares were banished.

"Say something, Melanie!" Mildred commanded me. "Don't just sit there! Talk to me!"

I told her what I knew: I described, for a second time, what I had witnessed in the parking lot, and later in the church between Matt and Daniel, and what Daniel had said afterward. As my words stumbled out, Mildred's eyes spilled over until tears soaked her collar.

"How could I have made such a mistake, Melanie?" Mildred asked. "How did I get so stupid and weak and blind? What kind of man is he, Melanie? What kind of man is my husband?"

Even now when I close my eyes I can recall the expression of grief and bewilderment on Mildred's face. Its memory holds a certain poignancy for me, because later that look would vanish and be replaced by something else—a certainty of vision honed by anger. At that moment Mildred seemed, simply, a young woman betrayed by love.

I answered her question, "He's a violent man. Someone you can't trust." Just speaking these words made Daniel's presence palpable to me. I shuddered inwardly when I thought of being bound by marriage and a child to a man like him.

"What happened to the Daniel Munk I was in love with all that time?"

"Maybe he evaporated like a demon, and went back to hell where he belongs," I said.

This statement seemed to cheer Mildred. She wiped her eyes on her sleeve and smiled. "I hope not," she said. "Because I still hope to be able to kill him in cold blood."

But then the look of bewilderment returned, and she asked, "How could I have been so fooled for so long? There must have been signs along the way, but I just didn't see them. It leaves me with such a lack of faith in my own perceptions. He fooled me! How could I have not seen? Maybe it's because he went away so much in Brazil—he had another life where he could act bad, and that's how he managed to act good around me. But he fooled me!" Her eyes filled again, and tears dropped onto my bedspread.

Mildred continued, in a voice full of grief and passionate indignation, "I let him hurt Ben! He hurt Ben, and I didn't see it. Even after he got violent with me, I didn't put two and two together about him and Ben until yesterday! But now I see it! I think of all the creepy things Daniel has done with Ben—like taking off his life preserver on the dock when we went fishing; did you see that? Once Daniel lost Ben in a crowd at a street festival when Ben was eighteen months old. And there's more. I see it now; I see that Daniel likes to frighten Ben. And I see that my son is scared of his father. He's frightened to death. What has Daniel done to him? What has he done to make Ben run away from him every time he walks toward him? And I didn't see it. Those black marks on his legs! What the hell was I looking at all this time? Do I just not see things the way other people do? Is there something wrong with me? Is it because my own mother was crazy, so I don't know when things are off?"

Her question hung in the air. I have never been good at commiserating. I want to lean forward, touch the person who is speaking, assure her that she is not alone in her feelings, and that the bitterness of the hour will go away. But such moments leave me paralyzed and timid. I tried to think of the right words to comfort Mildred, to speak directly to her as I had finally done with Matt, to allay her doubts and fears. But instead I said, "You need to think about hiring a lawyer to keep Daniel away. If he's run off, you need to find out how you might legally separate from him without being able to serve him personally with papers. And maybe you can press charges against him, or get an ex parte temporary order to keep him away from Ben, in case Daniel comes back—"

"A lawyer!" Mildred said. "Why waste money on a lawyer? A hit man is cheaper!" She snorted, looked at me, and laughed.

"Mildred," I said.

"He tricked me out of protecting my own child!" she answered.

"Mildred. It's not your fault that you didn't know. You found out fast, probably, compared to most women in your place. I didn't see through him until last night. Last night! It took us both the same amount of time—"

"But I lived with him," Mildred said. "I should have been onto him sooner."

"You can't afford to blame yourself—it just makes Daniel stronger if you do." Mildred frowned. I tried again. "There are plenty of decent women who stay with violent men for years, for decades even, because they're afraid of getting hurt if they speak up or run away—or they're afraid of losing their children, or of not being able to support them if they leave."

Ottilie startled me. Her pale hair glimmered in the dim light of the hall; her tea-colored dress lost itself in shadow. I wondered if she had stood there long, hesitant to enter until I had spoken the right words.

She came in, and sat down next to Mildred. "Melanie's right. Don't blame yourself," Ottilie told her. "You were in love with Daniel. He was your husband, the father of your child. Even after you begin to realize—to realize that your husband has acted wrongly, it's hard to pull yourself away from him if you've loved him. Your love can drag you back like undertow."

Ottilie looked past me out the window. There was nothing there, just the low fog dissipating over the lake. I wondered if Ottilie was speaking for herself. Was this why she had married my father when Matthew was seven? Something leapt in me—a small fish arcing over water, a trace of feeling, and then I lost it before I knew what it was.

"I even felt sorry for him!" Mildred said.

I found that I was crying. I patted Mildred's hand clumsily. Ottilie pulled Mildred's hair from her face and rested a hand on her arm. Mildred held it there, her eyes closed, and then wept loudly with hoarse, ungainly sobs.

"You've been married such a short time," Ottilie continued. "And love blinds people."

"Fuck love! Fuck love!" Mildred exclaimed. Then she sat up and wiped her eyes again on her sleeve. "I'll be fine. Just as soon as I can murder Daniel."

NONE OF US could sleep. We slipped downstairs for tea and coffee, moving quietly, ghostlike, past the couch where Reverend Steck lay. Ottilie covered him with an afghan and joined us in the kitchen. Outside, a bush shattered into sparrows. To me, their song seemed frenzied, deafening. I found it unbearable that we three women had been brought together by something I had no wish to speak of, by recollections of violence and fear. I wanted to be somewhere, anywhere else: I leaned against the wall and closed my eyes, and imagined that I was not there, and not myself. I was a small furred animal, tucked in a winter hole, breathing the dark smell of roots in earth, warm and mindless.

"Melanie, what are you thinking about?" Mildred said.

"Nothing," I answered, sitting down.

Ottilie set a kettle on the stove, and turned on its burner. The blue dress of the burner's flame blew upward and settled. She busied herself, throwing biscuits together from an instant mix. With her back to Mildred, Ottilie said: "I should have spoken earlier. I'm sorry. I suspected something a while before now, but I couldn't figure out how to say it to you."

"Naw," Mildred answered. "It wasn't your business until you knew for sure."

Ottilie joined us at the table. "I should have asked. I used to think I could tell just by looking in a wife's eyes whether she lived in fear of her husband. I used to divide the world between people who knew— people who know what it's like to feel terrified, and people who don't."

And then a memory crested, engulfed me, and receded: my father standing over me and my mother, his face inches from mine, his hand grabbing my wrist so hard that he left a bracelet of bruises afterward, my mother shrieking, "Let go of her! Let go! She's only five! You'll break her arm!" And then that picture of myself vanished, like water soaking into sand.

"Melanie," Ottilie said, "I wondered if the cancer affected you that way, if it left you—terrified. Because you aren't the same, Melanie. You're quieter than you used to be—sometimes it's like you're not even there."

"I'm still here," I said, trying a joke, but no one laughed. And in that moment I saw myself as a ghost haunting my own life. I had survived in spirit but not in flesh, as an insensate being who saw and recorded daily events. "I don't know," I said. "I have no idea if I'm scared. I don't know how I feel about it."

"It changes you, knowing terror changes you," Ottilie said. "It's not just—it's not just the way it snatches—snatches away love—it's the way terror clings to you. That dread that's always sitting there in the back of your throat." Ottilie had never talked this way around me before. I wondered how long she had harbored such a view of life. Since Matt's childhood? And then I felt it—a flurry of dread and anxiety that settled on my shoulders. I shook it off.

"It's a bad way to change," Ottilie said. "It's hard to look at things the same afterward. I admire your father, Mildred, because he's not afraid, because I want to remember what it's like not to—"

"I'm not scared yet," Mildred said. But then she contradicted herself, and an edge crept into her voice. "I'm scared for Ben, scared as hell."

I asked, "Have there been any other incidents with Ben?"

"Oh yeah, there sure have—" Mildred started to answer, and then stopped herself, wiped her eyes, and restarted. "I never wanted to say anything about this before because I didn't know what to make of it; it just seemed weird. But now I keep going over and over it." Mildred halted again and held back tears. Panic rose inside me. Mildred's habitual self-mocking tone was gone, and I missed it: I did not want to hear her words, stripped by sorrow and worry to a spare directness.

"Remember when you went out to get worms with Daniel for the fishing trip?" I recalled more clearly than I wanted to. "The night right before he met with you, I came into the bathroom while Daniel was giving Ben a bubble bath. Daniel was sitting in the bathtub with Ben, and Ben was, Ben had, Ben was holding on to Daniel's penis."

"He was doing what?" Ottilie asked.

"His penis was erect, and since it was moving, sticking up in the bubbles, Ben grabbed for it, you know the way babies and toddlers grab at things? I told Daniel to stop. But he just sat there until I pulled Ben out of the bathtub. Daniel joked about it and accused me of overreacting. We had a big argument later. I kept praying there was an innocent explanation for it, but it scared me."

Ottilie answered, "Well, maybe there was—"

"It happened a second time," Mildred said. "Yesterday, Ben climbed upstairs for a minute while I was downstairs, and when I went looking for him, I found him with Daniel in our bedroom. Daniel was changing his clothes. He had an erection, and Ben was reaching for his penis, and Daniel was just standing there, looking down at Ben and smiling. Encouraging him. When Daniel saw me, he laughed it off. We had another fight. He said Ben had come up on him while he was dressing, and I said, I didn't care, wasn't there anything he thought it wasn't all right to do—"

"Do you think Daniel has a thing for little kids?" I asked. "That he's a pedophile or something?"

Mildred sat, seemingly frozen, unable to speak, as if she were concentrating all of her energies on wrestling her emotions into place. Then her voice dropped, and she said, "I just couldn't make sense of it." I could barely hear her. I leaned forward, and then she spoke louder. "After that night before the fishing trip, I decided to watch things. I stopped leaving Ben alone with Daniel at home, and if they were outside together, I'd keep an eye on them. You know how it is when you get lost in a marriage? It's your world, everything in your world is centered by your marriage, and when the center goes, all of a sudden, it's, it's chaos! Just chaos whirling around you. You can't get a perspective on anything because your center's gone. I couldn't get my bearings for a while. I had to figure out where I was going to stand, find a piece of dry ground where I could look at things from. I thought that if Daniel was a goddamn creepy child molester, surely I would have known before now—"

"And I'm still not sure there's really enough to go by," Ottilie said. "What he did is certainly not right, and it's scary because it's—"

"Because it's not enough to press charges," I said, "but it's just bizarre enough to make you frightened for Ben—"

Mildred had begun to cry again, and I stopped. The kettle whistled on the stove, and Ottilie mixed us each a cup of coffee, and made herself tea. She pushed our mugs toward us. As she sat back down, I leaned over my cup's dark eye, and steam covered my face.

Mildred said, "I don't think Daniel's driven by some need to get off on children. It's worse than that, Melanie! If he were only some poor dumb pedophile who couldn't help it—but he can help it. He just doesn't care enough not to. No, it's more than that—Daniel has to be able to do whatever he wants. It's rules, it has to do with rules—any rules—even about safety, say, they bother him. He doesn't like to be told how to act, even around Ben, so he breaks rules to show no one can tell him what to do." Mildred halted, grasping at an explanation. "I think Daniel did that in the bathtub and bedroom because—it's the way he is with everything! Why would sex be any different? He let Ben play with—play with his father's penis because it proved that even that rule doesn't apply to Daniel. Daniel did it because he knew he shouldn't. And because he knew I wouldn't like it."

"Because he knew it would hurt you—" Ottilie said.

"Yeah, that too, he did it for the same reason he wouldn't put on Ben's life preserver, to hurt me. And to hurt Ben. I just can't get past that. Why would he *want* to hurt us?"

When Mildred asked this question, I felt such anger brush against me, suddenly, from nowhere: it rose like a cold current and grabbed me and threatened to pull me under. I felt my blood race, the muscles in my throat tightening, a rage that eddied around the top of my spine. It frightened me, and I stood up, walked to the counter, steadied myself. The rage soaked into my muscles, into my bone marrow. It did not feel like part of me, but as if it came from outside, like a chemical infusion replacing my blood, and discoloring the fibers of my being. My hands shook.

I reached for the fork in Ottilie's bowl of biscuit dough, to occupy my hands and govern them. I dropped dollops onto a tin, opened the oven, and put the tin inside.

"When did Daniel first get violent with you?" Ottilie asked.

I closed the oven, my back to Ottilie and Mildred, and now my hands were still. I leaned against the counter, folded my arms, kept my fingers locked above my elbows.

"A few weeks ago," Mildred answered. "When we went to Door County. Daniel hadn't ever been violent before then. Well, just once before. Maybe twice. In Brazil, one time, he got drunk and punched me."

"He punched you?" I asked. My voice was restrained, mine, colorless.

"Yeah, but he was drunk. He doesn't usually drink. He never did anything like that again, when we were there, so I didn't think it meant anything. The truth is, we got along pretty well. We only argued a few times, and when things got too tense around the house, Daniel would go off on one of his research trips, for a few days, and even, a few times, for a couple weeks. When he'd return, it was like a honeymoon; we'd fuck our brains out. Anyway, still, we once had a bad argument— Daniel got smashed during this big festival in the village where we were living, and a perfect stranger brought Ben home. I yelled at Daniel for getting drunk when he was in charge of Ben, and he hit me in the eye. But he's not a drinker. I never saw him drink like that again, so I just didn't think much of it. He's a big guy, but he didn't hurt me very badly. His aim was off, and he was falling all over himself."

I knew what all the justifications in Mildred's account meant. They were one woman saying to another: No man could get the better of me that way.

"He got drunk with me one night behind the halfway house," I told her.

"Daniel got drunk?" Mildred asked.

"Did he act different then?" Ottilie asked. "Did he show a side of himself that—"

"I don't know. I passed out."

Ottilie stared at me. "You drank that much?"

"Don't worry, Ottilie," I answered, glad for the digression. "It's never happened before. Except once, when I was in high school, and Matt and Aletta Knorr and I got hold of this Night Train and went up to the quarry—"

"It kills off your brain cells when you pass out," Mildred said. "That's why grass is so much better for you—"

"Don't change the topic—" Ottilie cut her off. Mildred and I both looked at her, surprised by her insistence. "You said Daniel got violent with you twice before you went to Door County. When was the other time?"

"After that fishing trip to Lake Muskellunge. This was only two days after we had the argument about—about the weird stuff in the bathtub. During the fishing trip, Daniel and I had another argument on the docks about the life preserver. After we came home, when my dad was out in the garden, Daniel got mad at me, and when I tried to leave our bedroom, he grabbed me by my hair and yanked my head back."

"He pulled your hair," Ottilie said.

"Yeah, at the time, I guess I just put it out of my mind. I didn't know what to make of it. He came up behind me and told me I had embarrassed him in public and yanked my head back by my hair. I told him he was hurting me, and he let go."

Mildred stood up suddenly and held her hands to the sides of her face. "He carried Ben across a field by his hair! I can't stop thinking how much it must have hurt—how scared Ben must have been!" She stood unmoving, as if transfigured by the picture in her mind's eye.

I thought of Matt: I saw my father dragging Matt up the stairs by his hair, Matt screaming, his face pressed against the stairway wall, one hand out to protect his eyes. When they reached the top, a hank of hair fell from my father's hand; he stormed away. Matt leaned against the wall, dazed, staring at nothing.

"What must have passed through Ben's head?" Mildred said. "He must have tried to make sense of it, but then just felt frightened!"

Ottilie took Mildred's arm, and pulled her back into her chair. "Tell us what happened in Door County," Ottilie pressed. She flushed, and looked in her lap. She explained quietly, "I want to know what Daniel's done, because I want to know how to stop him. Because I'm afraid for Ben, too. And I'm afraid for Matt."

I sat down.

Mildred answered, tentatively at first, but almost, it seemed, with a sense of relief, so that I wished someone had prodded her sooner, asked her weeks ago how she was doing, what was happening in her life. She spoke simply and straightforwardly, without emotion, as if the last weeks had knocked the feeling out of her, or as if the facts were easier to relate without having to feel them, easier to look at as cold empirical evidence, clues and pieces in a mystery we needed to solve, the mystery of who Daniel Munk was, how dangerous he was, what made him tick.

Mildred told us that when she had traveled with Daniel to Door County, "he acted like another person." He was irritable and short with her all the first day. In the evening they argued, and he lost his temper and called her a "bitch" and a "cunt." Later he apologized and said that he was under a lot of stress. "I swear," Mildred told us. "I never thought I'd live to hear the man I was married to use words like that on me. I wanted to snatch them out of the air and stuff them back down his throat."

Mildred related that two nights later, after Ben was asleep, she criticized Daniel, because he had allowed Ben to come too close to the camp-fire. Daniel accused Mildred of making Ben "a clingy mama's boy," and of jealously guarding Ben from becoming attached to his own father. They argued again, and Daniel told Mildred to "shut up" and attacked her with his fists, hitting her in the ribs and face and shoulders.

"I didn't even defend myself," Mildred said. "I was so surprised—even while it was happening, I couldn't believe it was."

"What did you think after he hit you?" I blurted out. My question surprised everybody, even me. Perhaps I had meant to ask what Mildred felt. Once, early in law school, I had dated an attorney for a few weeks. The first night I went home with him, he seemed, out of the blue, to change his manner. He grabbed me roughly by the arms, told me that I was "a hard woman, hard as ice," and forced me down into a chair. At that instant I experienced not merely a complete shutting down of every feeling I had had the moment before; my very thoughts and perceptions turned off; I felt myself rise mechanically, and I moved toward a dim light in the room, and found my way out of the apartment. I never talked to him again. And afterward, I wondered what had propelled me out of his building. It was as if an instinct had traveled with a pure certainty of direction, down a path so old that feeling had long since vanished, leaving the essential bone. I wondered whether when Daniel had attacked Mildred, a memory of helplessness had disarmed her, left her without the ability to feel and reason.

"What did I think?" Mildred answered. "I was pissed!"

Mildred elaborated that after the fight, Daniel stalked away into the woods with his sleeping bag, and did not return until morning. Mildred sat by Ben all night, feeling "as if a rabid skunk lurked nearby."

When Daniel returned in the morning, he demanded Mildred's forgiveness, and confessed that her criticism had angered him because it echoed his very thoughts, the words he had suppressed but wanted to say to her. How could she have endangered her son by allowing him to be left alone with a man who was psychotic? Daniel wanted to know if she had a sick need to force her son to spend time around a crazy person, because her own mother had been insane. He wanted to know if Mildred was insane.

"That was cruel," Ottilie interrupted. "It was calculated to be cruel."

Mildred drew a deep breath and said, "I thought Daniel was having a nervous breakdown. I felt worried for *him*." She continued, "When we got back home from Door County, I kept trying to get Daniel to speak about what had happened. But he refused to. He told me that it would be better just to let things drop. But I couldn't," Mildred explained. "I stewed for a few days, and I tried again to make him discuss what he had done. His reaction was really strange. He acted as if he had no idea what I was talking about."

"That must have made you feel crazy," Ottilie said.

"Well, maybe so," Mildred answered. She looked down into her coffee, her eyes watering, and then continued. "But it didn't matter, because after that I was watching Daniel every second. Once, one of the few times Daniel took Ben out by himself, I followed them, and I saw Daniel stick Ben way up high on a tractor seat, and then let go of him, so high that Ben would have fallen and hurt himself if he'd lost his balance. When Daniel saw me coming, he took Ben down. I wondered if Daniel had known all along that I was watching him—if he had done that with Ben just to bother me. Or what was worse, I wondered if he had done it just for the pleasure of it, without knowing I was there."

"I saw him do that," I said. "I was walking by the field when he put Ben up there."

Mildred looked hard at me and asked, "What did you say to him?"

"I didn't say anything," I answered. "It just didn't click before he'd already taken Ben back down—"

"That's how he works, isn't it?" Ottilie said. "He likes to cross the line, but to barely cross it, enough to upset you, but not enough to get himself in trouble. I think that's so strange! He must be such a strange person inside!"

I wondered how many times human beings had sat down to figure out a man like Daniel. Surely there were people smarter than us, more experienced and worldly. I imagined myself in another time and country, a merchant standing in the shadow of an exotic building, a pyramid or coliseum, joking with his brother about the cutthroat and megalomaniacal dealings of a business rival. When Ottilie asked, "Melanie, what do you think?" I felt so distant from the scene in the kitchen—from the three women huddled over the table trying to understand someone who had fooled them so easily—that it took me a moment to collect myself and answer.

"No one like that could keep from crossing the line every minute," I finally said. "There must be times when his brinkmanship goes too far."

"Of course he goes too far!" Mildred answered. "If he's confronted with himself, he loses it; that's what makes him lose it! Yesterday Daniel just exploded. I put Ben down for a nap, and then I cornered Daniel. I tried to force him to speak about what was going on with Ben in the bedroom, and about his violence during the trip. I asked him if he was the one hurting Ben."

Mildred's voice became flat, as matter of fact as if she had been talking about the events of another time, events that had happened to someone else, in which she shared some interest.

"This time he threw me to the kitchen floor and kicked me, and then put his hands around my neck. He said, 'Will you just shut up! I'm not a violent man! Shut up! Do you want me to strangle you?' He pressed on my windpipe until I couldn't breathe. When I started to feel dizzy, he stopped as suddenly as he had started. He stood up and pretended that nothing had happened. He sat down at the kitchen table and began reading a book." Mildred looked away when she said this. She did not wish to see her words reflected in our faces.

I took the biscuits out of the oven, and set the tin on the stove. I watched the oven's blue flames quiver like a feather boa. I turned off the fire, wiped my eyes on my sleeve, closed the oven door. I dumped the biscuits into a dish and placed them on the table.

Mildred waited for me to sit down and said, "I was shaking afterward. I asked Daniel what the hell had gotten into him. Was he a chicken hawk, or just a fucking asshole?"

I smiled in spite of myself: only Mildred would think to counter such a scene of violence with such a question. But I knew also that to ask that question, she must have been able to shut down every feeling, her fear and humiliation and confusion, in the very moment of his violence.

"And then do you know what he told me?" Mildred asked. "He came over to me and took my hand and said he wanted to make love with me right there. He said, 'Why can't you let things rest? You know I love you. When you're with me, people feel jealous to see what a happy family man I am. You're my wife, and I love you.' Christ! That's when I told him I wanted to separate."

Mildred related that Daniel then let go of her, and told her three things. He told her first, that if she discussed any of their "recent disagreements" with her father, he, Daniel, would expose the whereabouts of four Nicaraguan couples who had sought refuge in Reverend Steck's church, and for whom Mildred's father had found safe harbors in Fond du Lac, where they had now lived for two years without detection. Daniel had discovered a list of illegal aliens Reverend Steck had been helping over the last few years. If the couples' names were turned in to the INS, they faced instant deportation, poverty, and almost certain political assassination in their homeland. Second, he would have Matthew thrown in jail for child abuse. Third, Daniel said that if Mildred made any move against him, such as asking for a divorce, he would take Ben. He would have no trouble proving his grounds: She was crazy, after all.

Mildred had listened to Daniel, stupefied. She watched speechless as he departed out the front door. "Then I stood up," Mildred said, "and washed my face and sat frozen on the couch staring at nothing for half an hour. I felt all of Daniel's threats hemming me in until it was like I was in prison—and then I realized how much I'd lost perspective, how easily you believe someone you've been in love with! I was amazed that I had reached the point where mere words, where just a threat, could grab hold of me like that. And then I forced myself to see Daniel clearly in my mind: I saw, I finally saw that he was not the person I'd imagined. And all at once I knew absolutely that Daniel was the one who had left those marks on Ben, that Daniel was hurting Ben—it was awful, suddenly knowing it—I felt like someone had punched me in the stomach with it. I ran upstairs. But Ben's bed was empty! Daniel had circled the house, come up the back stairs, and taken Ben. I saw Ben's sheets all snarled in a ball around the empty place where he had been sleeping. And that's when something snapped in me. Then I understood exactly what I had to do. I didn't feel anything about me and Daniel anymore. Not heartbroken or afraid or anything."

I wondered if Mildred's confrontation with Daniel—her direct challenge to the person he needed us all to believe he was—had unbalanced him with a force he could not counteract. Perhaps she had upset him just enough that he had continued to reveal himself all day—in the Kmart parking lot, in the Park and Pray with Matt, and so, to me.

"I felt a kind of relief in the middle of all my fear for Ben," Mildred said. "After Daniel left, I realized I had been holding things back so long, seeing and not seeing and never talking about any of it. I just hadn't been able to bring myself to tell anyone about it. But now I knew I had to talk. I called Dad and asked him to wait at home for Daniel while I looked for Ben. I told Dad about Daniel's violence, and the weird stuff in the bathtub and bedroom, and everything. I told him Daniel had lost it. I said that Ben wasn't safe with him."

Mildred related that she had driven all afternoon, back and forth in Muskellunge's small residential area, and then to Sheboygan, and then up to Manitowoc. She thought she saw Ben on every corner. She slowed beside every toddler, every man of Daniel's build. She chased a man walking a little girl with overalls like Ben's into a movie theater. She frightened the little girl by suddenly grabbing her shoulder, mouth open in anger, ready to yell at the man who wasn't Daniel. The man had called for the movie manager, and Mildred had run off, not wanting to waste time explaining. She sped away in her car and hunted for another hour. She finally called home and raced back, her heart in her throat, after her father told her Ben was safe. Chief Komar flagged her down outside of Muskellunge and gave her a speeding ticket.

When Mildred finished this account, she said, "Ottilie, it's different with me. I don't love Daniel anymore. I don't feel that undertow you're talking about pulling me back to him. When I found out Daniel had taken Ben, that he had used Ben as a weapon against me, to scare me, I went cold as a snake inside."

"That's lucky, that's good," Ottilie said, almost to herself.

"Oh, yeah, I feel really lucky," Mildred answered.

Reverend Steck knocked on the kitchen lintel and said, "Ben's crying, honey."

Mildred rose, but Ottilie said, "No, listen—he's already fallen back asleep." We all fell silent, straining to hear.

"You see, he's okay," I told Mildred.

She still looked uneasy, and Ottilie said, "I can check him." But I followed her into the living room and told her, "Go sit down with Reverend Steck and Mildred. I can look in on Ben." It was a strange thing for me to do. I don't have a manner or appearance that calms children.

Ottilie touched my hand and gave me a look I could not make sense of—not simply worried, but apologetic or defensive. "Of course I loved Joel for a long time!" she whispered. "Of course I did! Passionately! Why else would I have married him?"

I wanted to tell her it didn't matter—of course she must have loved my father at some time. But Ottilie turned and fled back into the kitchen.

I walked up the stairs slowly. When I reached the bedroom where Ben was, he said, "I didn't like that noise!" He closed his eyes when I kissed his forehead.

I lay down beside him, and listened to Reverend Steck and Mildred talking below. Mildred's voice rose and fell, sometimes broken by crying. At one point I heard Reverend Steck say, "Why didn't you tell us? Why would you keep this to yourself?"

Ottilie answered, "Because she felt humiliated!"

Ben cried out in his sleep, "Only if you say please!" I pushed back his hair, but he stirred peevishly and said, "Don't take my pillow." So I withdrew my hand. I tucked him in, and fell asleep there, watching his chest rise and fall under the blue coverlet.

2

DANIEL DID NOT return the next Sunday, as he had promised. But Sunday evening, Joel Ratleer appeared on the local news: he was defending a man named Frank Worlfordt, who had been staging one-man protests outside a Madison abortion clinic. Worlfordt had waited in ambush outside the clinic's door, thrown pig blood on doctors as they were leaving work, and attacked one of them with a stick.

I was alone in Ottilie's house when the news came on, and to see Joel Ratleer that way, so unexpectedly, was a shock. He had aged very little: His gray hair was thick and curly, the lines in his face had etched more deeply but handsomely. His voice boomed into a microphone held by a newsman: "Mr. Worlfordt is guilty of one thing only: exercising his First Amendment privilege of free expression! I'll defend his right to throw pig blood anywhere he wants until the day I die!"

Joel Ratleer and Frank Worlfordt were interviewed in the Madison paper, and Reverend Hatch was quoted in the *Muskellunge Eagle* and *Manitowoc Courier* as saying, "Frank Worlfordt has thrown the blood of the first American martyrs upon the land, and I'm standing in line behind him."

That evening Reverend Steck came to Ottilie's house, and startled me by climbing the stairs to my room before I could answer the bell. He wore mechanic's coveralls over a minister's shirt and collar, and his ponytail was secured with copper wire. He had been working with Matt on the halfway house's van.

"Melanie?" Reverend Steck asked, leaning into my room. "Your father is a well-known lawyer, isn't he? It's not too soon for Mildred to be thinking about talking to a good lawyer."

My mouth must have dropped open. "Joel Ratleer would *not* be a good choice," I said.

"He wouldn't?"

I pictured them in battle, Daniel and Joel Ratleer, and for a moment, I savored the idea of two devils facing each other off. But then I dismissed it. I doubted my father would understand the danger Daniel posed to Mildred and Ben. "He's way too expensive," I answered. "And he's a criminal defense attorney. He doesn't practice domestic relations law. He's probably better equipped to represent someone like Daniel—"

"What kind of man would defend Daniel Munk against Mildred!"

"A lawyer. That's what kind of man would defend Daniel Munk."

"You're a lawyer," Reverend Steck answered. He waited for me to respond, then asked, "Is there any chance that a man like Daniel could get custody of a child Ben's age?"

At first, without thinking, I said, "Reverend Steck, anything is possible in a court of law," but I checked myself when I saw the worry in his face.

"Melanie, why do you keep calling me 'Reverend'? I'm a man, not an office. How long are you going to hold me at arm's length? My name is John Steck."

I asked him to sit down. He chose Aunt Mimi's blue armchair. "Mr. Steck. John. Courts usually let small children stay with their mothers. But men often get custody because of judicial prejudices about women, or because men fight dirtier, or because they have the money to hire better lawyers and experts—"

"Daniel would have to lie to convince a court to give him custody, wouldn't he?"

"Yes," I affirmed. "He would have to lie."

"But men like Daniel make very convincing liars, don't they?"

"I would guess—"

"Imagine him telling Mildred what he did about the immigrants I've sheltered! As if I would be foolish enough to keep a list of their names. Imagine me sending helpless refuges to godforsaken Fond du Lac! I'll pray Daniel's other threats were just as meaningless."

I smiled.

"It's such a surprise to see you smile; you don't do it very often." Mildred's father tugged at his collar, as if it made him uncomfortable.

"Melanie, Mildred told me that she once thought Daniel might be having a kind of nervous breakdown. Do you think there's any possibility that he's a good man? Just a good man who's fallen apart under stress?"

"Daniel doesn't act crazy the way Matt and Dr. Eatman and the other guys at the halfway house do. He's not incoherent or confused. I don't think he's having a nervous breakdown."

"No. I didn't think so either. I just don't want to judge too harshly. I keep asking myself, is he a bad man, or just a troubled one?"

"I wouldn't know," I said.

"Should we try to help him? Maybe he commits these acts of violence when he loses his temper—maybe he's a good man with a bad temper, who has to learn to control it. Surely a part of him, some good part knows he's troubled, and tries to swim to the surface like a soul gasping for air."

I answered jokingly, "Matthew thinks Daniel's the devil."

Reverend Steck frowned and cocked his head as if considering this statement at face value. His ponytail curled on his shoulder like a small animal whispering in his ear. He answered, "It's essential that we men of religion try to penetrate the deep mystery of the devil. Some would say we need a sense of the devil as a spirit who names himself with his specific personality for every occasion."

I must have looked baffled, because John stopped his rumination and, in a different tone, said, "Well, in the end, it doesn't really make any difference whether Daniel is troubled, or just plain bad, does it? What matters is that he doesn't hurt my daughter, or my grandson."

I said, "There's something so calculated about Daniel—he doesn't seem to me like a guy who just has problems controlling his temper. He led us all on so well for so long. But the more I look at him, the less clearly I see him. I haven't figured him out yet."

John answered, "I guess we all need to give Mildred time to detoxify, to get Daniel out of her system. After all, we merely had the wrong impression of a person we barely knew. Mildred has to deal with a whole man turning out to be false. And she's been very much in love with Daniel." I saw that I had underestimated Mildred's father, that he was not as blinded by goodness as either I or Mildred had supposed him to be.

"We have to be patient," he concluded, standing up. "Perhaps Daniel has redeeming qualities. In any case, he doesn't strike me as the kind of man who wants the full charge of a child. Maybe he's stolen my daughter's car and run off. I'll pray that's what's happened." He turned and took the stairs, his ponytail bobbing on his shoulder.

A WEEK PASSED, and then another, and Mildred did not hear from Daniel. John Steck visited the local police, but they told him that there was insufficient evidence to charge Daniel with abusing Ben. Mildred's father believed Chief Komar seemed sympathetic, however. He must have remembered Mrs. Steck—Mildred confided that he had been the one to drive her mother to the hospital the time she had walked naked down the yellow center line of Walleye Street. Chief Komar agreed to put out a bulletin for the stolen Cadillac, but cautioned that a son-in-law's brief disappearance with a car his wife happened to have title to, was, in the law's estimation, a far cry from grand larceny.

In those first weeks after Daniel's disappearance, it seemed possible to believe that this destructive man paradoxically had left in his wake a wealth of harmonies. We huddled together around the fires of our dread, and drew close to one another. Ottilie arrived early one evening at the halfway house with one of Mimi's brilliant fuchsia scarves woven in her hair, and she joined John Steck for a supper cooked by Rockefeller, embellished by Dmytryk's dandelion wine, and commented upon drolly by Dr. Eatman. The following morning she allowed herself to be seen walking arm in arm with John Steck in the church garden, as his parishioners turned under the September soil.

Matthew came to Ottilie's house often, and he, Mildred, Ben, and I could sit together at a single table. Matt would sing over lunch, "I know an old lady who swallowed a fly," and Ben would conclude merrily, "Perhaps she'll die." Mildred joked easily with Matt. She even announced over dessert one evening her theory that crazy men have more hair than other men. Matt replied, "What about John Brown?" and then, grabbing his thick hair in two fists, answered himself. "He was crazy as the day was long."

Matt still teetered between clarity and confusion, but freed from Daniel's influence, my brother gained a certain equilibrium. Either Mildred's attention focussed Matt in some way, by reflecting back the joy in him, or he simply hid less from her behind the tangle of his illness than he did from the rest of the world. When Mildred was present, Matt opened himself to me also. He brought me gifts at once touching and off-base: a musty book on the history of Great Lakes shipping law;

a pink shirt with a high prim collar, much too small; a chipped Wedgwood plate with a hole in the center of it; and a series of Chinese boxes, red fitted into blue, fitted into green, with a poem called "In Fear of Harvests" by James Wright, clipped from a book's printed page, and folded into the smallest box like a fortune:

> *It has happened*
> *Before: nearby,*
> *The nostrils of slow horses*
> *Breathe evenly,*
> *And the brown bees drag their high garlands,*
> *Heavily*
> *Toward hives of snow.*

While I read this, Matt hovered above me, peering into the last box as if it were bigger than it seemed. I wondered how much he relied on the poetry books people had given him to construct a lyrical underworld more bearable to inhabit than his actual life.

Matt also found me a car, an old Volkswagen Beetle that had been sitting unused in a garage for a year. He must have known about it for months, but told me he did not like the color, "a mean yellow," and he would not deal with the owner directly or discuss questions of money. When I bought the Volkswagen for three hundred dollars, Matt fine-tuned it in a day, telling me its motor was "less complicated than a sewing machine—a moron could fix it." He repainted it pink with black fenders.

Matt gave Ben a checkerboard for his third birthday, and afterward, during gatherings at Ottilie's, he and Ben would play a three-year-old's version of checkers that had no rules or protocol. At these times Matt almost seemed sane. He let Ben pick off the pieces one by one, and pretended to be upset when he lost, crying "No fair! No fair!" Ben called back, "Fair, fair!" mounting his men into columns that towered over Matt's triple kings. With Daniel gone, Matt seemed as happy as a new groom.

As Daniel's absence grew longer, sometimes, at odd moments, I felt myself longing for what I thought he had been, for the kind of person I had felt like around him, for the image of that land Daniel had conjured up, Brazil of the frontier, the country of narrow escapes, of lawless defiance of death. And then I would check myself, fearing superstitiously that such thoughts might call him back home.

I assumed that if I had such moments, Mildred must also, despite what she had told us about her blood running cold as a snake. She had been so crazy about Daniel such a short time before. There must have been hours when she ached to touch the man she had believed she loved, when her temperature rose as she recalled afternoons she had spent in bed making love with the man she believed Daniel was. Her body must have had moments of rebellion against her, not understanding the logic of her conscious reason. She must have missed him. She must have felt widowed, as if the real Daniel had killed off his better, imposter self, leaving nothing behind but a smell of violence and the hollowness of loss.

But I began to see that Mildred was not like the rest of us, that her response was to forge herself into a weapon, to prepare for battle against Daniel, to understand him so that she could outwit him. I think she tried consciously not to look shaken, not to look eviscerated by loss. She laughed loudly and often, as if she were being observed by an enemy she wanted to convince of her invulnerability.

When Mildred watched Matt play his old, invented variations on checkers with me, she enticed him into showing the games to her, and then asked him to put away the checkers and teach her what he knew about chess. When Matt told her that the secret to the game lay in knowing every possible outcome, every permutation that extended from a single move, Mildred smiled darkly. And when he explained how to misdirect her opponent by sacrificing a rook, she watched carefully as he drew her toward the bait and checkmated from another corner, and then she made him reenact the play several times. Matt taught her to keep control of the middle of the board, and never to play defensively. She was a good player: I could not beat her. And Matt would not allow himself to. But he also would not let her win. He loved to always end in a draw, to tantalize Mildred toward winning, and then stop her just short of victory and chortle over her exasperation.

"You're too tender-hearted," she told him once. "You shouldn't be so careful not to win. I'm not made of glass. I won't break."

Sometimes, watching Mildred, I found myself wrestling my fear of Daniel into place. I thought of Reverend Steck's words regarding the devil as a spirit who names himself as a specific personality in every life, and I wondered if I had exaggerated Daniel in my mind—if I were seeing him as a figure far more powerful than I believed he could be, more menacing and dangerous, more wily, more successful in his machinations. And then I would shrug off images of him, the edginess that seemed to cloak me all the time now, and I would remind myself that Daniel was only a man, albeit a violent and deceptive one.

To me, Mildred's conduct during this period seemed extraordinary. Years later it would be my memory of her then that let me believe she was capable of the things she did later. It was the way she steeled herself and adapted so quickly to what she had learned. I knew that in her place I would have taken months to "detoxify." I would not have been able to see Daniel so well so soon. And I would have been more frightened. I would have woken at night with terrible images of his violence reverberating in my dreams.

And even from where I was situated, on the periphery of Daniel's violence, my nightmares were so frightening that I rose in the morning feeling apprehensive and disoriented. I dreamed that I was bathing Ben, and discovered on his back words, runes, that someone had carved into his skin with a sharp instrument. I dreamed that I was half human, half sea animal, an otter-child, the last of my species, lying hidden behind a breakwater, as men wielding axes chopped at the wood around me, hunting me. I dreamed I was carrying an infant, and when I unfolded the cloth swaddling him, I discovered he was gone; I had let him slip from my grasp and lost him somewhere on the vast, darkening shore.

But Mildred plotted strategies for overcoming Daniel. One morning, as I approached the halfway house, I saw her talking animatedly to her father in the empty squash bed. She had made him a series of minister's collars in wild patterns and colors—tie-dyes and paisleys and bright solids. That day John wore a bright orange circle, cut from the same fabric as Mildred's overalls. It flashed like a warning when he threw up his arms in exasperation at something Mildred said.

As I entered the garden, John was trying to persuade Mildred to press assault charges on her own behalf against Daniel, but she refused, and her refusal baffled him.

"You're asking me to go tell Chief Komar what it felt like to be beat up by my own husband? So that later he can go jack off to my description of what it's like to be strangled?"

Mildred's father looked stung when she addressed him this way. She stopped in midspeech, and tried to pull her outrage into place. "I'm sorry, Dad. The last thing I want to do is to sit down with some stranger and tell him the gross details of my married life. You know how these things go—the police say it's only a family dispute, they don't take it seriously, and then you suffer all the humiliation for nothing."

"How would you know that?" John looked tired. He worried a hardened clod of dirt with his heel, and a small mottled beetle scampered behind him down a gully.

"I found out! You know that lady Veronica who sits in the last pew in church? The one whose husband beats her up once a week?"

"Russell Pease?" John looked at me, in astonishment, as if I could tell him something. "Russell Pease does that?"

"Sophie Pease found out that Mr. Pease had gotten mad at her mother, as usual, and held a gun to her mother's head. *Held a gun to her head*. So Sophie got her mother to go down to the station to report it. And do you know what Komar's little deputy said to her mother?

"He said, 'Do you have any evidence?'

" 'Yeah, she's telling you it happened,' Sophie said. 'It was her head, so she saw it. She's an eyewitness.'

"He told her she needed 'corroboration.' Now, get that. If some guy holds a gun to your head to rob your store, and you go to the police and say, 'That man just robbed me,' do they say, 'I'm sorry, we need some extra proof—' "

"Mildred, if you don't want to talk to the police right now, you don't have to."

"If I go in there and start crying about myself, they'll never take me seriously. I have to focus on getting them to help Ben. To make them believe Daniel's violent at all, I'll have to—What I want to do is set Daniel up somehow. I want to trick him."

"Set him up?"

"Yeah, I want to lure him to some deserted place, get him in an argument, provoke him into doing something illegal, let him take a swing at me somewhere where I've already got a witness watching—"

"That's too dangerous, Mildred—"

"And then I'll nail him. I'll trick him, the same way he likes to trick other people."

"You're not talking sense."

"Don't be so damn innocent!"

"Don't you be," John Steck answered. "It's not as easy to fool people as you think. You're not the devil."

Mildred looked at me, and then John did, and then they continued talking, facing each other. I felt a little out of place, and walked away.

I visited Matt in his room, and as soon as he saw me, he told me that he was worried about Mildred. "She could do something drastic," was how he put it. And it was during the same visit that Matt told me Daniel had visited the halfway house repeatedly. He said that Daniel liked to sit on the top of the stairs and tell the men about his exploits in Brazil. Once Daniel had told Matt about an anthropologist named Taussig, who wrote on a Colombian custom of christening money during baptisms. Daniel had added that he had played a trick on Brazilian miners. Borrowing from Taussig's writings and changing them just a little to adapt to his Brazilian setting, Daniel had convinced several miners that he had brokered baptized cruzeiro notes from men who had stolen the souls of the miners' own children during their baptisms. Daniel had then convinced the miners to give him research information and even, in one instance, small lumps of mined gold, in exchange for the cruzeiros he carried. It was such a bizarre story, I shuddered; it must have frightened Matt to hear it. And it made me profoundly uneasy that Daniel had copied Taussig the night he told me similar stories, that the morning we had gone nightcrawling, Daniel's very conversation with me had been plagiarized.

AT THE END of September the Kiwanis Club joined forces with the Shriners and Lions and Masons to help organize the annual Pferd Beer Parade. Preparations were disrupted by an announcement from Reverend Hatch: inspired by Frank Worlfordt, Hatch intended to lead a protest march against abortion in the wake of the great float carrying Miss Muskellunge, drawn by the twelve Pferd Percherons. Pro-choice groups in Madison learned of Hatch's march, and announced that they would arrive in busloads to stage a counter-protest. The local police were alarmed, and at Chief Komar's request, the state police agreed to send extra troopers to Muskellunge.

Mildred was tickled by Reverend Hatch's vocal identification with Frank Worlfordt, and she escalated her antiabortion activities in preparation for the parade. Mildred seemed to welcome discord, to relish the thought of dissension, as if honing herself for an anticipated fight with Daniel. In a single week, she made one hundred placards to be carried by demonstrators, each with a provocative slogan: PROUD TO BE UN-

BORN, WORLFORDT WOULD BE BETTER OFF IF HE'D NEVER BEEN HATCHED, FIGHT OVERPOPULATION IN MUSKELLUNGE, and even FORMER FETUSES FOR ABORTION.

Three months before my return to New York City, I walked to the Stecks' house to help Mildred paint posters. I found Ben and Matt playing alone together in Ottilie's side yard.

Ben appeared suddenly from behind the house, dressed in a mail-order Halloween costume: a jack-o'-lantern mask, and a black silk cape spangled with orange glitter.

"Ho, ho, ho, Melanie!" he yelled. "I need a head!"

Matt came up behind him and said, "Ben's going to be the headless horseman on Halloween." Matt spoke so clearly that it was hard to think of him as crazy. His apparent sanity took me off guard as much as his craziness sometimes did.

"And I'm going as an escaped lunatic." Matt laughed, parodying the cackles of madmen in old movies.

I laughed, too, at how it was possible to be crazy and know you're crazy at the same time. "I'm going to scare people on Halloween," I told him, "by sneaking up behind them and dipping my hand in their pockets, dressed as a lawyer."

Now Matt let his own laugh slip out, easy and heartfelt. "What an old, old joke, Melanie," he said. He tied an electric orange scarf around Ben's neck.

"What's that for?" I asked.

"Because it's going to be cold," Ben said patronizingly.

"To see if it matches his costume," Matt said.

"Pick me up by my feet! Pick me up by my feet!" Ben commanded.

Matt leaned over, grabbed Ben by his ankles, and carried him across the yard, his head suspended over the grass, his scarf trailing.

"Help me! Help me, Melanie!" Ben screamed. "This is dangerous," he called happily, looking at me upside down. "Very, very dangerous!"

When I entered the house, Mildred was alternately chuckling over her signs and scowling whenever she remembered her situation. She had grown angrier, more worried about Ben, less puzzled about Daniel. As we worked, she would joke about Frank Worlfordt, and then fall silent as she sorted through the facts of her marriage. She turned Daniel over in her mind as if she were polishing a dark gem, as if she were testing the feel and weight and density of him. She asked me questions I usually did not have the answers to. Once, she asked, "Do you think all violent men are like Daniel? Do you think they all come to lead double lives, because they have to hide their violence? Or is Daniel different? Is he worse than most?" Twenty minutes later, she looked up suddenly and said, "Do you think Daniel has a piece missing somehow? I can't get his parts to fit into a whole. I can't pin down who he is anymore." And then a few minutes later, she said, "Do you know why I think he latched on to me? He thought it was more of a challenge to fool me. I think he wanted to conquer me, somehow. Or maybe it was the opposite." She looked at me, her eyes flashing angrily, and demanded, "Was it because he saw some vulnerability in me, that made me easy prey to him?"

"No," I answered, "I think Daniel miscalculated. Maybe he thought that because you were so much younger than him, and a minister's daughter, you'd be easy to push around and wouldn't see though him. But he bit off more than he could chew."

"Oh, yes," Mildred said. "He sure did." She laughed. "You always look so serious when you answer questions, Melanie," she said. "I'm going to miss you when you go back to New York." I saw that I would miss her, too.

THE PFERD BEER PARADE occurred on a sunny, chilly day, the air crisp with the smell of impending snow. Cars and buses full of Frank Worlfordt's followers and Madison pro-choice groups parked in front of the elementary school. The parade marshal looked over his shoulder, uncomfortable and anxious as he led a group of shivering baton twirlers up Main Street, past the Pferd beer stands selling strawberry ale. Behind the baton twirlers were fifty Shriners dressed in maroon fezzes and dazzling silk balloon pants, their scimitars raised in preparation for war. Chief Komar stood on the curb in his dress uniform, which fit him awkwardly, as if it had been borrowed from a much larger man. He watched the parade with a belligerent expression, his dress hat resting insecurely on his bristly hair. But the counter-demonstrators from the capital proved well schooled, reacting with stony passivity before the wild jeers Reverend Hatch shouted through a megaphone as he walked backward behind the Pferd Percherons. He carried a poster-size picture of the 2001 fetus. His followers, who, like a foreign army, had come mostly from outside of Muskellunge, carried identical placards. But even they were relatively subdued, marching in step behind the Percherons, and the police relaxed, no trouble seeming imminent.

The Pferd Percherons lumbered slowly up Walleye Street, as if they had been watered on beer before the parade, their red tassels wobbling on their arched necks, their spangled headbands crooked, the ribbons braided prettily into their tails unravelling, their massive hooves stumbling on potholes. They did not strain in their traces, but moved lazily and effortlessly as they pulled the immense float carrying oversized beer kegs and Miss Muskellunge of 1977, a brown-haired girl dressed like an exotic queen in purple crinoline.

Matt waved to me from across the street, with Ben perched on his shoulders. Mildred accepted a sheath of leaflets from a man in a suit facing her and engaged in a conversation with him. He seemed to terminate the talk abruptly. As he turned away, I recognized the bottom paper in Mildred's hand as the unmistakable pale periwinkle blue-back of a judicial subpoena or court order. I realized that the man must be a process server.

The Percherons pulled between us, stopping to realign their harness, and Reverend Hatch's rally flowed around the sides of the float, up to the shoulders of the hindmost horses. Reverend Hatch disappeared into the crowd ahead, and a commotion gathered around him near the lead horses. When I tried to cross in front of the Pferd team to get to Mildred, the Percherons lunged forward suddenly, pushing Mildred away from Matt and Ben, and blocking my path. Reverend Hatch re-emerged before the horses and pulled from behind his back, as if by some sleight of hand, a ten-gallon jar of formaldehyde containing a human fetus.

Chief Komar stepped forward and demanded, "What the hell is that?"

"That's the most beautiful seven-month-old fetus you ever saw!" Reverend Hatch cried.

"You're under arrest," Chief Komar answered. He grabbed Reverend Hatch by his spiky elbow, and hauled him toward the curb.

That is when chaos broke loose. Reverend Hatch's followers cried out in protest, "What's the charge? Arrested for what!" and the horses shied from the tumult and reared in their traces. They tossed their spangled heads as if in anticipation of some ancient battle their forebears had been bred for, flared their nostrils, tossed their foamy manes, and trumpeted like elephants, joyful in their remembered wildness, and threatening to tip the Pferd Beer float on which Miss Muskellunge teetered. Dmytryk and Dr. Eatman nabbed Stretch Rockefeller by his collar and pulled him away from the horses: Rockefeller was shouting with alarm.

On the other side of the street, in the middle of this chaos, Matt saw Daniel Munk.

Daniel was watching over everyone from where he sat, perched on the roof of Mildred's car, which he had parked on a side street. He had transfigured and disguised the Cadillac: The hood ornament had been removed, and the body repainted a mustard green, so that the golden script bearing Mildred's name was no longer legible, and the fenders were no longer turquoise. He had not gone to Chicago, as he had informed the Stecks. He had driven instead to Milwaukee, established residence there, and consulted a Milwaukee matrimonial lawyer.

Matt watched Daniel get out of the car, approach a state trooper, and show the officer a paper with a yellow back attached. With Daniel close behind him, the officer approached Matt, and handed him the paper: It was a temporary restraining order, enjoining Matthew "from assaulting, harassing, threatening, or approaching the child Benjamin Munk from within a distance of one hundred yards."

I did not see any of this. I can only imagine how Ben cried and shrieked when the officer tried to help him down from Matt's shoulders, how Ben clung to Matt when Daniel came to pry him away, how Matt struggled against Daniel and then kicked him hard, how Matt wrestled with the state officer, who tried to subdue him by yanking his arm into a half nelson, and then called for help when Matt resisted. I cannot imagine how Matthew felt when two state policemen held him down while a third handcuffed him as he looked around frantically, and saw Daniel push Ben into the back seat of a beige car parked beside the Cadillac, moments before the police forced Matt into a state patrol car.

LATER, DANIEL parked the beige car in a lot behind the Sears store that had been closed by fire. The car belonged to the process server. Ben, exhausted from fighting something he did not understand, sought refuge in sleep. He curled up in the back seat with his eyes closed. When the process server returned to his car, Daniel left Ben with him and walked to the Stecks' house, where Mildred sat on the front porch, waiting for Matt to return with Ben. She had lost sight of them in the commotion, and was worried.

I also headed toward Mildred's house. I tried to push my way through the roiling crowd. "The charges," I heard Chief Komar shout, "are disorderly conduct and obstructing an officer! How do you like that!" The crowd formed a wall and forced me backward along Main Street and into an alley. I circled a row of buildings and doubled back toward the Park and Pray.

As I reached the church's road, I spied Daniel, standing in the Stecks' yard, talking to Mildred.

He was dressed oddly, in a suit and tie, and had trimmed his hair, so that he did not look like the man I remembered from a few weeks before, but instead like an imitation of Daniel Munk, a stranger. He and Mildred faced each other. When I was within twenty feet of Daniel, he turned and said to me in a voice that was cold and businesslike, "Matthew Ratleer has been arrested. I have obtained a protective order restraining your brother from coming near my son."

"Where's Ben?" Mildred demanded.

Daniel faced Mildred and smiled: It was an odd, meaningless smile, neither humorous nor ironic. "He's fine. He's asleep in the car."

"You left Ben alone in the car?"

"Mildred, honey, you're my wife, and Ben is my son," Daniel answered. "Come with us to Milwaukee now." He dangled the Cadillac's key in front of him, and slid it into his shirt pocket. And then Daniel repeated "Milwaukee" in a succession of sentences, until the word seemed full of meaning and unintelligible, the arcane syllables of a cabalist incantation. "Join us in Milwaukee," Daniel said. "I'm keeping Ben with me in Milwaukee. Ben and I are going to live in Milwaukee now. If you don't come with us to Milwaukee"—Daniel inclined his head slightly toward me—"I'll press charges against Mr. Nutto."

"Why are you doing this?" Mildred asked.

"But Matthew's helpless," I said. "He's insane."

Daniel frowned irritably, looked briefly at me, and then turned back to Mildred and said, "Decide. Come on home with me, and I'll just forget the court papers you got today. We'll tear them up and throw them away. We've got our own place now. That's been the trouble all along. We haven't had any privacy from everyone here."

"Maybe you're the one who's insane, Daniel," I said, but then I corrected myself. "No. You aren't crazy. You're something else that doesn't have a name—"

Daniel patted his pocket, pulled a paper from it, unfolded it one-handed, and said, "Why don't you look at this, Melanie? Mildred already has a copy."

The paper that Daniel presented to me was a petition for temporary and permanent custody of Ben, filed before a Milwaukee Family Court commissioner, and ordering Mildred to appear before him on October 19, 1977:

> I, Daniel Munk, petitioner in this case, being duly sworn under oath, depose and say:
>
> 1. On August 20, 1977, I separated from my wife, Mildred. I and my son, Benjamin Munk, age 3, are currently residents of Milwaukee County. I am filing this petition for legal and physical custody of Benjamin, because I reasonably fear that his safety and well-being will be endangered if he remains with his mother, and reasonably believe that she is an inappropriate custodial parent, for the reasons set forth below.
>
> 2. On or about July 1, 1977, my wife, who had sole charge of my son on that day, indulged in the use of marijuana.
>
> 3. Between the dates of January 1 and July 31, 1977, my wife left our son in the care of a severely disturbed schizophrenic, Matthew Ratleer, and continued to do so even after learning that he had physically injured my son, to wit: pulled his hair, punched, hit, and kicked him.
>
> 4. Between the dates of January 1 and July 31, 1977, my wife alienated my son from my affections, by permitting and encouraging said Matthew Ratleer to frighten my son with stories to the effect that I would take him from his bed at night and kill him. Such conduct has raised legitimate concerns about the mental stability of my wife and the safety of my child.

As I read the petition, a fear deeper than I had known in all my adult life overcame me. To me, the petition's words were not just words: each one was imbued with the arbitrary power of the law; each carried such a potential for harm that I caught my breath at the bottom of the document and could not read on. I lifted the affidavit's last page. Underneath was a single sheet stamped with a judicial seal. It was a temporary restraining order, signed by a Milwaukee County Court judge, enjoining Mildred from "assaulting the child Benjamin Munk, or approaching his person" before October 20, 1977.

"What kind of lies did you tell to get this?" I asked Daniel.

"I told the truth," Daniel answered.

"Mildred," I said, "do you know this order gives Daniel legal right to keep you away from Ben until you appear in court two weeks from now?"

"Decide," Daniel repeated to Mildred. "If you come with me, I'll just tear up that paper and all the others. But if you don't—" Daniel shrugged.

"I won't live with you anymore," Mildred answered. "Where's the car?"

"The man who served you with the papers is driving Ben to Milwaukee right now."

"You let a stranger take Ben away in a car?" Mildred broke then. She lost her grip, as a mother trying to rescue a child from a river might momentarily let go of his shoulder in order to get a tighter hold on his arm. She staggered back for a moment, caught her balance, and continued. "All right, fine. It's over. I'll go with you, and the three of us will live together."

Daniel tilted his head back in unrestrained, heartless laughter. "Mildred, honey," he said, looking at her and then both of us, and smiling flatly at our dumb faces. "Mildred, you know I would never threaten you. I just want you to be happy. I want you to know you're doing this of your own free will. I'm a good husband and father, and Ben needs his family. I just want us all to be happy together. I only want you to come with me if you want to. Now let's go."

3

THE STATE POLICE took Matt to the local jail, which was already overcrowded. Forty of Hatch's parading followers had formed a barricade between him and Chief Komar, who had charged them all with obstructing an officer and disorderly conduct, and detained them. In jail they crossed their arms in front of themselves and held hands like that, and sang hymns. And Matt, Chief Komar told Ottilie when he called her house, "was not acting like he belonged." Komar wanted us to come pick up my brother, but the charges, resisting arrest and battery to a law enforcement officer, were serious, and Komar wanted to get back in touch with the arresting officers before he released Matt. The state police had cleared out of Muskellunge that day and had their hands full in Madison—a dozen of Worlfordt's followers had chained themselves to a fleet of police cars in front of the jail, and hundreds of others were trespassing on police property, alternately holding a silent candlelight vigil, and chanting "Baby killers!" in thirty-minute outbursts.

Worlfordt had issued a statement praising Reverend Hatch, the kind of declaration that would get Worlfordt into trouble with the law, and that must have irritated his defense attorney, my father. What Worlfordt said was, "The police officer who arrested Reverend Hatch deserves to be executed. Let his bloodstained hands change places with the unblemished bodies of the unborn."

Chief Komar told a Madison radio reporter, "Tell Mr. Worlfordt I'd be glad to sit beside him in any electric chair in the country."

Chief Komar had placed Matt in a room by himself at the back of the jail. Eventually, Hatch and his followers stopped singing, and held a silent prayer in imitation of Worlfordt. Matt, they complained, disrupted their vigil. As soon as they had announced their silence, he began crowing hymns in a loud voice. When Ottilie and I reached the police station, we heard Matt singing hoarsely, "Oh you can't get to heaven on a pair of skates," a little off key. But when we came to him, he acted confused and withdrawn, and would not talk, even to Ottilie. He seemed sunken into himself, his shoulders hunched, his eyes flat and inward-looking. Torn from Mildred and Ben, he seemed unable to sustain any belief in his own sanity.

Ottilie held Matt's hand and said nothing, while I read a copy of the restraining order. "Matt," I said. "Don't worry about these papers. We'll get the order vacated," although I was unsure that we could. The charge of assaulting an officer buttressed Daniel's accusation that Matt had been violent with Ben.

Matt did not respond. He stared hopelessly at the cement floor. When Chief Komar told us the jail was closing, and Ottilie and I rose to go, Matt did not seem to notice.

By then it was long past dark. Musky's neon light flickered like a constellation on the edge of the world, and the sky spread above us, cloudy and ash-colored. John Steck stood outside the station, his hands in his pockets, his white minister's collar glowing like a sickle moon.

"Chief Komar told me what happened," he said. Then, his voice breaking, John told Ottilie, "Mildred's in trouble, she and Matt are both in trouble—" Ottilie took John's arm and followed him to the van, abandoning her car in the police station parking lot.

As John drove us home, he told us that Mildred had called him from a pay phone outside the women's room of a Sheboygan gas station. He had pleaded with her to return, but she told him she had to find Ben first. "She said Daniel told her that if she tries to take Ben with her back to Muskellunge, she'll be violating a court order, and never have any chance of getting custody after that. I pleaded with her to come home, but she says she won't leave Ben with Daniel, even for a night, and she won't come back until she can check with a lawyer to find out if what Daniel told her was true. She thinks Daniel's setting her up to lose Ben. She asked me to find her the name of a good attorney. She says she wants to know how she can 'trick' Daniel, and get Ben safely away from him."

John stopped the van at the end of Walleye Street and leaned his forehead on the steering wheel. "Ottilie," he said. "My wife. Mildred's mother, Annie. There was a period when she was not herself, and sometimes became unpredictable and violent. I don't think she knew what she was doing half the time. It was bad for Mildred. Could this be why she—"

"Daniel might have found her and courted her anyway," Ottilie said.

"Annie died in a car accident. She had been drinking while on medication."

Ottilie leaned against him. I felt embarrassed by this intimate interchange of grief. I looked out the window: the bright wings of an owl flashed over a field and plunged suddenly into darkness.

"I'm terrified," John said. "I'm terrified for Mildred, I can't seem to persuade her—"

"Mildred's right," I said quietly. "If she violated the restraining order by taking Ben from Daniel and absconding to Muskellunge, the Milwaukee Family Court might see her conduct as a reason not to entrust her with legal custody of Ben. If she were my client, I wouldn't want her to even think of it—"

"That's crazy!"

"Yeah," I said, "the law is crazy, but Mildred isn't. The law just makes her look like she's crazy. She's banking on the chance that Daniel won't call the police if she stays with Ben in Milwaukee, as long as she does what Daniel wants, as long as she lives with Daniel, too."

"Surely a good lawyer can help Mildred!" Ottilie said.

John drove in silence until he parked in front of Ottilie's. Then he said, apologetically, half to himself, "Before Mildred left, I called around to see what matrimonial lawyers cost—I don't have enough savings to hire a good attorney. According to Mildred, Daniel has a great deal of money—it seems his family was wealthy. I remortgaged my house when my wife got sick, years ago, to pay off bills from private hospitals. Radical ministers don't make much of a salary. I'm going to have to call some friends and cash in on old favors."

"You must have a lot of friends—a lot of favors coming to you," Ottilie told him.

"Mildred calls them the body snatchers," John said, "my old comrades-at-arms. She means it as a compliment. A provocative compliment."

Ottilie laughed quietly.

Beyond her, at the end of Walleye Street, the tall windows of the

Park and Pray glinted. I missed Mildred, as badly as if she were already gone forever from us. I cleared my throat and said, "Where will Matt stay now?"

John answered, "At the halfway house. He's going to need a lawyer, too, right away."

Ottilie opened her door and asked, "John, will you be okay?" I wondered if she meant for him to stay at her house, but John answered, "I'm going to keep busy. I'll be on the phone all night, scaring up lawyers."

We got out of the van. Ottilie leaned into John's window and pressed his hand, whispering something I could not catch.

When we entered the house, Ottilie picked up the telephone in the hallway, without removing her coat. She dialed information, asked for a name and number. I heard her sigh. Then she said, "Joel? I'm calling because—it's me." My father did not recognize her voice.

"It's Ottilie. Matt's in trouble. He's been arrested, he fought with the police, and he violated a restraining order, but the order was based on facts that were lies—

"He's your son!" Ottilie said. "You have to help him!" There was a pause, and then Ottilie shouted, "You're a monster! A monster!"

Ottilie looked at the receiver: my father had hung up on her, and her angry words had fallen into deafness.

JOHN CONTACTED a prosperous Chicago attorney with offices in Milwaukee, an old friend who had drawn up legal papers for the halfway house. He agreed to allow a young associate in his firm to take on Mildred's case pro bono, under his supervision; she was interested in legal claims involving the newly recognized battered wife syndrome, he said. John gave Mildred the law firm's number when she called him from a pay phone the next morning. John again insisted that Mildred come home, but she refused to linger and talk. "Daniel watches me all the time," she told him. "Ben's a wreck. He's here with me; he knows things are all wrong." John made Mildred promise to call him after she talked to the attorney. When she did, he told her he wanted to rent a hotel room near wherever Daniel was living, to keep an eye on her, but Mildred told her father frantically, "Please, don't. Please! You'll tip Daniel off. He'll get suspicious if he sees you."

John came to Ottilie's house the following morning, looking sick with worry. He wore jeans with his black minister's shirt, his minister's collar forgotten, and sat down at the kitchen table without touching the coffee I gave him.

"She thinks she can fool Daniel!" John told us. "She wants to stay with him for two weeks until he tears up the court papers, or lets the dates go by when the court orders expire. The lawyer told her that she should wait it out. The lawyer! Maybe this young associate is inexperienced and doesn't know the seriousness—"

"It's probably the right advice," I said. "If Daniel doesn't show up for the two court dates—the one for the restraining order and the one for the custody proceeding—the courts will probably dismiss his legal actions."

Ottilie fumbled with some pans under the stove. Finally she stopped and asked, "Would this young woman also represent Matt?"

John stood up and reached for Ottilie, saying, "I'm so sorry, I was so absorbed in my own—" Ottilie pulled away. "I should have told you already that I found Matt a good lawyer, David Vogelsang. He's from Madison, and knows the police there."

Ottilie flushed. "I'm sorry," she said. "All I can think about is how Matt looks sitting in that jail!"

"You thought I wouldn't remember Matt," John said quietly, placing his hand lightly on her arm.

Then he sat down, as if nothing had happened. He said, "Vogelsang and I are old cronies. He's semiretired from a general practice and was just about to head south for a winter vacation when I called him. We were in jail together during the Vietnam War. He helped Mildred get her job with *The Progressive*."

I thought Mr. Vogelsang might be a bad choice—a radical Madison lawyer would only ruffle a small-town judge. However, I did not say anything, because Ottilie seemed so relieved. She sat down across from John and took his hand. I stood back and let them talk, and when the hallway telephone rang, I left them alone in the kitchen.

"Melanie?" Mildred asked when I picked up the phone.

I was so surprised to hear her voice that I experienced a moment of confusion and answered, "No, it's not, it's—Mildred?" I told her, "Your dad just got here. I'll go get him."

"No, Melanie. I wanted to talk to you. I have to be fast. I've kept away from Daniel for over an hour. I don't know when I can get away again." She had called to ask about Matt, and I was moved. I tried to make light of the situation; she did not know the police had charged Matt with resisting and attacking them, and I chose not to tell her. I did not want to increase Daniel's control over Mildred by telling her that he also held my brother's life in the balance.

"I'm not going to let Daniel hurt Matt," Mildred said. "I'm going to be the perfect little wife for three weeks, and the second those legal papers expire, I'm heading home, and then I'm going to swear out a protective order against Daniel, to keep him away. Whatever he does to us, I'm going to do back to him," Mildred said. "Daniel got his protective orders just by filling out a bunch of papers! I didn't know it was that easy!"

"When you get back here, you can file a divorce complaint and petition for custody before the Muskellunge Family Court commissioner, and ask for a protective order then."

"You should be my attorney," Mildred said.

"There's a law library in the courthouse here, so I just looked up a few things," I said. "But I don't have a license to practice in Wisconsin. And anyway, I'd never do matrimonial law."

"Why not?"

"It's too sad."

After a short silence, Mildred answered, "Well, it's only two weeks until blastoff." There was another pause, and then she said, "Melanie, now that everyone knows Daniel's not—that he's not what he presented himself as, he's not even trying to seem like a nice guy. He's so afraid I'll leave him, he can't think of anything else. He acts like Ben's not even in the room, it's so weird—" She hurried off the phone, and hung up without finishing.

When I returned to the kitchen Ottilie and John were both wearing their coats. Ottilie told me, "We're going to talk with Matt." She pulled on a rabbit fur hat that blended into her own hair. I put on my parka and hooded my face without telling John and Ottilie about the phone call; I did not want to reveal how afraid I felt for Mildred.

It had snowed during the night. When John opened the kitchen door, a chill wind met us, and we walked slowly to avoid slipping on the icy road. White silhouettes of bushes lined the street and a ragged, solitary black butterfly passed over us, blown upward like a dark shawl, and settled on a mound of snow.

When we walked to the jail together, Hatch's followers were on the street corners, in the pet store and drugstore, and Shove's. "Do you remember that scary movie *The Birds* that Matt and you liked so much when you were little?" Ottilie asked. "They remind me of that part where all the blackbirds are flocked together on the ground, waiting for the people to come out—they look as if they'll attack us if we move too quickly."

John laughed and said, "Maybe they will."

"There must be an arraignment today," I said.

When we arrived inside the police station Matt was pacing the floor, frantic, as jittery now as he had been stunned the day before. He talked almost too quickly to understand, sat in his chair, and sprang up from it. He was distraught when John told him Mildred had left with Daniel. Matt grabbed his hair, covered his face with his arms, and moaned, "How could she do it? How could she?"

John took Matt by his wrists and sat him down on a folding chair. John did not let go; he grasped Matt's hands tightly, as if to keep him from sinking into himself.

"She thinks she knows what she's doing," John tried to console Matt. "She thinks if she stays with Daniel a little while, she can convince him to drop the custody suit."

"Tell her to come back!"

"She won't listen," John said. "Mildred won't leave Ben alone with Daniel. She told us to stay away. She wants to handle it." Reverend Steck's voice broke; he reassembled it. "A bright young woman lawyer in Milwaukee is helping her. Matt, we have to focus on getting you out of here right now. I've also hired you a good lawyer. He'll be here tomorrow, to discuss your arraignment."

"I'm going to Milwaukee," Matt said.

"You can't," I told him. I tried to explain that the restraining order barred him from seeing Ben, but Matt already understood its implications. He just didn't care about them.

"Why did she leave?" Matt hissed.

"She feels trapped," I told him.

"She is trapped," Ottilie said.

Ottilie's words hung in the air. Matt stood and looked out the square barred window of the room. A field of mud stretched from the courthouse to the horizon.

"Mildred should just run away," Matt answered.

MATT'S LAWYER, Vogelsang, arrived on Sunday evening. Ottilie answered the door, and men's voices chased one another around the living room and settled there. I heard, "There I was, standing in front of the Un-American Activities Committee, wondering where the hell young Reverend Steck had left our thermos of whiskey!" and a burst of laughter. And later, "the most capitalist commodity, marriage—" After this, a man's bass voice, insistent as a beehive's buzzing, vibrated without pause under the floorboards.

When I came downstairs Vogelsang was bending over the shelf where I had left my cross-referenced digest of insurance law. I was relieved that he at least did not look like a radical lawyer. He was in his late sixties, conservatively and even elegantly dressed. One of his hands was badly scarred from a burn. The hollows in his cheeks might have been dimples when he was a younger man; now they were long and curved and made me think of the f-holes in a fiddle.

He sat down, and his voice fell, bass, sonorous. "Lofty stuff," he said. I must have moved an eyebrow, because he explained, "Your work over there—lofty ACLU-type stuff."

When he failed to draw me out, Vogelsang turned toward John as if he did not want to bother me further, and pontificated in the way of radical lawyers: "Now, what Mildred's going through—being held prisoner in a marriage because of a man's threat to take her child— that's the dark underbelly of the law. Women will lose ground in the home long before they gain it in the workplace. Wisconsin has abolished the maternal preference in custody cases and replaced it with—what? With nothing but the absolute arbitrariness of unhampered legal process. For the next fifty years, women will be fighting desperately to keep their children from being taken from them by husbands who have better paid, more unscrupulous lawyers. If I were a young, feminist attorney, this is where I would concentrate—not on the lofty rulings of appellate courts, but in that sewer of the legal system, Family Court." He sipped from a cognac glass. It looked aflame, distorting in its curve a reflection of the fireplace.

I felt a desperation to absent myself from the room. I thought, suddenly, of the quarry pit in McCarthy where I had fled as a child. There had been copper in the soil, and the water that filled the pit was like a turquoise eye. I remembered the feeling of warm potatoes in my pockets, the surprise of being burned by the roasted skin.

As if to outwit my silence, Mr. Vogelsang looked away from me, and stared at the fire thoughtfully. The hearth's flames shone in his eyes, and flared brilliantly in the circle of his onyx ring when he gripped his knees.

"I wish this didactic old lawyer would shut up," he said. "I can't stand it when men try to tell me what's good for women. And I'd like to be left alone to continue my research. I'm trying to read every law review article ever written on insurance, from the first monks with their worldly annuities right through TIAA-CREF."

I laughed.

"So, are you going to second seat your brother's case with me?" Vogelsang asked. "Daniel's attorney has agreed to adjourn Matthew's TRO hearing, but the criminal charges will have to be dealt with immediately."

"What's been adjourned?" John asked.

"There are two things going on here, John," Vogelsang answered. "First there are criminal charges for resisting arrest and assaulting an officer stemming from Matt's alleged violation of the restraining order here in Muskellunge. Second, Matthew also has a right to be heard in civil proceedings in Milwaukee on whether the restraining order should have been issued in the first place. But Daniel's lawyer doesn't want the civil hearing—he could lose, and then his case against Mildred would weaken considerably. On the other hand, I don't want the hearing, because *I* might lose. Moreover, if we postpone it long enough, maybe Daniel will lose interest." Vogelsang looked at me as if waiting for confirmation, and then told me, "This was supposed to be my long winter vacation. I was going to Miami to bet on jai-alai. But I couldn't resist. I've been fighting on the losing side my whole life. That's one of the ways I can be sure I'm right."

"You think Matt's case is hopeless?" I asked, without hiding my irritation—if Vogelsang thought he would lose before he even began, he was a bad choice for a lawyer.

"Of course," Vogelsang answered with a courteous detachment. "If Matt goes to court on criminal charges here, he will certainly lose—an insane young man against a state police witness? But there's our strategy—we'll just make sure he never gets into court here." Before I could answer, Vogelsang peered behind me and said, "What the hell? This must be the doings of Reverend Hatch of Muskellunge."

I turned and saw a procession of people advancing up the road, carrying candles.

"You've heard that Mr. Hatch has asked your father to represent him?" Vogelsang asked me. "Mr. Hatch has decided to take all his cues from Worlfordt. I doubt Joel Ratleer will want to help Mr. Hatch—the publicity would be cumulative and redundant."

Hatch's followers passed the house, looking like carolers who had lost their way, eerily songless, their lights jostling one another and crossing like fireflies, or a current of stars.

THE WEATHER turned severe in early October: Canada geese broke the brittle air with their overhead honkings and stretched their masked faces southward. During the day Daniel rewrote his research at a desk in the small furnished apartment he had rented from a graduate student on leave from the University of Wisconsin. The apartment was above a store in a rundown neighborhood several miles from the university. There was no room for Ben, just an alcove where Mildred set up a child's cot. Daniel had not paid for phone service.

Mildred took Ben outdoors early in the mornings, so that she did not have to be in the same room with her husband, but it was too cold to walk outside for long. During her first two days Mildred took Ben to the indoor section of the Milwaukee zoo, to a children's matinee, and to a tour of the Budweiser beer factory. She visited a cathedral-sized basilica in Daniel's neighborhood, and let Ben run up and down the center aisle while she prayed that God would kill Daniel. She told me later that the basilica gave her a sense of confidence. She felt it showed God she was serious.

Mildred called her father from the basilica's pay phone. They had cut a deal: He would ask Mildred if she was safe or frightened, and if Ben was well, but he would not ask what it was like to share a home with Daniel, to eat across from him at the table, or where she slept at night. John wanted her to return home immediately. Mildred told her father that she never let Ben out of her sight and repeated that she planned to stay with Daniel until he "tore up the papers," or until he failed to show up for court proceedings.

What she did not tell us at the time was that, isolated from anyone who knew them, and obsessed with the thought that Mildred might leave him, Daniel had become more frightening. When Mildred went on walks, she would find him following her. He waited for her and Ben at the entrances outside the Milwaukee zoo, and the matinees. He sifted through her purse for telephone numbers and continually asked her whether she had talked to Matt or any other man, even her father. Daniel demanded that Mildred not call Muskellunge, telling her, "Your whole family's come between us for too long. I'm your family now." Daniel rarely played with Ben or spoke to him. Ben would not let him come near.

Matt had Ottilie send Ben things after he arrived in Milwaukee—a box containing a nest of robin's eggs, a kazoo, a magician's hat from a catalogue. Mildred wrote him not to. She called and told me that Daniel became irate when the presents arrived. He did not want Matt exercising "further insidious influence" against Ben and took the presents outside to a Dumpster before Ben ever saw them. "The weirdest thing," Mildred told me, "is that Daniel acts like he believes his own theatrics." She sounded as if she were crying when she said this, but then she laughed, and told me jokingly that she wished she had the starter's pistol with her. "I could fool him the way he has me," she said. "At least I could scare him."

After three days Mildred was able to arrange to meet in person with the attorney she had spoken to on the phone. Mildred enjoyed eluding Daniel by taking Ben into the lingerie section of a department store, and then climbing out a window in the women's bathroom adjoining the dressing rooms. However, when she arrived at the law firm, the associate who interviewed Mildred told her, "I'd never let a man call *me* a cunt. And if a man ever laid a hand on me, I'd divorce him the next day."

Mildred answered, "I didn't *let* him; he did it of his own accord. And I'm here because I'm trying to figure out how to get away from him without leaving my son behind."

Mildred was steaming when she left the lawyer's office. She called me from the basilica and said, "This lawyer told me that I'll have to explain why I stayed with Daniel—you have to show why a wife would have lived with a violent husband if he was so bad. Was she a battered child? Did she have a low opinion of herself? Did she develop some odd syndrome?" Mildred paused as if expecting me to answer.

"Well, that's a lot of crap," Mildred said. "The main problem people who are beat up have is the creeps who are beating them up. Why doesn't the law ask what's wrong with the creeps? This lady lawyer wanted to know if my mother was violent? Does this explain why I like being beat up? I told her, 'What makes you think I liked it, and leave my mother out of this. Daniel Munk doesn't get his orders from my mother's ghost, you know.' I just need to find out what holds Daniel Munk together, so that I'll be able to take him apart when I have to. Why's the law so full of pigshit, Melanie? Doesn't it worry you to be going back to some legal job where you have to stare at the law every living second?"

I wondered how Mildred maintained her equilibrium, cohabiting with Daniel and trying to keep clear-sighted about him at the same time. The stress she must have felt was unimaginable to me.

I asked Mildred what else the lawyer had said. Her attorney had advised her to watch Daniel all day on October 19 and 20, to see that he did not appear in court. If he did, Mildred should follow him and appear as well. If Daniel defaulted, the attorney would assure his actions were dismissed, and Mildred could return to Muskellunge and file for divorce and custody there. However, the associate was not willing to initiate legal proceedings in Muskellunge County. Mildred suspected that the lawyer was glad for an excuse to free herself of the case. "We didn't exactly hit it off," Mildred said. "Maybe I got too upset."

When I told Vogelsang about Mildred's interchange with the Milwaukee lawyer, he agreed to draft her divorce complaint, and petitions for custody of Ben, and a protective order. The custody petition was simple: it set forth in Vogelsang's courteous, restrained language that Mildred had always been Ben's primary caretaker, that Daniel had taken long absences from Ben during the marriage, and that Mildred would be able to prove that Daniel, because of his "tendency to violence and inability to observe accepted sexual boundaries between adults and children," would be "an imprudent choice as a custodial parent."

Vogelsang came to Ottilie's house in the morning and asked me for a second opinion after he had drawn up the papers. He made ceaseless small talk about the law, until I took the complaint and petitions. While I perused them, he read over my shoulder, mumbling aloud until he suddenly asked, "Am I irritating you?" Then he moved restlessly around Ottilie's living room, scavenging articles from the shelves, which he picked up from their usual places and absently deposited elsewhere. When I was finished, Vogelsang said, "Do I have you in my clutches now? Are you going to be my associate on Mildred's case as well as your brother's?"

I answered, "I've never been the type of female attorney who fastened herself onto mentors. I like working by myself." The words came out more angrily than I had intended, but I did not retract them.

"For God's sake, I'm not Joel Ratleer, I'm not going to eat you up," Vogelsang answered, sinking back into a chair and fastening me with that look of courteous detachment.

I sat for a while without answering. I reread a few paragraphs of the complaint and redlined a few sentences. I made a note to myself to look up some sections of Wisconsin's Annotated Statutes. Finally, I put down my pen and asked, "So, you've met my father?"

"He's known to just about everybody in the Wisconsin bar," Vogelsang answered. "We've crossed swords a couple of times."

"I see."

"If I were in jail, your father is the man I'd want for—" Vogelsang caught himself. "Of course, *you* will accompany me this morning to the police station to speak with Chief Komar about your brother."

"Right now?" I asked.

"I'd like a ride. I froze walking over here."

Vogelsang buttoned his coat and waited for me to offer to drive him to the station. As we walked to my car, grass broke under our steps, and Vogelsang's voice rose in smoky curls in front of us. "I always feel like a pupating insect when I ride in one of these VW Beetles. What will I have turned into by the time I step back onto the street? A giant metamorphosed beetle? Or worse yet, a giant lawyer? 'One morning, Gregor Samsa awoke to find that he had transformed into a giant lawyer.'"

As I drove to the station, we saw Hatch's followers everywhere: They stood along Walleye Street, wearing black armbands, and passing out pink pamphlets; they gathered outside the pet store; they huddled in the entryway of the bridal apparel shop; they blocked the doors of the pharmacy.

"I see the occupation army is hungry," Vogelsang said.

Along the road, signs had been posted at twenty-yard intervals, like a low fence, each bearing the same slogan: ABORTIONISTS LIE TO WOMEN FOR MONEY.

"Catchy," Vogelsang said.

A truck carrying caged chickens skidded around a corner in front of the Volkswagen and almost fell over. A flurry of white feathers settled on the road. Vogelsang caught the dashboard as if in sympathy with the chickens. When the truck regained its balance, he let go of the dashboard and said, "Melanie, you're a vivid conversationalist." I did not answer. "I've never felt comfortable with people who don't talk. I myself can't think clearly with my mouth closed."

I parked at Shove's. When I stopped inside for a coffee and newspaper, the counters were past overflowing with Hatch's followers. Vogelsang handed me a copy of the *Muskellunge Eagle* with a headline announcing that Hatch sympathizers were sleeping in the Walleye Church's pews. The front page featured a large photograph of Hatch, looking deliriously happy, standing with his hands raised in front of a packed church. (Underneath him, a smaller headline ran, "Tour Guide Continues Lone Search to Solve Mystery of Pferd Percheron Drunkenness." Under this were two short paragraphs in which Pferd's tour guide avowed that he had been "personally upset by the evening's events and the horses' escape," and had found "evidence of breaking and entry into a padlocked storeroom where Pferd by-products are kept.")

We walked to the jail. A police dog suffering from the cold came up to Vogelsang growling and shivering. Vogelsang stepped away and said, "Police dogs never act like dogs. And cold dogs always look unnatural to me. A dog should be lying puffing on a hot dirt road."

Chief Komar stood on the jail's front steps wearing a khaki hunting jacket over his uniform. The fur of an unidentifiable animal rimmed his hood.

"You here for Hatch?" Chief Komar asked menacingly.

Vogelsang said, "No, I'm here to chat about Matthew Ratleer."

Chief Komar looked relieved. He led us into a back office, where he sat down at his desk without removing his furred jacket.

Vogelsang slipped out of his coat. The suit underneath was impeccable, gray with an illusion of pinstripe. He opened his briefcase, set it on the desk, sat down beside me, and said, "You know why I'm here. I want to lessen the court's load by getting the charges against this girl's brother dropped."

"I don't care about the court," Komar answered. "I just run the jail."

"You know the temporary restraining order that led to Matt's arrest never should have been issued."

"You tell me why," Komar answered.

"Reverend Steck was in here complaining about that son-in-law days before he took out the TRO."

"That's the same one?" Komar asked. "The boy who likes to beat up on his wife and kid? I called the police in his hometown, Ripon. They hadn't seen him."

"Well, I can tell you now, it would have been better if he'd remained unfound," Vogelsang said.

Becoming animated for the first time since our entrance, Komar continued irrelevantly, "That Mr. Munk's family comes from Green Giant money. His family used to own everything down there."

"You don't say," Vogelsang answered. He acted as if he were writing down this information, but when I glanced at his legal pad, it said, "Sousa, Sousa, Sousa!"

"Mr. Munk's family sold out to Green Giant and then tried to buy up every farm between Ripon and Oshkosh, how do you like that? Now they're out of agriculture—they're all dead!"

"Ah," Vogelsang said.

Komar walked to a small window in the office and peered into the muddy field behind the station, as if something might be hidden there. "When I was little," he said, "my granddad owned this land. From right here, to there." He tilted his chin slightly toward a bright thread of horizon that seemed to separate the very sky from our world. "Now an agribusiness and some bank own all this. Everything you can see." He spread his arms wide, a look of feigned incredulity on his face. "And all I have is this teeny little badge." Komar lifted the tin shield on his parka, with mock admiration. "You know what this is?" he asked. "It's the law. Do you know what the law is? I'm the law."

"So you are," Vogelsang said amiably.

The conversation that followed left me in the dark.

"Matt's situation sounds a hell of a lot like the Sousa case, doesn't it?" Vogelsang asked. He even seemed polite when he swore.

Komar narrowed his eyes, and answered, "I don't see it."

"Why did one of those state troopers yell 'Man gone berserk!' at Matt? It's a strange thing for an officer to say about a boy who's just standing watching a parade." Vogelsang lowered his voice and said, "It would be pretty embarrassing for those state police if—"

"I'll tell you when they're embarrassed," Komar said.

"Then there's that choke hold. What made them use that particular choke hold?"

"What choke hold? Who'd you talk to?"

Vogelsang rustled the stack of papers in his hand and examined them as if the answer lay there: They looked like affidavits. But when I leaned forward, I saw that they had nothing to do with Matt—they were pages from the will of some other client of Vogelsang's.

"And there's no evidence Matt ever saw the TRO before they assaulted him for violating it—he says they never showed it to him. You don't think they made the mistake of assuming that because he was crazy, he just wouldn't understand legal process?"

"Who told them he was crazy?" Komar answered.

"Anyone can tell from a mile off that *Joel Ratleer's* son is psychotic," Vogelsang answered.

I did not understand the emphasis on my father's name, but it had some significance to Chief Komar, because he whistled, and then looked at me as if sizing me up. "That boy is *Joel* Ratleer's?"

Vogelsang smiled.

"Worlfordt's Ratleer? Sousa's Ratleer?"

"It makes these charges look more than a little vindictive—"

"Those officers had no idea—"

"Sure they didn't. They didn't know Matt Ratleer was crazy, even though the underlying affidavit stapled to the TRO said he was psychotic. They showed him the TRO and talked nice to him. The name on the paper, 'Ratleer,' didn't ring any bells." Vogelsang also leaned back in his chair and lowered his voice a little. *"Ratleer?"* he asked. "How many Ratleers do you know?"

Chief Komar held up his hands and said, "I take the Fifth. I have nothing more to say. Nothing at all."

"I'll get back in touch with you day after tomorrow," Vogelsang said, rising. He extended his hand, but Komar merely looked down at it. He studied my face, shook his head, and laughed.

As we exited the police station, Vogelsang said, "I'm hungry. Let me take you out to dinner." He did not explain what had transpired in Komar's office.

As I drove him outside of town to Musky's, Vogelsang regaled me with a lively and sardonic summary of custody law. "Just last year, one of the most respected appellate courts in the country addressed the question of whether a man's murder of his wife rendered him an unfit custodial parent. The court held that depriving a convicted murderer of his children would be detrimental to *them*. The court forced them to leave their maternal grandparents and live with their father after he was paroled, and then—What on earth? Is that to attract customers, or frighten away all but the brave?" Musky's yellow neon fish towered over us. After I parked, Vogelsang walked directly under the sign and stared up at it. "Absolutely bizarre," he said. "It looks custom-made. Wisconsin is one of the strangest lands on earth."

When we entered the restaurant Vogelsang stooped in front of the fish tank and peered at Musky Senior. "My God!" he told the head waitress. "Do they feed him to the customers, or the customers to him?"

Vogelsang seated himself, read his menu, and said, "Flounders always give me the same uncomfortable sensation you feel when someone runs his fingernails over a blackboard. The idea of having both eyes set on the bottom of your face, scraping along a rocky lake bed—"

"Their eyes are on top," I said.

"Their eyes are on top?" Vogelsang asked. "Then how do they see their food?" He studied his menu a little longer and ordered rainbow trout. After sitting quietly for a period, he smiled, leaned back, and said, "You're dying to ask me what happened with Chief Komar, but you won't ask! You are absolutely the most paralyzed young attorney I've ever met."

"Okay," I answered. "Who's Sousa?"

"Sousa was a psychotic man who lived in public housing in Milwaukee," Vogelsang answered delightedly. "The police got a disorderly person call from one of Sousa's neighbors, who described him as 'a crazy old nut.' Seven officers arrived at the scene, on what police radio tapes termed a 'man-gone-berserk call.' The police broke down the door and scared Sousa to death. He was sixty-eight years old. He had been watching television at high volume, disturbing his neighbors, and he was still watching it when the police arrived. He explained that the television had been conversing with him, warning him of an imminent attack by the Vietnamese. When the police interrupted, Sousa ran to the kitchen and pulled out a baseball bat. One of the officers got him in an illegal choke hold and broke his arms and collarbone. The other one used a nightstick. By the time Sousa arrived at the hospital, four of his ribs were cracked and they had shattered every bone in his right hand. He lost his hand. Of course they charged him with resisting arrest and assaulting an officer. It was in all the papers for months, a few years ago. The officers involved lost their jobs, there was a big shakedown in the police department, big civil rights lawsuit later. Sousa ended up a rich man. A psychotic rich man with one hand. Police procedure changed— after that, when they trumped up charges of resisting arrest or battery to an officer after an incident of police brutality, they were careful to invent an underlying charge for the arrest too: resisting arrest *and* gun possession, battering an officer *and* drinking in public."

"I didn't hear about it," I said.

"You must have been buried in some appellate clerkship," Vogelsang answered. "Maybe you were debating the fine points of search and seizure law? Pondering provocative legal questions like, 'If a German shepherd, trained to sniff out drugs for narcotics officers, snuffles a sealed cardboard box in an airport and smells hashish, does he have probable cause to tear open the box?'"

When the waitress brought our dinner, Vogelsang thanked her graciously and said, "I worried that Musky had eaten you." He studied his supper, a rainbow trout buried in parsley, and said, "I wish they would remove the eyes. I can't stand to be stared at by my dinner." He continued, "Your father convinced the jury that 'man gone berserk' was the police code alert for a call to subdue a psychotic person, and that it meant, essentially: you can do whatever you want to this guy because he's too crazy to defend himself. Joel Ratleer had a heyday with the case. His first press release went something like: 'It's a damn shame we're going to have to triple the size of the police force, because Milwaukee needs five officers to wrestle a sixty-eight-year-old psychotic man to the ground.' This was right in the middle of negotiations between the city and police department about increased hiring."

"Well," I said.

"You eat fish without lemon or butter?" Vogelsang stared at my plate. "A telling detail. In my youth I worked with a secretary from Utah who wouldn't eat any kind of fish because she thought it was too exotic. She only ate what she called 'American food,' and for some reason she didn't consider fish American." He continued, "Joel Ratleer became celebrated, briefly, as a champion of the rights of the mentally disabled. When I saw him on another case at the time, he whispered in my ear, 'Every place I go, I get followed by loonies who think I'm one of them. Sousa is a mean, crazy son of a bitch who'd beat in your grandmother's head with a baseball bat just for the hell of it.'

"Imagine," Vogelsang said, "if five years later the police trumped up a false charge against Joel Ratleer's mentally disabled son out of vindictiveness, yelled at him that he was a 'man gone berserk,' and did the same illegal choke hold on him."

"That's not what happened," I answered.

"No," Vogelsang said. "What really happened is that a man named

Mr. Munk, a divinity student, trumped up charges against an insane man, Matt Ratleer. Why? Because Mr. Munk thinks it will hurt his wife, and he likes to hurt her? Matt Ratleer, on the other hand, is a gentle soul—psychotic but gentle—and as proof of his proclivity for nonviolence we have the fact that after he was arrested once before in Chicago for battering an officer, those charges were reduced to disorderly conduct on the condition that he receive psychiatric care."

I did not answer.

"A jury would have to know a hell of a lot about life to believe that one." Vogelsang mashed his baked potato: He sprinkled it with what seemed like half a pepper shaker, and then added four pats of butter, sour cream, and all of his parsley.

When he had finished, I said, "You could waive your right to a jury and ask for a judge trial."

"A bench trial!" Vogelsang guffawed. "That would be worse! Melanie, the face that leans over the bench, swaddled in black rayon, is not Solomon's. It's a *lawyer's*. A lawyer dressed up in a black costume. And what kind of judge would we get? How much will he know about people? Is he stupid? Prejudiced? Does he lack imagination? Failure of imagination is the heart of the law. There's a much better chance that someone on a jury would have met a Daniel Munk before, or that at least one juror would believe in the infinite possibilities of the human character. But a judge!"

"And you're going to solve this problem," I said, "by committing perjury." I confirmed then to myself what I had long suspected—that I was the only honest lawyer I had ever met.

Vogelsang dropped his fork, gave me an assaying look, sighed dramatically, and said, "It will never go to court, so it's not perjury. It's just plain *lying*. I'll tell you the whole truth now, Melanie Ratleer: Matt loves Ben. Ben was scared. Matt tried to protect him. Valiantly and fiercely. Matt couldn't let the police make the mistake of handing Ben over to a man who would hurt him. And Daniel Munk sought the protective order against your brother in order to send him down the path of his own destruction, because that's what men like Daniel Munk do. Look behind Daniel and you'll see that everyone whose life he's brushed against has been injured irreparably, in some way, great or small. And here's the rest of the truth: If Matt's convicted, he'll probably go to jail for a while. He may or may not survive prison—he will certainly suffer the greatest miseries life can devise there. And Daniel: Daniel will get his temporary restraining order made permanent. If the custody battle continues, Daniel will use Matt's conviction and that order to prove Mildred's a bad mother, and perhaps, to succeed in getting custody of Ben. Then Daniel can chuckle over his victory, and hurt Ben and Mildred until Ben is grown. If Ben makes it that far whole. Because a child raised by Daniel Munk probably would not end up whole."

"So," I said, "you see it as your personal mission to initiate me into the corruption of my profession."

"I've got a better idea. Let's let Daniel Munk sell his lie to the court. Daniel's lie will shape our world, but at least our bright little truth will sit safe with us in a dark bag."

"There must be a better way," I said.

Vogelsang glared at me until I felt like a witness under cross-examination. "We're lucky we have any way at all, Melanie. I'm not interested in convincing a Muskellunge judge to believe the truth. I just want to keep Matt out of jail, and to make sure Mildred doesn't lose Ben. *Your* job is to see what's true, to know when we're lying, and to know when the truth, no matter how it's uttered, will never be believed. To keep your eyes open. To see everything."

"I was born with my eyes open," I said, annoyed.

"Good, because you're going to need that kind of clarity of vision to deal with Daniel Munk."

I felt my face redden.

Vogelsang picked up a dessert menu and said, "Baked Alaska. I haven't seen it on a menu in years. Do you think Baked Alaska is exotic, or one hundred percent American? When I was young, it was always on the menu. When I was released from prisoner-of-war camp after World War II, I and a man I had met there named Gustave dined at a restaurant in France owned by an American expatriate, where we ordered Baked Alaska and cognac and argued politics. He believed civilization had ended with the death of Napoleon, and I did not. By our fourth cognac, we were agreeing with each other. I loved France the whole time I was there, but afterward, I wondered if this was because Gustave and I drank cognac the entire month I traveled in France. Perhaps, for me, it turned an entire country into something it was not." Vogelsang ordered us both Baked Alaska and cognac.

After the desserts arrived I said, "Your plan could backfire. The police might double their efforts to go after Matt, when they find out

he's the son of the Joel Ratleer who's defending Worlfordt and his followers."

"Yes, it could," Vogelsang answered, "but it probably won't. Worlfordt's just a pain in the ass. Joel Ratleer would cause them a world of
trouble if they went after him." Vogelsang put down his fork and said,
"Do you want to just forget everything, Melanie? You don't have to
work with me on this case."

I hesitated. "Yes," I said. "I'd like to be anywhere else right now.
And I'd like to be anyone at all, other than Joel Ratleer's daughter."

"But you will work with me?"

The invitation seemed so personal. Listening to Vogelsang's charming, low, grumbling voice, I could not turn him down. "I don't have
much choice," I said.

Vogelsang answered, "If that cognac affects you that quickly, you
are probably the kind of person who shouldn't drink at all, or the kind
who should drink all the time. Maybe liquor is too much of a relief for
someone who's so tightly wound. Do you think you'll wake up to regret
this decision?"

"I already do," I told him.

Four days later Chief Komar called the house to say that although
the temporary restraining order was still in force, the state police had
withdrawn criminal charges and Matt had been released.

THE FOLLOWING WEEK Matt stayed in his room in the halfway
house, only coming out for meals, talking to no one. When I visited, he
played chess or checkers with me silently. He did not want to talk about
Mildred. On October 16 I called and invited him to Shove's for lunch,
but he declined. On October 18 I received a letter from Matt by mail,
which had taken two days to traverse Muskellunge. The letter was addressed correctly, but instead of a stamp, Matt had drawn a picture of a
stamp, and the envelope arrived postage due. Matt's message was as
disoriented as his first letters to me had been, in the worst years of his
illness. His anxiety about being in jail, or the effects of his forced separation from Mildred, had plunged him deep into the lonely whirling of
his own thoughts:

*Dear Melanie, why do you call instead of coming in person? It is beginning
to happen again, when I look from my window, blues and yellows seep*

away and I see in green and red, and the lines will not stay straight, pathways are wide at the openings but lead to pointy closed ends. They are triangular. And everything, always, smelling like stinkbugs. Although others may believe they can look through the holes in my head, I see better out of them, and I can see right back, and I have no choice anyway, they all drag me like nets with their colossal who-they-ares. Picture it: Daniel on the left, and after him Mildred (he is much much bigger, and she is in danger!), and then Reverend Steck in the middle and then Ottilie, and you are either beside her, or somewhere near Daniel, depending on who you are deciding to be—a human being or a lawyer. And then Ben, way off to the right, and I am not in the lineup at all, because I am Ratleer depending on what net I am in, but sometimes really just a slippery little Fisch-pez-fishy wending my way down the river. Too small to eat, so throw it back in! But I like seeing Mildred best. And that is why I am here, watching all of you people my trembling places. Don't step on my small fears! You must help Ben! I send this as a warning, and out of love. Your beloved brother, and as you know, only up the road—

The letter ended in midsentence.

I walked to the halfway house that evening, but when I arrived, Matt was already asleep in his room. Above his bed, he had tacked an incongruous triptych: a magazine reprint of Brueghel's *Massacre of the Innocents* taped neatly to a bookplate of Dürer's *Great Clump of Turf,* taped in turn to a crayon picture drawn by Ben. On the left, mothers wailed as soldiers speared infants before the stony figure of a bored captain; in the center, dandelions and seed-laden grass sprang vigorously, unharmed by the tumult beside them; to their right, a fiery tornado of red crayon swirled upward with wild and lively joy.

I found John downstairs in the halfway house, and he told me that Matt had come to the office in the back of the church earlier that day and asked for Mildred's address and a map of Milwaukee. Matt was agitated, and John had difficulty calming him: Matt predicted a disaster on the twentieth. He had heard John and Ottilie discussing Mildred's court date in hushed whispers. Matt told him, "The twentieth is a bad day. The numbers and whispers are all wrong." Eventually John believed that he had convinced Matt to sit tight, to avoid violating the restraining order, and to stay away from Mildred and Daniel, because this was what Mildred wanted.

However, after I left the halfway house, Matt disappeared from his room. He must have been pretending to sleep when I visited him. He hitched a ride to the Manitowoc bus station (he had no driver's license; the state would not issue one to a schizophrenic). From there he took a Greyhound to Milwaukee.

I can imagine my brother boarding that bus, as passengers turn to look at him in his not-quite-right clothes, his flannel shirt buttoned wrong, the scowl on his face unconnected to any manifestation in the physical world around him. His hair is dishevelled, his beard a new stubble. He sits down in a window seat and exclaims something to himself. The woman in the seat next to him rises and moves farther back in the bus. He is on his way to find Ben and Mildred. Matt is going to save them, wrap them in his arms, carry them home. He travels in cold darkness, wearing familiar sorrow like an old sweater, the woolliness of anxiety and despair cloaking him. He is afraid and exhilarated.

In Milwaukee it took Matt three hours to find a taxi willing to ferry him: He looked too large, too disoriented, for most of the drivers to risk him as a fare. When he arrived in Mildred's neighborhood he waited a full day in the cold alcove of a closed store beside her building, stomping his feet and clapping his hands, and attracting the stares of passersby. Once around three-thirty in the afternoon, Daniel passed Matt as he stood there, but Daniel did not see him. He was following Mildred, who had walked with Ben to the basilica's pay phone to call her attorney, who told her that the custody proceeding that had been scheduled for October 19 had been dismissed. Matt trailed them at a careful distance.

When Daniel found Mildred at the phone, he became angry, and accused her of calling her father. Daniel yelled, "I'm your husband! He's not!" and held Mildred in an argument for thirty minutes. Just as Matt decided to intervene in the argument, Mildred seemed to make up with Daniel. She kissed him and took his arm, and they went out to lunch at a local cafe, while Matt watched them through the window. At five o'clock they left, holding hands like young lovers. And during those hours, the County Court dismissed Daniel's restraining order, and Daniel lost his last legal hold on her. Daniel's lawyer did not appear in either Family or County Court—Daniel must have been so confident of his power to win Mildred back, that he had not paid for further legal services.

Matt slept on the basilica's floor, until a night watchman threw him out. The following morning Matt watched Daniel leave the apartment, carrying books. Matt followed Daniel to a store, and watched him catch a bus. Then Matt returned to Mildred's building, and rang her apartment's bell. He was so relieved when Mildred opened the door that he cried out. He was a godsend, Mildred said. He carried Ben and half her luggage to the Cadillac. Mildred called her lawyer again from the basilica, to confirm that Daniel's protective order had expired. Then, according to Mildred, she and Ben and Matt "lit out of there, like three bats out of hell."

When they arrived in Muskellunge they were in a high state of excitement, as if they had both been paroled. The Cadillac pulled into Ottilie's driveway, honking, and I rushed out to greet them. "Checkmate," Mildred told me. "Checkmate."

4

THE MORNING AFTER Mildred and Ben returned to us, Vogelsang filed divorce papers before the Muskellunge County Family Court commissioner. When Daniel did not appear in court two weeks later to contest the papers, the commissioner granted Mildred's request to have Ben placed with her while the divorce was pending, as well as her request for a protective order against Daniel. We all felt a little giddy with triumph when Vogelsang returned to Madison, so that when he rang Ottilie's doorbell only three days later, I opened the door and looked at him with a sense of shock, as if he had come from much farther away than the state's capital.

After Vogelsang apprised me of new turns in Mildred's case, I accompanied him to Mildred's house, already feeling that I was no longer a friend to her or Matt, but instead, one of the law's grim harbingers. Vogelsang's black winter coat flapped in the icy wind like a malignant omen, and I walked in his boot prints through the snow, my dark coat also fluttering. When we knocked on the Stecks' door, I already believed that as the law took hold of our lives, it would isolate Matt from Ben and Mildred; that it would change Mildred's motherhood, so that she would weigh every action she took and had ever taken in light of whether it could separate her and Ben; that she would have to use her own son as a pawn in order to protect him.

No one answered our knocking, and so Vogelsang and I entered the Stecks' living room uninvited. We heard Mildred's voice at the back of the house, and then Ben's and Matt's, and then laughter. We found Rockefeller in the kitchen, mixing pancake batter. The remnants of a pancake breakfast were on the table, and several jars of peanut butter stood at its center.

"Smooth it on like this." Mildred's voice echoed inside the tiled walls of a bathroom adjoining the kitchen. Matt's laugh followed. When I opened the bathroom door I found Mildred, Ben, Matt, and Dmytryk standing in front of a long mirror, slathering peanut butter on their faces, and pretending to shave with plastic rulers.

When Mildred saw me in the mirror she said, "I'm in disguise." Peanut butter covered her cheeks and upper lip.

"Melanie!" Ben said. "I have a goat!"

"A goatee," Mildred told him. She explained to me, "It works because it's creamy, but you have to water it down."

"We're teaching Ben to shave," Matt said in that sane, humorous voice he used in Mildred's presence.

Dmytryk, a bottle of dandelion wine in his left hand, was shaving with his right; he turned to show me a peanut butter beard. Beside him, Matt grinned; a pencil moustache, exactly like Dmytryk's, rimmed Matt's lip.

Matt looked into a corner of the mirror, at something outside my field of vision. He saw Vogelsang, and stopped smiling. Then, without turning around, Matt reached behind him for the bathroom door and slammed it closed.

"Matt!" Mildred said. "Let her in."

I stood outside, uncertain what to do. It seemed ridiculous to knock on the door of a bathroom that already harbored four people. I felt a tug on my sleeve, a small hand scurrying to open mine; Rockefeller deposited a warm pancake there, wrapped in a napkin.

"It's bad news. It must be bad news," I heard Matt say.

Mildred opened the door. She and the others had wiped their faces, and now they stared at us.

"Mildred, Matt's right," Vogelsang said. "I'm here to discuss all kinds of bad news."

Matt carried Ben upstairs, shielding him from us.

As soon as I joined Mildred in the living room, Vogelsang said, "Daniel has fired the attorney who was representing him in Milwaukee and has hired a well-known Chicago lawyer, Gordon Trippler. They've appealed the Family Court commissioner's rulings to Muskellunge County Court."

"At least I have him in my own territory now," Mildred said, sitting down on the sofa and spreading her arms.

Vogelsang folded his coat over the back of a chair: The fabric was glossy and made me think of cricket wings. His face took on a lawyerly expression, and he said, "Trippler will also be representing Daniel in a hearing on whether the temporary restraining order against Matt should be continued permanently. I had hoped Daniel would default on the order's adjournment date. Now we'll have to contest that order. Naturally, we'll seek to dismiss. From now on, you can't imperil Matt or yourself by violating the TRO. You have to keep Ben away from Matt."

"That's outrageous," Mildred answered. Everything we had come to tell her would take away her gaiety bit by bit, until, by the end of our talk, Mildred would be quiet and grave.

"Mildred," Vogelsang said. "What this appeal means is that Daniel is renewing his efforts to get custody of Ben. He wants a full hearing in County Court to determine whether Ben should live with him permanently. And until the court finds time to hold a hearing, Daniel's asking that it reverse the decision about where Ben should live in the meantime. For several reasons, I don't think the judge assigned to the case will tamper with the commissioner's temporary custody ruling. However, even if that ruling is affirmed, Daniel will continue to use Matt to help his standing in his suit for permanent custody. If you encourage Matt to violate the TRO, Trippler will use it as grounds for proving your unfitness as a mother."

Mildred asked, "And what happens to Matt?"

Trippler has requested a second and longer adjournment of Matt's TRO hearing, and I've agreed to it. Neither of us wants to litigate the charges against Matt, for the same reasons that led to the first adjournment. I'm hoping that if we wait, we may be able to force dismissal of the TRO as a condition of a divorce settlement. But right now, Trippler is just betting on the fact that you two will collude to violate the TRO. Do you understand?"

Mildred answered, "If I consent to Ben's being with Matt, doesn't that make it legal? Doesn't it prove he's not dangerous? If he's around Ben and doesn't hurt him—"

"What if Ben *does* get hurt again?" Vogelsang said. "In that case, you'll want to be able to show that Daniel is the only other person who has access to Ben when you're not with him."

"What do you mean?" Mildred asked. She looked at me, confused, and then she stood up and shouted, "How will Daniel get access to Ben? I thought you said Ben will be staying with me!"

"Daniel's entitled to visitation while the divorce is pending, Mildred. You need to prepare for that. I'll try to see if the court will order visitation to be supervised by a social worker, but—"

"The court will make Ben visit Daniel? I never leave him alone with Daniel now!" Mildred's face settled in a mask of anguish. "It's impossible! It's impossible!"

I almost stood and took her hand and said something consoling, but I could not: I felt arrested by my understanding that we, Mildred's lawyers, did not represent her in any real sense, or empower her at all. We were simply there to guide her down into the dark windings of the law, where she would relinquish all control over the battle she had set herself to win single-handedly.

Vogelsang waited for Mildred to sit down before he continued. "Daniel is also appealing the commissioner's decision on the temporary restraining order that enjoins Daniel from coming near you or Ben. That's the rest of my bad news. Your case has been assigned to Judge Bracken, and he's fairly conservative. He may reverse that order because he'll think it's the result of a ploy to further your interests in a custody battle."

"The judge will assume I'm lying?"

Vogelsang said, "It's possible that he won't be willing to believe at this juncture that you're telling the truth."

"I think I can get this lady in Milwaukee to be a witness for me. She'd testify that Daniel socked me in the stomach."

"Daniel hit you again?" I asked her.

Vogelsang answered quietly, "You should be prepared for the probability that the court won't consider evidence of Daniel's violence against you in determining whether he can visit with Ben. A judge of Bracken's generation will just see that as a problem between you and Daniel."

Mildred glared at Vogelsang as if he were her enemy. "The judge will think it's good for little kids to see their mothers get hit? Or that a man who can't keep his temper with his wife can keep it around a three-year-old? Which is it?"

"I'm sorry, Mildred," Vogelsang answered. "The law in this area has been idiotic for as long as I can remember."

We all sat quietly for a moment, pondering Vogelsang's statement. Vogelsang rose and walked restlessly around the room. He leaned his forehead against the front window and said, "Can you see that big neon fish from anywhere in Muskellunge? Imagine if you were from Jupiter, and your spaceship landed here. That sign would be the first place you would go. You would immediately identify it as the most significant thing on the horizon. You would assume it was a headquarters of some king, the throne of the King of Earth, or the king himself. You would probably spend days, weeks, trying to get it to communicate with you. You'd never even guess that something called *the law* existed: an invisible force that wreaks havoc with ordinary human lives, secretly destroying what it openly purports to assist. It's a comforting thought that an alien people might never be able to understand quite what lawyers are—"

Mildred finally laughed.

Vogelsang sat down. "Where was I? I was going to talk about getting a guardian. We can ask the court to appoint a guardian *ad litem* to represent Ben in court—the Wisconsin Supreme Court is requiring guardians more and more frequently in custody cases. A guardian might ask for supervised visitation, since his sole aim would be to represent Ben. And we do have evidence that Daniel has hurt Ben, which will be admissible. We have the fact that your father and Ottilie saw those bruises, and there's Mrs. Shove's testimony; it's a ghoulish aspect of the law that you're now to consider the existence of such evidence a good thing. You must focus in the meantime on the fact that you have temporary custody. Bracken's likely to think children of tender years belong with their mothers, even though Wisconsin law has eliminated a presumption in favor of mothers in custody cases. And Bracken's likely to believe that fathers don't know how to care for children. We'll just count on one prejudice cancelling out another. If he affirms the commissioner's temporary custody ruling, Bracken can't change that before the final custody determination without a hearing. And the longer Ben stays with you pending the case's resolution, the more likely it is that the judge will adopt the status quo in the end."

Mildred tugged her braid nervously; its amber filaments broke between her fingers. "Ben won't understand why Matt can't see him anymore," she said quietly.

"You could tell him Matt has chicken pox," I offered.

"Chicken pox?" Vogelsang asked.

"Yeah, that might work," Mildred answered.

"And maybe," I ventured, "we can set the judge up somehow. Maybe we can bait Daniel's lawyer into saying something about Daniel that we know isn't true. Then we can reveal that Daniel's lied to the court, and even to his lawyer. The judge will feel hoodwinked by Daniel, just like we all did. Then the judge will begin to understand how Mildred has felt, and he'll take it out on Daniel."

Vogelsang drew back in his chair and studied me. "Melanie, you're talking about intentionally leading Trippler into making fraudulent representations to the court about his client."

Mildred smiled. But her smile was fleeting.

"That's right," I said. "It's well within the Code of Legal Ethics."

"Ah, 'legal ethics,'" Vogelsang answered. "One of the great oxymorons of the English language."

Mildred stood and said, "I want to be the one who breaks the news to Matt, all right?" Without waiting for an answer she bolted upstairs, as if she could not bear our company any longer.

Vogelsang and I sat uncomfortably on the couch as Matt's and Mildred's voices commingled above us. They talked until we realized that there was nothing left for us to do but leave. Then Vogelsang and I crawled back into our coats and headed into the cold. We took the back door and walked through the garden, where the snow humped over buried flower beds. The wind sang and rattled in my hood like a locust. (I remembered Dr. Eatman informing me what insects did in the winter in Wisconsin: "This climate is too chilling even for beetles. They crawl down into the dark places and cling to the sides of houses and the bottoms of rocks until the world makes sense again.")

I don't know what Mildred told Matt, but she must have used the right words, because Matt honored her request without self-pity, and the disequilibrium that had possessed him before he left for Milwaukee became less marked. Perhaps Matt's success in retrieving Mildred from Milwaukee had left him with an enduring sense of triumph. He reacted creatively to our bad news, and delighted in technically obeying the letter of the order while subverting its spirit. He kept away from Ben but found a dozen ways to affirm the ties between them. Matt repainted Mildred's car in its old colors, and he left secret messages in the glove compartment for Ben, instructing Mildred where to find treats Matt concocted with Rockefeller's assistance: chocolates, imbedded like insects in amber in a sheet of ice clinging to an oak; snowballs flavored with maple syrup; Popsicles lining the Stecks' walk in a colored picket fence. Matt missed going out with Ben on Halloween, and every day for two weeks thereafter, my brother deposited a present for Ben on Reverend Steck's desk, and the presents were so outlandish (a baby hognose snake, a set of vampire teeth, a wolf tail attached to a leather belt) that Ben might have enjoyed the weeks before the custody proceedings and their sudden unravelling, were it not for the frightening intrusions of the legal case on his life.

ON THE NIGHT before our first court appearance in front of Judge Bracken, I dreamed I was a spectator at a trial in which my father represented the defense. He stood before the bench, and announced something in a foreign language, causing a flurry of commentary. I asked a woman seated to my left what had happened. Translating from the common language of the courtroom, she explained, with a pronounced accent, that the defense attorney had stated that he was not really himself: He was Melanie Ratleer. I protested this interpretation in a frantic whisper, but the woman smiled with a knowing look, opened a brocade handbag lined with green satin, and pointed inside to what I knew was conclusive evidence of my self-deception: It was Mildred's derby hat, but shrunken to the size of a robin's nest. Inside it were the red roe of a lake fish. To my horror, I told the woman that I wanted to eat the eggs. Before she could respond, I found myself standing in front of the jurors, and now I laughed to discover that I was Joel Ratleer. My huge chest expanded, my voice sailed toward the witness stand, and although I knew that my arguments were wrong—twisted and illogical and underhanded—I enjoyed them because of this. I felt intoxicated and omnipotent.

The following morning as I entered Bracken's courtroom, the dream clung to me and increased my sense that my father's spirit haunted any involvement I might have in legal affairs in any state where he practiced. Daniel sat at a table in the front of the courtroom, dressed in the same business suit he had worn the day he served Mildred with papers. He carried a briefcase and looked like a lawyer. When Mildred saw Daniel, her expression communicated pure fury: her face was always like that, open as a book. Daniel nodded to her and leaned back, reading a copy of John Dillinger's *Martin Luther* until his attorney arrived.

Daniel's lawyer, Gordon Trippler, was an influential member of both the Illinois and Wisconsin bars and Judge Bracken's contemporary. Trippler's style was eccentric: he appeared in court carrying a walking stick and wearing a dark fur coat and a Tyrolean hat with a blue jay feather. When he removed the fur coat, he revealed a velvety green sports jacket underneath. He had the odd effect of making Daniel seem regular. That first day, when he argued before Judge Bracken, Trippler was ingratiating without being obsequious. He never looked at Judge Bracken when speaking; Trippler looked instead at Bracken's portrait—a red-faced judge robed in Rembrandt browns, surveying the court with a challenging expression. The painted judge, like the real one, wore an extravagant pompadour that crested over his forehead in a white wave.

Halfway through Trippler's third sentence, Judge Bracken interrupted him and said, "What is that, Mr. Trippler, a Tyrolean? I don't allow hats in my courtroom. Gentlemen, off the record—"

The stenographer, a small woman with frosted hair and a mint-green pantsuit, looked up, and lifted her hands above her keyboard.

"—I'd like to make clear to both you gentlemen that my courtroom is my own private country. I am the president and vice president and secretary and treasurer here, do you get my meaning? And I expect you to observe my rules. I don't allow hats in my courtroom."

Trippler's response was riveting—he smiled broadly, but his smile was humorless, a frown twisted onto its back. He removed his hat with a flourish and an expression I have never seen before or since—it was at once a parody of compliance and a look of suppressed rivalry.

The stenographer's hands then returned to her keyboard. When Trippler finished speaking, Vogelsang addressed the court with his customary detachment, and with a brevity that suggested the judge should not waste much time entertaining Daniel's appeal. "There's no reason for this court to disturb the commissioner's order," Vogelsang said. "Obviously, the three-year-old child belongs with the mother, to whom he's closely attached. The divorce complaint and petition for custody set forth facts regarding Mr. Munk's violence toward his wife and child. He's too dangerous to be left alone with a small boy."

Judge Bracken listened inattentively; as Vogelsang spoke, Bracken perused the complaint and petition and appellate papers as if he had not seen them before. When Vogelsang concluded, Judge Bracken waved the attorneys to the bench and, turning to the stenographer, said, "This is off the record, too." The stenographer glanced up as we approached, and then opened a romance novel. She did not seem to hear a word of the ensuing discussion.

As soon as we assembled before the bench, Judge Bracken fastened an eye on me. I met his stare without speaking, not realizing that he intended for me to name myself. After almost a minute, he said with annoyance, "Parties should remain seated!"

"This is my associate, Melanie Ratleer," Vogelsang answered.

"It's an honor," Trippler told me.

"Ratleer's daughter?" Judge Bracken asked. I nodded. "So Ratleer's turned out a lady lawyer? And she wants to second seat a matrimonial case?" Again, Bracken looked me in the eye; I had the sense he did this to disconcert young attorneys. "Well, all right," he said. He then turned to Trippler and said, "Are you two jokers really going to tie up my court with a hearing?"

Most civil cases consist not of a dramatic public spectacle like my father's notorious criminal trials, but instead of a series of court appearances and adjournments in which judges as well as parties grandstand, bluff, and bully one another toward settlement. "I hope," Bracken said next, "that you two gentlemen will walk over to Tikalsky's this evening and hammer out a settlement. I'm throwing out the protective order, and the temporary custody order remains as it is. Now settle."

"This is an outrage," Trippler said, smiling as if he were not outraged at all.

Vogelsang told Bracken, "The protective order is essential for the safety of the mother and child. Mr. Munk's repeated violence against his wife shows that he's unable to control his temper, and is likely to lose it with a child, who could be severely injured by him. And we have three witnesses prepared to testify that he's abused his little boy before."

"Your honor, if Mr. Vogelsang wants theatrics," Trippler began, looking not at the judge, but at his portrait, "wants to act like Wild Bill Kunstler and F. Lee Bailey, maybe we should transfer this proceeding to Chicago. I wouldn't know—I'm not Flea Bailey. For God's sake, your honor, my client is a Yale Divinity student; the girl has problems; the accusations are hysterical." Trippler's words fell randomly, unconnected as flumes of snow, and settled into meanings as stark as icy fields. He pretended, like the judge, to read his copy of the papers for the first time. Trippler guffawed. "What's this, you're saying my client does what? Your honor, I can't, I can't repeat in words what this affidavit says. Look here!" He pointed to a sentence and ran his finger along it, holding up the paper before the bench. "She says he lets a toddler toodle with his—I don't know—of course, you can bring all these fancy histrionics here to try to prove a point, but what does it all come down to? Is it fair? You tell me, I don't know. Do people do things like that?"

"Not in Muskellunge," Judge Bracken answered ambiguously. The phone rang in an adjoining room. He stood and said, "Clerk's out," and disappeared through a back door. A minute later Judge Bracken returned to his desk with a bellicose expression, his pompadour curling high above his head as though he had twisted it in a moment of exasperation.

"Hatch," he said, sitting down. "The Reverend Hatch has refused to plead to disorderly conduct. He wants the public exposure of a full trial on charges of obstructing an officer and disorderly conduct. On misdemeanor charges and less! He and each and every one of his coterie! Did Chief Komar lose his senses when he decided to arrest that man?" Judge Bracken glared at us. "Now, what do we do here?" He rustled the papers before him. "The boy is thirteen?"

"Three," Vogelsang corrected blandly.

"Well, let's set up a visitation order. Let's not separate a father and son."

"Your honor," Vogelsang answered. "I don't have to remind you that Mr. Munk can't have unsupervised visitation. He's violent. He encourages a three-year-old child to play with his penis—"

"Whose penis?" Judge Bracken said. "His or the boy's?" Judge Bracken lifted a page of the divorce complaint. "He lets the boy play with his *own* pecker, or he lets the boy play with *his* pecker?"

"With his pecker," Vogelsang said.

"With whose pecker?"

"With Mr. Munk's pecker," Trippler answered in an incredulous tone.

"Mr. Munk is a troubled man," Vogelsang continued, "without impulse control, who has beaten his young wife badly and attempted to strangle her—"

"Not important! Not important!" Trippler interrupted.

"—and he's left marks on his own son. A three-year-old child."

"He's a Yale Divinity graduate completing Fulbright research," Trippler countered.

Judge Bracken turned a little in his swivel chair and narrowed his eyes exactly like the judge in the portrait above the bench. I wondered if he had practiced this pose as a private joke. "Mr. Vogelsang," he began, "I'm not prejudging this case, but I do find it a little hard to believe allegations of this kind against a man of this caliber. Yale Divinity School!" Judge Bracken added jocularly, "This isn't Reverend Hatch we're dealing with. And the father's supposed violence toward the complainant is not relevant to the issue of custody."

"Why not?" Vogelsang asked.

"Because I say so," Judge Bracken answered.

"Ah," Vogelsang said.

"Let's get a visitation order together and return in three weeks," Bracken said. "By then this Hatch business will have blown over."

"Your honor," Vogelsang said, "from now on, I'd like everything on the record." The stenographer set down her novel, and poised her fingers over her keyboard.

"Fine," the judge said. "Temporary custody order affirmed. Temporary restraining order dismissed. A nice compromise. Visitation as follows: The child will visit with the father Tuesdays and Thursdays, 4:00 P.M. to 7:00 P.M., and Saturdays, all day, from 9:00 A.M. to 5:00 P.M."

Vogelsang placed his elbows on the bench, leaned forward, and fastened Bracken with a judicial look. "This case is not about compromising between two parties to a lawsuit. It's about protecting a child. And I don't want any more off-the-record sidebar conferences in these proceedings."

"Take your hands off my bench!" Bracken commanded.

"Pay attention to this case," Vogelsang answered sternly, without moving. It was the first moment in which I was acutely aware that Vogelsang was a generation older than Bracken, and it was also the first time I had seen an attorney talk down to a judge. "This court has just ordered a toddler to spend three days a week with a psychopath. That child better be in good shape at the end of this mess. If visitation occurs at all, it will have to be supervised."

Before Judge Bracken could answer, Trippler stepped to the side of the bench, stood level with the judge's elbow as if counseling him, and said: "Your honor, I'm sure every other day a lawyer comes to this court with a simpering, crying housewife complaining that her husband has slapped her. Just because a man hits his wife, this doesn't give her the right to keep him from seeing his child. And the Muskellunge County Court certainly can't waste its resources supervising visitation in every little matrimonial case that comes scampering in here."

"Exactly," Bracken said.

Vogelsang stepped back from the bench and let his low voice drop, so that Judge Bracken had to tilt forward to hear him. "If you will not consider that man's repeated, willful, terrorizing of his wife as relevant to his fitness as a father—"

"Oh, yes, Mrs. Munk's so terrified of her husband that she flew to rejoin him after he moved away to Milwaukee," Trippler interrupted. "Threw herself in her husband's arms and moved back in with him right before filing her allegations—"

"Is this true, Mr. Vogelsang?" Judge Bracken asked. "Is it true that she followed the father to Milwaukee after he had left her?"

"Of course—"

Judge Bracken frowned.

"Of course she followed him," Vogelsang answered. "He took the boy with him. What mother would leave a child alone with a man like that? I want it on the record that this court has been fully apprised of Mr. Munk's violence toward his son."

"I'm sure the child will survive," Bracken said sardonically. "Visitation is as ordered: Tuesday, Thursday, Saturday."

"Without supervision?" Vogelsang asked.

"Trippler, tell your client not to stray too far from Muskellunge. That's supervision enough. You two lawyers can come back in three weeks," Judge Bracken concluded, lining up the edges of the papers in front of him with efficient precision. "Put your heads together and choose a psychiatric expert to evaluate the parents. Get your clients interviewed."

"We'd like to request the appointment of a guardian *ad litem* to represent the child's interests," Vogelsang said.

"Not in my court. Not in a run-of-the-mill custody case. Besides, the attorney in this area who takes that kind of work is tied up with this Hatch business right now."

"Run of the mill?" Vogelsang asked. He began rattling off cases and citations to legal reporters and told Judge Bracken, in a friendly, informative way, as if he himself were surprised by the information, "Section 247.045 of the Family Law Act requires a guardian to be appointed in any action where there's special concern as to the future welfare of the child. The Wisconsin Supreme Court seems to have reversed a number of cases recently where trial judges haven't followed the statute."

Judge Bracken reached out his left hand, spread it over the stenographer's keyboard, and whispered, "Well, we're not in appellate court here, are we? We're in my court." Then he removed his hand, gestured to the stenographer to continue typing, and said, "It's within the discretion of the hearing judge to determine whether a guardian *ad litem* is necessary. A guardian's opinion would just be cumulative here, wouldn't it? There's nothing special about the child's interests here that you two lawyers won't bring out when you start going at each other. Bailiff, move these lawyers out of my courtroom!"

As I turned to leave, the judge detained me. "Miss Ratleer," he said. "I hear that Reverend Hatch has asked your father to serve as counsel on his case as well as Worlfordt's. Your father has refused. It seems that Hatch is mortally offended by this, but the last thing we need is a time-consuming public spectacle in this court. You can tell your father I'm mighty thankful for that refusal."

THROUGHOUT Judge Bracken's sidebar conference, I had not looked once at Mildred; I had been afraid to. Now, when I turned, I saw Vogelsang bending over her, whispering. Mildred sat pale as a pillar of salt, perfectly still, without speaking. As I approached, I heard Vogelsang say, "Don't let Trippler and Daniel see you react. Just walk out of the courthouse with me to the store. And Melanie, don't look so morose: At least wait until Daniel leaves. Don't let him think he's won anything. Talk to me in a leisurely way, Melanie. Talk!"

I fumbled for words as we crossed the street. "What about that bit the judge pulled with the stenographer?" I asked him.

"Oh, that was nothing," Vogelsang said. "I once saw a judge throw a stenographer's keyboard out the courtroom door. But it's good Bracken's denied our request for a guardian—if we got a bad final ruling, we could use it as grounds for an appeal, and I'll just keep reminding Bracken of that fact."

"How long does an appeal take?" Mildred asked. I could not see her face in the darkness, but her voice was strained and anxious.

"Well, there are immediate appeals from interim orders—but appealing a final custody determination would take about eighteen months."

"Eighteen months!"

"Or longer," Vogelsang said. "An appeal from a custody ruling is utterly useless from a practical standpoint where a small child is concerned. However, most judges will do anything to avoid allowing their

brethren in the higher court to insult them by overturning their decisions—a judge like Bracken does not like to be reminded that he is
not the Almighty God. So we'll just keep letting him know when he's
wrong."

Mildred pulled away from us as we walked the rest of the way
toward Shove's.

When we sat down, and Vogelsang reviewed what had happened in
court, Mildred simply cried. Mr. Shove, dressed in his bright orange
overalls, kept ducking from behind his shelves of inventory to stare at
us. I assumed he was concerned we might scare away customers.

"What's wrong with the judge?" Mildred exclaimed. "How could
it hurt him to order someone to watch over Ben? I can't send Ben off
with Daniel every other day!"

"You have to obey Bracken's orders to the letter," Vogelsang told
her.

"And what if I don't?" Mildred shouted. Mr. Shove stepped closer,
lingering near the Hubbard squash.

"Then Daniel will win!" Vogelsang said emphatically.

"What's wrong with the judge?" Mildred repeated. "Is he stupid,
or does he just not care about children?"

"I don't know yet," Vogelsang answered.

"How can I let Ben face Daniel alone?"

Mrs. Shove set down her pad and paper, closed the cash register
with a bang, and joined us at our table. She patted Mildred's hand and
told her, "Don't you worry. If that husband of yours comes in here,
we'll watch him like hawks."

Mildred wiped her eyes on her napkin.

Mrs. Shove waved to her husband like a customer summoning a
waiter. Mr. Shove approached, carrying a small purple cabbage the size
of a baby's bonnet. He sat down beside his wife, and raised his bushy
eyebrows as if surprised that he would talk to us.

"And I'll tell everyone I know to keep an eye on your little boy,"
Mrs. Shove said. "I know plenty of people in Muskellunge with nothing
better to do."

"Thanks," Mildred said.

"My sister-in-law," Mrs. Shove said, looking pointedly at Mr. Shove,
"was once in a bind with her ex-husband—"

"She married a turkey!" Mr. Shove broke in.

"Her little girl had asthma, and her ex-husband—"

"Gobble, gobble," Mr. Shove said.

"—wouldn't give the girl her medicine on visits, hey. So her friend Laurie went over to the ex-husband's house every day, hung around the park when he went there, followed him everywhere, pretending to write things down, asking him when the girl took her medicine."

"It worked," Mr. Shove said. "It was my idea. It drove the turkey crazy."

"I could do that," Mildred said.

"No, you can't," Vogelsang told her. "I don't want you near Daniel. And I don't want you involved in anything that can be construed as interference with visitation."

Mr. Shove scowled. "It was a good idea. It was my idea."

"It certainly was," Mrs. Shove affirmed.

Vogelsang said, "But *you* can do it, Melanie. You can be the one to deliver Ben to Daniel, and then you can sit outside his place in your car, or follow him around at a courteous distance. Of course, Trippler will object vociferously, but we'll just let him do that."

Mr. Shove said gruffly, "What a character! I wouldn't want to be standing in front of that judge in a courtroom." He crossed his arms.

Vogelsang asked him, "So, what can you tell me about Mr. Bracken?"

" '*Mister Bracken*'? Don't call him by his name—he makes everyone call him 'the Judge'!"

"Even his wife calls him 'the Judge,' " Mrs. Shove said with a puzzled look. "I've always wondered whether she—"

"He even makes us do it!" Mr. Shove interrupted. "Us, his golf partners! What's more, he cheats, hey. That's what I know." Mr. Shove laughed at something he had not said yet, and looked around the table, letting his stare rest dramatically on each one of us. He continued, "I and my pals used to play together on Wednesdays, and Bracken used to cheat on five-dollar bets. Makes you think, doesn't it? What kind of guy would cheat a man out of five dollars in a friendly game of golf? And do you know how he did it?" Mr. Shove waited for someone to ask.

Vogelsang obliged him. "How did he cheat?"

"If the judge took a swing and missed the ball, he'd pretend it was a practice swing. He'd squib it off the tee and put it back when no one was looking. Once he lost his ball in the woods and I saw him drop a new ball through his pants leg!"

For the first time since we sat down, Mildred laughed.

"He must have cut a hole in his pants pocket!" Mr. Shove told her.
"My God," Vogelsang said.

A group of men carrying canvas rifle cases entered the store, and
Mrs. Shove rose. Outside, a buck lay stretched over the roof of the men's
van, looking like a sacrifice offered up to a modern god: the deer's
frozen blood streaked the windshield. Mildred stared out the window
unseeingly. She looked exhausted and defeated.

"You know," Mr. Shove told her, patting her hand. "Your dad
would get a lot more people at that church if he didn't do all those
things. Talk about poetry and composting. Ask people to an Arab Sunday lunch where they have to eat food called falafel. Play those songs
that don't have any tunes to them. Give a church a name like the Park
and Pray."

DANIEL DID NOT move to Muskellunge. He rented the only house in
Eklundville, the blue home that I had passed in Mildred's car on the
day of my arrival. Mr. Eklund, the house's owner, lived across the road
in a Winnebago trailer behind his gas station. Perhaps Daniel sensed
that he might be watched in Muskellunge or he hoped that his isolation
with Ben would frighten Mildred.

On Saturdays Daniel cancelled visitation, and drove to Chicago to
be interviewed by the psychiatric expert Trippler and Vogelsang had
chosen. Vogelsang was optimistic about the expert: He was more progressive than any local psychiatrist available for court work, a graduate
of the University of Chicago, and aware of recent advances in the law
of custody. Daniel's lawyer had agreed on him, to avoid the usual local
Department of Social Services experts recommended by the court,
whom Trippler feared would be prejudiced in favor of a Muskellunge
resident. (I pictured the Chicago psychiatrist outsmarting Daniel, expli-
cating his duplicity with intellectual zeal.) The expert did not ask to see
Ben in those first weeks, and Mildred was relieved that Daniel would
not be taking him to Chicago. However, the few times Ben spent alone
with his father affected him profoundly, and the hardest fact for all of
us was that we did not know precisely what Daniel did to Ben during
visits. We only saw Ben grow from the talkative three-year-old we knew
to someone else: a taciturn, anxious child with an old face.

Every other day I drove Ben out to Eklundville, to the pale blue
lozenge of house dissolving into an utterly stark, blinding white snow-

scape that stretched from the road to a nearby shore of eastern Lake Muskellunge. Ben would sit quietly, strapped in his seat belt, a plastic King Arthur sword clamped between his knees.

On the first day, when I tried to hand him to Daniel, Ben held to me so tightly that I had to pry his fingers one by one from my arms, and then he grabbed me again when I lifted him toward his father. Daniel had parked a large blue Galaxie 500 in front of the house. It looked almost new, like a rented car, and Daniel leaned against it and watched us. I finally brought Ben back inside the Volkswagen, rebelted him, stuck his sword in his hands, and then sat in the front seat while Daniel unbelted Ben again.

Ben looked at me accusingly, and said, "I'm not even talking to you!" while Daniel carried him inside.

I waited in the car, thinking: Good, let Ben hate me, instead of mistrusting his mother and everyone else. I sat staring at the snow: at Mr. Eklund's gas tank with its arm raised, its metallic finger in its solitary ear; at his three red pigs snuffling a murky tunnel in the muddy snow; at Mr. Eklund's toothless face, impermeable to more knowledge, hovering behind the green plate-glass window of his gas station. I hoped that my presence outside the house would unnerve Daniel, that it would make him perform every move as if he were an actor auditioning on stage, every gesture assessed. But he knew that whatever he did with Ben behind the blue house's closed doors could never be proven, and he must have weighed the effect of this on me and Mildred.

Sometimes, sitting in the Volkswagen during visits, I imagined I was the expert interviewing Daniel in Chicago, delving into his heart with psychological omniscience, delivering an exegesis of his soul. In fact I was incapable of anything of the kind. Before I had met Daniel, I believed it was possible to slip into the skin of almost any person, to feel what he thought, to invest him, if only momentarily, with sympathy. But Daniel still defied my understanding; I could not imagine any redeeming qualities for him that would not be negated or twisted by his duplicity and dangerousness. Sometimes I speculated that Daniel must be lonely, with only his lawyer to talk to; that Daniel's desperation to keep Mildred revealed a terror of falling into the cold isolating darkness of himself. I wondered if Daniel was the most profoundly solitary person I had known—he seemed to have no connection to anyone but us, the people he had chosen as his antagonists. Once, I lay back in the car seat and closed my eyes, and pretended to myself that I was Daniel

Munk. I imagined myself slightly less tall, heavier, my hair that extraordinary dark red. I stretched out my *sapatões* in front of me, and adjusted my wire-rim glasses on my nose, and felt—contentment, an absolute expectation that I would triumph in my desire to claim Mildred from herself. My mind plunged into an edgeless, vast universe in which the possibility of loss had no place—and then I opened my eyes, my heart racing.

On Ben's first visit, the Volkswagen's primitive heating system left me too cold to move. After an hour I had no feeling left in my hands and feet, although I had dressed as I had learned to from a lifetime in McCarthy: in three pairs of socks, shoes within boots, gloves tucked into lined mittens, a hat worn over a ski mask, snow pants pulled over blue jeans over long winter underwear, layers of sweaters under my parka. It was a wonder that any of us had felt a connection to the world at all, muffled so completely from our surroundings half the year.

Matt had told me that the cold would freeze the Volkswagen's motor. He had given me two extension cords, one to plug into the engine, if the temperature fell too far below zero, and another to connect to a small space heater from the church, which Matt advised me to prop up in the seat beside the driver's—this seemed to me a crazily dangerous suggestion. I walked to Mr. Eklund's gas station to see if I could get a cup of coffee and warm myself inside. But when I entered the gas station office, I found that it was barely heated, and there were no refreshments.

Mr. Eklund stood behind a counter, staring vacantly out the green plate-glass window, immobile as if he had turned to ice. Only his curiosity about what I was doing could have held him there. Under the bill of his winter cap, his weatherbeaten face collapsed into his wrinkled mouth like an eroded streambank. I tried to enlist him in conversation, but he was more taciturn even than I; he simply nodded or shook his head when I gave him a jumbled story in which I explained myself as a kind of social worker appointed to oversee the visits of his tenant's child: The child, I clarified, was sick. I don't know why I fabricated such a story. It seemed easier than telling the truth, and Mr. Eklund barely listened. When I offered him a pile of dollar bills, after asking if I could use his electricity from the outdoor outlets and store the space heater in the gas station garage between visits, he accepted the money without asking questions. I plugged in one extension cord, returned to the Volkswagen, and turned on the space heater. For the rest of my visits, it roared quietly beside me in the front seat, glowing so ferociously that I had to open the windows periodically to keep from baking.

An hour before Ben's first visit should have ended Daniel brought him back outside. Daniel looked tired and irritable. Ben had fallen asleep, and Daniel handed him to me saying, "He's wet," and then returned inside without addressing me further. I hurried Ben into the car, and pulled off his boots and pants and wet underwear. I wrapped him in my parka. Ben screwed up his face but remained asleep, as if by an effort of will.

Each of the first five or six visits began and ended this way, with Daniel returning Ben early, and with Ben taking refuge in sleep. After the second visit I started knocking on the door an hour after Ben's arrival, asking to use Daniel's bathroom. The first time I tried this, Daniel begrudgingly allowed me to enter his house, although he must have divined that I was there to spy on him. Ben lay asleep on a sofa, clutching his sword. Daniel sat at his desk, writing. Beside him both a radio and a television played at low volume: Their voices crossed tinnily in an unintelligible dialogue.

I covered Ben with his coat, and rattled around in the bathroom long after I had finished. When I opened the bathroom door, Daniel startled me: he stood directly outside, so close that the door knocked against him.

"Melanie," he said. "What have I ever done to you? You used to be friendly to me. Do you remember when we drank that wine behind the halfway house? You trusted me then. Boy, I was so plastered, I don't remember how I walked home! Now, you wouldn't even sit down with me for a talk over a beer. You've joined with all of them—" He spread his arms in a gesture that seemed to take in all humanity.

When I did not answer, Daniel stepped to the side, and I slipped past him. He followed me into the living room; under the lamplight his dark red hair made me think of sumac. He looked different, somehow: He hadn't shaved in a few days, and this gave his face a disordered, mildly desperate look.

"Melanie, I'm doing my best. I'm just trying to be a father to my son in the only way I know how."

I believed Daniel might be telling the truth, that he really might not know how else to act, presented with the prospect of losing Mildred.

"I guess the blush is off the rose," he told me. "You got close enough to see me, and you don't like what you saw?" Daniel's voice broke, and for the life of me, I could not tell whether his self-pity was genuine or feigned. "You think I'm not like the rest of you—" Daniel nodded to the window behind me, as if "by the rest of you," he meant the whole world. "When I was a kid, I used to wonder, how do I know I see colors the way everyone else does? What if when they say 'orange,' they're seeing what I call 'green'? How would we even know? How would you know if you feel life the same as other people do, if you're even put together the same?" His question seemed rhetorical—I could not tell if by "you," he meant himself, or me, or any of us.

"I always thought I was basically like other people," I answered. "Just a little gloomier."

Daniel took a step closer. "Please reason with Mildred," he said; there was almost a pleading tone in his voice. "She must have to convince herself I'm an ogre to carry on this way. I know that lawsuits do this to couples—the attorneys turn them into archenemies when they really care for each other."

I drew back and spoke cautiously, as a lawyer rather than a human being. I did not ask Daniel what I wanted to—whether he recognized that he was dangerous, whether he knew that he had hurt Ben and Mildred, that he had driven away someone who once loved him. I wanted to say, "Daniel, you fucked up with Mildred. Now let her go." But I feared he would turn anything I said into a weapon against Mildred. And so, I did what lawyers and confidence men do: I formulated a question instead of providing information. "What do you want, Daniel?" I asked.

Daniel's answer might have come straight from a legal handbook on witness preparation in matrimonial cases: "I just want Ben to have a solid upbringing under a father's supervision."

"What do you want from Mildred now, Daniel? What do you expect her to—"

Daniel slammed the wall with his hand and shouted, "I want Mildred to see me the way she used to! She's not seeing me right! She's not seeing me right!" He kicked a chair so that it fell backward, and Ben started in his sleep. Daniel must have believed that I had never seen him lose his temper before. The anger in his face vanished in a moment, but afterward I felt wary.

"You need to calm down," I said. "As long as Ben's here, you'll have to be calm."

"I am calm," Daniel answered. And the face he turned toward me was as peaceful as if he had been sleeping. "You can leave now." Daniel walked to the front door, swung it open, and looked at me with a sarcastic expression. As I walked down the front steps, he said, "You have no right to come between me and Mildred."

The second time I knocked on the door, Daniel allowed me to use the bathroom, but as I entered, he called me a "carrion crow," and did not attempt to speak with me again. I don't know why Daniel continued to let me in; maybe he wanted to watch me for a while, to give himself a rest from being watched. Or maybe he wanted company, even hostile company. Then, and on each later occasion I entered, Ben lay asleep on a sofa, and Daniel sat working at his desk, his papers scattered around his typewriter. Mildred seemed relieved when I reported this to her. She stopped putting Ben down for afternoon naps, and kept him up later at night, to assure that he slept through his visits with Daniel. She told me that she herself had "given up sleeping, and laughing at jokes." Neither Mildred nor I said anything about the fact that Ben always sidled away when I entered the house, as if I were a malevolent god who had come to bear him away to my underworld.

However, it was apparent to both of us that Ben could not have slept all the way through every visit with Daniel. Ben was changing: He had become brooding and angry. When Mildred tried to hug him after visits, he would curl into a ball, hiding his arms and legs and making himself unembraceable. He threw things, and hit us, and had tantrums. Sometimes, he would hurl himself to the ground in an odd kind of fit, where he would lie immobile, his arms and legs tucked under him instead of kicking.

Those visits were strange for me also. I would sit in the Volkswagen, the space heater roaring, perched beside me like a hellish companion, and I would try to keep from imagining what went on inside between Daniel and his son. I never brought my law articles to read on such occasions. I just watched Eklundville, and the hours passed like days: That part of Wisconsin in winter seems half alive. There is little movement between anywhere you stand and the horizon, and any gesture of activity seems out of place, disruptive. I once saw an orange fox, his pretty face pointing westward, his slender, black-stockinged legs picking their way daintily through a snowdrift. He seemed surprised when a white rabbit leapt from under him as if kicked loose—he froze like a pointer, and watched the rabbit jackknife away. People rarely stirred outside near Lake Muskellunge's eastern shore. When they did, they dressed in thick parkas and lumbered like half-hibernating animals. The windchill factor hovered at twenty-five degrees below zero, and sky raced over the fields at breakneck speed toward the lake. After the first visit, I kept the car's motor plugged in to Mr. Eklund's garage wall, and I turned the space heater so high I thought the car's upholstery would catch fire.

On Ben's second Tuesday visit I saw a flock of crows chasing an owl. As a child I had witnessed the antagonism of crows toward owls before. My father had once stuck a stuffed owl in the lower branches of an apple tree, his feathers ruffled and his beak skewed from cut-rate taxidermy. A horde of crows circled the tree, screeching and dive-bombing the owl to frighten him away. Finally, one knocked it to the ground, and then they all rose in a raucous triumph.

As I waited for Ben I saw this drama repeated, but with a larger, live owl, white and brown-speckled, who sailed on muscular, curved wings from the high branches of an oak. Behind him a mob of crows whirled and twisted, cawing and calling to one another. The owl soon outdistanced them, his wings pushing through the air with such profound quiet that his flight seemed to hush their cacophony. He moved as if driven only by the joy of his own power, without acknowledging the crows hounding him. I wanted to believe he was symbolic of something about one of us, that he proved that the righteous should prevail. The crows settled back into the tree branches, exclaiming loudly, joking among themselves.

Afterward I got out of the car and knocked on Daniel's door. No one answered. I peered through the cracks in the curtained windows, but the living room and kitchen and study were empty. I could not see into the other rooms. Daniel's car was still in the driveway. I walked around the barn beside the gas station, but only Mr. Eklund was there, poking a boar with a pointed pole.

Mr. Eklund looked at me but did not say hello. "Soo-wee," he told the pig. "Soo-wee." The boar lifted his head and focussed on us with long-lashed, intelligent eyes. He looked as if he comprehended far more about the world than Mr. Eklund ever would. Mr. Eklund shook his head when I asked if he had seen Daniel.

I returned to the house. Between the lake and the road the snow stretched flat and shadowless to the end of the world. Only a set of deer tracks approached the blue building, and then doubled back before reaching it. Far off, on the lake, two men were ice fishing, about fifty yards from shore.

One fisherman stood beside a bluish vein that zig-zagged over the pale gray surface. I shook my head, wondering at the audacity of some hunters and fishermen, who seem to love tempting the laws of nature—the lake was only just setting, far from safe for ice fishing. Both men wore red ski masks, and the one who was standing tapped the ice with a thick pole. At first I thought the other fisherman was a person squatting, hunched over the lake as if to examine a flaw there, or to test its thickness for ice fishing. I could not make out the image clearly: The cold wind billowed over him, and snow jumped from the ice like pounded flour. When he moved, a swirl of electric orange flapped flaglike beside him. The flag fluttered again and then extended three or four feet, too long for the marker of an ice fisherman.

I recognized the scarf Matt had given Ben, and I realized with horror that the squatting shape was the standing figure of a little boy, and the adult next to Ben, Daniel in his parka. Daniel turned toward Ben and enveloped him. He kneeled beside him and placed his head beside his son's, as if whispering to him. Daniel stood and prodded Ben forward, and then strode ahead of him, proceeding not hesitantly, but confidently toward the center of the lake. Ben watched from where he stood and began edging sideways, slipping as he went.

I ran until I slid down the snow bank that led to the shoreline. "Ben! Ben!" I screamed, waving my arms. The wind snatched my voice from me. Ben saw me and tottered in my direction. Daniel continued to walk forward, picking his way over the ice without looking back, as he had that time in the parking lot.

The ice cracked and echoed under my feet until I reached Ben. I picked him up just as Daniel turned and saw me.

"Ben, it's me, Melanie, Mommy's friend," I said.

Ben clung to me as if he didn't care who I was. "Cold," he said. "Cold."

Daniel did not move. I understood then that he had wanted me to see him, and that he expected me to tell Mildred what he had done, in order to frighten her. I carried Ben back to the car, and when I turned on the ignition, I saw Daniel still crossing the lake, heading toward its far shore with easy, gliding steps, like a water strider walking on water.

5

DURING THE PERIOD covered by Judge Bracken's first visitation order, Mildred told me that her thoughts were possessed by two things only: whether Daniel would injure Ben irreparably, and whether there was a way she could murder Daniel and get away with it. She had terrible attacks of anxiety at odd moments, as she drove down Walleye Street, as she was sorting through produce at Shove's, when her heart would race and her pulse flutter like a frightened bird's, so that she could not bear any longer the exquisite torture of being locked inside her body.

Ben fell sick with a cough and fever the evening after I drove him back from the lake. Mildred seized on this as a reason to keep him home for the week, and Vogelsang informed Trippler that Ben was too sick for visitation. Daniel was incensed. The following Thursday morning he insisted on entering the house and taking Ben to an out-of-town pediatrician to verify that he was ill. John would not let Daniel in the door.

Ottilie surprised Daniel by pushing angrily past John, and shouting, "Get out of here!" She spat out the words. "Or I'll testify that you tried to force your way inside!" Ottilie had not even put on her coat. The wind tugged at her dress and worried the cuffs of her white hospital technician's pants.

"That would be perjury," Daniel told her.

"It will be your word against mine!" Ottilie snapped.

Reverend Steck looked astonished by Ottilie's outburst. But then he placed a hand on her shoulder and stood next to her.

"Whatever you do to Mildred," Ottilie said, "I'll do back to you!" Her tone was icy.

I liked John Steck immensely in that moment. Another man, I thought, might have been moved by discomfort to silence Ottilie, or to take charge of the situation, or to retreat from it. Instead, John stayed where he was, one hand in his pocket, until Daniel turned and left.

From Chicago Trippler called Vogelsang's Madison law office and vigorously protested Mildred's "interference with a father's sacred right to visitation." Vogelsang countered that Daniel's imprudence in taking a toddler outside in subzero weather had caused Ben's illness, and that Mildred had only exercised "a mother's sacred right to protect her young from predators." Trippler insisted that Ben was not sick, and when both attorneys arrived in Muskellunge for their next court appearance, Trippler requested an increase in Daniel's visitation rights to include overnight Saturday visitation, to "make up for father-son time, already tragically lost."

The judge waved us into his chambers, but Vogelsang insisted on remaining in the open courtroom and commanded the stenographer to "record every word spoken here today, however few that might be." The stenographer placed her fingers in the air above her keyboard.

"I want to state on the record," Vogelsang began, "that Mr. Munk decided to take the three-year-old child on a stroll across Lake Muskellunge in early November, before the lake was entirely frozen. Mr. Munk's conduct is part of a pattern of recklessly and intentionally endangering his son. My client is reasonably concerned her child will come to serious harm if there is no oversight of Mr. Munk's conduct—"

Judge Bracken answered, simply, "Mr. Trippler, is your client a city man? Tell him to stay off the lake. It won't set for another month."

Trippler said, "This is disgusting. This is the most disgusting thing I've ever heard. Not only is this woman turning her child against his own father. She's filling his mind with such twisted thoughts about Mr. Munk that she's doing the boy psychological damage. Now she's opposing increased visitation with the father. If she's so hostile to Mr. Munk, maybe the father should have temporary custody for a while."

"Mr. Vogelsang," Bracken said, "if the father's willing to take added responsibility for the boy on Saturdays, why stand in his way?"

"And the mother's been flagrantly violating this court's orders," Trippler continued. "Flagrantly. She's pretended for a week the boy's too sick to visit—"

"Mr. Munk took a three-year-old on an outing in twenty-five-below weather," Vogelsang said. "And now Mr. Trippler can't understand how the child got sick. It's a miracle the boy's not frostbitten. Apparently, Mr. Trippler knows as little about caring for a small child as his client—"

"I love children!" Trippler exclaimed. "How dare you imply I don't care about children."

"The boy had a bad cough and a one hundred and two fever, and Mr. Trippler sent his client over to the house demanding that the child be forced to go out."

"Children get colds all the time," Trippler answered.

"I renew my request for a guardian *ad litem* to represent the child's interests," Vogelsang said. "For the record." He nodded at the stenographer.

"Denied," Bracken said.

"Then at the very least, I demand that visitation be overseen," Vogelsang pressed. "There's no earthly reason to imperil a small child in this manner. Appoint someone from the Department of Social Services to supervise visitation—"

"I will not babysit parties in matrimonial cases!" Judge Bracken answered. "Apparently you think this court is not overburdened." The judge leaned forward and said, sotto voce, so that the stenographer stopped typing and strained forward to hear, "Why can't you settle this case, Vogelsang? If you don't like things the way they are, settle!"

"Mr. Munk has unequivocally represented that he won't settle."

"Nonsense. We've offered and offered," Trippler said. "But they won't back down."

"Vogelsang," Judge Bracken answered angrily, "I'm telling you right now, if your client runs interference between Mr. Munk and his son, and continues to unreasonably oppose Mr. Munk's requests for visitation, I will seriously entertain a change in temporary custody."

Both lawyers, especially Trippler, seemed surprised by this announcement. Trippler stood, his mouth open, and then he shut it on whatever word he had intended to utter. Fear somersaulted in my chest. Until that moment I had not entertained the remote possibility that the judge would take temporary custody from Mildred: Everything in the law was in her favor. I imagined the tearing of Ben from Mildred, and the notion was so painful that it paralyzed me; again I found that I could not even turn around to witness how Mildred had received the judge's pronouncement.

Vogelsang recovered first. "Any change of temporary custody at this juncture will require a hearing. And I'm sure you're not seriously contemplating taking a child away from the mother who has raised him, day in and out since birth, in order to hand him over to a man with a history of violence?"

"What history are we talking about?" Trippler followed. "What history? My client is a Yale Divinity graduate!"

"That man *did not graduate from Yale!*" Vogelsang announced. "According to Yale, Mr. Munk was asked to leave their program after three months."

Now I looked at Mildred; she seemed as surprised by the revelation as I was. She turned toward Daniel: Her eyebrows were lifted in immediate surprise, but a more profound shock underlay all of her features. Her profile was empty of feeling.

Daniel did not move. He studied a crossgrain of wood on the table in front of him and betrayed no embarrassment.

The judge faced Daniel and said, "Is this true? You're not a minister? Have you allowed your attorney to represent to this court that you had a degree from Yale Divinity School?"

"He had a crisis of faith," Trippler suggested, "and he left before completing his degree."

"According to Yale," Vogelsang said, "his crisis of faith consisted in a little irregularity in his application for admission."

"That's outrageous!" Daniel stood precipitously, looking genuinely indignant. "There was no irregularity—"

"It's all right, Daniel," Trippler answered. "Don't let these attorney tricks ruffle you."

"But he's not a Yale Divinity graduate?" the judge asked.

"And there's no Fulbright, either," Vogelsang said.

"No Fulbright."

Now Bracken scrutinized Daniel with a judicial look. Above him the eyes of the painted judge surveyed us all.

"I'm completing research for my doctorate in comparative religion at the University of Wisconsin," Daniel explained. "Your honor, these stories about Yale and the Fulbright are things my wife told her family to impress them. You see, her father is a minister—"

"Later, later," the judge said. "Let's put together the next visitation order." There was a brief silence while all of the parties collected themselves. Trippler tapped his cane absently on a hollow wooden table leg, and Bracken arrested him with a look of annoyance. Vogelsang sat down with a sigh.

"As long as we're increasing visitation," Trippler said suddenly, "tell Vogelsang to call his dogs off. He's had Ratleer's daughter following my client around like a bloodhound during visitation—"

"*That* is not 'Ratleer's daughter,'" Vogelsang retorted. "She's my associate, Melanie Ratleer, top of her class at Columbia. If Mr. Munk wants to agree on a court-appointed social worker to supervise visits, I'd be glad to call off Ms. Ratleer."

Judge Bracken studied me. "Trippler, what's the harm if this girl's there to supervise? She's not really acting as second counsel on this case; she hasn't opened her mouth once since entering this courtroom." Then he muttered, so that the stenographer cocked her head to catch his words. "Weekend visitation will be from 5:00 P.M. on Saturdays until 9:30 A.M. on Sundays."

"How is Ms. Ratleer to protect the boy," Vogelsang said, rising with exasperation from his chair, "if he's forced to stay overnight with his father? With a man whom any seeing, thinking, rational person would identify as an antisocial character. He lies. He breaks basic rules of safety with a three-year-old. He beats the wife he's promised to cherish."

"Save that song for another day," Bracken said, waving the attorneys away with an imperious gesture. A wine-colored suit gleamed within the cuff of his judicial robe. "And Vogelsang, leave the evaluation of Mr. Trippler's client for the psychiatric expert. I expect all psychiatric evaluations and the expert's report to be complete by the next time I see you. Come back in three weeks. Hatch will have blown over by then."

As Daniel rose to leave the courtroom, Trippler said in a hearty voice, "Thank God the little boy will be with you overnight now, Daniel. A boy this age needs a father."

Mildred glared furiously at Trippler. Vogelsang took her by the arm and said, "Don't say anything until we get outside. Trippler is just trying to upset you in front of the judge. Do not appear upset."

But as we entered the hallway, Daniel circled us, and stood in front of Mildred. She looked at him blankly. Daniel held out a note to her.

"Stay away from her," Vogelsang growled.

He took the note. As Daniel walked away, Vogelsang read to us:

"Meet with me tonight, without any lawyers around, to see if we can end all of this. I'm asking you as a person now."

Vogelsang said, loud enough for Daniel to hear, "This phrase, *'as a person now,'* is peculiar. What does he mean, that he suddenly considers you a person, or that he's going to take human form for the night?"

When Daniel reached the courthouse entrance, Trippler slapped him on the back. Vogelsang waited for them to disappear around the corner before he let us leave the courthouse.

When we were inside the car, Vogelsang told Mildred, "Meet with Daniel. Who knows what he has to say? Maybe he's grown tired of babysitting a three-year-old, and wants to work out a financial settlement advantageous to him. If you agree, I'll tell Trippler you'll talk to Daniel in a public place. In the police station lobby, where he won't try to assault you. Say as little as possible, and just listen. Whatever you say will be evidence if the hearing proceeds. The same is true for Daniel."

Mildred barely seemed to hear him. "I can't let Ben stay with Daniel overnight," she said. "It's gone too far now—it's just too far."

"Let's see what Daniel wants," Vogelsang counselled.

Mildred leaned her head against the car window, and stared at the scenery: A yellow dog rocketed across a field of ice. When he disappeared, nothing remained behind, just a white expanse stretching to the horizon, but Mildred continued to watch the field. I saw that her hair had begun to turn: silver strands frosted her honey-colored braid. Before that moment I had not believed that anxiety could turn a person's hair gray, and I had not realized how frightened Mildred really was.

I DROVE MILDRED to the police station that evening. Low clouds reflected the town lights so that the starless sky seemed too close. A man in a fur coat trotted down the street. He slowed in front of the bridal apparel store and peered inside, so that I thought of myself looking in the same window weeks before. Then the man walked on, and as we passed him, I recognized Trippler. After I parked near the police station, and Mildred exited the car, Trippler appeared again in my rearview mirror. He turned into the pet store opposite my car, and I watched him through the plate-glass window as he joked with the proprietress and allowed a white mouse to run up and down his sleeve. Twice he came out and looked toward the police station, but he did not see me.

Mildred waited in the lighted lobby of the station until Daniel approached her. He spoke and reached for her arm. She stepped back and jerked her arm away. Then she returned to the car, slid in beside me, and slammed the door.

"Daniel told me he'll fire his lawyer if I come back to live with him." She looked into the street and said, half to herself, half to me, "I have to get away! I have to get away!"

We drove on in silence to the Stecks' house. When we entered, Ben was asleep upstairs, and Vogelsang and John were talking in the living room. They stopped when we came in.

Mildred sat down next to her father. She appeared jittery; she looked at him, and then away from him; she pulled off her mittens and fidgeted with the empty finger holes. "I need your help," she told John in an earnest voice. "I need you to find me a fake Social Security number, so that I can change my name and live someplace else with Ben."

Before John could answer, Vogelsang said, "It's too soon to start considering that kind of alternative, Mildred."

"I can't hold out any longer," Mildred answered.

She sat, seemingly oblivious as her father unzipped her coat and slipped her arms out of the sleeves.

"I won't leave Ben with Daniel overnight." As Mildred spoke, the skin over her cheekbones grew taut and whitened; she had lost weight. I tried to ascertain what was different about her profile, and the phrase that came to me was: The law has taken the light out of her face. Its sly subversiveness was gone. I could no sooner picture her driving down Walleye Street in her Cadillac, honking at pedestrians, than I could see myself doing it.

"Mildred," John said to her gently. He was wearing a cheerful green paisley collar, and it set off his expression of pure grief. I remembered him declaiming poetry in his garden, sermonizing about insects and wiggling his eyebrows in imitation of Mr. Shove. My sense that Daniel had irreparably altered everyone within his sphere deepened.

John balanced a Bible on his knee; this was the first time I had seen him carry one outside of church. "Do you know how hard it would be for you and Ben if you just absconded?" he asked Mildred. "And it's immoral—what if Daniel had run off with Ben?"

"He did run off with Ben! Daniel just used the law to do it!"

"What if you were found out? If Daniel tracked you down? How would you get work without any history? And if someone discovered that your Social Security number wasn't really yours, what would you do, move someplace else and start over again, with a small child? How would you support yourself and care for Ben, too?"

"You should know how!" Mildred said. "You help undocumented immigrants every day. You tell me how!"

"Do you believe life is easy for them? And what do you think it's like for their children? They move from one place to another; they live in constant fear of being deported—an illness, an arrest for a driving violation, any little thing could devastate their lives. They can't ask the police for help if they're attacked, they can't be quoted in a newspaper, or ever stand out in any way. They live in fear and silence. Is that what you want? Because they also have one another, people who share their stories and fears. You'd be alone. It would be intolerable."

"What I live with now is worse than intolerable. Sending my child over and over to stay with a dangerous man—it's like a punishment thought up in hell! Anything would be better than waking up every day to the threat of Daniel's violence. Every day, every day!"

"But I might never see you and Ben again," John answered. "It would kill me."

Mildred fell silent.

John said, "Maybe I'm arguing against you out of selfishness. But please wait before you give up hope. Trust in the courts a little longer."

"Please sit, Melanie," Vogelsang told me. "You make me nervous, hanging over the couch like a vulture." When I dropped down beside Mildred, Vogelsang continued, "It's way, way too soon for you to talk this way, Mildred. And moral arguments aside, child snatching is risky and illegal. If you took off with Ben and were caught, the court might fix it so that you never saw him again. Right now you're a ways from losing custody. We haven't begun to show the court our evidence. That's for the full custody hearing."

"I can't just sit back hoping that Ben doesn't get hurt too badly," Mildred answered. "What if he doesn't last until the hearing? And when the hearing finally happens, what can you tell the judge that will matter to him? That judge is not going to protect Ben." Mildred stood up, very agitated, and said, "I could have fought off Daniel! But the court makes him bigger than he is. The judge gives Daniel so much power over us!"

"You're despairing, Mildred," John said. He stood and faced her. "You can't afford to do that. You—" He pulled her toward him, and patted her back, holding her close. I was touched, and embarrassed; their knees knocked against mine, and I felt I should not be watching them from such a peculiar angle.

"The judge threatened to take Ben from me," Mildred told her father, crying. "He said he would send Ben to live with Daniel if I didn't agree to whatever kind of visitation he wanted."

Vogelsang waited for them both to sit down again. I moved over and they wedged in beside me. Then Vogelsang counselled: "You can't start predicting disaster yet, Mildred. You haven't even seen the psychiatrist's report. The judge said what he did about changing temporary custody in order to pressure you toward a settlement—"

"To *pressure* me? He thinks it's OK to pressure me by threatening to hand my child to a man who hurts him?" Mildred's voice rose angrily. "What makes him think he has the right to do that?"

"Let's talk legal strategy," Vogelsang answered. "That's why you have a lawyer."

Mildred sat back and crossed her arms. Then she closed her eyes, as if she hoped that the rumbling tones of that bass voice might hypnotize her.

"The opinion of the psychiatric expert is crucial," Vogelsang said methodically. "It would be extraordinary for a psychiatrist to recommend custody to Daniel. First, Ben is a young child, attached to his mother. So, there's the fact that you've always been Ben's primary caretaker. And whether or not Bracken cares about wife beating, most normal people would be a little appalled by it—surely it will affect a psychiatrist's judgment of Daniel."

"A psychiatrist is not a normal person," Mildred said. "Ask Dr. Eatman." She laughed a little.

"And then, Mildred, there's the fact that a man who beats his wife and children, and succeeds in hiding it from everyone else, usually leads a double life in other ways. It's always easier in a case like this if the husband is white-collar or educated. Subpoena his bank records, his work records, his tax forms; you'll find other crimes of deception lined up there, evenly as teeth. If Daniel had a responsible job, he'd embezzle. A check of his credentials was sure to turn up some irregularity. We'll find more on him. We gained a little advantage today. The judge backtracked a little from his threat about temporary custody—"

"That was good," Mildred said, opening her eyes. "The Yale and Fulbright." She looked at her father and said, "Did you hear?"

John said, "I've just learned," and shook his head. "Daniel Munk is all mirrors to the bottom of his being."

"It seemed to be the only thing that gave Bracken pause," I said to Vogelsang. "Why didn't you tell us before?"

"Because I needed to guarantee an element of surprise. You all looked genuinely surprised—you and Mildred, and even Trippler. And the judge noticed. Bracken looked—he looked like he realized he'd been bamboozled."

"Bamboozled," Mildred said, as if tasting the word.

"I thought Trippler was going to disappear into a puff of smoke right there," I said.

Mildred snorted, and then we all laughed, a little hysterically, a little uncontrollably, half-relieved.

"Before we go to court again, Mildred," Vogelsang said, "I'm going to draw up affidavits to submit to the psychiatric expert, affidavits on every incident we can think of that shows duplicity in Daniel's character. And his dangerousness. I want one from Melanie, on what happened at the lake, and in the parking lot, and with Ben's life preserver. And one from you, John, and from Ottilie about Ben's bruises. The judge might ignore the affidavits, but the psychiatrist shouldn't. If the judge dares to raise the prospect of temporary custody again, the psychiatrist's report should stop him. And Mildred, you'll get that affidavit from your neighbor in Milwaukee, and you yourself need to write something up now about Daniel's violence toward you—that will make it easier when you have to talk to the psychiatrist."

"My mother once convinced a psychiatrist she *was* a psychiatrist," Mildred said.

John drummed his fingers on his Bible, smiled, and said, "I remember that. It was at a World Council of Churches gathering, and Annie showed a newly published psychiatry book to a renowned psychoanalyst—"

"It was called *The Female Mind*—" Mildred said.

"And Annie told him she had written it, and she signed it with the author's signature for him! The author's name was Cecil Bone, and he was really a man."

John and Mildred dissolved together into laughter.

Vogelsang put a damper on this, saying, "I wouldn't dwell on the fact of your mother's mental illness when you're interviewed by the forensic expert. If he doesn't bring it up, don't tell him."

"What do you mean?" John asked. "That Mildred shouldn't reveal her mother was troubled because it will make the psychiatrist doubt Mildred's mental stability?"

Mildred took her father's hand. "Well, I've always been a little off the wall, Dad," she cajoled.

"Some psychiatrists believe mental instability is inherited," Vogelsang answered, "and some don't. Most wouldn't make assumptions about you. But don't take any chances with the legal expert."

"Oh, great," Mildred said. "He'll think I'm deluded when I tell him Daniel assaulted me." She made an effort to keep her voice light, to spare her father, I thought.

No one responded. Vogelsang cleared his throat and looked at me. I finally thought to say to Mildred, "I guess it's going to feel weird, telling some guy you've never met about what Daniel did to you, just because he's being paid—"

"Maybe I'll get really stoned first," Mildred answered jokingly. And then she stood, and told everyone, "I need about fifteen years of sleep. I'm going to bed: Wake me up when the court case is over." Then, abruptly, she left us.

John whispered, "Melanie, don't let her be alone right now. It's just that—"

I followed Mildred upstairs.

Ben cried out "Mommy!" He slid off his bed and rushed to Mildred. "I had a dream about a nightmare!"

Mildred picked him up and said quietly, "What did the nightmare look like?" A bedside lamp threw a circle of light on Ben's pillow. Mildred had told me Ben would no longer sleep in the dark.

"He was a ghost," Ben said.

"Was he inside or outside our house?"

Ben concentrated. "He was standing on the window."

"Do you know what I used to do when I was little girl and I was afraid of ghosts?" Mildred asked, setting Ben back on the bed. "I slept with a big stick next to my pillow. Then, if a ghost came near, I would wave the stick, snicker-snack! and say, 'If you take one step closer, I'll wallop your ghosty head off!'"

Ben laughed.

"And after that, he was a ghost of a ghost," I said. Ben gave me a quizzical look.

"Now where's *your* sword?" Mildred asked Ben, pulling up his covers.

"On the floor!" Ben answered.

I searched the room and found several swords: a toy wooden one, and a plastic pirate sword, and the King Arthur sword, and a rubber dagger. I brought them all over to Ben.

"Just put these all right here next to your pillow," Mildred said, "and nobody will dare bother you. In fact, if any ghosts try to bother me tonight, I'm going to say, 'You better watch it! I wouldn't come around here, because Ben will slice you in two.' "

Ben stuck each weapon under the elastic of his pajamas, down into his pants leg. He turned over, the bundle of swords looking immensely uncomfortable, his arms circling their hilts. He closed his eyes.

I stood beside Ben's bed for a while, until Mildred decided he was asleep. Then Mildred said to me, "Melanie, have you ever wanted to trade in your life for a new one? I keep feeling like my life has ended somehow—like it's been made too small. As if Daniel has succeeded in fencing me into a world where all the joy was left on the other side of the fence. As if my life isn't mine anymore."

THE FOLLOWING DAY Ottilie returned home early. Around five in the evening, I heard her clattering angrily in the kitchen, opening and slamming drawers and cabinets. I descended the stairs and found her in the den, clinking her teaspoon against a steaming cup and reading a stack of Aunt Mimi's postcards. Ottilie had not removed her parka. From behind she looked like a stranger, twice her bulk. For a moment I saw her as Aunt Mimi herself, returned from the Antarctic to rest in Muskellunge and tell us stories of her travels.

"I'm such a fool," Ottilie told me. "I was foolish to want to believe that Mr. Vogelsang might help Mildred."

"You think we'll lose?" I asked.

"Melanie, I've just visited Daniel in Eklundville—"

"You visited Daniel? Ottilie, that might have been dangerous, not letting us know beforehand—"

"Daniel doesn't want anything," Ottilie answered, ignoring my warning. "He doesn't care if he gets Ben, or what shape visitation takes."

"What do you mean?" I asked, baffled. "You think he'll back down?"

"No!" Ottilie said. "I mean that now that Daniel knows how much the court proceedings hurt Mildred, being in court is an end in itself to him. He'll ask the court for whatever Mildred doesn't want, and fight to the death over it. He *likes* being in court."

I considered what the effects of this would be, if it were true—Judge Bracken would exert increasing pressure on Mildred, bullying her with threats of changing temporary custody, and never believing that we had no power to settle the case.

"Maybe Daniel's bluffing, and wants us to think he doesn't want to settle."

Ottilie answered, "Melanie, you have to see what he's doing! He told me that the court—the phrase he used was that the court is 'his weapon of choice.'"

"It won't be the first time someone has abused court process to—"

"I think that if Daniel keeps getting the visitation he demands, he'll just look for something new to fight over. He's going to keep changing what he wants," Ottilie said, "so that he can keep Mildred in front of that judge, so that he can keep her terrified that she'll lose Ben."

I thought of how many of my father's cases Ottilie had watched unfold in the papers. Ottilie pulled on her hat, and her hair disappeared in a circle of rabbit fur. "I'm going out," she said. "I can't stand being locked inside the rest of the evening." She departed without inviting me to join her. Her car coughed in the driveway and moved restlessly along the snowy road.

WHEN I LEFT the house, it was long past dark, and snow sifted lightly from the trees under a brilliant, starry sky. I headed toward Tikalsky's, where I ordered knockwurst and beer. I had drunk a second Pferd, and was almost finished with the knockwurst, when I saw Trippler's Tyrolean hat only two tables away. He was staring at me. I wondered how long he had been there.

He signalled to me and then came over to my table without being asked. He wore his green velvety jacket and carried a mug with him. When he sat down in the chair opposite me, I saw that he was drinking cocoa.

"You're a hot young lawyer, no?" he asked me. "Top of your class at Columbia? Clerked in the Second Circuit?" He sipped his chocolate noisily and lowered his eyebrows. "You didn't know I went to law school in New York, did you? Fordham. When I was your age, I worked for a Manhattan trial judge, New York Supreme Court. First case, a divorce action, the mother alleged that her husband had beat her up for years. Put her in the hospital. Broke her ribs, broke her nose, broke her jaw. Fled the marriage for her life, there were four kids. By the time she came to court two years later, she and the kids were living with an accountant, decent guy. She couldn't get alimony without proving the husband was at fault. Married fifteen years. Housewife. So the judge finds her at fault for abandoning the husband, and the husband refuses to divorce her. No alimony, no remarriage. Later the judge told me, 'I'm old-fashioned. I don't like the idea of a woman shacking up with a man without being married. Maybe this will encourage her to marry the accountant.' Well, she couldn't have remarried, could she, since she couldn't get a divorce? Same judge ordered another guy to pay his ex-wife ten percent more in maintenance than he'd ever made in gross salary. No one should ask how law and sausage are made."

"Why are you talking to me?" I asked.

"And that's New York! 'New York, New York!'" Trippler sang. "Imagine what happens in our little town midwestern courts."

"Why are you talking to me?" I repeated.

"Because you're not even born yet." Trippler sipped his chocolate, smiled, and said, "To warn you."

"I already know what you're trying to teach me."

"Of course, you're Miss Top of Her Class at Columbia! All a man like me needs is a little bit of a woman in his life, and he's fine. But you're too much woman, aren't you; you want a lot more, Miss First at Columbia."

"You're as crazy as your client," I said.

"Crazy like a fox," he answered. "And what's your role, second-seating a custody case? Without ever saying a word? I could call you as a witness. Smoking marijuana? See the writing on the wall? Why keep spending your client's money when you're bound to lose?"

I did not tell Trippler that we were representing Mildred for nothing. Nor did I betray any reaction to Trippler's allusion to marijuana— although I wondered whether he would make something of my having told Daniel that I had smoked with Mildred. Instead, like any lawyer, I bluffed.

"Ask your client about the time he got drunk behind the church," I said. I remembered nothing of those hours, but then, Daniel didn't either. "And I hope you have a big retainer. Daniel won't pay you just because he promised to. He won't deal any straighter with his lawyer than he did with his wife."

Trippler pursed his lips, sipped his chocolate, let out a bark of a laugh. "My retainer's plenty big," he answered.

"A lawyer should be willing to defend anyone—as long as they pay him, right?" I asked. "How do you look at yourself shaving in the morning, knowing who Daniel Munk is? Knowing what you're doing to a three-year-old?"

"Well, I guess I should go shoot myself," Trippler answered. "Why don't I do that, I'm that sorry. I'll just shoot myself." Trippler laughed again. "I'm a mouthpiece," he concluded. "A very expensive mouthpiece."

I signalled for the waiter and paid my bill and tip at the cashier's counter, leaving Trippler sitting alone at the table. I counted my change, and set all of it down but one dollar bill—it was one of Mildred's. I thumbed the red, taunting writing and tucked the bill in my pocket.

WHEN I LEFT Tikalsky's, the moon was large and orange as a sun, and the black branches of trees stood out starkly against it. The bank clock gave the temperature at ten below zero. I almost felt warm. I remembered how, as a girl, I had considered any temperature above zero to be mild.

As I approached the halfway house I heard voices. Three people stood in the turned-under tomato beds, looking at the sky. High above them the diamond silhouette of a kite somersaulted across the moon. I stopped to watch. The kite swam upward into the air like a joyous sea animal, floated downward, and rose again.

"Stupendous!" Dr. Eatman's voice said. "It's like something out of a dream." As I came up behind him, the smell of tobacco smoke engulfed me. A struck match illuminated his face momentarily inside the hood of his parka; he grinned like a jack-o'-lantern, and smoke curled behind him.

"Hey," Matt said. He tugged an invisible line, and the kite dove in a devil-may-care swoop and then uprighted itself.

"Can Ben see it?" Matt asked.

"Yeah, everyone's watching from Ben's room," Mildred answered.

In a high window three faces pressed against the glass—Ottilie and John and Ben.

Matt tugged the string again, and now the kite swam upward over the moon and circled it, fell and ascended. I wondered whether, in the entire history of the world, anyone had ever thought to fly a kite at night.

"It looks like it's moving by itself," I said. "It's strange, not seeing the string." I reached for the slender path that connected Matt and the kite and felt the tug of fish line. Matt handed me a reel. I must have stood there for twenty minutes, feeling the line grow taut and slacken, watching the kite climb and soar, and in that time, I forgot myself and the universe I inhabited and the circumstances of our lives.

"Don't hog the line," Dr. Eatman finally said. "Give me a try."

I passed him the reel. "It's mesmerizing," I told him.

Mildred said, "It makes me feel like I don't live here in Muskellunge. I feel like I'm somewhere else, you know? In some undersea place. Heaven. Mars." She and Matt both looked longingly at the kite, and I wanted to follow them to it, far from our oppressive and confining world.

6

JOHN STECK suggested that I use the halfway house van on the three Saturdays before the next court date; I could stretch out in the back when I slept. It did not occur to him that I would do anything but spend the night in Eklundville during Ben's weekend visits. John and Matt stocked the van with a butane stove, the space heater, an arctic-quality sleeping bag, and a radio. Matt gave me a flashlight and said, in a voice that sounded purely sane, "When it's Ben's bedtime, you can shine this flashlight out the window, and Ben will shine his back." I experimented with potatoes, roasting them, wrapping them in tin foil and then towels for insulation, and piling them in the van, hoping they would retain their heat longer than I would.

"Melanie, you still might freeze to death," John told me, but he did not suggest that I make another plan. "Thanks, I haven't thanked you. It will help Ben just to know you're nearby."

The first Saturday, Mildred took a bus to Chicago to be interviewed by the psychiatric expert. She had decided to hold two interviews back to back, to avoid being so far from Ben two Saturdays in a row. At that time we assumed Ben would have to travel to Chicago to be observed with his parents on the final Saturday. I drove Mildred to the bus station, and on the way, she checked the inventory of Ben's overnight bag: his flashlight, a sword and dagger, a stuffed tiger, a toothbrush, pajamas, his wolf tail, and a piece of Petoski stone from Ottilie he called his magic rock. Mildred hugged Ben so long before she got on the Greyhound that I thought it would leave without her.

When Mildred boarded the bus, Ben twisted in my arms and

shouted, "Don't go! Don't go!" As the bus pulled away, he cried hysterically. I tried to calm him, saying, "Ben, Mommy's coming back tomorrow." He kicked me so hard in the stomach that I lost my breath. I sat
down on a bench, and he wrested himself from me and ran toward the
highway. I ran after him, swooped him up like a predator, and held him
tightly while he struggled. He cried out and kicked until he exhausted
himself. I carried him inside the bus station and bought him a warm
cider.

He stared at me sullenly with those minnow eyes. He looked so
small, so new—as if his three years on earth were not weighty enough
to hold him to our world.

"You know, Ben," I said, "you won't always be so little. One day
you'll be bigger than Mommy, bigger than Daddy."

"Bigger than Daddy?" Ben answered. "Bigger than you?"

"Probably," I said. "You'll probably be bigger than me, too."

"I'll be bigger," he said. He smiled, just a little, an inward smile.
"I'll grow like popcorn," he concluded.

I could not bear the thought of taking him to Daniel.

It was dark at four-thirty when I drove to Eklundville. I gave Ben
his flashlight to play with in the van, and I told him to shine it out his
window at me that night. I tried to joke with him in a way I never had
before with children. I told him that if I were a spider, I would crawl
into his room and sleep under his pillow; that if I were an old shoe, I
would snuggle under his covers and sing to him; that if I were a nightmare, I would put on a nice dress, and sit on the foot of his bed with
my hands folded on my lap just so he would talk to me.

"That's not true!" Ben said.

When we arrived at Daniel's, the moon rested on the roof of his
house like a pumpkin, and I told Ben, "Look, the moon is waiting for
you."

Ben answered, "No, it's in the sky." But then he said, "A kite was
flying on the moon!"

"That was your Mommy and Matt out there, flying that kite," I told
him. "They're friends with the moon." I took Ben from the car and led
him up the stairs to Daniel.

THAT NIGHT BEN did not ever shine his flashlight out the window;
perhaps Daniel confiscated it. My flashlight dimmed down until it threw

a frail target on the books I tried to read. I turned the space heater up, and I pushed down deep in my arctic sleeping bag until I was sweltering. I burned my hands on the roasted potatoes. I listened to the only radio station with late-night reception: A revivalist preacher predicted the end of the world until his voice shut off at two o'clock. My rustlings mingled with the noises of half-dreams, distorting my sense of time and awakening me from half-sleep. Late into the night I thought I heard a child's cry but it was so high, I wondered if I had imagined it—it was like the cry of a summer insect, eerily beautiful, racing upward in a scale out of reach of the human ear. In the morning the squealing of Mr. Eklund's pigs woke me. I wondered if I had slept ten straight minutes.

At nine o'clock I knocked on Daniel's door, but he refused to answer. I returned to the van, warmed up the motor, and played the radio loudly. Mr. Eklund's face appeared behind the gas station window, swam backward, and then reappeared and hovered there.

At ten Daniel came outside. He put Ben down in the snow in front of the blue house and returned inside, without speaking. Ben stayed where he was, looking at his feet. I picked him up, and he did not fight or hug me. I belted him in in the back seat. On the ride home Ben at first eluded every attempt I made to talk with him.

"Ben, did you have a good time?"

"I don't know."

"What did you do?"

"I don't know."

"Did you play checkers?"

"No."

"Did you go outside?"

"No."

"Did you stay inside?"

"No."

"Did you eat lunch?"

"No."

"Do you like saying no?"

"Yes," Ben answered, and tilted his head back against his seat. He looked weary, like an adult after a long week.

"Matt and Stretch Rockefeller made you icicles out of Kool-Aid," I said. "They hung a can from a hot-water pipe on the roof, and it dripped down Kool-Aid all night."

"Will it give me chicken pops?"

"You can't get chicken pox from things," I said.

"Daddy says all the presents will give me chicken pops."

"Daddy made a mistake. You can't get chicken pox from things. Believe me, I know. I've had chicken pox, and worse."

Ben didn't answer.

"The icicles are green and purple," I said. "Everybody missed you. You were gone so long."

"Daddy took away my sword," Ben said miserably.

When I looked in the rearview mirror, Ben was crying quietly. His head tilted forward and he whimpered. "Oh, oh, oh!" he said. "Oh, oh, oh."

I pulled over the car. I crawled in the back and put Ben on my lap. His clothes smelled like stale urine, and his hair was acrid. "What's wrong, honey? What is it?" I asked him. I remembered my mother saying the same words to me, in a scene whose details I had all forgotten, other than her voice saying, "What is it, honey? What is it?"

Ben kept sobbing, in that way children have, where their chests convulse and they hiccough as they cry. I could not help him stop. After a while he exhausted himself and curled sideways in my lap. I stroked his hair and felt his forehead. It was hot and soaked with tears. I held him until he relaxed in my arms, and then I drove him home.

When I carried him into the Stecks', Mrs. Shove was there, talking with Vogelsang and reading over an affidavit he had prepared for her. She wore an auburn pantsuit and a new hair style that made me think of a bantam.

Mildred rushed to the door, lifted Ben, and said, "Sugarbeet, you're back." She whispered to me, "He smells like an old drunk."

He roused, pressed his face into her shoulder, and said, "I do not!"

"He feels a little hot," I said.

"I came back," Ben said.

Mrs. Shove walked over to Mildred and touched Ben's cheek. "It's not really a fever," she told me. "He's probably just overtired. It seems like ninety-nine or a hundred. I used to give my boys a sponge bath when they were like that."

"That's just what I'll do," Mildred told her. "This boy needs fumigating." She kissed Ben's hair.

"Well, let me help," Mrs. Shove said. She followed Mildred up the stairs, to the bathroom, talking. I heard Ben cry out, and Mrs. Shove say, "Why, his pants look like he pooped in them a day ago. Look at this rash!"

I reached the top of the stairs as Mildred was settling Ben into the bathtub.

"Hey you," Mildred was saying. "Hey you, hey you."

Mrs. Shove sat on the toilet lid and poured bubble bath into the tub.

I picked up Ben's soiled pants and ran them under the sink tap. They reeked. I reached under the sink for soap, filled the basin with soapy water, and scrubbed at them.

"Try this, Sugarbeet," Mildred said, and handed Ben two orange aspirin tablets.

"They taste like candy," Ben said.

"How was the interview?" I asked her.

"I don't know," Mildred answered. "It was awkward. The doctor is sort of full of himself. He's not going to ask to see Ben. Don't you think that's strange? That he wouldn't want to see how Ben acts around Daniel?"

"What did that Munk-man do, run him around in those wet clothes?" Mrs. Shove asked, peering at the sink.

"Do you have a penis?" Ben asked Mrs. Shove.

Mrs. Shove raised one plucked eyebrow and answered, "Not that I know of."

Ben looked at the bubbles rising around him, and said, "I took a bath last night."

"Well, it looks like you need another one," Mildred told him.

"Daddy made me take a bath, and then he made me sleep in dirty clothes!"

John poked his head inside the bathroom. "How's it going up here?" he asked.

"Oh, we ladies are just having a to-do," Mrs. Shove answered.

"Everyone's in the bathroom!" Ben said.

"Matt and Stretch Rockefeller sent Ben this," John said, holding up a long icicle, striped green and purple. "It's lime and grape flavored."

"You can't come in!" Ben told him. "There's no more room in the bathtub."

"I'm not getting in the bathtub," John said. "I'm just handing you your icicle."

Ben reached for the icicle and said "It's hot!" and withdrew his hand.

"I'll take it," Mrs. Shove said, and wrapped a washcloth around the base. "Hold it here, honey." John's footsteps receded down the stairs.

"Daddy made me take a bath with him, too."

"Daddy took a bath with you?" Mildred asked.

"Why, he's too big for that! There wouldn't be enough room," Mrs. Shove said.

Ben took the icicle, stirred the bubbles with his free hand to clear a circle in the water, and stuck the icicle's point into it. "It turns the water purple," he said.

"It's melting," Mrs. Shove told him.

"Do you have a penis?" Ben asked Mildred.

"No, sweetheart," she answered. "I'm a lady, so I don't have a penis."

"*I* have a penis. Daddy has a big penis. A big penis that gets bigger when you touch it."

Mrs. Shove frowned. I stopped wringing the clothes in the sink.

Mildred drew a breath and asked, "Did Daddy let you touch his big old penis?"

Ben looked at his mother's face, puzzled, and said, "I don't know."

"Christ," I said.

"He got into the bathtub with me!" Ben answered.

"He did?" Mildred asked.

"It was my bathtub!" Ben said. "I hit him with my sword."

"You had your sword in the bathtub?" I said.

Ben smiled. "Yes." Then he frowned. "He took my sword! He hit me back with it."

"He did? Which sword?" Mildred asked. "The wood one with the red handle?"

Ben nodded. "It's my sword," he said.

"Where did he hit you?"

"He smattered the side of my head."

"Did he hit you on the head?"

"He *smattered* it. It made noise right through my neck." Ben touched his ear. Then he repeated, "It's my sword." Almost as an afterthought, he added, "And then he punched me on the side."

Mildred wiped the bubbles from Ben's shoulders and pulled his hands up.

"Show me where," she said.

"Here," Ben answered, touching the fold of his upper arm. And then we all saw it, on the right side of his rib cage, high up, a yellow bruise like an enamel rose on china.

MILDRED WOULD NOT release Ben for further visitation. "Daniel found something that would force me to keep Ben away. Now he'll accuse me of interfering with visitation," Mildred said. "His lawyer will use this to argue that I shouldn't have custody, won't he? And it won't matter to that judge that Daniel hit Ben, or did anything else to him, will it?"

When Mildred asked me this, she was seated in Ottilie's peacock-blue armchair. The hair in Mildred's braid had unwoven in feathery tufts, as if she had been pulling on it out of nervousness. Her flannel shirt was buttoned wrong, the collar slanting on the left side to meet a low buttonhole. Ben lay asleep in her lap. After the Saturday visit Ben clung to her as if he feared she would disappear if he strayed so far as another room by himself.

Vogelsang had filed a new petition in court the Monday after Ben's overnight visit, asking to terminate unsupervised visitation and attaching affidavits from all of us, and a letter from Ben's pediatrician. ("I assured the mother that there is no evidence of a concussion," he wrote, "and the hearing is intact. But the bruises on the upper torso and behind the ear are large.") Judge Bracken sat on the papers. He did not want extra work, and set the return date for the new petition on the same day he had originally scheduled for us to appear in court.

Even before this result, I thought the judge would merely find the further suggestion of Daniel's lack of sexual boundaries with his son distasteful, and shun our papers, and dismiss the evidence of Daniel's violence. Daniel was too hard to assemble into a picture, and an understanding of Daniel's motives would never be within the grasp of Judge Bracken's court: Daniel's love of brinkmanship, his desire to know that he could get away with anything. Even now it is unnerving for me to remember how effectively a man like Daniel, who subverted every code, fit the law into his hand like a well-worn tool. It was as though the law had been designed specifically for him all along.

On Monday afternoon, when Vogelsang rapped on Ottilie's door and entered, his grim face already told us the bad news.

Outside, behind the house, Ottilie and Matt's laughter rose incongruously. Ottilie had bought a five-year-old Impala, and Matt was standing in front of it with the hood open, as Ottilie pressed the accelerator. Ottilie had told me that her old car would never make it through the winter, but I thought she had purchased the newer car to keep Matt occupied. Now the car motor roared, and Matt jumped in the air and danced a little jig. Ottilie exclaimed something, and vapor streamed like cirrus clouds behind the Impala.

Vogelsang kicked the snow from his boots and frowned.

"Sit down, Melanie," he said, seating himself on the couch.

I sat down. The image of Daniel's face flashed in front of me—that handsome, red-haired, angular face—and it struck me then that Daniel Munk was the scariest man I had ever known.

Vogelsang said, "Mildred, I received a copy of the psychiatric expert's report from the court clerk. It's going to upset you. It's a piece of work, but a good cross-examination will reveal the expert's bias and poke holes in his report. And we're going to hire our own expert, to challenge this report."

Mildred looked at him suspiciously and leaned back, physically bracing herself for the next blow. Vogelsang handed us each a copy of the report and said to Mildred, "Maybe you'd like to be alone when you read this, and then we'll talk about it."

Mildred lifted Ben's head gently from her lap and resettled it on the chair, as if she were afraid that the force of her emotional reaction to more bad news might injure him. She stroked his hair and said, "If he wakes up, call me right away." She climbed the stairs to the spare bedroom and closed the door.

Vogelsang folded his hands in his lap, closed his eyes, and pressed them with his fingers. I read the report:

Preliminary Comments

I, Arthur Pale, received my doctorate in child psychiatry from the University of Chicago in 1963. I am the author of *Children in Crisis: The Experience of Single Parenthood* and several scholarly articles, and have practiced in a clinical setting for thirteen years, five of those in a supervisory capacity. I have served as an expert witness in over forty custody proceedings. In my work, I strive for even-handedness and objectivity. For this reason, I have never, in my career, accepted payment as a hired witness for one side in any custody case. I contract my services only when I am at liberty to examine both parties and to draw independent conclusions. Before undertaking this evaluation, I met with each party for two eighty-minute sessions, and studied documents provided to me by each.

Interview with Mr. Munk

Mr. Munk, a graduate of Yale Divinity School and a doctoral student in comparative religion at the University of Wisconsin, made a great effort to control his emotions during his interview. However, at several junctures, he was unable to hold back tears as he told how his wife had abandoned him after his prolonged efforts to hold together their marriage.

According to Mr. Munk, his wife, Mildred, comes from an unconventional family. Her father is an avowed communist and Unitarian, and her mother was apparently institutionalized after a clinical diagnosis of manic depression, and died in a drunk-driving accident. Mildred's mother believed in free love, and gave her daughter unbridled access to psychedelic drugs such as hashish and marijuana. Mr. Munk smiled ruefully when he said that initially he had been drawn to Mildred's "iconoclasm." He speculated that as a man of religion, he foolishly had felt that her ideals were a salutary challenge to his own theological views.

The couple met while Mr. Munk was doing research in Brazil on a Fulbright scholarship. Their marriage occurred in January 1973, and ten months later, their son, John Munk, was born. The child was named after Mildred's father, "John Benjamin."

According to Mr. Munk, as long as the couple resided in Brazil, their lives were quite conventional and peaceable. However, six months before his research was completed, Mildred received a letter from her father, and insisted on returning early to the United States. Mr. Munk believed that Mildred's father, whom he believes now exerts an "unhealthy" influence on her, pressured her to return, despite the devastating effect this would have on the family and the child. The child was approximately two years old at the time, a bad age, Mr. Munk felt, for the boy to be deprived of his close relationship with his father.

When Mr. Munk completed his research and rejoined his wife in Muskellunge, he found that she had changed dramatically—the word he used in explaining this change was that she had "fooled" him. Every aspect of her character, her speech, her dress, and her social habits, was different. Mr. Munk stated that he considered himself a "moderate conservative," and fairly open-minded, but that he found his wife's clothes inappropriately revealing. She also began to express views which echoed her father's and which Mr. Munk described as "atheistic" and "leftist." Mr. Munk paused to clarify that he believes each person has the right to maintain any lawful religious or political perspective. What troubled him, he said, was that his wife either had concealed her views during their engagement, or had proven herself extremely suggestible to family pressures. He said he felt "unnerved" by her ability to dissemble facets of her self as important as her religion and politics.

Mr. Munk's greatest concern, however, was that upon his return to Muskellunge, he discovered that his wife frequently indulges in the use of hashish and marijuana in the presence of their child. He stated that after he had made several attempts to counsel and dissuade her against the abuse of such drugs, the couple had a serious argument, and he flushed her drugs down the toilet. Mr. Munk states that his wife intends to deny in court they ever had any altercations about drugs. However, he has supplied an affidavit from Mr. James Piening, an employee of Pferd Beer Factory, who states that Mildred came to his factory during a tour one evening, clearly "inebriated" from the effects of drugs, and producing a disruptive influence on his tour. Mr. Piening averred that Mildred "reeked of marijuana" during this incident. According to Mr. Munk, Mildred bragged to him about her conduct on this occasion, in a manner which made him fear that "she lacked all sense of right and wrong."

After the incident in which Mr. Munk flushed her "stash" down the toilet, Mildred told him that if he ever took her "stash" again, she would "turn everyone against him." Thereafter, he said, his wife conducted a campaign to persuade her father, and all acquaintances Mr. Munk had made during his brief stay in Muskellunge, that he had been mistreating her.

Mr. Munk showed anger only at one juncture in the interview, when he said that his wife had acted with "unbelievable self-centeredness." However, he then contained his anger, and explained that he had been genuinely embarrassed by her stories. He has always considered himself to be a "gentle soul," and as a man of religion, he is particularly chagrined by the accusations. He consistently denied allegations that he had ever injured or threatened his wife, and will produce witnesses to testify that there was "no violence whatsoever" in their relationship. He is concerned that under the guidance of her lawyers, his wife will be forced to stick to her invented story. He says that the last weeks for him have been "Kafkaesque." When questioned whether he believed his wife is deluded, he answered, "I don't have the expertise to answer that question," and then rose a little to her defense, saying that she might say things in anger which she later regrets.

Generally, rather than express vindictiveness toward his wife, Mr. Munk showed genuine concern for her. Upon further questioning, however, he confessed that he had at times been afraid that Mildred, like her mother, might be suffering from mental illness. Mildred's father apparently runs a halfway house for the severely disturbed, and Mildred preferred to choose her friends from that place. Mr. Munk became especially concerned when Mildred repeatedly permitted her son to play with a dangerous schizophrenic, who has two prior arrests for assault on a police officer.

In early September, Mr. Munk once again surprised his wife smoking marijuana in the same quarters where her son slept, presumably under her sole care. Mr. Munk thereafter removed his child from the home, and took him to Milwaukee for his safety. After three weeks away from her family, Mildred, he felt, made "great strides," and they once again coexisted peacefully. However, after receiving repeated phone calls from her father, Mildred "played an ugly, nasty trick picking up the kid and leaving," without any warning to him. At this time, Mildred returned to Muskellunge, and since then has acted under her family's influence.

Mr. Munk stated that although his child is still of tender years, he often babysat his son in Brazil while his wife took trips of as long as a week to visit local tourist attractions and to "get away." He says that he became "an old hand" at changing diapers, and "quite a cook." Otherwise, they shared equally in caring for Ben.

Mr. Munk concluded that he wished to do what was "right for his family." He presented a compelling case for continued close supervision of his son's upbringing. Despite the sad story he relates of his marriage, Mr. Munk remains forgiving of his wife and states that he only wishes for Mildred to return. "I believe in marriage, and I want our marriage to last," he concluded.

Interviews with Mrs. Munk

Mrs. Munk commenced her interview by volunteering that she had been compelled to leave Mr. Munk because of his violence toward her and his "inappropriate conduct" toward his son. When asked to clarify these allegations, she complained that Mr. Munk had struck her on occasion, and that he once had "placed his hands around her neck and squeezed."

Throughout her interview sessions, Mrs. Munk spent the bulk of her time complaining about Mr. Munk's mistreatment of her and his inadequacy as a father. She complained that he does not care for the child when he is sick, does not change his soiled clothes, fails to adhere to basic rules of safety around boat docks, etc. She believes that he has lost his temper with the boy, and is offended by her husband's practice of showering with and disrobing before the three-year-old John. She seems unwilling to acknowledge the contribution her husband is willing to make to his son's upbringing.

Using legal terminology, perhaps as directed by her lawyer, Mrs. Munk asserted that she always had been her son's "primary caretaker." She denied that she ever had left her son alone with his father while she vacationed, and averred that she would never have left John alone with his father "even overnight." She stated that Mr. Munk's contact with the child had been "sporadic," and as an example she stated that he had remained alone in Brazil for six months after she returned to Wisconsin with the child. She stated that she was uncertain whether Mr. Munk was "able to enjoy or really connect with children." When asked whether she believed children need fathers, she answered, "It depends on the father."

On the one hand, Mildred stated that she would "not interfere" with Mr. Munk visiting his son. On the other, however, she had "grave reservations" about leaving the child with Mr. Munk. Apparently Mildred initially saw no contradiction in her statements. When asked for clarification, she said that she felt placed in a "double bind," because she had been told that the law would penalize her if she did not allow visitation. However, if she did not voice her objections to visitation, no one would believe she was serious in her reservations.

Mrs. Munk denies that she is a habitual drug user. She says that she has never "indulged" in marijuana use in the company of her son. She denies having used hard drugs.

Mrs. Munk denies that she is romantically involved with anyone at this time.

Mrs. Munk then returned to the theme of her husband's violence, and asked why she was expected to deal with a violent husband without help from the court, a man who, she maintained, "would be more than any one person would be able to deal with." She said that she found the court proceedings exhausting, and that she felt that her motherhood had been overshadowed and undermined by her fear of losing her son, which had made her feel "numb" and "distant from the world." When questioned, she said she did not know whether Mr. Munk harbored similar feelings.

Mrs. Munk has collected several affidavits to bolster her assertions that Mr. Munk mistreats her and acts inappropriately with his son. I have read the affidavits submitted by Mildred, her father, and friends of the family, but I am unable to determine whether these people tailored these affidavits at Mildred's behest.

Mrs. Munk impressed as anxious and depressed during her interviews. She expressed intensely negative feelings, such as anger and fear, during the course of the interview. One would hope that she would be sensitive to the boy's need for seeing his father frequently, and would allow his relationship to flourish in spite of her negative feelings against Mr. Munk. However, she was unable to show any commitment in this direction. This, and her apparent involvement in drugs may make her an inappropriate choice as custodial parent.

Conclusions

Several unfortunate themes run through this unfortunate case. The main one advanced by the mother is that her husband has been violent toward her, and, presumably, the child. I do not possess the expertise to determine whether Mr. Munk is violent toward his wife. However, I saw no evidence, gesture or word indicating that he is a danger to the 3-year-old John, and it is my belief that Mrs. Munk, who is ten years her husband's junior, may be exaggerating without meaning to. Mr. Munk presents as one of the most concerned and dedicated fathers I have met in my career. He is like both a mother and father, in his concern for the child.

Ideally, this couple would undertake counselling with a mental health professional who can help them work out their problems. In particular, this professional may be able to guide Mildred through those troubles which she currently finds "too large for any one person." This interviewer does not accept the now outmoded supposition that only a mother can provide for a child of tender years. Clearly, either parent in this instance has the experience and skills necessary to provide for the boy, and both have divided primary responsibility for his care. If the allegations of drug use are substantiated in court, I therefore would recommend Mr. Munk as a more mature choice for custodial parent.

Please feel free to contact me if I can be of further assistance to the Court.

Sincerely yours,
Arthur Pale, M.D.

AS I FINISHED this report I heard Mildred cry out with anger and outrage. Ottilie entered the house in her parka just as Mildred shouted, "It's a nightmare! They all belong in a nightmare!"

Ottilie climbed the stairs, and I listened to her quiet voice, low and soothing, talking to Mildred. I walked to the back porch, and peered through a small frost hole: Matt leaned over the Impala's motor, pouring antifreeze into the radiator.

"Every last one of them is crazy!" Mildred said. "Any one of them could have protected us! They all had the power to help us, but none of them did!"

Ottilie and Mildred talked for a long time. When I was sure the tumult had died down I carried Ben upstairs and set him on the bed where he had lain asleep, months before, the day we believed Daniel had left our lives. Mildred perched beside Ben, hollow-eyed; she held a fistful of her own hair in her hand.

"He didn't even get Ben's name right," she said.

I groped for something to tell her, but there did not seem to be any word that could help us.

Outside, the low grumbling song of the Impala lifted in the chill air.

Ottilie said, "Mildred. I know when you feel trapped, sometimes you don't see your way clear—I lived whole years at a time once, like that—but you aren't as trapped as you must feel." She lifted Mildred's hand, pressed it between her palms as if it were a small, scared animal, and said, "Do something, Mildred."

ALL WEEK the pending court appearance weighed on all of us. I felt, impossibly, that whatever happened, the custody case could not continue—that, if necessary, the sun should fail to rise, or the ocean cover the land, or any act occur that would pause Daniel and Trippler and Judge Bracken in their orbits. I could not concentrate on my work, or any book I read; I could barely follow a sentence of dialogue when anyone spoke to me. I found myself daydreaming compulsively. When Vogelsang explained the strategy we should take—"the creation of an evidentiary foundation for exposing expert witness bias, a renewal of our request for a guardian, and then we provoke the judge to commit reversible error. We'll appeal immediately and make Bracken act under fear of appellate review"—I thought of how Mildred's starter's pistol would feel in my hand, dense and smooth and arched. How I would tell Daniel, "If you move, I'll shoot you," while Matt stood by, waiting to rescue Ben as I held Daniel at bay. In my mind's eye, in a setting more brilliant than any painting, I saw Matt whirl beside me, a tornado of bright greens and reds. I heard the triangular side window of Daniel's car shattering, the car lock's quiet thump as Matt pulled it upward, Ben's sleepy voice as Matt cradled him from the car, and carried him, loping, to somewhere where Ben and Mildred would be safe. I heard too, the quiet of Matt's fear as he ran, knowing the severe consequences he could suffer for his actions.

When Daniel stepped forward to chase Matt, I dropped the imposter gun and wrapped my arms in a wrestler's embrace around his ribs. As Daniel tried to pull away from me, I reached out to catch my balance. I grabbed his shirt so that he toppled onto me. I felt Daniel's breath on my face, my eyes met his, and I clamped his wrist with both hands, twisted his arm behind his back, and held on to him as if he were part of me, as if he could be subsumed in me. I believed in that moment that Daniel could be pinioned there forever, that whatever shape he assumed, I could wrestle him into place. "Hold on," I commanded myself. "Don't let go."

Vogelsang stopped talking and said, "You haven't heard a word I've told you, Melanie."

IN MID-DECEMBER, the Madison district attorney's office leaked to the press that all charges against Worlfordt and his followers had been dropped. Worlfordt's picture appeared on the front page of the *Milwaukee Journal*, and my father stood behind his right shoulder, grinning like the Cheshire cat—understandably, for while we had secured the dismissal of a single set of charges against my brother, my father had effected the dismissal of hundreds of charges against a legion of defendants.

"It's unprecedented," Vogelsang said. "What could Joel Ratleer possibly have done? Does he have something on the prosector's office? And what about the doctors? Surely they didn't consent to the charges being dropped? I believe that man could talk the stars right out of the sky."

Worlfordt was not smiling in that photograph, however: He looked sullen and disappointed, like a general who has arrived at the battle scene, fully prepared to fight, only to learn that a peace treaty has been negotiated with the enemy the day before. After that week Worlfordt vanished from the news like a vaporous spirit.

In Muskellunge, however, the prosecutor, backed by Chief Komar, continued unwilling to withdraw charges against Reverend Hatch, although it was rumored that Judge Bracken pressured Chief Komar and the prosecutor for such a result. On the return date of the custody hearing, Hatch stood on the front steps of the Muskellunge County courthouse and announced in a sepulchral voice, "The rights of the unborn remain unsung in the state capital, but not in Muskellunge. We are here not to represent ourselves before this earthly tribunal, but instead before the higher court of the Almighty." The slow process of adjudicating the cases of Hatch's followers had begun that morning, as one defendant after another demanded a full trial on the charges of obstructing an officer, resisting arrest and disorderly conduct. All day Judge Bracken listened to cases, and by four, he had resolved only two; there were thirty-seven more defendants in line, each with a separate story and different set of witnesses, each asserting that he had obeyed "a higher morality than the law in defending the unsung rights of the unborn."

When we entered the courtroom shortly after four, Judge Bracken was in a state of high irritation. At first he seemed not to recognize any of us: He looked up from the bench and said, "Where did the prosecutor get to?" The court clerk whispered in his ear, and exited carrying a pile of papers. Then Bracken faced us and said, "Well, gentlemen, haven't you settled your case yet?"

Vogelsang walked up to the stenographer and told her, in an intimate tone, as if the proceeding concerned only her and not the judge, "I'm renewing my request for a guardian *ad litem* to protect the child's interests in this case."

"Denied, denied, denied!" Bracken answered. "And talk to me, not the stenographer."

Without moving at all Vogelsang continued, "And I'm placing further evidence of Mr. Munk's violence toward his son on the record." He then read aloud all of our affidavits attesting to Ben's explanation of his injury. He showed Judge Bracken photographs of the bruises, and described the photographs for the record. Trippler watched indifferently as Judge Bracken added the affidavits and photographs to the pile of papers in front of him.

"Your honor, we've filed an order to show cause with this court, asking for immediate suspension of visitation—"

"We have a report here!" Trippler interrupted, pulling a neat folder bound in vellum from his briefcase. "My client has willingly submitted to an evaluation. A psychiatric expert has thoroughly examined him. A former divinity student! The smartest psychiatrist from the University of Chicago! We have a report! And it says there is no evidence that this man would abuse a child. None whatsoever."

"The psychiatrist who wrote this report needs his head examined," Vogelsang said. "Apparently he was under the delusion that Mister Munk is a Yale Divinity graduate with a Fulbright."

"The girl told him that, not my client."

"So that's the little defense you've cooked up," Vogelsang told him.

Mildred's voice rose behind us: "But the psychiatrist never even met Ben!"

"Admit it! You're wrong, admit it!" Trippler told her, turning around.

"And he never saw how Ben acts around Daniel!" Mildred shouted. "How afraid he is!"

"Admit it!"

"The party will not address opposing counsel directly!" Judge Bracken shouted.

"Mildred, sit down; don't bother with this man," Vogelsang said, gesturing with annoyance toward Trippler or Bracken. "He's not worth it."

"You'd think," Trippler said, "that Mrs. Munk would be glad to learn that her child hasn't been abused. But instead she's actually upset that this report says he hasn't been! Imagine, she's upset!" He focussed on the judge's portrait with such intensity that I almost expected the painted judge to lean forward out of his gilt frame and make a ruling. "Read this, your honor, and this." Trippler opened the report to the last page and pushed it in front of Bracken. "Note the conclusion. The girl's a drug user. Note the marijuana." Bracken took the folder and held it at arm's length, as if he were farsighted.

"Your honor," Vogelsang said, "these conclusions are based solely on a biased acceptance of Mr. Munk's allegations. Mr. Munk obviously has succeeded in fooling this prominent representative of the field of psychiatry. However, we lawyers are more familiar with and better able to identify the seamier side of humanity. After all, we deal with lawyers all day. We're much less likely to be tricked than a member of the psychiatric profession, which is so renowned for its wobbliness of mind."

"Vogelsang," Judge Bracken answered. "I urged you before to settle this case. If you persist, and this marijuana business proves true, I'm not likely to award custody to the mother. Right now I think temporary custody might sit better with the father."

"You can't change temporary custody without a full hearing!" Vogelsang answered angrily. "Or do you intend to do it by judicial fiat? Let the record reflect that Judge Bracken has described himself as 'the president, vice president, treasurer and secretary' of this court.'"

Bracken glared at him.

"Perhaps," Vogelsang said, "you're thinking you don't need a hearing because you've prejudged the case already. Change temporary custody now, and I'd appeal within seconds. Reversal would be automatic." Vogelsang's tone was almost jeering. He was doing what he had planned—trying to provoke the judge into an immediately appealable ruling, on the chance that scrutiny from a higher court might make Bracken less cavalier in his treatment of Mildred.

The judge leaned forward, looking furious, even unravelled. But before he could speak, Trippler stepped in front of Vogelsang and said, "We have a disinterested witness who corroborates the father's statement that the mother in this case is a drug user. A Pferd factory tour guide saw the mother in a state of extreme drug intoxication on the evening of July 24 this last summer. Your honor, that witness has no reason to invent testimony that the mother is a drug user. He's never met either party before." Trippler slipped a paper under Judge Bracken's nose.

"That ridiculous affidavit!" Vogelsang said. "Written by a petty man with an axe to grind." Vogelsang waved a copy of the affidavit in front of him, and read aloud with a cutting sarcasm:

I, James Piening, being duly sworn under oath, depose and say:
In my five years as a Pferd Company employee, I have never neglected to shut the doors of the storeroom where excess fermented materials are deposited, or to firmly secure those doors with the heavy padlock designated for that purpose. I would never have embarrassed the company in this manner. I would never have failed to observe that the company's horse team was not securely confined. The horse paddock was discovered open in the very place where the two girls were giggling uncontrollably and disrupting the tour which over a dozen people had traveled to hear. Afterward I discovered the disruptive

smell of marijuana, so strong that the storeroom where the horses had partaken reeked of that smell for several days. There I saw evidence of breaking and entry.

"He couldn't possibly have smelled anything over the stink of that storeroom," I interrupted. Bracken and Trippler looked at me as if I had risen from the dead.

I almost felt that I had. In that moment I pictured Mildred seated behind me with a look of absolute hopelessness; Hatch on the court-house steps, his arm spread; and the judge perched before me, his pom-padour disarrayed like the crest of an infuriated bird.

"And this court may take judicial notice," I said, "that it's not possi-ble to smell marijuana in a room days after someone's smoked inside. Especially a room where 'excess fermented materials are deposited.' If the witness lied about that, how can you trust anything he says?"

"How would you know?" Trippler asked.

"I had a troubled roommate in college," I answered. "And I was with Mildred on the evening of July 24. I can tell this court in no un-certain terms that she never smoked anything. We went to church together."

"According to the same witness," Trippler told Bracken, "Miss Rat-leer was present at the Pferd factory during that very incident. Equally intoxicated."

"Well, that's easy enough to disprove," I said. "I can't smoke, your honor, because I'm recovering from cancer." My voice took on a note of ersatz tragedy, parodying every moment of actual suffering I had en-dured in the last year. As I spoke, I felt like pure lawyer, disembodied, gutted of my own pain, eviscerated of human feeling. "And Mr. Munk, on the other hand," I continued, "once got drunk in my presence behind the Unitarian Church and went after me in a way a married man shouldn't. I had to send him home. He's certainly not divinity student material, believe me—" I lied and lied. Vogelsang watched me, his face grave, and I felt my lie spread out like a cloak of many colors, exuberant, lively, and cover us all.

"All right, let's have a temporary hearing to resolve this matter," Judge Bracken said. "We'll visit the crime scene. We'll all walk the three blocks up there and sniff the room, and I'll decide whether it's possible to smell marijuana over the smell of the factory. Then we'll all come back here and I'll decide if Mr. Piening's allegations are credible."

"That's ridiculous," I said.

"Control your associate," Judge Bracken directed Vogelsang.

Vogelsang let out a strange noise, halfway between a laugh and a crow. "In my forty-five years of practice, this will be the first time I've visited a crime scene in a matrimonial case." He told the stenographer, "Judge Bracken believes he can order us to walk up to the Muskellunge beer factory in fifteen-below weather to sniff a storeroom in order to determine if marijuana could have been smelled there five months ago. Did you get that? This may be the first time the Wisconsin Supreme Court will be asked to examine the record of a three-ring circus."

"That's Wild Bill Kunstler's favorite phrase," Trippler said. "Three-ring circus."

"He stole it from me," Vogelsang answered.

"For the record!" Judge Bracken said to the stenographer, as if she, suddenly, had become the judge of the proceedings, "MY COURT-ROOM IS NO CIRCUS! And what I order is law. Do you under-stand?"

The stenographer, of course, did not answer: Her fingers flew over the keys, and she looked straight before her, at nothing at all.

Vogelsang addressed Judge Bracken in a needling tone, "You don't have the authority to order it!"

"I surely do!" he answered.

There was a moment when the courtroom seemed hushed by that counterchallenge: I witnessed it in disbelief, looking first at Vogelsang and then Bracken, stunned by the simple thought that this man who called himself a judge had power not just over Ben, but countless children, year after year. Then the law filled that courtroom and took on a life of its own. As it buffeted me, I felt like the floating figure in a dream: The judge shouted to the bailiff to close the court, coats flew on, the stenographer returned to her novel, and we, the law, marched up the only hill in Muskellunge to determine whether the smells in the Pferd Beer Factory storeroom were too pungent and noxious to allow an ordinary human nose to detect through them the aromatic scent of hemp burning.

Even the cold did not arrest us: Judge Bracken led the way vigor-ously, the passage of a hundred golf games apparently having primed him for any test of physical prowess. Trippler and Daniel followed close behind him along the road's shoulder, braced against the wind, the late afternoon sky already loosening its darkness over them. Mildred walked beside Vogelsang, and suddenly, she laughed long and hard. I remember thinking that the absurdity of things must have overcome her despair in that moment, and grabbed her and shaken that laugh from her.

When we arrived at the factory, Judge Bracken sallied forth in search of the tour guide. He returned without him, and with news that Mr. Piening did not work that day. Another employee, a tall, bony man built like a scarecrow, who recognized Bracken, calling him "The Judge," led us around the Percherons' paddock. The floodlights threw a birdcage of pale blue outside the storeroom. The Pferd worker removed the huge padlock on the storeroom doors, and returned it, half-open, to its resting place. He asked us to lock up when we were "done with whatever we had in mind," and then he lingered at the door, looking a little confused, until Bracken told him, "You may leave!"

We entered the dark storeroom, and a blast of hot air from a factory furnace caressed our faces and swaddled our parkas. The smell was both noxious and pleasing, but overpowering.

"I'm really sorry about this, Melanie," Mildred's voice whispered in my ear, and I could not make sense of her words. "I want to apologize ahead of time." Someone nudged me forward, and I did not have time to ask what she meant. I settled into a position in the corner, behind Vogelsang. I heard the judge take a deep, appraising breath. Then the doors closed behind us. There was the quick rattle of a lock, and the sound of footsteps in snow.

Judge Bracken's voice said, "Open the door! It's impossible to see at all with the door shut."

"We're not here to see; we're here to smell," Vogelsang answered. "And my view is, your nose couldn't detect the odor of a decomposing body over this stench. It smells like ancient urine."

I heard a shuffle of feet, and another rattle, and then Trippler's voice: "The door is not open; it's closed. Closed shut. Locked." He knocked on it. No one answered. He knocked again.

I heard Daniel's sharp intake of breath, and then he said, angrily, "Where's Mildred?" There was no reply.

Vogelsang asked, "Melanie, are *you* here?" I touched his sleeve in affirmation.

There was an exclamation, a short pause in which we rubbed against and bumped into one another—it was impossible to tell where one of us started and the other began. We heard the clinking of the bottling machine, the thumps of horses' hooves and whinnies, the sounds of each other's mutters, and nothing else. Someone pounded on the galvanized aluminum doors, but no one heard us. Whatever workmen operated the machinery at night were lost in their occupational deafness, their earplugs locking them into their silent, contained worlds.

And there we were, trapped in our own darkness. I didn't say anything. I wondered exactly when the idea had come to Mildred to shut us in there, and realized she must have made the decision in a split second. I wondered why she hadn't just waited and run off with Ben in the middle of the night, without incurring more of the law's wrath than absconding with her son would bring down on her. Perhaps she needed to make the extra gesture of putting the court in its place, in order to reestablish a certain equilibrium in the world, a balance between law and lawlessness, or an imbalance between lower and higher law. Or perhaps the law had pushed her too far and unhinged her mind just a little, just barely past the point of good judgment.

Muffled by the increasing volume and outrage of the voices around me, I felt an intensifying joy fill me—it sprang in that darkness from the soles of my feet, and fountained and trumpeted upward, flower-shaped, spreading into my extremities. I decided in that moment that I probably never had felt real joy before. Although Judge Bracken and the others would not be able to agree, I was prepared to tell them that we had all been freed by Mildred's escape, and if they asked me where she had gone, I was going to say: she's sailed to Tierra del Fuego, or rocketed to Mars to charter its first frontiers, she's threaded the whorls of a cat's ear, she's at the bottom of the sea, speaking Portuguese with the whales.

"This," Vogelsang said, "is the most startling experience I have had in my long career as a lawyer. I should retire today, on the pinnacle of my astonishment."

When the Pferd workers arrived in the morning they did not hear any of us banging on the wall of the storeroom. We had removed our coats in that sweltering noxious place, and slept on top of them, stretched out on the floor like barn animals lying in a manger—Daniel and his lawyer, and Vogelsang and me, and the presiding judge. It wasn't until 10:00 A.M., when one of the bottlers stepped outside for a cigarette, that any Pferd employee heard Judge Bracken call to him. No one could find the key to the padlock, and eventually Chief Komar arrived at the factory with a crowbar. When his face appeared in the crack of light in the doorway, he looked unequivocally amused. Judge Bracken commanded him to open the padlock and release us.

7

THE LAW had no sense of humor about Mildred's transgression. Judge Bracken demanded that she be charged with felonious false imprisonment "of a high member of the Wisconsin judiciary." He was furious at Vogelsang, but Mildred's decision to lock us in with the rest of them saved us from any appearance of complicity in her actions.

Daniel was certain that Matt had helped Mildred get away, although there was no proof of anything, and the temporary restraining order against Matt was dismissed eventually for mootness. (Daniel never noticed that Ottilie's new Impala was missing; Ottilie and Matt would not discuss the car with Vogelsang or me.) Daniel pressed charges against Mildred for kidnapping and he carried on a private crusade to apprehend her. He badgered the local and federal police, and for years he tried to trace her through private detectives, who would knock on Ottilie's door, looking cold and clueless. She never let them in.

Mildred resurfaced only briefly among us. She and Ben hid for a week like two fugitives, at a hotel in Wisconsin Dells. John arranged for Mildred to have a new Social Security number and a new name. And then Mildred disappeared, with Ottilie's Impala. After that John received a photograph of Ben every Christmas, and several letters a year, always disguised with pseudonyms, always with different postmarks. He hid them in a file. Matt also received letters and photographs—like John, Matt hid them, but he perused them often, and showed them to me with bittersweet pride whenever I visited. I expected Matt to fall apart after Mildred left, but he did not. He and Ottilie both seemed to have borrowed some meaning from Mildred, which they clung to when she was gone.

John donated his home to the Park and Pray, turned it into a second halfway house for women, and lived in a room in the church. When he could not bear the quiet of the office where he slept on a rollaway cot, he moved into the halfway house with Matt and the others, until a year later, when Ottilie consented for him to move in with her. She would not marry him, which became a small scandal. In the end this, and John Steck's final sermon on "free love and marriage as a capitalist commodity," cost him his pulpit. Another Unitarian minister arrived in Muskellunge to direct the Park and Pray, and John ran the halfway houses, expanded the garden, and occasionally gave guest sermons.

I returned to practicing in New York, and submerged myself again in work. Every now and then, as I walked through New York crowds in the subway or on the sidewalk, the thought of Mildred would pierce me suddenly: I would imagine her lying low, clerking in an Idaho drugstore while Ben attended the local school, or I would picture her working as a court interpreter in Arizona, a fox in a nest of chickens. And then I would think I had glimpsed her face suddenly in a crowd. But the person's profile would come into view, and I would know I was mistaken—from the front Mildred had such a common face, easily confused with so many others.

A year after Mildred left, I visited Ripon, Wisconsin, when I returned to Muskellunge on vacation. I wanted to learn something about Daniel; I needed to believe that somewhere at the center of him was an explanation, that someone in Ripon would remember him as a child, simple and likeable and possessing potential. But no one did—his family had lived on a gentlemen's farm at the edge of town, now sold, and had not socialized much. Most of the other families who had occupied the neighboring farms had moved away, or had been bought out or foreclosed on. Only one neighbor remembered the Munks: He said that Daniel's father used to like to stand in the apple orchard behind his house, and have his son pitch apples to him. Daniel's father would whack the apples with a baseball bat from the top of the orchard into a field, one after the other, for hours, without pausing to talk. He would do this all fall, until the apples were gone. He resisted every invitation to join the town baseball league, although he had a powerful swing: The apples would explode when he struck them, and the pieces would fly thirty yards through the air.

I looked through high school yearbooks in Ripon's public library, but Daniel wasn't among the seniors in any of them—perhaps he had attended private school. Finally, a 1956 yearbook offered the only relic of him I would find in that town. It was a picture of the school band, of clean-cut boys, and girls with curled hair. Daniel stood to the left of the group, not quite part of it. The caption said, "Daniel Munk, freshman, front row." A French horn curled gracefully like a golden snail in the crook of his arm. He was smaller than the other boys, with a narrow, pointed, bewildered face, and his right hand rested tentatively on the shoulder of the boy in front of him.

BOOK FOUR

MIRROR UNIVERSE

1

HISTORY OF THE RAILROAD:
AN INTRODUCTION

Steck's underground railroad primarily aided women, which resulted in criticism that it condoned "reverse discrimination." Steck rejected such criticism with her customary mixture of earnestness and irony: "It may be," she stated after her now famous Wisconsin Proclamation, "that one effect of the Railroad is to even the score in the so-called Gender War, but our principal aim is to protect children. And we try to prevent needless homicide."

By "needless homicide" Steck probably intended to be ambiguous. She initially seemed to be referring to homicides of women and children resulting from domestic violence, but, taken in the context of later statements, this phrase appeared to encompass, in addition, that situation where a woman had come to feel she had only two choices: to murder her husband or boyfriend, or to risk, in the alternative, serious harm or death for herself or her children. Accordingly, Steck later clarified, "In some cases, we appear to have been working in the interests of the men involved."

The use of legal measures by the Railroad should not be discounted. Many experienced attorneys were secretly members of, or in contact with the Railroad. Through the help of such attorneys, legislative reforms were enacted, and free legal services provided for obtaining protective orders and divorces, and securing custody of children. Of course, some sympathizing attorneys introduced clients to the underground, and Mildred Steck's antagonism to legal process is well documented. She considered herself an outlaw.

from *The Ratleer Chronicles*

2

JOY CAN BE as surprising as loss, and with time, terror can become so attenuated that it is almost forgotten. In 1992, with the advent of the new antipsychotic drug Clozapine, Matt's schizophrenia ebbed, leaving his mind as calm as a battered lakeshore after a storm. Matt was suspicious of Clozapine: He said that he did not like the idea of being controlled by a substance manufactured in Switzerland and approved by the Food and Drug Administration. He distrusted anything with the label "antipsychotic." However, Matt told me, "for the first time in twenty-five years, I have periods where the only voice in my head is mine. It's as if a radio had been blaring inside me, a radio broadcasting advertising jingles and pork prices and static, and suddenly it's been turned off."

His powers of concentration were heightened. He could read more easily and focus longer on things that interested him. Matt courted by mail a woman named Sophie Tipton, who lived three blocks away at the women's halfway house and had a tendency to catatonia. He composed twenty "Sonnets of Love and Madness" and sent them to her twice each week for ten weeks before she responded. Thereafter, Ottilie wrote me, Matt and Sophie began "dating seriously. Sophie is a nice girl when she comes out of her shell."

The same year, John Steck bought Matt a computer and software for playing chess. Within a month Matt had outsmarted the program: He learned how to place a bug in his adversary's highest levels, so that the computer would be fooled by certain simple moves and allow itself to be checkmated. In a period of a few weeks, Matt mastered Windows, and then WordPerfect and Quicken. John maintained that the computer was ideal for an intelligent man afflicted with schizophrenia: It required no social skills, no adjustments of his personality, no conforming of his physical appearance and mannerisms to the world of the sane.

In the fall of 1992 Matt obtained a part-time job in the Pferd Beer Factory's controller's office. (Pferd had expanded greatly in the eighties with the introduction of a new line of cooler called Red Hoof.) His boss was an accountant named Henry Nummelin, who wore Orlon shirts and pants too short in the leg and lived alone in a small brown house at the end of Walleye Street. Apparently Henry was so lacking in conventional social skills that he noticed nothing unusual about Matt. The two men sat in a back office at the Pferd factory, playing chess and computer games, journeying on the Internet, and logging in payroll figures and shipping orders.

Henry taught Matt about the Internet with an intensity possible only in someone who has collected the lonely knowledge of computer science year after year without outlet. Henry's log-in name on the Internet was "idsavant." According to Matt, Henry was the kind of man who could add up thirty numbers by picturing in his head a pyramid of black digits that swarmed like ants and resolved into a bright sum. My brother absorbed everything Henry taught him, and he came to love the Internet. Matt called it "the common electronic consciousness" and fed it with information he deemed useful or enticing, such as Dmytryk's recipe for dandelion wine and a taxonomical chart in progress, intended to contain the names of 300,000 beetles, designed by Dr. Eatman, who now worked as a curator for a small natural history museum. (Dr. Eatman's mission was to give a common name to every beetle that had only a Latin one. *Plusiotis gloriosa* became Glory of God Beetle, and an obscure species of weevil, Ratleer's Curculio.) Matt liked to use the Internet to break security codes and plant incongruous data in computer files: "How to Ferment Dandelion Greens" appeared on page 117 of the local power company's 1992 computerized credit records; a poem by James Wright titled "The Jewel" replaced an employee disciplinary file at Budweiser; and a detailed description of an Eastern Hercules Beetle ("that changing milky green of jade") multiplied through the shipping logs of Green Giant industries. On a private bulletin board of the Internet labeled "job opportunities in Alaska," Matt posted a list of Social Security numbers belonging to the dead.

At this time I had been settled in for several years as a New York Appellate Division judge. My presidential appointment as a federal judge in the Southern District Court had just been announced, and I had received the requisite FBI interview. When Matt's activities transgressed the law, I worried. I called and explained to him that criminal statutes were being drafted daily to check the budding lawlessness of the computer world. Matt would promise to be careful, but a few months later, some new challenge would possess him and Henry. After the confirmation of my appointment to the federal bench, Matt boasted that he and Henry could break into the personnel files of New York's federal district courts, and I swore to Matt that I believed him, and admonished him not to demonstrate his powers. This was in April 1993, before I knew anything about Mildred Steck's political activities.

In early June 1993, while I sat in my chambers, scanning Lexis for articles on the "colorable claim of innocence" standard in the law of habeas corpus, my computer screen became blank, and a message appeared:

TASTE OUR MANURE COOLER:
DRINK RED HOOF.

I laughed aloud. Two law clerks standing outside my chambers exchanged glances. They thought I was tickled by an arcane nuance of the law. When I was in my twenties and clerking for the federal judiciary, I was acquainted with a few justices who were serious jurists, and very strange people. They were men who stayed late in their chambers every night and on weekends. They lived alone, or with their mothers, rarely socialized, and spoke stiffly and uncomfortably with their clerks. They dressed without thought or style, since what they wore was cloaked inside their judicial gowns. Lawdust gathered in their nostrils, in their pores and ears and wrinkles. In old age they seemed sepulchral, in middle age, old. By 1993, at age forty-three, I had become one of those judges.

The screen flickered. A sentence erased itself and reappeared:

BULLETIN FROM THE UNDERGROUND RAILROAD:
HELEN NOBEL IS ALIVE AND WELL!

This pronouncement puzzled and surprised me. I had never heard of an underground railroad other than the one Harriet Tubman helped run. Helen Nobel had been a party in a notorious Wisconsin divorce trial. I had written an article on her case earlier that year and sent a copy of my article to Ottilie. A few weeks later Helen Nobel disappeared, and she was presumed dead. My brother now claimed to know where she was, and I did not like the idea of Matt having access to knowledge whose possession might be a violation of criminal law.

I did not offer to assume the role of chronicler for Mildred Steck's underground railroad until after the Nobel crisis and the Steck Uprising. In late 1993, Mildred accepted my offer in a brief reply note:

> We need a historian, like you Melanie, who can tell our tale with the necessary bias and sympathy. Your tendency to methodical analysis will make you especially convincing in conveying the Railroad's goals. Besides, Matt and Henry can show you how to obtain information from the Railroad through the Internet.

Mildred signed this message, "Yours affectionately, Martina Luther." (These are some of the aliases Mildred used in the early days: Martina Luther, Mildred Crail, Mrs. John Brown, Mrs. Munk-Daniels, Mildred Muffet, Mrs. Ratleer.)

I HAD FOLLOWED Helen Nobel's case, because as an active member of the women's bar association, I had always charted progress and backtracking in matrimonial law. I kept a file of hair-raising cases: a Manhattan judge who ordered an eight-year-old girl sedated during visitation, because she became hysterical when forced to spend nights with the father who had molested her; a Westchester judge who took a toddler from his mother, deeming she had abandoned her children when she fled home to escape her husband's violence; a Brooklyn judge who jailed a pregnant mother of two during her third trimester, because she could not pay support for a son taken from her in a divorce proceeding ("women cannot assume that by burdening themselves with a new child they will lessen their duties to the previously born," the judge reasoned); judges who parted infants from their mothers because the mothers were gay, or worked full-time, or had committed adultery, or because of judicial vindictiveness and prejudice. (I had a file marked "questionable judges," although, after the Clarence Thomas hearings, this no longer seemed as rewarding.)

The gaudy scandal of the Nobel case began in early 1992. Frederick Nobel was the CEO of Nobel Grain Industries of Skelter, Wisconsin, and a well-known personality in the Midwest. Before Nobel Grain's stock went public, Frederick Nobel's family had owned the company for several generations. It specialized in a limited array of bakery products: bread, sweet rolls, and hamburger and hot dog buns. Frederick Nobel's father had forged a bond with the Oscar Mayer company in Madison, bought farmland all over central Wisconsin and northern Illinois, and maintained a midwestern monopoly on packaged breads throughout his lifetime. The Nobel company's curious slogan, emblazoned on all of its products, was, "At least we're American." Nobel Grain employed a third of Skelter's populace, and the town's Main Street terminated at the entrance to the Nobel Building, a behemoth stone structure surrounded by a spiral of silos set at one-hundred-yard intervals, so that from a distance Nobel Grain seemed to rise out of the flat countryside like Stonehenge. The smell of lard baking into flour permeated Skelter's air as far away as the town dump.

In the early eighties Frederick Nobel married Helen Othersall, a society girl from suburban Kenilworth, Illinois, whose father's family had strong ties to Kraft Industries of Chicago. Thereafter Nobel became a household name by performing in his own advertising campaign, which played on the American dairy and pork industries' fear of growing consumer aversion to foods high in fat. Nobel was robust, with football player shoulders and an incongruous and expansive vocabulary: he belonged to the Dartmouth Club, but he had the style of a people's man. In one local commercial Nobel appeared on a playground, offering five Wisconsin children each two paper plates, one containing a cheeseburger and hot dog, and the other what he described as "baba ganoush on a whole wheat bagel," or "sushi on seven-grain health bread," or "bok choy pita pockets." His arguments, directed at children between the ages of two and six, were mildly comical. He would admonish them about fat content, extol the virtue of whole grain, and ask whether they really believed that "pork is the other white meat." The children would invariably choose the hot dogs and cheeseburgers. Every commercial would end with the slogan, "At least we're American." In a similar series of commercials run in Illinois, Nobel wandered through the bleachers of Wrigley Field, attempting to convince children to eat "tabouleh tacos" instead of hot dogs. These commercials concluded, similarly, "At least we're American."

Between 1985 and 1990 Nobel Grain's stock tripled in value, and in late 1991 the company engineered a hostile takeover of the largest baked goods distributor in the Northeast. *Forbes* magazine ran a feature story on Frederick Nobel in which he described himself as "the heartland's answer to health food," and "a cross between Lee Iacocca and the Jolly Green Giant." He hinted that he envisioned running as a Wisconsin congressional candidate on the independent ticket.

In January 1992, Frederick Nobel's wife, Helen, filed for divorce, on the ground that her husband had subjected her to "severe and repeated physical abuse." She petitioned the Milwaukee Family Court for permission to leave Wisconsin in order to ensure her personal safety. Two days later, before a Family Court commissioner had acted on her petition, Helen Nobel fled Milwaukee with her six-year-old daughter and returned to her recently widowed mother in Kenilworth, Illinois. Mr. Nobel pursued his wife and created a disturbance outside her mother's home, a delivery man called the police, and the *Sun-Times* ran a lurid series of photographs depicting Mrs. Nobel being carried into an ambulance, her face bruised and her arm splinted. The Cook County state's attorney brought felony charges against Frederick Nobel for aggravated battery. His wife refused to speak to the press, but a week later, Frederick Nobel told a *Sun-Times* reporter that he "saw it as his job not just to vindicate his name, but to clear the name of every man who has been subjected to the darker side of the Gender War." When the reporter asked Nobel why his wife would fabricate assault charges, he responded, "Tomorrow, it could be you. Tomorrow, your wife could accuse you of beating her and having sexual intercourse with your own children. What will you do then?"

At the Chicago criminal trial, Helen Nobel testified that her husband had attacked her in the presence of their daughter. X rays revealed a fractured skull and a broken arm. A resident of Skelter, Wisconsin, one Mr. Nachtwey, told the press that he had once seen Mr. Nobel "pick up his wife and throw her like a rag doll" across the back yard of the Nobels' vacation home in Skelter, but this evidence of past violence was excluded from trial. The defense discredited Nachtwey in the press by revealing that he was a disgruntled former employee of Nobel Grain.

Frederick Nobel's defense attorney, a prominent authority on the battered wife defense, told the press that not only would there be no guilty plea; she invited the jury to pronounce Mr. Nobel "innocent beyond a reasonable doubt." She called witnesses who described Helen

Nobel as "reclusive" and "unsociable," and who depicted Frederick
Nobel as a solicitous husband burdened with an agoraphobic spouse
who had not furthered his career. Business associates and neighbors attested to Frederick Nobel's integrity and his record of philanthropy. A
forensic expert testified that Helen Nobel's injuries were consistent with
a fall from a diving board into a neighbor's unfilled pool. There were
intimations she had been drinking. The defense argued that Helen
Nobel had fabricated criminal charges to enhance her position in her
divorce action; following Nobel's arrest, the Milwaukee Family Court
commissioner had granted her request to leave the state with her daughter. The jury acquitted Frederick Nobel, and the forewoman, before the
judge could stop her, pronounced him "innocent beyond any shadow of
a doubt."

After the trial Frederick Nobel stood before the Cook County
Courthouse and told television reporters, "My wife's selfish rampage has
ended. Now it's time to help my little girl, who is the biggest victim of
her mother's slander." Helen Nobel again refused to speak to reporters.
She was a well-dressed, matronly woman, somewhat stuffy-looking, and
in a news photograph taken of Helen outside the courthouse, her
daughter peered up at the blinding photographer's lights with her face
hooded in a brown wool jacket, her mouth open like a baby bird's. The
following day newspapers reported that Nobel Grain's board of directors had held a congratulatory celebration for Frederick Nobel in a Chicago tavern.

Immediately after his acquittal, Frederick Nobel appealed the Milwaukee Family Court rulings to the County Court. He demanded that
the court order his wife to return from Illinois to Milwaukee, or in the
alternative, to forfeit custody of their daughter. In the nineties courts
were increasingly granting noncustodial spouses power over where custodial parents could live, and New York matrimonial lawyers routinely
complained that abusive husbands exercised this power to prevent their
wives from fleeing to safety. Thus, the Nobel case seemed of immense
juridical import to me, and I undertook to write an article on it for the
women's bar journal. At this time Helen Nobel's attorney protested,
"Frederick Nobel bought his acquittal. No intelligent person believes he
is not a dangerous man. Should Helen Nobel return to the state of
Wisconsin, within the sphere of her husband's violence and away from
the shelter of her extended family, the law, which has failed her once
already, will now become an accomplice in terrorizing her." He con-

demned the jurors at the Chicago criminal trial as "bamboozled innocents" and reminded the press that Frederick Nobel's history of past
violence would be admissible evidence in Milwaukee civil proceedings.

However, the Milwaukee judge assigned to the divorce case, Honorable Frank Hochwald, expressed the opinion that "false charges of domestic violence might well justify a change of custody because of the
psychological damage inflicted on the child. In any case, the mere fact
that a woman is abused by her husband does not give her the right
to move hundreds of miles away." Before hearings commenced, Judge
Hochwald questioned whether Helen Nobel's flight to another state was
"a ploy to interfere with a girl's affection for her father," and warned
that Frederick Nobel would be granted temporary custody of his daughter unless Helen Nobel returned to Wisconsin with her immediately.

Helen Nobel's lawyer demanded that Hochwald recuse himself, for
his "bias in prejudging the issues of Helen Nobel's credibility and the
seriousness of her claims," and for "foaming at the mouth to make
Nobel the Bakke of custody cases. God help us if Mr. Nobel champions
his side of the Gender War so well that women will be frightened from
asking the courts for protection from violence. Judge Hochwald already
has given Frederick Nobel the right to restrict his wife's freedom of
travel to an area the size of a postage stamp. This is just a new Fugitive
Slave Law by another name."

Although I wrote my bar journal article for sound jurisprudential
reasons, I found that the Nobel case haunted me in that way news stories
occasionally do all of us—as if they implicated us personally. I could not
read or hear about Helen Nobel without feeling a stab of personal fear
and being swept up in a whirlwind of empathy for her and her daughter, without picturing Frederick Nobel shot accidentally in police cross-
fire or envisioning a scenario in which Judge Hochwald, ignominiously
dethroned, was led from the bench in handcuffs after his arrest for
influence-peddling or embezzlement. And I could not think of Wisconsin without picturing Hochwald's airless courtroom, inhabited by that
cast of sorrowful characters.

Shortly after I sent Ottilie my article, there was a swell of public
support among women's groups and bar associations for Helen Nobel.
One investigative journalist, Richard Sparrow, hounded Judge Hochwald with near obsessiveness. Sparrow unearthed information that
Hochwald had sentenced a piano teacher, a mother of four, to jail when
she proved unable to furnish $17,000 in back support he had ordered

her to pay after granting her ex-husband custody of their three children. In Hochwald's twenty-year career on the bench, he had never jailed any father for failure to pay support. In a pointed editorial commentary, the president of a prominent women's rights organization accused Hochwald of "enacting a crude egalitarianism where women will share the punishments but not the privileges of so-called equality under the law."

Around the same time, Nachtwey, the disgruntled employee of Nobel Grain Industries, wrote a letter to the *Sun-Times* maintaining that he "had a whole iceberg of information on Mr. Nobel, and all the jury in Chicago knew about was the tip." Nachtwey repeated that he had once seen Mr. Nobel "pick up his wife and throw her across the yard like a rag doll." In addition, Nachtwey used the opportunity to complain that Nobel had wrongly fired him after a job-related accident in which Nachtwey "twisted his neck when a sack of flour was heaved onto his head." Furthermore, Nachtwey noted, Nobel Grain had cheated him out of ten days of sick pay.

In early May, 1993, before any legal resolution of the custody issue, Helen Nobel and her daughter vanished without a trace. The manner of their disappearance riveted the Chicago press and led to the extensive national broadcasting of what had been primarily a midwestern scandal. The Monday Helen vanished, she called a family friend, a Mrs. Felicia Grove. "What Helen said," Mrs. Grove told the *Milwaukee Journal*, "was that her husband had kept up a campaign of terrorizing her after she returned to Milwaukee with her daughter, and that he had threatened to come to her house and 'Do justice to her' that very night." When questioned by skeptical police officers, Mr. Nobel said that he had not visited the marital home in Milwaukee the Monday night of his wife's disappearance, because she had invited him to meet her at an Italian restaurant on the edge of town.

At this time the Milwaukee police already suspected homicide. They discovered traces of blood shown to be Helen Nobel's in her bedroom. There was no evidence of the daughter's whereabouts. Helen Nobel had left a frantic letter under her bedroom pillow that said, "Please, someone, confine my husband." Frederick Nobel could provide no alibi. Upon further police questioning, he claimed that when he had arrived at the Italian restaurant, he had discovered it was closed on Mondays. After waiting an hour for his wife, he had driven back to his condominium in downtown Milwaukee.

A gun registered in Frederick Nobel's name and a bloodstained

scarf were recovered from a Dumpster near his condominium, and finally, the police arrested him. They theorized that Nobel had murdered
his wife and had killed their daughter accidentally in the process. The
Sun-Times retreated from its position of support and questioned his
guilt. Tabloids speculated that Nobel had intentionally killed his daughter because she was a witness to his wife's homicide. Nobel protested his
innocence, maintaining, "I couldn't be more distraught about this tragic
event." He was arraigned on murder charges and held without bail in a
special cell, under heavy guard.

And so, when I received my brother's message in early June, 1993,
that Helen Nobel was alive and well, I felt both curious and worried; I
wondered where he had obtained his information and how. My concern
increased about a week after Matt's message appeared on my computer
screen, when there was a twist in the Nobel case. Under the headline,
"Wife Rises from the Dead," the *Chicago Tribune* printed the following
letter, handwritten on embossed ivory stationery in the delicate, round
script of a society matron:

> *To the Kenilworth Public:*
> *I wish to inform the community that my child and I are well, particu-*
> *larly now that we are no longer within the sphere of my husband's influ-*
> *ence. We could not remain where he could find us, without risking great*
> *danger. For this reason, it was necessary for us to feign our deaths. I greatly*
> *regret, and am a little shocked still, that the courts were unwilling to help*
> *us when we turned to them for solicitude. I am somewhat comforted to*
> *know that Mr. Nobel has served at least some time in jail for his criminal*
> *actions.*
>
> > *Sincerely,*
> > *Mrs. Helen Nobel*

The detail on which the newspapers lingered, and which seemed to
stick most in Mr. Nobel's craw, was that his wife had invited him to the
closed Italian restaurant on the night of her disappearance for the sole
purpose of making it impossible for him to furnish an alibi. He told
reporters, "I never would have believed her capable of such a diabolical
maneuver."

He pressed kidnapping charges against Helen and revived his action
for custody before Judge Hochwald. Nobel appeared on television with
a picture of his daughter and wife, and asked that the public "help
return my little girl to the father who loves her and deliver her mother

into the hands of the law." Helen Nobel's apprehension seemed certain: her face had been in the papers too often. The value of Nobel Grain stock, which had plummeted after Mr. Nobel's arrest and confinement, rose significantly, then fell slightly, and hovered at its original level.

3

IN EARLY SUMMER, of 1993 I planned a two-week visit to Muskellunge because I was worried that Matt's activities on the computer
would lead him into trouble. I had last seen Matt two months before,
but then only for a few days. From 1978 until 1993 I had never taken
more than a week's vacation from my work, although I traveled to
Wisconsin each year for Christmas and for a few days each summer.
And Matt visited me, with Ottilie and John Steck, once each year
around Easter. When they arrived in New York, John always wanted
to see St. John the Divine Cathedral and Riverside Church; Ottilie attended operas (she thought they were exotic, and would leave them with
eyes shining, as if she had taken a narcotic); Matt liked the Village; and
no one wanted to see the Statue of Liberty. When Matt strolled ahead
of us as we walked through Manhattan, he was the only one who did
not turn heads. Ottilie and John looked like tourists from a mile away,
with their pale hair and practical midwestern clothes, but Matt, with his
derelict's beard and haircut, fit right in. It was probably the only time
in his life that he knew the luxury of walking down the street totally
ignored. He loved New York and was terrified of it.

I arranged for a vacation in August. My tenure as a federal judge
would not commence until Labor Day, and I apportioned myself the
first two months of that summer to bone up on new federal law. Ottilie
invited me, during a phone call, to stay with her and John. Her description of life in Muskellunge almost jarred me from the despairing vision
of Wisconsin Helen Nobel's case evoked in me: "Yesterday Matt and
Henry planted a bed of orange milkweed in Dr. Eatman's insect garden,
and afterward we roasted a whole pig in the back yard according to

instructions Aunt Mimi sent me from Madagascar. Dr. Eatman brought an ironclad beetle to dinner." Ottilie elaborated that Dr. Eatman had stopped in Muskellunge in early spring, and he and John had designed the insect garden. It consisted of stands of weeds and wild plants known to attract not only butterflies, but also beetles: milkweed for monarchs and milkweed beetles, roses for rose weevils, dogbane for dogbane leaf beetles, spicebush and pipevine for swallowtails. Sophie, Matt's new girlfriend, liked to sit in the garden with an easel and paint butterflies, and her works were exhibited on the walls of the food co-op where John sold the organic vegetable garden's produce.

Ottilie's call made me waver in my plan to work straight through the first two months of New York's oppressive urban summer before visiting her and Matt. I already felt a growing ambivalence toward my career, for while outwardly I displayed an attitude of commitment, excitement, and gratitude for my ascendancy to the federal bench, inwardly I had begun to experience an increasing aversion to my work. Even the word *career* made me think not of the trajectory of a profession, but instead of reckless speed, of a life careering crazily toward a fatal consequence. As I continued preparations for my federal appointment, leaning over yellowed law books until my neck ached, I found myself sinking beyond the small print of the pages into a dark maze of legal reasoning where I searched not for knowledge of the law, but instead for its weaknesses and vulnerabilities, the soft tunnels that if pressured, could crumble and bring the mighty edifices of the courts tumbling to the earth. After hours of study late into the night, a lawless delirium sometimes overcame me and forced me to close my books and rush outside into the city night, until its noises reminded me that days had passed since I had spoken a word to anyone.

Early in the summer, I felt more exhausted than I had since my months of illness as a young attorney, and I considered extending my vacation in order to pass a restful month basking in Ottilie's yard and wandering through John's garden. But while I vacillated, the decision was made for me. I booked a flight to Wisconsin more than a month before I'd anticipated, in late June, in order to attend my father's memorial service.

My father died of heart failure while sitting at the defense table in a Milwaukee courtroom. He and the prosecutor had entered the court around one in the afternoon to await the verdict. The jury deliberated only forty minutes before the foreman emerged, followed by the jurors, and announced that my father's client had been found not guilty of intentional murder. The defendant had shot a man in a bar, twice, with a crossbow. After the bailiff called, "All rise," the judge turned to my father, who had not risen, and said sternly, "Ratleer, you are subject to the rules of this court like every other mortal soul who enters here. You better have a damn good reason for sitting when the court tells you to stand up." There was an uncomfortable silence. The defendant looked at the judge in mild alarm. The prosecutor approached my father, felt his pulse, and was later reported to have said, "Even dead, that bastard Ratleer won his case."

My father was seventy-seven in 1993, and still maintained a full law practice the year of his death. He was not survived by many people. His third wife, Molly White, had died three years before of pneumonia. In his will my father had directed: "I ask only that, after the anticipated memorial service by the Wisconsin and Chicago bar associations, etc., a small ceremony be held by my family and the Booths, my wife's close friends, near their vacation home in Spring Green, Wisconsin. I wish the service to be at dawn on the first day of the month following my demise." This directive was both confusing and embarrassing to the Booths, who were aware that my father had had little contact with us. By "family" he must have meant Molly White. However, Mrs. Booth called me in mid-June and asked if I "or anyone else in the family" would join her and her husband on the first of July for a small memorial service in Spring Green.

My father did not want to be buried under the earth; he wanted to be cremated, and his will directed that his ashes be "scattered over the grounds of Taliesin, Frank Lloyd Wright's estate in Spring Green." I recalled my father's dog-eared copy of *The Fountainhead*, and a picture of Taliesin he had kept in his study when I was a child, that had been captioned "A work of genius—a manmade landscape." I thought Joel Ratleer must have identified in more ways than one with Wright—he would have admired the architect's arrogant, maverick lifestyle, his flaunted public affair with his mistress, those buildings which, godlike, he proclaimed part of the natural world.

Ottilie felt that she and Matt should both attend the funeral. The Booths told me they would bring my father's ashes from McCarthy to Muskellunge, and drive on to Spring Green early to arrange their summer house, where Mrs. Booth offered to host a dinner for us the evening before the ceremony. (*"The idea of a funeral breakfast struck me as odd,"*

Mrs. Booth wrote me. *"Please let me know in advance how many will be attending."*)

I agreed to contact the funeral home where my father's ashes were located and to handle other arrangements. I did this with an efficiency that I found mildly objectionable. I was used to funeral services: Death clustered around those who had populated my life, so that at the age of forty-three, I sometimes believed I knew more people who had died than I could still count among the living. My grandfather Klonecki lay next to his wife and my mother in Tampico's small cemetery. The doctor who had treated my cancer when I was young was dead from cancer. Judge Bracken, too, was dead: He died from ptomaine poisoning after eating fish at a country club reception held in his honor. My judicial predecessor in the Southern District was killed by a prostitute, and his cause of death was listed in a *New York Times* obituary as "a fall down a flight of stairs." Mr. Shove died from emphysema, his wife moved away to Los Angeles to live near one of her sons, and for years afterward Shove's general store lay empty as a new coffin until John Steck rented it for his organic food co-op. Vogelsang died at eighty-five, not of old age, but on a passenger plane shot down en route to China, where he had determined to take a three-month excursion with an interpreter from the World Council of Churches. (Daniel Munk, of course, had not died. After completing his degree, he had been granted tenure as a professor of comparative religion at an Indiana college, where he would later become provost.) Dmytryk died not from liver failure, but from old age, while sleeping on a bench in the organic garden. A birth certificate among his effects revealed that he was ninety-three years old. Rockefeller's family placed him in a home for mentally impaired adults in Milwaukee, which Dr. Eatman described as "a living death—carrion beetles must clamor at the entrance." Shortly afterward Rockefeller moved into the house of a girlfriend none of us had known about, a woman twenty years his senior, who managed a restaurant in Sturgeon Bay.

IN 1993, GREYHOUND ran directly to Muskellunge from Milwaukee, a result of the prosperity of Pferd Beer, which now employed workers from towns as far away as Manitowoc and Sheboygan. I took a redeye flight to Chicago and an early morning bus that deposited me in front of Pferd. As I stepped off the Greyhound after a sleepless night, the muggy heat rose from the ground with such a soporific effect that I felt as if I were sleepwalking. The factory loomed over the road like the figment of a hideous dream: Pferd had tripled in size, and a new building annexed to the horse paddocks had been painted to look like a six-pack of beer.

Unlike many northeastern towns Muskellunge had thrived during the recession. Sears had reopened, Tikalsky's bar had expanded and become Tikalsky's Family Restaurant, and Musky's sign flashed in full daylight on the horizon. The courthouse looked recently sandblasted. A funeral wreath made of dried twigs and purple crepe hung on the door of a renovated building sporting the sign, CHRISTIANSEN, FISK, AND CHRISTIANSEN, ATTORNEYS-AT-LAW, the first name crossed off, and the third recently painted on. Walleye Church was now Episcopalian, John Steck's produce market sprawled onto the sidewalk that Shove's had once fronted, and the Park and Pray, renamed Muskellunge Unitarian, bore a sign on its door announcing that its minister, a woman, was vacationing in Rio for four weeks.

John Steck's garden swelled around his old church, dazzling and enormous. A plot of purple cabbages extended from the road to a back field, looking like the helmets of a buried army; beside these filed unending rows of string beans, their flowers like bright tassels, jostling one another over the long green blades; stands of tomatoes, exploding in reds and yellows, ran westward to a yellow field. A wide band of privet, swarming with butterflies, separated the vegetable fields from the insect garden, where a red banner reading DR. EATMAN'S INSECT PARADISE fluttered over a chaotic flowerbed overrun with thistles and dogbane and electric orange milkweed plants. When I leaned over the fence, the smell of spicebush commingled with the medicinal odor of Toreador marigolds. I imagined myself forgetting everything I knew in the perfumed heat of the garden, my memory's cells erasing themselves. I would arrive at Ottilie's door and say, *Do you know who I am? Take me in.* Then I shook off the daydream—it was eccentric and embarrassed me. I turned down the road and walked quickly toward Ottilie's.

Aunt Mimi's house had been newly painted. Its top windows changed color with that introverted shimmering of stained glass viewed from the outside. A black car was parked out front. Before I could knock on the door, John Steck threw it open and rushed out to greet me. He wore a faded black minister's shirt, open at the neck and frayed at the elbows, and his silvered ponytail was over six inches long. He pumped my hand as though I were about to celebrate my own graduation. He looked, oddly, as if he were bursting with joy.

A man in a lawyerly dark suit sat in the living room. A fiftyish woman hovered beside him, wearing a gray silk dress, heavy pearl earrings, and a bun as small and tight as a pearl onion.

"Molly never complained," the woman in the gray dress murmured. When she saw me, she said, "Oh!"

"The Booths," John whispered in my ear.

Ottilie rushed through the kitchen door and down the back steps without seeing me. John rubbed his hands together and watched her.

"Melanie, I'm afraid something's come up," he told me. "Can I just leave you here for a minute? Your room upstairs is all fixed up for you." Before I could answer, he ran out the back door after Ottilie.

Mrs. Booth said, "There seems to be some kind of commotion about a child being stung by a bee. It seems she's allergic."

"A child?" I asked.

"They were talking about taking her to the hospital."

Mr. Booth, a man with the narrow-set eyes and long nose of a moray eel, examined me. "So, you're a young attorney?" he asked. "I'm an old veteran of securities law. What's the nature of your practice?"

"I'm a judge," I answered.

"Ah," he said. "Ah. You don't say."

"A federal judge–designate," I added.

"Ah."

"New York Southern District."

Mr. Booth straightened his necktie, and said, "Joel never mentioned it."

I had sent my father a notice apprising him of the nomination but received no reply.

"We've brought the—" Mrs. Booth said. "We've given it to your mother. It's a little white milk carton."

"She means the ashes," Mr. Booth said.

Behind Mr. Booth, on the mantel, was a framed photograph of Aunt Mimi, standing on the steps of a foreign airport, under a sign that said, SAMY MANDEHA, SAMY MITADY. A small airplane rose beside her from a dusty airstrip. A scrawl at the bottom of the picture read, "Antananarivo." Ottilie had told me that Mimi, now in her seventies, was leading a zoological expedition in Madagascar. In the discomfort of that room, trapped with the Booths, I wished that I were Mimi, that I could stride down the porch steps to the back yard to where an airplane awaited me on the grass.

"Will both Ottilie and the Reverend Crail—is he her husband?" Mrs. Booth asked. "Will he be coming to Spring Green?"

I told her I thought so, and thanked her for the dinner.

She looked vaguely dissatisfied. As if to remedy my failure to divulge Ottilie and John's relationship, Mrs. Booth looked at my left hand and asked, "You're not married?"

I raised my eyebrows. This was a question I no longer answered. (Although facing Mrs. Booth I was tempted to reply, "No, but I lived on and off for seven years with a writer whom I met in my twenties, and after we decided not to have children, he ran off without notice to marry a kindergarten teacher from Montclair. After that I dated another lawyer, who did not like mouth kisses, and after that, an unmarriageable archeologist, George Wrath, who drank too much, but liked staying in bed all day, making love until both of us were asphyxiated from hyperventilating. We remained friends, and then there were a few others, after which I went back to George for a while, and then four years ago, when I became a state judge, I threw myself into my work, and gave up dating, but I do see George now and then, just to keep sane.")

Upstairs there was a flurry of laughter: an unfamiliar man's laugh, and Matt's chuckle. Footsteps sounded down the back stairs, and the back door slammed.

"Have we interrupted something here?" Mr. Booth asked. "Everyone was sitting with us in the living room, and then they vanished."

"Maybe they took the child to the hospital," Mrs. Booth said.

"You can't be too careful," I said. "I once presided over a case involving the estate of a man who died at age sixty-two from a bee sting. He was deathly allergic but never knew. He had never been stung before."

Mr. Booth said sardonically, "I've never been stung and I'm sixty-five."

I thought then, while looking directly at him, that he would die one day, that like me he was a lawyer, and that somehow the law was carrying us both toward death. I pictured a place, heaven or an underworld, where my father stood on a shore, his hand raised in greeting: We had come to join him in that other world where dead lawyers go. Mr. Booth raised his eyebrows when I continued to stare, and I looked away.

"Perhaps we've come at a bad time?" Mrs. Booth asked.

"We need to be getting on our way—" Mr. Booth told me.

"And there doesn't seem to be anyone to say good-bye to," Mrs. Booth finished.

"I accept your good-bye," I answered.

"And you must be exhausted, too," Mrs. Booth said hopefully.

"I've been traveling since midnight last night."

"Well, of course!" Mrs. Booth said with relief. "You must be dying to go upstairs and freshen up." She smiled and added in a conciliatory tone, "You *are* awfully tall. I guess it's hard to find a man who's both tall and nice at the same time."

"What?" I asked. George Wrath was my height, a ridiculous-looking man, with a goatee and wild, wiry hair, and feet and hands as slender as an El Greco saint's. I used to like to believe as I lay in his arms and smelled his sweet breath, a cross between clover and gin, that he was coddled in forgetfulness, that he could not even remember my name (*Judge Ratleer*), but only the way our bodies fit together.

"We'll see you at our memorial dinner on the evening of the thirtieth. At six o'clock," Mrs. Booth said. She reached for her bag on the front table, a gray cloth purse that opened and shut like an oyster.

Mr. Booth grasped my hand and said, "Pleasure." His wife followed him out the front door.

I ascended to the room I had occupied in 1977. I set down my bags and hung my black lawyer's suit on a hook. Laughter echoed through the window facing the back yard. Outside, Ottilie and John stood in the grass. He caught her waist and kissed her on the back of the neck. She turned around with an eager expression. Neither of them looked worried, and there was no child in sight.

I lay down on the bed in my slip. Mrs. Booth's face above its sea of gray silk flashed before me, and as if commanded by her belief that everyone was exhausted (was she exhausted?), I closed my eyes.

I thought of my father, of his enormous absence in our lives for the past twenty-five years, and an oppressive sense of loss opened inside me. Even in middle age, when I pondered men like my father, I could not guess what it felt like to have their hearts beating in my chest instead of my own. I wondered now, as my mind drifted toward a more forgetful sleep, if that was why such a barrier had risen between me and the world—that trying to make sense of Joel Ratleer had left me doubting the intelligibility of other people. I felt sorrow when I thought of my father, but not the true misery of piercing grief, or even regret that in his advancing years, I had never come to know him well. Instead, I realized with chagrin that I mourned his failure to know me. I wondered if this failure had made me in some way unintelligible even to myself. My father's face appeared to me, a face from my youth, with its thick gray hair and crooked teeth and handsome, brilliant eyes, and then a broad darkness opened its wings, a black butterfly, and I fell asleep.

WHEN I AWOKE, afternoon light slanted and shimmered in the windows like yellow grass. In the room beside mine Matt's voice lifted, and then a woman's laugh, and the voice of a second man discussing a computer program.

"Try Control V, 728," he said.

"Here it is, Henry, it's coming up!" Matt answered. I heard tittering, a chair being moved, bustling sounds, and then silence.

"Now scramble it," Henry answered. "*Now* try to decode it. There! You see, it's uncrackable. That's why the FBI outlawed this encrypting program."

I listened with curiosity, but nothing else was said, and I sank back into sleep. In my mind's eye the two FBI agents who had interviewed me after my nomination sat at a desk before me, dressed identically and writing observations on notepads. Their questions had been short and perfunctory. Never in their careers had they investigated a potential federal judge with so unobjectionable a life. They had not brought up the 1977 incident with Mildred and Judge Bracken: Questionable clients are the stuff of which great legal careers are made. With that fluidity of thought that sleepiness permits in its dreamward descent, I understood that the FBI had asked me nothing about myself, because there was nothing about me to know. By contemplating the law, the very brick and mortar of our world, I had reduced my life to an emptiness, almost removed myself from society.

I opened my eyes, wondering why Matt was discussing the FBI. I tottered to the bathroom, showered quickly, and put on a light sundress, a green thing that would have made another woman willowy. Under the neckline my collarbones looked like coat hangers.

When I entered the adjoining room, Matt and Henry were gone. A young woman in cutoff overalls and a baseball cap bent her slender neck over a portable easel with a photograph of two butterflies taped to it. She moved her pencil languidly, and the drawing before her looked nothing like the butterflies. It was a series of petal shapes that began near the left margin high on the page and repeated themselves until they tilted off the paper's bottom right corner.

"Sophie?" I asked.

She turned slightly and gave me a brief, acknowledging smile but didn't answer.

"I'm Matt's sister."

She nodded and returned to her drawing. (How crazy was she? I imagined Matt opening a door into the back of Sophie and stepping in, the inner angles of her thoughts intimately familiar to him.)

The room was quiet in that way of hot summer days, the humid air heavy with silence, buzzing with it. Dust motes glittered over me, and shadows deepened like mines in the corners. Beyond Sophie, to the left of the bed, the turquoise rectangle of a laptop's computer screen hummed. On the bed was a pile of chess books whose titles suggested a rational world as hermetic and insular as any madman's, although one that was expansive, international, boundaryless: *The Latvian Gambit Made Easy; The Siesta Variation; The Maróczy Bind; Trends in the Czech & Schmid Benoni; Winning against 1d4 (Play the Nimzo-Bogo-Indians); Mr. Chess: The Ortvin Sarapu Story; The Semi-Slav Defense;* and Alexander Alekhine's *My Best Games of Chess,* in two volumes translated from the Russian.

"Is Matt coming back up here?" I asked.

Sophie looked dreamily in front of her, inclining her head slightly, a goddess of languid, hot days. "Probably," she said.

I decided to linger a while and walked around the room idly, looking out the window, admiring Sophie's picture, catching a glimpse of myself in a mirror between the bed and the computer: a tall, emerald blur that merged with the luminous whites of Sophie's paper. Behind me brown shadows fluttered on the floor and swam upward to the ceiling.

I stared absently at the laptop's monitor, then returned to the top of the screen and reread it carefully:

UPDATED INFORMATION ON IDENTITY CHANGES

1. *Mary*: Hair colorers: Cleopatra's organic Henna #4 looks more natural than past red hair dyes.

2. *Red Rosa advises:* Avoid small towns: people in small towns tend to have satellite dishes, and to watch shows like America's Most Wanted. Anonymity is easier to achieve in a medium-sized city.

3. *M. Tubman:* Need a new Social Security number? Remember, you can usually use anyone else's number for a year without

being detected. Always feel free to use mine. It's [*chk unscramble:*] ▐┶—┳┼-ᴸ-┌ᴸ

SAFEHOUSE CODE:

Today, safehouses may be identified by the following sign: [*chk
unscramble:*] ♂☺●♣♪♥▼→►◄

NEWS FROM THE RAILROAD:

"Honorable" G. Hochwald has set an August 30 court date for the
Frederick Nobel case. Watch out, Hochwald!

PERSONALS

40-year-old single mother, sporadic income, about $12,000 a year, 2
children, looking for single parent to share expenses. I'm a good cook,
good with children, ok housekeeper, otherwise very reliable.

32-year-old single mother, $55,000 annually, long work hours, one
child, seeking full-time single parent to share childcare responsibilities,
part-time income ok, will pay rent. Young children a plus. Must be
good with kids.

54-year-old, no income yet, separated, children grown, seeks temporary residence. Great housekeeper, can help with childcare, errands,
etc.

17, pregnant, and nowhere to go, but I better move fast. Good
housekeeper, babysitter.

NEW SUGGESTIONS REGARDING ECONOMIC OBSTACLES TO ESCAPE

Advice from R.R.: If your husband has control of family bank accounts, get his bank card from his wallet, go to a location far from
your home, and withdraw money from an ATM machine. Encourage
him to believe that his card was lost or stolen, and then used by a
robber. Remember: ATM machines usually have hidden cameras. Find
the camera lens and keep your back to it. Keep your face hidden, and
consider dressing like a man.

A thin hand snaked past me and hit the escape key. "Careless to
leave it on!"

In the mirror beside the computer a man's face appeared, gaunt and
shadowed, almost cadaverous, black-haired.

The face darted away, and a second arm enclosed me in a bony embrace. Its hand danced over the keys, making me think of a daddy longlegs. The voice behind me said, "Control this, control that, Alt 29, control this, this, this, escape exit." The writing before me vanished, replaced by a dark screen.

The man stood back and held out his hand: it felt like a bundle of pencils. "Henry Nummelin," he said. His eyes were clear and steady, the exact color of oxblood shoe polish.

He held my hand longer than I felt comfortable, but he apparently did this unself-consciously, because as he continued to talk, he did not let go. From Ottilie's description of Henry I had expected a socially awkward man—but perhaps he was so out of it that he did not know when to feel awkward.

"What was that?" I asked.

"Only a little Internet bulletin board," Henry answered. "Your brother and Ottilie are down in the kitchen. I popped up here to get Sophie."

"I'm just sitting in this chair," Sophie said.

Henry walked two steps toward her, still holding my hand. "Are you sure, Sophie? Everyone down there would love to have you."

"I'm sure."

"And you?" Henry asked, looking at me. Only then did he notice that the thing pressed between his palms was my hand. He looked at it and said, "Oh, well, you'll be needing this." He returned my hand to me.

"Matt!" Henry called. "Your sister's awake. Risen from the dead!" He laughed inwardly when he said this; his cadaverous face contorted into a smile-grimace. "She was up here looking at your computer and talking to Sophie."

Footsteps clattered up the stairs. Ottilie entered, and Matt followed. He walked to the desk immediately and snapped shut the laptop.

"Is everyone all right?" I asked Ottilie. "I heard that a child got—"

"Oh, Melanie," Ottilie said. "I meant to come right to the door when you rang, but we had a kind of emergency, and now everything is fine." She embraced me. Ottilie's hair had turned a translucent yellow. When she stood back, she smiled: crow's-feet gripped her temples. She looked profoundly happy—the emergency could not have been that bad.

"You're—luminous," I said.

She laughed.

I like to believe that the idea of reincarnation is based not on the hazy recollection of past histories, but arises instead from our observations of this life alone, since widowhood, illness, the deaths of children, or divorce can end a person's life, and force that person to begin again as someone else. My father, of course, had many lives—a public and private one; and the three successive lives of each of his marriages, two with children, and one in which his children, by his own choice, played no part. But most remarkable to me was Ottilie's biography, which had commenced in such hardship, and then became something else entirely, a world she pieced together after her first life ended in deadening grief.

"I mean, you look happy," I told Ottilie.

"Well, I might be," she answered.

Matt handed Henry the laptop and hugged me. I smelled a subtle odor of musk; my brother was wearing cologne. He had become heavier, a side effect, he later told me, of the Clozapine. The weight made him look more like my father than Matt ever had. In middle age Matt was a plainly handsome man, although he still seemed off center. He wore high-top sneakers and a boy's haircut, parted on the side.

"Judge Ratleer," he said.

Matt walked to Sophie's chair and touched her elbow. She rose as if levitating on his arm, the easel still in her hand, and kissed him behind the ear.

"Matt and Henry, can you come here for a minute?" John called from downstairs. "The van's ready! Bring the laptop and the modem."

"You better hurry," Ottilie said. She almost added something, looked at me, and stopped herself. Apparently no one intended to give me any details about whatever had been going on when I arrived.

"Why do I get the feeling that everyone but me is in on some big secret?" I asked.

"Because you're paranoid," Matt teased. "Because—"

"Because everyone but you is in on some big secret," Henry said.

"Because I'm your psychiatrist," Matt told me, "and you think I'm really your brother."

"Lock her up," Sophie said.

"Because," Henry continued, "while you were sleeping, our bodies were taken over by aliens who are here to eat you."

Sophie looked at him in dismay.

"Not really, Sophie," Henry said, laughing sweetly. "It was a joke."

He left, bearing away the laptop. Matt followed, prodding Sophie gently in front of him. She walked like a woman in a trance.

"I must be moving," she said.

When they had left, Ottilie told me, "Henry is Matt's closest friend now. I didn't realize until recently that he may be the only sane friend Matt has made in ten years."

A dark van pulled into the part of the driveway visible from the window. A hand opened its side door, and Matt, Sophie, and Henry slipped in. The door closed furtively, as if hiding a dignitary from the press. What I felt distinctly then was that Matt no longer needed me—he had Sophie and Henry as well as the love of Ottilie and John. I was glad that my brother had finally gained a foothold in the world, but I found myself thinking: *I still need him.* I felt left behind, wandering beyond the pale of the world.

Ottilie looked at her hands, seemed to consider something, turned them over, and told me, "I like Henry. He reminds me of that boy who used to be in your fifth-grade class. What was his name? Alonso Volpe? The one who had to wear that patch on his eye to correct his vision. He was the same—off in his own world, but you got the feeling it was a nicer world than ours."

"I can't remember him," I said.

"Really? You had a crush on him. He owned a telescope. He used to let you look through his telescope and he told you that Pluto was named Melanie. You don't remember?"

I frowned and shook my head.

Ottilie then talked on in a way I had never heard her do. She gave me the impression that she was stalling, trying to distract me and prevent me from leaving the room where we stood. "John knew Henry when Henry was little. He told me Henry used to unsettle adults with his love of mathematics. When he was five years old, he used to approach John in church and say, 'If I'm 5 and you're 29, when I'm 7, you'll be . . . 31!' He'd run off, and in a few minutes, he'd reappear and say, 'When I'm 9, you'll be 33!' And then the same thing again: 'When I'm 12, you'll be 36!' Or he would look up at you and say, 'I can count by 14's. 14, 28, 42, 56 . . .' Or, 'Do you know what my favorite number is? Pi!' John says Henry was so smart, people in Muskellunge thought he was secretly retarded, or a little crazy. Maybe that's why he gets along so well with Matt."

I must have looked bewildered by Ottilie's prattling. She stopped, and folded her arms. She looked at the ground, then at me, then at the ground again. "Melanie, as a judge, would you be disciplined or fired if you were party to illegal information?"

"It depends—" I began.

The van honked outside.

"Hold on," Ottilie said. "Let me see what they want."

She left the room, returned a minute later, and told me, breathlessly, "John needs to leave right now. I'm sorry to rush off like this. We'll be back by tonight." She slipped out of the room, and I listened to her feet descend the stairs, stop, and then reascend.

"The Booths brought this!" she called from the stairs. A moment later, she reappeared in the doorway, carrying a white carton. She handed it to me: it was light, made of a waxy paper.

"I almost forgot your father!" Ottilie said.

4

OTILLIE AND JOHN did not return until after midnight. I wandered aimlessly through the house's large, empty rooms, snooping in desk drawers that looked as if they hadn't been opened in years, pilfering food from the refrigerator, perusing old scrapbooks with crumbling pages that shed dark corner-holders shaped like blackbirds. On John and Ottilie's beside table I found snapshots of Matt and Sophie, and a postcard from Aunt Mimi that read: *Why, when Madagascar has flora and fauna like pachypodia and aye-ayes, as if it had been separated from the rest of the world since before the first volcanoes, does this country also have hedgehogs? Could it be that all evolution, no matter what its course, bears swiftly toward hedgehogs?* I wondered what a life would be like where mornings were spent pondering such questions.

"Melanie?" Ottilie entered the room quietly behind me, while I sat on her bed, holding Mimi's note. I stood, embarrassed to be caught in Ottilie's bedroom. I gestured lamely toward the postcard, as if it could explain my violation of her privacy, and said, "I always wanted to be like Aunt Mimi, traveling around the world. I'm the only person I know with my level of education and salary who's never been out of the country."

"Why haven't you?" Ottilie asked.

"Work, I guess. I just haven't had time." But even as I said it, I knew this wasn't true. "I think I don't travel because I remember how much Matt wanted to voyage around the world when we were young. I feel bad for him that he can't, and so I don't."

"Matt wouldn't expect that," Ottilie said.

"I know."

John appeared beside Ottilie, and took her arm. He also, graciously, did not ask what I was doing in his bedroom. He said only, "Hello, Melanie."

Even so, I questioned him: "What was going on here when I arrived?"

"We had to take a little girl to a doctor," Ottilie answered. "She got stung by a wasp and—"

John cut Ottilie off. "We have to be circumspect. You know I still do work sheltering immigrants, and medical care is always complicated, now that many hospitals feel compelled to report to the INS." He looked down as he spoke, so that I thought he was lying. I was sorry he felt that he had to dissemble with me.

"Where is the girl now?" I asked. John turned away, embarrassed, and I didn't pry further. We said good night to each other. Afterward I heard John and Ottilie talking for almost an hour in their room. The following morning, when I arose late, they were still in bed. They had fallen asleep with the door open, and lay on top of the covers and with all of their clothes on. Ottilie's arm rested on John's neck, and they faced each other, so close that they must have breathed each other's breath in their sleep.

BY LATE MORNING of my second day in Muskellunge the air grew sultry, and the sky was yellow and overcast, still as a hurricane's eye. At noon I found Sophie in the back yard, her head bent over the portable easel, a pink tent-dress obscuring her from the neck to the ground.

Matt and Henry entered the back yard carrying long bamboo poles and stood under a large, papery wasp nest.

"Melanie!" Henry shouted when he saw me. "Stand back there with Sophie. These guys are going to swarm!" He circled the nest. "John and Ottilie keep putting off doing something about this nest. And now look at it; it's the size of a watermelon."

Matt poked the nest, and wasps billowed forth. He threw down the pole and he and Henry ran around the house.

Sophie looked up when the pole clattered to the ground, and after that her face remained with its chin jutting forward, as if resting on a shelf of air.

The men returned and Matt told Henry, "The nest's too big to knock down with a pole. They'd be all over us before we got it loose."

"They were coming out at a rate of about three and a half wasps per second," Henry answered. "Within a minute, there'd be 210 wasps."

"Maybe a hose would work," Matt suggested. The wasps were settling back onto their nest. Two or three lunged belligerently at nothing.

Matt walked over to Sophie, kissed her cheek, and then whispered something in her ear.

"I like it here. I won't get stung," Sophie answered.

"It could be too many wasps to tackle with a hose," Henry said. He was wearing cutoff pants—not blue jeans, but cutoff suit pants. Brown leather shoes without socks. A short-sleeved shirt with a front pocket. His arms and legs were long and sinewy, tanned dark up to the rims of his clothing—evidently he had dressed this way frequently.

"We could smoke them out," Henry said.

"You'd have to use a big torch," Matt answered, "to generate enough smoke. John keeps citronella torches in the shed. I'll show you." I followed Matt and Henry into a low cinderblock structure that was well over a hundred degrees inside. We sorted through rusty garden implements, chipped pots, and one-hundred-pound bags of fertilizer.

Matt found a broken torch and said, "No good—the stick's not long enough. They'd sting us to death before the smoke lulled them." I watched him as he rummaged in some boxes: his sanity glittered like an iridescence. "Maybe we could tie a torch to one of the poles to make it longer."

"You could light the nest on fire," I suggested. "It looks like it would burn."

"Well, Judge Ratleer," Henry said. "That would be a brilliant way to rid a wooden house of a wasp nest."

Matt chuckled and told him, "Melanie could set fire to the front of the house, just to be safe, and wait until the fire burned its way around to the back where the wasps are."

I laughed.

"Now *this* would do it," Henry said. He pushed a heavy piece of equipment across the concrete floor. "Electrolux," he announced. "These things really suck." It was the long, low kind of vacuum cleaner, shaped like an old house trailer.

"I don't know," Matt said.

"It's got to work," Henry told him. Henry fit together two yard-long metal tubes, attached them to the Electrolux, wheeled it through the shed's clutter to the porch, and plugged the vacuum cleaner's cord into an inside wall socket.

"It might just make them mad," Matt said.

"Stand back," Henry told us. "Stand back about thirty-two feet, at least."

We all retreated. I perched on a low stone wall. Matt's laptop computer lay open below me, a few feet from Sophie. On its screen a graphic drawing of a building's interior changed color, magically extended into a three-dimensional design, and chased itself down a corridor.

Matt lifted Sophie by the easel and steered her to a bench on the other side of the yard before rejoining Henry. In her pink tent-dress Sophie's ankles were invisible, and she appeared to move as if on wheels, like a float.

Henry turned on the vacuum cleaner. A deafening wind rose from its nozzle. Wasps poured from the nest, maddened by the noise. Henry lifted the nozzle in the air, within an inch of the nest. A dozen wasps flew furiously at it and then disappeared.

"It works!" Henry shouted. "A wasp-sucker! We'll apply for a patent!" One by one the wasps exited the nest, raging, crested in the air, and then dipped over the lip of the nozzle, their menacing buzzing unheard over the noise of the Electrolux.

When the last wasp had vanished, Henry stood back, the vacuum cleaner still on. He watched the nest until three or four stragglers appeared. These he also vacuumed up. Then he set down the nozzle, turned toward us, and said merrily, "Impressed?"

"Good work, Dr. Jekyll," Matt said.

"Thank you, Mr. Hyde," Henry answered.

I asked, "Now what will you do? If you turn it off, they'll all fly out."

Henry laughed, as if he found my doubt preposterous. He stopped, and in one quick motion, switched off the Electrolux and opened the back compartment containing the vacuum cleaner bag. "Built like a lobster trap!" he said. "So the dust can't get out."

Even so, Matt fetched duct tape from the garage, and he and Henry sealed the hole in the vacuum cleaner bag before lifting it out. The bag buzzed in their hands like a radio. They dropped it in a plastic garbage can and hastily clamped the can shut. They were an odd combination,

Matt a psychotic man with a surprising component of sanity, and Henry, a sane man with an apparently profound lode of eccentricity.

"What do you do next?" I asked. "Maybe you could pour gasoline on the vacuum cleaner bag and light it."

Matt and Henry grimaced at each other—they seemed to concur that my idea was gruesome. This mutual exchange, which seemed so outwardly ordinary, arrested me: It was the first time I had witnessed Matt engaging in that kind of easy communion with another man, a sane man his age. I thought that the Clozapine's effect might be even more dramatic than Ottilie had described. For the first time in more than a dozen years, I let myself see my brother as a grown man unburdened by mental illness, amiable and carefree. Matt then told me, "Those hornets scare me a little, Melanie, because sometimes if you listen to them too closely, you can sort of hear a voice in the buzzing, and it's the hive talking to you."

Henry did not seem to register the strangeness of this remark but merely said, "We should carry off the nest, too, or they might fly back to it." He knocked down the nest and picked it up with a fishing net from the garage. "Lift the lid!" he shouted. Matt unclamped the garbage can and shut it hastily after Henry dropped in the nest.

"We could stick the bag on the lake for the fish to eat after the paper dissolves," Henry said.

"What if some kids find it?" Matt asked. "What if they hear the bag and open it up?"

Henry asked, "What about the Dumpster behind the police station?"

"The garbage men will get stung."

"Tenderheart," Henry said.

"Why don't you drive the wasps to the cemetery?" I asked. "They can't hurt anyone there."

"Ho, ho," Henry said with admiration. He jingled some keys in his pocket and circled the garage. A motor turned on with a quiet noise, like a cough covered by a polite hand. An ancient Lincoln Continental backed along the driveway. Henry and Matt lifted the garbage can, and loaded it into the Lincoln.

"Do you want to come, Melanie?" Matt asked. "You could sit here with me and the wasps." A muffled, irate buzzing arose from the back seat.

"I'll sit up front," I told him.

"You can drive, then," Henry said, getting out of the car and handing me the keys. He sat down in the back beside the garbage can. As I slid behind the wheel, he rolled down his window and said, "If those hornets get out, I don't want them trapped in here with nothing but me and the air conditioning."

Matt retrieved his laptop computer and whispered something to Sophie. "I won't come," Sophie told him. "You've already moved me once." She sat planted on the bench, her feet braced in front of her, a figure of pure resistance.

After Matt joined us, the Lincoln rolled noiselessly forward, while the wasps raged inside their vacuum cleaner bag, a compressed swarm of anger. As we drove through Muskellunge, I felt like a terrorist carrying a car bomb or secret weapon. A heavy quiet hung over Walleye Street. The bank clock showed ninety-nine degrees, and people were staying inside, near their air conditioners. The occasional explosion of a premature Fourth of July firecracker only made the town's quiet seem quieter, profoundly silent outside the muffled, furious buzzing of the car. Thunderheads hung ponderously at the humid edge of the horizon, heavy-bottomed, still, threatening never to burst.

"Wait a minute!" Henry said. "I want to get a Saturday newspaper. There should be something in there about Hochwald."

"Judge Hochwald?" I asked.

"The very man you wrote your article on," Henry answered.

"You read my article?"

"Matt showed it to me. Frederick Nobel and Judge Hochwald are the scandal of the hour right now in midwestern news, so of course I had to read your article."

When I pulled over to the curb, Henry jumped out and ran into Tikalsky's Family Restaurant. He appeared about five minutes later, carrying a *Milwaukee Journal* and three cans of Red Hoof.

"We'll celebrate your sister's arrival," he told Matt.

"At the cemetery?" I asked.

"It was your choice," Henry answered. He searched through the newspaper and said, "Matt, it's in here! You've got to see it, you've got to read this." As I drove on, they unfolded the newspaper across the garbage can and read it together, snickering.

"Listen to this, just listen," Henry said. "A transcript of the custody hearing, forwarded in full to the *Milwaukee Journal*, contained what the sender described as 'unequivocal evidence of dangerous physical injury to Mrs. Williams in the form of hospital and police records, introduced, unchallenged, by Mr. Williams's attorney.' It goes on to say: 'The husband perjured himself copiously on the stand and was soundly impeached by his wife's attorney. Mrs. Williams attested to her husband's repeated acts of brutality against her and the two children, ages five and eight, and her testimony was corroborated by eyewitnesses.'"

Matt and Henry laughed ghoulishly.

"And then Judge Hochwald refused to issue a protective order to keep Mr. Williams from coming to the marital home, and after that took custody! Took custody from the mother because she 'clearly could not provide a stable home environment for the children in the safehouse where she resided.'"

I drove the Lincoln through the cemetery's archway and parked it under a lone sycamore. "Why are you laughing, Matt?" I asked. "Why is that funny?"

Henry read aloud from the *Milwaukee Journal:*

> An organization calling itself the Railroad has announced that a group of actors performed a "mock custody hearing" in the courtroom of Milwaukee judge, Honorable G. Hochwald. Two of the actors pretended to be Mr. and Mrs. Williams, parties in a custody suit involving domestic violence. The Railroad claims that the purpose of the mock hearing was "to reveal Judge Hochwald's insurmountable bias in the Frederick Nobel case and general unfitness to judge other human beings."

Henry handed me the newspaper, and pointed with a long finger to a column written by the journalist Richard Sparrow and titled, "Judge the Judge." I read:

> When contacted by the *Milwaukee Journal* about the ruse, Judge Hochwald deplored "the gross monopolization of an overburdened court's time." He expressed outrage and called for sanctions against the lawyers involved: "They should be disbarred. Never has such outrageous vigilantism been perpetrated against the courts of this state."
>
> The Railroad has issued a letter replying that

even disbarment would be ineffective, because the attorneys were in reality actors. The letter further states: "We regret Honorable G. Hochwald's embarrassment at the revelation of his personal bias and unfitness for his position, and also regret that judges throughout the area may feel, occasionally, an anxiety that the parties before them are not real, but instead actors who will expose and judge the judges.

"We regret, also, Honorable G. Hochwald's casual resort to the term *vigilantism*, a word which conjures images of Jim Crow Era mobs, and of young Aryans armed for survival in Idaho, stockpiling ammunition for the post–Nuclear War Age. We are not vigilantes. We are simply outcasts. *We call that woman an outcast who is denied protection of the law.* For most of us on the Railroad, the 'legal means' used against us have placed us outside society."

The article continued that the stenographer who had recorded the hearing had been "totally unaware of the trick they were playing. It just seemed like all the other goings-on I've heard in court. I feel sorry the judge was fooled. But they must have been very good actors." She noted that she had been paid in full for her services, and bore no ill feelings against them.

"What an idea," I said.

Henry teased, "Does it make you anxious, Melanie? Imagine, one day a man walks into your court, charged with a serious crime. You ask yourself, Is he guilty? Innocent? Or is he just an impostor, judging you?"

"The idea makes me nervous," I said, laughing uncertainly. The whole ploy was preposterous.

Matt slid from the car and shut the garbage can in the Lincoln. "This is really off the wall, Melanie," he told me. "Driving to a graveyard to let a bunch of wasps go."

"Henry," I asked. "How did you know there'd be an article on Hochwald in the paper?"

"The Internet," Henry said. "There is nothing left in the universe that is not on the Internet. "There, you can find the $250 recipe for cookies served at Neiman Marcus's exclusive cafe, free of charge; you can read the demands of unheard-of revolutionaries in far-off countries; you can request to have pi calculated to the one millionth digit."

"You heard about Hochwald on the Internet before it came out on the news?" I asked.

"Of course," Henry answered. "Half the world is on line before the media gets wind of it." He distributed the Red Hoof and told me, "Unlike Pferd beer, this does not taste like urine. It's more like a combination of urine, vodka, Boone's Farm Strawberry wine, and floor cleaner."

"You can leave my can in the car," Matt said. "I'm not swallowing any of that stuff."

We wandered around, Henry and I sipping our Red Hoofs. The cans were oversized, sixteen ounces, and the labels boasted that Red Hoof's alcoholic content significantly exceeded that of beer. My Red Hoof seemed to be a distillation of the sultry air: It went down woozily.

Henry walked systematically through the mossier gravestones and announced: "Buth, Tikalsky, Dahmer, Sielski, Sielski, Sielski, Nummelin, Piening, Gelbke, Godke, Godke, Godke, Godke, Ziolkowski."

I turned down an alley of gravestones and found the bas-relief angel that the Pferd Percheron had cooled his forehead against fifteen years before: I thought of Mildred and Ben, in happier times, standing in front of the angel, posing for the *Muskellunge Eagle.* The name on the stone was worn away, as if a thousand escaped horses had been there since, or the wings of countless fleeing souls had brushed it.

There were no Ratleers in the cemetery, although I looked for them. As I searched, I found myself thinking that after my death, my real life might start, and in that later life I would know all the great loves: my own mother's unconditional love, a father's doting, an unbroken kinship with siblings, and all the intimacy that grew from these. I imagined that in that life my blood would feel like wine in my veins, and that I would finally understand I was connected to the human race by a thread of light like the billowing golden outline of a cloud, and then I caught myself and wondered why I was yearning for my own grave.

Matt crossed in front of me, rubbed the faces of two stones, and said, "I like these names: Juniata Mesmer and Seth Smoke."

"Matt," I asked him, "where does the Internet's news on Hochwald and the Nobel case come from?"

My brother laid his hand on my shoulder, ducked slightly, and peered into my face—I thought of how few people would have to duck to see me. The pupils in his eyes dilated, as if he were looking into darkness.

"The Clozapine makes it hard for me to focus," he told me. He continued to stare until he said, "There," as if I had resolved into a clear image. He asked, "Does it really make you nervous, as a judge, hearing that story about Judge Hochwald?"

Although Matt had not answered my question, I tried to answer his: I worried I might have been unrealistic to expect an ordinary conversation with my brother, simply because he was taking a new medication, and I clung to whatever dialogue we could create between ourselves. "I don't know. Sometimes I'm not even sure I want to be a judge."

"Melanie," Matt told me then, "maybe now that Mr. Ratleer—now that our father is dead, you don't have to be a lawyer anymore."

"Don't have to?" I asked.

"I heard on the radio that you became a lawyer and then a judge to out-Ratleer Ratleer."

"You heard it on the radio?" I asked.

Matt looked at me, a little confused. "Oh," he said. "No, I couldn't have."

"It doesn't matter where you heard it," I said. "I know what you mean." The possible accuracy of his odd statement unsettled me. Even more, I was startled by the revelation that my brother was studying me as intently as I was him. I had been watching Matt for evidence of a new drug-induced sanity, and all along, he had been observing me, hoping for some change that he would not find. I could not remember the last time anyone, sane or insane, had looked inside me and unearthed anything there.

"Oh, Matt," I answered.

"I'm not making much sense," Matt said. "I wanted to say something to you because you were looking so sad, Melanie. I was thinking about the memorial service, too."

But I hadn't been, and the realization made me feel inhuman—I had walked around a cemetery shortly after my own father's death and not once had I thought of him. I had not contemplated his downward seeping into the earth we walked on, or his ashes' upward mingling with the air we breathed. I had not considered that the violence of his needs no longer invigorated a man but now fed only on the density of our feelings, lived in the gloomy caverns of my recollection. I had not thought of the lost shape of my father's broad hands, or the hushing of that voice, with its relentless, passionate, cruel charm, its words that twisted in the air with such virtuosity that jurors could not remember, moments afterward, what had convinced them.

"No," I answered Matt. "I wasn't thinking about him. Maybe his death just hasn't hit me yet."

"It takes a while to sink in," Matt answered. "He's kept apart from us for so long, it's hard to believe he's *really* gone. Now he's gone to himself, that's the difference."

Again I shifted to catch what was rational in my brother's words. Grief showed plainly on Matt's face, but I did not know whether it was grief at our father's death, or because in dying my father had made his abandonment of Matt permanent.

"Well," I said. "Maybe I'll listen to the radio, and it will tell me how to feel about everything."

Matt laughed. "I still hear voices, sometimes," he told me. "But usually now I know it's just craziness. Sometimes, though, they seem pretty real, especially the ones on the radio."

Down the street a pink triangle moved imperceptibly, like a windless sailboat, in the direction of the insect garden.

"Look, it's Sophie! Moving under her own steam!" Henry cried.

Matt turned to watch. Then he walked to the car and lifted out the garbage can. Henry joined him, and together they carried the wasps toward the Smoke and Mesmer markers. The two graves were set askew. Juniata Mesmer's faced away from that of her husband, Hugh Mesmer. Seth Smoke's solitary grave turned toward her, as if attracted by an invisible force, so that the inhabitants appeared to be conversing.

Henry lifted the garbage can's lid slightly and peered in. "No escapees," he said. He took the nest gingerly from the can and laid it against Seth Smoke. Matt set the vacuum cleaner bag beside the nest. It hummed like a live bomb.

Henry pulled a pencil stub and a pencil sharpener from his pocket. "Accountant's weapons," he said, sharpening the pencil. Then he yelled, "Stand back! At least thirty-two feet!" He speared the vacuum cleaner bag and jumped away. We retreated, and a wasp emerged and buzzed skyward: it was burnished red with gold wire legs and antennae like the filigree on Victorian brooches.

Afterward we headed through the somnolent air toward Sophie in the garden. In front of me, my brother and Henry kicked Matt's full can of Red Hoof up the street. The can clattered and echoed off the curbs until it burst against a stop sign and ricocheted into a storm sewer.

Henry dropped back and walked alongside me, carrying Matt's laptop computer. "Matt's managed to call up a kind of virtual reality replica of Frank Lloyd Wright's Taliesin on the screen," Henry told me. "He wanted to see what it looked like. Well, it's not really virtual reality. It's more like computer-aided design. We like to call it 'computer-aided reality.'"

"Matt did what?" I asked.

Henry flipped open the laptop while still walking, as if he had operated a computer on the run many times before. Without pausing in his progress up the dusty street toward the organic garden, Henry hit several function keys and typed in a series of numbers.

"You need a lot of memory and disk space to do this," Henry said. "We couldn't pirate the whole program." A delicate image, like a pencil blueprint, appeared on the screen with the name "Taliesin" in block capitals underneath it. A rectangle pushed into a three-dimensional passageway that leapt up a flight of stairs and disappeared. "You can walk right through the building," Henry said. "It's a simple matter of projecting perspective from a blueprint in order to create a three-dimensional image. A little geometry, a little trigonometry. We tried it with a builder's blueprint of the Pferd annex, and it was child's play."

I have since learned that such computer-aided design programs are commonplace in architectural firms, but in 1993 I had never seen one before. I found myself falling into a geometrical whorl of patterns that contracted and widened into hallways and antechambers and an auditorium.

"Where did you get this?" I asked.

"Oh, it seems the architecture school at Taliesin is working on a computer-aided design project, turning blueprints of Wright's buildings into three-dimensional representations. Since a couple of students use the same computers on the Internet, it's just a matter of jumping files."

"Jumping files?"

Henry patted the computer and said, "We didn't think we could do it, but we did. The Internet is organized anarchy. Of course, you could argue that the whole use of computers is antidemocratic, if you think of all the world's illiterate already relegated to comparative powerlessness, and how computers will widen the gap between the educated and uneducated. But on the other hand, I called this program up myself just by doing a general search and then hitting . . ."

"Henry, is breaking into Taliesin's files legal?" I asked.

He studied me, as if my question posed a mathematical problem of certain solution.

"Oh, well, I wouldn't call it *breaking into*. And it's not as if we intend to sell the files for profit." Henry pressed a button and snapped the top closed; his long hands caressed the computer. "And then, we aren't hurting anybody, are we, Judge Ratleer?"

I stopped walking.

"Don't worry, Melanie—there's no way for them to catch us—we do everything by modem through remote locations so we can't be traced. By the time they think up enough laws to govern the Internet, it will be obsolete, replaced by something even more impossible to restrain. I always make sure we're ahead of the law. The technology is *always* a few steps ahead of the law."

"Ahead of the law?"

"Yes, I try to verify that we're not illegal *yet*. You just call up Lexis and check the federal statutes."

"That sounds dangerously smart," I said.

Up the road John appeared suddenly, beside the church; his face emerged at ground level, and then his whole body, as if he were ascending from the earth itself.

"Does John still use the church?" I asked.

"No, it's closed for part of June and July. He was probably just checking up on the basement stairwell as a favor to the minister. It tends to leak when there's rain."

John climbed into the van and drove back toward Ottilie's.

"Henry," I said. "Please don't do anything that would get Matt in trouble."

Henry answered, "You have my personal guarantee." He laughed in a way I found less than reassuring. "Melanie," he said then, fixing those clear oxblood eyes on me, "Matt's a grown man. He makes his own decisions; he could handle the whole Pferd shipping office with one eye closed. But if the ax fell, I'd let it fall on my neck." Henry lifted his hair in a comical gesture: his tanned neck nape met a paler olive line under his shirt collar; the skin on the undersides of his hands was olive, his wrists burnt olive, his hair dark as soot.

When he straightened, I said, "I'm glad Matt can concentrate well enough to run computer programs. But his thoughts on other things seem kind of tangled."

"I've often speculated that knowledge of numbers is so fundamental it doesn't use the same brain circuitry as our rational thoughts," Henry answered. "Numbers make sense. Numbers never lie. They never insult your intelligence. They're reliable. The rest—the rest is just madness!"

I smiled. "Matt was always good at math when he was little. But he was good at everything he did, before he went crazy."

"You care so much about Matt," Henry answered. "You're much nicer than I'd expected."

"That must be a compliment of some kind," I answered.

"You don't say much," Henry said. "So it's hard to tell about you."

"If you don't say much, people are always attributing qualities to you that they want you to have. You wouldn't believe how much they see that's not there."

"But the resemblance to Matt is uncanny," Henry continued, in a musing tone. "You have the same ears and shoulders and eyebrows."

I laughed, and we continued walking.

"I imagine you don't talk much," Henry said with an earnest expression, "because words have a way of pulling up thoughts."

I answered mockingly, "Yeah, most of the time, it's just blank in here."

"I meant thoughts and memories. Words hook onto memories."

"Well, not always—" I began.

"Matt says that you're haunted by memories. He has a recurrent dream where you keep a little yellow box under your pillow, and he takes it out, it's full of fall leaves, yellow and red and blue, and he says, 'Look at this, a red maple! Look at this, a live oak! Look at this, hackberry!' And then you say, 'Put them back, put them back, they aren't there to look at!' It's a remarkable dream if you think of its straightforward clarity—"

"Matt tells you his dreams?" I asked.

"We log our dreams into a computer file first thing every morning and assign numerical equivalents to certain recurrent images and themes. Next we'll cross-reference them, then do some kind of compendium that makes all the connections we can't figure. Of course, we talk about our dreams, too—we talk about everything, the workdays drag on so. Everything except Pferd and shipping orders, which we try to avoid as much as possible."

It had been years since anyone besides Ottilie or John had spoken to me about Matt: Mildred had been the last. I felt a surge of warmth toward Henry. I believed Mildred would have liked him.

Henry led me into the insect garden. We took a side path that led past the locked doors of Muskellunge Unitarian. Bags of mulch and fertilizer, dried beef blood and bone meal were piled high beside a basement door. The thought of John storing fertilizer in the Unitarian Church made me laugh aloud.

Sophie sat drawing within a thicket of orange milkweed. Matt plucked a bright beetle from a silvery leaf and, cupping it in his hand, showed it to me. It looked like a jewel, dark iridescent blue with flashes of green and orange.

"It's a dogbane leaf beetle," he told me.

"It doesn't bite?" I asked.

"Dr. Eatman claims that no known living beetle bites," Henry said. "Of course, some of them pinch."

A shutter slapped on a high window of the church, and I thought I saw a small face peering over the sash. I asked, "Is someone in the church? I read it was closed for the minister's vacation."

Henry answered, "It is—there's no one there," so that I had the strange and eerily satisfying feeling that I glimpsed a daydreamed figment of myself.

Sophie lifted her head slightly and told me, "I like to dance at church dances with Matt. And in bars. He whirls me around."

A monarch hung from a leaf behind Sophie, heavily, like a cluster of grapes. She inclined her head toward her pencil and, except for the movement of her hand over the paper, sat motionless in her tent of pink. Matt bent over Sophie and pressed his lips against her hair in a humorous, infinitely slow kiss, as if he intended to remain balanced there for the rest of the day.

5

FOR DINNER on my second night in Muskellunge Ottilie prepared aromatic white rice, spinach floating in watery bowls, and fish with coconut-banana sauce, all recipes Aunt Mimi had sent from Madagascar. When I leaned over my plate, a spicy steam masked my face. Ottilie announced at the beginning of the meal that she had heard that Frederick Nobel would be interviewed later in the evening on a local radio show with a right-wing bent and purportedly Christian agenda.

"You should listen, Melanie," she told me. John and Ottilie had read the newspaper story on Hochwald, and like Henry and Matt, seemed to derive unusual pleasure from it.

"It makes me physically sick to listen to those ultra-conservative radio personalities," I said. "Even to ridicule them, even to keep tabs on them."

"When Mr. Reagan was president," John answered, "I used to have to get up and leave the room if he appeared on the television. I found his voice more irritating than I could humanly account for."

"You have to listen the hardest to what it hurts to hear," Ottilie said.

"Stop sounding like a minister," John told her, and they both laughed.

After dinner Matt and Henry came to the house with a radio and plugged it in beside the living room couch. Sophie sat down in the peacock-blue armchair, while Matt and Henry fiddled with the radio's dials.

"This radio gives me the creeps," Matt said.

"It won't hurt you as long as I'm here," Sophie answered.

"Better than a sack of wasps," Henry said.

Sophie turned slowly toward me when I came up behind Henry. She asked, "Why do you always stand up when everyone else is sitting down?"

Matt said, "Ho, ho, ho, Judge Ratleer's joining us." My face must have revealed annoyance, because Matt told me, "I was just teasing, Melanie."

"You were just teasing Melanie?" Sophie asked.

Henry turned a button on the back of the radio, and Matt twisted the tuning dial. There was a burst of static. Henry hit the top of the radio, and the static quieted. "The bureaucrat who issued the patent for this radio should be hunted down and killed," Henry said.

When I laughed, Sophie whispered loudly to Matt, "Melanie's in love with Henry." I turned red, as if she had some power of divination that I lacked.

"No, it's me sending off lovelorn vibrations, Sophie," Henry said. "What man could remain unsmitten by Matt's tall, tall sister? She looks like the right half of the number eleven."

Sophie squinted at Henry and asked, "You're the left half?"

There was a sudden, short blast of religious music. Henry drummed his spindly fingers on the radio. He told me, "twelve-eight." I must have given him a blank look because he explained, "Gospel music in twelve-eight time—an unusual rhythm that embraces the two fundamental time signatures of Western music in a single meter."

John and Ottilie snuggled next to each other on the couch. I almost sat beside them, thought better of it, and remained standing. Sophie slid to the floor, and she and Matt leaned against the armchair, their legs intertwined. Ottilie tucked a pillow behind their heads and patted Sophie's hand. Everyone leaned together toward the radio. I felt a little envy for that happy gathering of people, for the fine world they had knit together among themselves.

Henry tinkered with the radio's dials, and a voice assembled itself and scattered. "They shouldn't call this channel Radio One-O-One-Point-Eight," he said. "It's closer to 101.8437."

When Henry located the station, the talk show host was already interviewing Frederick Nobel. Nobel's voice entered the living room and burst over us so loudly that his first words were unintelligible. Henry turned down the volume.

"Who can condone judicial witch hunting?" Nobel asked. "Judge

Hochwald is a public servant, doing his job well, and he's being abused by a secret society that has shown no respect for the law whatsoever. None at all. We already know this group tried to frame an innocent husband." Nobel's voice, a vibrant baritone, called up his image from the covers of a half-dozen financial magazines: a small, almost delicate nose perched over a knowing smile; eyes an innocent, bright blue; a wedge-shaped jaw; a face slightly too large even for his thick-chested body.

A listener phoned in to complain that his child support payments were too high. "What if I want to loaf around with the kids?" he asked. "Let my ex-wife go out and get a job. See how she acts when the shoe is on the other foot and *she* has to pay child support. I tell her, that's what we'll do, my mother will look after the kids and you can go out and work and pull your own weight—"

"I want to remind all you callers out there that the topic of this broadcast is men falsely accused of domestic violence," the talk show host said.

Sophie alone seemed focussed elsewhere. She looked out the window: a gray triangle of sky shuddered under a tree branch.

The talk show host's voice stopped in midsentence, as if the radio had been unplugged. A new burst of static followed, and gradually diminished until a woman's familiar contralto momentarily superceded it. This was followed by a ringing tone like the emergency broadcast system's.

The woman's voice returned. She said, "We're demanding amnesty for your wife and daughter, Mr. Nobel. We want the State of Wisconsin to provide Helen Nobel and her daughter, and all similarly situated persons, with safe havens, new identities, and shelter from the laws of other states. In other words, we're demanding that Wisconsin declare itself a free state."

I sat down, astonished, beside Ottilie: The voice was Mildred Steck's.

"Cut the call," the radio host directed. His words sounded tinny and distant, as if his microphone had ceased to function.

A commercial broke in, but static drowned it out, and a high, wavering soprano came on the line. "Fred? Fred—"

Nobel apparently believed that the call was off the air because he answered, "Helen? Helen, where the hell are you? What kind of crackpot have you hooked up with? You're in deep shit, Helen. That was some stunt you pulled with the police. How long do you think you'll last before the law catches up with you?"

"We're not really worried about being caught. We're asking people not to turn us in."

"You're doing what?"

Mildred returned to the line. "Frederick Nobel, we're demanding that Judge Hochwald step down in your custody case, so that there might be some semblance of a fair hearing. While we're waiting for that, we want a full investigation by an impartial tribunal into your past brutality against Helen. Otherwise, we're conducting a hearing and investigation ourselves. And finally, Fred, we're asking you to vacate the state of Wisconsin, to make it safe for Helen and the rest of us. Think of it as a kind of reverse parole."

There was more static. Matt adjusted the dial again, and Henry said, "It's because she's radioing in from a remote location."

There was a click, and then another call, without any intercession from the talk show host. The new caller did not immediately identify himself. He had a deep voice with an undercurrent of gloominess. "The reporters forgot to ask," he said, "why I was inspecting the flour." The speaker paused. "It was because of all the rats. The flour sack fell on Mr. Nachtwey because he was up there on top of the sack pile trying to do something about all the rats in the Nobel company's batter room. That's what I was doing."

The broadcast terminated in deafening white noise that forced us to turn off the radio. I looked at the faces around me, and all of them, except Sophie's, watched mine. As if by prior agreement everyone except John rose. Matt lifted Sophie gently and pushed her in front of him toward the door, behind Ottilie and Henry. John leaned toward me and said, "The cat's out of the bag, Melanie, isn't it?"

ONCE, when I was eighteen or nineteen, I visited Matt on Christmas at a Chicago state mental hospital. A nurse called Matt out of the room, and he and Ottilie left me alone for a few minutes while Matt stumbled down the hall for medication. While they were gone, Matt's roommate entered the room, dropped his pants, and flashed me: His penis rose and crooked to the left. "My feet are cold," he told me, smiling, and watched my face for a reaction. I stepped into the hall, waiting for Matt and Ottilie's return. As I stood there, I heard an inmate across the hall carry on a conversation through a window. I leaned forward and saw no one was outside: The hospital lawn sparkled with snow under the lamplight, and behind it, the grounds stretched out blackly.

I watched the man's reflection: His shadowy mouth scowled and grimaced, smiled and gaped. He seemed to be conversing with his own image, mirrored in that dark glass, and I stepped forward to eavesdrop. I discovered then that he was not talking to himself, but to his God. "Jesus, my Lord," he said, "I hate this place. Why couldn't you have taken me from here just this one night? Why couldn't I walk with the angels for just one goddamn Christmas? What's it to you?" He leaned over a heater in front of the window ledge, and I understood then that Jesus was not even outside, on the hospital grounds: The man had not been talking to the glittering night, but instead, to the heater itself. He leaned on the heater's metal grate and rattled it.

He raised his head then, and his reflection stared at my image in the glass; the shadowed pool of his eyes moved toward mine. He scowled and said, "You think it's strange that I think Jesus lives in this heater, don't you?" He took a menacing step toward the reflected me. "It's no stranger than believing He lives in the sky!" Then he laughed, long and loud.

Ottilie and Matt returned, and we reentered the room together. Matt's roommate had curled up under his covers on the bed, and lay facing the wall, ostensibly asleep. Ottilie and Matt and I resumed whatever conversation we had started earlier. I wanted to tell Matt and Ottilie that Matt's roommate had exposed himself, that the man outside had found Jesus in the heating system, but I let it pass: I guessed events like this made up much of Matt's usual day, and Ottilie looked too tired and sad to take in more. However, for the rest of the afternoon I felt that I had somehow remained caught in the shadowed glass of the hallway, in that reflected world. The little things left unsaid pinned me there, held a wholer version of me.

Now, as I faced John in Aunt Mimi's house, that afternoon with Ottilie and Matt came back to me. John inclined slightly toward me, poised, ready to divulge a secret, but what I thought, irrationally, was that it was I who held a secret, I who had chosen to inhabit a shadowy realm where I would bear witness but never retell. It was an odd thought: I had nothing to impart to John that could have been of any interest to him in that moment.

"Melanie," John began. "We've been hesitant to speak to you because, after all, you're a judge. A federal judge." He waited—for what, I did not know.

I felt uncomfortable and joked with him. "Matt thinks the only reason I want to be a judge is to out-Ratleer Ratleer."

John did not laugh. He answered, "I've always asked myself whether you became a judge because you feel safer from the law's arbitrary power and cruelties up there on the bench—because you hope the law's power can't get you up there."

"It can still bite my toes, John," I said.

"It certainly can," John answered. "That's why I'm not sure how much to tell you. Ottilie doesn't want you led into anything that could imperil your career."

"Any legal consequences for me are my worry, not yours, aren't they?" I answered. "Why is Mildred on the radio, and why is she with Helen Nobel?"

When John did not answer immediately, I pressed him. "Are you worried you can't trust me? Do you think I'd give Mildred away? Matt's involved in all this, somehow, isn't he? And Ottilie? Do you think I'd do anything to get them in trouble?"

"Of course not," John answered. "Ottilie trusts you without reservation. She just doesn't want you pulled in because you've worked so hard to get where you are. Melanie, you live in a world where—"

"What could you possibly know about my world?" I answered. I felt like a lost soul calling to a living man across gray water. "I spend all day with these jackass judges, glorified lawyers who like to lord it over other lawyers. The same assholes I went to law school with, twenty years later, even more full of themselves, twice as pompous and arrogant as they were before. How could you imagine I'd feel any loyalty to my world?"

"Is that really what you think about it?" John asked, astonished.

"It must be," I answered.

"I never suspected. You've never talked about your work before."

"Well, John, I'm kind of a strange person," I answered. "Half the time I surprise myself when I say out loud what I've been thinking." I had meant to say this with light-hearted irony, but John nodded gravely, and paused, looking straight at me before continuing. In my discomfort of the moment, I found myself thinking for no reason at all of how much I had loved to ice fish as a girl, to sit perched on the back of a lake as it moved darkly under the bright creaking ice. Immediately before John resumed speaking, I saw McCarthy's black lake startlingly, as a part of me, as a breathing animal, sleek and lively, intoxicated by an immense exuberant anger. I reached for the words to express that thought, could not find them, and waited for John to talk.

"Melanie," he said, "I worry about telling you more because there's no turning back from certain kinds of knowledge. If you do, you'll be like Lot's wife—you'll change into a pillar of salt!"

"Lot's wife?"

"Or like what's her name, Orpheus's wife? It's funny how Lot's wife is just remembered as Lot's wife, not by her name, and now for the life of me, I can't remember the name of Orpheus's wife. The one who died from snakebite. The gods told Orpheus, 'If you go down to Hades, we'll let you lead your wife back out, but if you turn around to make sure she's following, you break the rules, and back to hell she goes!' But Orpheus couldn't resist—he thought he heard her stumble behind him, he thought about her sore ankle where the snake had bitten her, he turned around, and she was gone! And they wouldn't let him descend again to get her. Lot's wife couldn't resist either—she turned to salt because she looked back at the city God had allowed Lot to lead her from. Who knows, maybe she had a lover there."

"What are you saying to me, John?" I thought that his years of retirement from the ministry had certainly affected his religious views. His resort to parables called my attention to how little like a minister he looked now: his broad chest seemed more massive inside his faded T-shirt, and his large, short-fingered hands were faintly stained with tar or paint. Mud clung to the cuffs of his blue jeans. His manner of speaking and fervor alone betrayed his years in the pulpit.

"What I'm trying to tell you, Melanie, is that if I impart to you knowledge of things that are illegal, I'll be leading you away from one world into another. Won't I? And at some point you won't be able to turn back. You'll have crossed the line, as they say. And then, if you try to return to where you were—a federal judgeship, for example, you may find you won't be able to."

"I want to know what's going on," I answered, adding, "Why don't you just tell me the basics, John? I'll let you know if what you say makes me uneasy."

"All right, Melanie. I'll give you what I can." John then measured his words carefully, withholding specific names and dates and places, and never identifying the source of his information. He explained the

Railroad to me in a general, straightforward way, and I have tried to recall and set down here exactly what he told me in that hour, because with time I would understand that his description, although simple, was also thorough, because the Railroad's success and durability lay in its simplicity.

He related that Mildred ran an underground network called the Railroad, which helped people who, as John put it, were "forced to flee adverse court rulings." Mildred had built the Railroad over a dozen years. It had started in Chicago and branched outward from cities on the Amtrak line that ran from Chicago through Buffalo, Syracuse, and Albany into Manhattan. It now extended throughout the country and into several foreign countries, some of which had started similar networks of their own. In 1993 the Railroad had hundreds of members in the United States and many more sympathizers. They included lawyers; doctors; policemen; a secretary in the Bureau of Alcohol, Tobacco, and Firearms; journalists; actors; nurses; and computer experts, including Henry. The Railroad provided free legal and medical services, Social Security numbers, and birth certificates. It had a relocation system that paired single parents through personal ads; safehouses throughout the United States that identified themselves by predesignated daily codes released on the Internet; and means of transporting people across international boundaries, when necessary.

John told me, "My daughter has resurrected the Underground Railroad of Harriet Tubman, but it's a railroad at once freer and less hopeful. Tubman could lead people to only one Promised Land, the North, but the Railroad leads to every possible destination. And while Tubman's enemies lay principally in the South, this railroad's enemies live everywhere." John stopped, self-conscious of his sermonizing tone. But he looked genuinely happy, so that I thought of him almost sixteen years before, when he had strolled through his garden with electric joy, his grandson and daughter nearby.

"The fundamental principle of the Railroad," John continued with unconcealed pride, "is that it should act in situations of domestic violence when legal means prove dangerously dilatory or ineffective." He explained that the Railroad was organized along the principles of the original Underground Railroad, also employing a loose cell system, so that very few people knew the identities of more than three others in the network: usually one person above, one of equal status, and one below. Many of those aided by the Railroad, and even those who gave

329

assistance through it, were not ever aware that their actions were part
of a larger structure. They were approached by concerned individuals
who ostensibly acted out of altruism or female camaraderie.

According to John, before 1990 the Railroad spread almost unhampered. In the early eighties, before the advent of systemic computeriza-
tion, it was still fairly easy for an average housewife to disappear into
the vast United States with her children. The Railroad offered her an
identity, a location where work and childcare were provided, and basic
training to avoid discovery by private detective agencies and the police.
The Railroad's work became more difficult in the late eighties, with the
development of computerized police identification systems and networks for discovering missing children.

"Mildred's political ingenuity is evident," John said, "in her early
recognition that the Railroad would not survive without computer experts who could crack such systems and encode information to protect
the Railroad from outsiders. Many computer hackers were among its
first members."

John spoke with the enthusiasm of a convert. When I asked him
whether the Railroad might not serve to further child snatching, he said
that every effort was made to verify the validity of claims in order to
avoid cooperation in "unjustifiable kidnapping." He believed that the
Railroad's investigations were "far more trustworthy than most legal
proceedings." Police and hospital records were examined, children carefully interviewed, and investigations made into the lives of those alleged
to be violent.

When I asked whether the Railroad had ever made a mistake, John
stopped talking and looked at me as if he had forgotten what he intended to say, or as if he suddenly sensed such doubt in me that he
decided to censor himself.

"Of course the Railroad has made mistakes," he answered, "but
there have also been hundreds of times when it's prevented women and
children from being maimed or killed." He spoke somewhat defensively, although I had not meant to put him on the defensive: I felt
myself drawn in by his description of the Railroad, but I had been a
lawyer and judge for years, and my mode of assessing information was
almost automatically adversarial.

John continued, "And there are even two known cases where the
Railroad identified previously kidnapped children—that is, children
wrongfully taken from a home where there was no history of violence.

The Railroad secured their return without involvement of law enforcement authorities, and since then there have been several instances where parents who have kidnapped children impulsively and come to regret it, have contacted the Railroad in order to secure some form of conditional amnesty for returning them. It's complicated, because Mildred won't deal with the courts or police. But then, of course, neither will kidnappers."

"Why hasn't anyone turned the Railroad in?" I asked. "Haven't there been ex-husbands who have become suspicious and gone after it?"

John frowned. "That's bound to happen sooner or later. But for every potential detractor, countless sympathizers come out of the woodwork. So many people out there have been up against what Mildred once was, or their family or friends have. Not that interference isn't sure to come. And now that Mildred has decided to make a public statement—"

"Why does she want to go public?" I asked.

"She's done it against my advice," John said. "But she's chosen this time to come forward because she believes Helen Nobel's case is a ripe opportunity to air exigent grievances." John said that he knew I must feel a little peculiar, being the link between Helen Nobel and Mildred: If I hadn't sent Ottilie the article on the Nobel case, and she hadn't passed it on to John, Mildred might never have planned to aid Helen Nobel's escape by staging her murder.

THE NIGHT after I learned about the Railroad I lay awake for hours, worrying about the very predicament of which John had forewarned me: whether I was about to enter a world concocted by Mildred that effectively would end my judicial career. I thought of Mildred living in nameless anonymity for most of her adult life. (I remembered her, in 1977, saying that "Steck" would come to mean what she would make it mean.) Then I calculated the number of years that had passed since Ben and Mildred had fled Muskellunge, and I realized that the timing of Helen Nobel's disappearance was not fortuitous—Ben was eighteen, and this was the year in which Mildred had become, in a sense, free, because Daniel would have lost his hold on her. A vicarious elation rushed through me, when I imagined how Mildred must have felt the morning she awoke and could say to herself: *No one can use the threat of taking my child from me ever again.* Because time had rescued them—

carried Ben on its crest to adulthood and deposited him safe on the shore. I wondered how the taste of Mildred Steck's name would feel in her mouth the first time she felt free to utter it. And then I worried what Daniel would do if Mildred's identity became public.

I could not have slept long, but my nightmares seemed endless. They stretched into an eternity where I journeyed shakily in a two-dimensional world of projected computer blueprints leading through corridors of Frank Lloyd Wright's Taliesin. I felt substanceless, a mere sketch of a ghost, and I soared into an open area where architectural students worked intently on their drawings. One of the students looked up at me with the face of Gary Cooper in *The Fountainhead* and asked, "Who are you?" "I'm the judge," I answered. "I'm the judge of all of this." "Ah," he smirked, "that must be why you think you can stop us." He pointed out the window at a turbulent sky: A pale tornado swirled over an opalescent snowscape, beautiful and lethal, threatening to bury us all. It prodded the snow until it found me and pushed me down under a cold thickness. A face bowed over me, indistinct as an image under frozen water. "It's me," the face said. "Mr. Nachtwey. You're going to miss your coronation if you're buried."

I felt the weight of a slight figure on my sheet, and I awoke to find Ottilie perched on my bedside in her nightgown. Morning light dusted the windows behind her.

"Melanie," she said. "Can you talk?" She leaned over me as if looking for something. Ottilie was sixty-one years old at this time. Her wrists and ankles and collarbone were as delicately curved as the wings of a small bird. I could understand the attraction my father must have felt for her forty-five years before. In that moment of awakening I tried to feel what it was to be Joel Ratleer, my voracious appetite swelling as I gazed on this pretty woman in her girlhood. A pleasant wolfishness filled me, a sense of how delicious it would be to go through the world seducing and devouring.

"My God, Melanie," Ottilie said. "You should see the look on your face! You must have had some dream!"

"I was dreaming I was dead."

Ottilie frowned and said, "Can I talk seriously with you, Melanie? You need to know that things happening with Mildred right now are about to—to take off. If you're worried your career will be compromised by your association with us, then you need to go home, now." When I did not answer, Ottilie asked, "What do you want to do?"

"Since I don't know what I'd be getting into," I told her, "it's difficult for me to answer your question."

"We didn't anticipate things moving so quickly, or I wouldn't have invited you to come this summer."

I wondered how long Ottilie had been involved in Mildred's network. For years? Since the beginning?

"I should surely go to Spring Green for the memorial service, Ottilie, shouldn't I? How much can happen in a few days?"

"All right," Ottilie answered. "Maybe you'll want to leave as soon as the service is over. John says even that may be too late, but—" She smoothed my hair and pushed it back, examining my face. "It's up to you, Melanie."

She left me there, struggling under my web of dreams. All through the morning and afternoon I felt that Ottilie and John were watching to see how I would adjust to the revelations of the day before. I believed John probably knew where Mildred and Ben, and Helen Nobel and her daughter, were staying, but he did not furnish this information. I assumed that he was testing me to see how much news I wanted to swallow—and I was not at all sure after I rose that morning whether I wished to cross the line between lawful ignorance and knowledge that might make me a criminal accessory. However, events involving Frederick Nobel escalated so precipitously that I found myself clinging to the bare facts John had offered.

MILDRED'S HIJACKED broadcast was picked up by the June 27 *Chicago Tribune*, which also noted Nachtwey's call with some humor. That Monday, Nobel Industries' board of directors met in its central headquarters in Skelter, and the *Milwaukee Journal* ran a photograph of Nachtwey pacing in front of Nobel Grain's impressive building in Skelter, wearing a sandwich board that read: PAY MY SICK PAY, MR. NOBEL! on one side, and LEAVE THE FREE STATE OF WISCONSIN! on the other. Nobel issued a press release stating that Nachtwey had been fired for omitting to note on his original job application that he had been dishonorably discharged from the army in the sixties.

On the same day, the *Milwaukee Journal* received a statement by e-mail from "the Railroad, an organization describing itself as 'a network of people fleeing domestic violence and the courts that encourage it.'" The newspaper printed the Railroad's message in its entirety:

WISCONSIN PROCLAMATION

It is a shame that women don't riot—hit the streets en masse, smash windows, plunder, pillage, destroy property, intoxicated by their unified rebellion and individual angry selfishness all at once. How do we protest?

Martin Luther King said that a riot is the language of the unheard. We are unheard: we live in hiding, under assumed names, while dangerous men like Frederick Nobel walk the streets.

We demand that an inquiry be made into Frederick Nobel's history of violence. We demand that the "Honorable" Frank Hochwald recuse himself permanently from the Wisconsin judiciary.

We demand amnesty for Helen Nobel, and all similarly situated persons, so that they may return to raising their children openly without the threat of criminal prosecution. We demand that Wisconsin declare itself a free state.

We are fighting the devil, and the devil is the law.

On the evening of this proclamation, I heard John and Ottilie arguing in their room while I drank coffee alone in the kitchen. Later, they came downstairs to the kitchen together. John sat tensely at the table beside me, while Ottilie made tea without uttering a word. When she leaned over the stove, her face seemed a mirror of that simmering water. I felt edgy and excused myself.

Around midnight the house's front door slammed, and John's van rumbled in the driveway. From my bedroom I watched the van move up the road and stop in front of Muskellunge Unitarian. The headlights turned off, and John disappeared into the blackness of a moonless night. I pictured him, agitated by his disagreement with Ottilie, strolling through the organic garden. He would be testing his land to see whether its fecundity held up in darkness: He would tap the sleek, dark purples of the eggplants, smell the alkaloid bitterness in the midnight mouths of tomato flowers, touch the squash blossoms, black silk under his fingers.

A light flickered on in the church and quickly turned off. I thought of the face I had believed I had daydreamed bending over the high window sash, and I knew John had entered the church to visit someone there.

When John returned two hours later, I cornered him in the upstairs hallway and asked, "Where is Ben? What will Ben do now that Mildred is—more in the open? Now that things are like this?"

John answered, "For God's sake, Melanie, you're still a judge!" He glared at me as though I were the law itself. Not only did he seem completely disinclined to give me further information; I thought he regretted having told me anything at all. "Don't ask me," he concluded, "to supply you with facts that could compromise my own daughter's child."

My face must have revealed hurt or embarrassment, because he relented, a little. "Melanie, it's not that I don't trust you. I'm sorry I spoke to you that way."

But he did not answer my question. He said good night, shutting his bedroom door behind him. Now, looking back on the events of those two days, I suppose that it was my sense of being excluded from a larger society, of being a stranger standing at the gate looking in, that compelled me to do what I did next. I waited in the hallway to hear Ottilie's and John's voices, comforting and reassuring each other. When they stopped, I returned to my room and dressed. Then I exited the house into the warm summer night.

Over the Pferd factory hill the stars looked like holes poked in a tin lantern. As I walked, the darkness thickened and collected along the road's edges, and I spooked myself. I heard footsteps ahead of me, but it was merely the sound of my own feet echoing from the walls of Muskellunge Unitarian. I believed I saw a light in the church, the rustle of curtains. However, as I came nearer, all of the windows looked dark.

I stood outside the church for a long time. A solitary car honked on the edge of town; crickets shrilled; a dog howled at the invisible moon. A sense of isolation descended over me; I felt like a solitary night animal mourning for its kind. The smell of the Pferd factory, that odd mingling of fermented hops and manure and fish oil, flowed around me, and traveled on in a current of sultry air into the garden. Then the voice I expected to hear came—not on the road behind or ahead of me, but up in the air. It fell through the balmy night from a high church window; I leaned against the church wall and turned my head sideways to listen to the dark sky: I heard it again—a few words cut short by a laugh.

I circled the church, testing the ground until I found stairs. I followed them to the basement door. My foot knocked against something, and an iron object clattered to the floor. I felt for the doorknob; the door was locked. I rattled the handle, feeling absurdly desperate—even being shut out in a literal sense seemed more than I could tolerate. I bent down and groped until I found the cold iron of a trowel. I stood, touched the door's window glass, and tapped a square pane with the trowel; I felt surprised to hear the pane break, although surely this was the predictable result of what I had done. I set down the trowel and stood back from the window. I felt the sharp edges of the glass, tested the size of the hole, reached inside, and turned the knob. A shard of light, small and yellow, fell onto the wall near the door; someone had thrown on an upstairs lamp in a neighboring house. It illuminated steps into the church basement, the bags of mulch and fertilizer, a garden hose. I slipped inside the church. As if in response, the light in the next house shattered and vanished.

The door gave way easily to a denser darkness. I walked through a corridor as lightless as a mine shaft. I felt along the wall for a switch but could not find one. My hand hit a corner, and then, a few feet beyond, a stair rail, and I walked cautiously up a small flight of steps to the church's ground floor. I stopped to test the double doors into what must have been the area behind the pulpit where John had once preached, but the doors were bolted. I thought of scenes in a dozen horror movies in which women lured by noises crept into unlit church naves only to find a handsome preacher conducting a devilish ritual, a human sacrifice perhaps, or in which dogs, larger than life and familiars for Lucifer, leapt out of sacristies to devour the pious. I climbed the stairs, enjoying the velvety danger of that darkness, and by the time I had reached the top landing I was imagining that I was a devil myself, or a criminal, a burglar or vandal.

And then I stopped, and asked myself what I was doing. I realized that the voice might have belonged to a nightwatchman—if I had in fact heard a human voice after all, and not a cat's meow, or a tree swaying creakily, or an echo from a neighboring building. I briefly considered that a nightwatchman might mistake me for a prowler and shoot me. At the very least I would be required to explain why a federal judge-designate had broken into a church late at night. It occurred to me that this was the kind of impulsive, self-destructive step a person took to undo the course of a life. But I continued climbing, blindly; when I closed my eyes to test the depth of the darkness against my own inner darkness, I saw the maze of corridors in Matt's computer-aided design program.

As I reached the final flight leading to an attic floor, I heard the voice again. Now it was, distinctly, a woman's voice. A dull brown light leaked under the door at the top of the stairs. I climbed to the next landing.

A hand grabbed me from behind. In that instant, I felt real terror, believed I had met the very thing I had imagined myself to be—a burglar or a devil. I was pushed forward, against and through a door, and then wrestled onto a cool floor and pinned there on my back, in pure darkness.

A flashlight switched on. Its beam blinded me, so that I had to turn my head.

"What the hell are you doing?" This was followed by laughter. The hands pinning my arms shifted.

"Christ, Melanie, you always were such a goddamn snoop!" The person stood and switched on the light. A yellow, forty-watt bulb glowed over a mirror. We were in a woman's bathroom.

This was how Mildred and I first met again, after fifteen years.

She wore a man's hat, so that when the light flickered on, I experienced an irrational rekindling of fear, an instinctual wariness triggered by that silhouette of a man, a male assailant. When I then recognized Mildred, I wondered if she had intended to disguise herself as a man. She was dressed in jeans and a man's button-down cotton shirt, and her hair looked as if it had been cut short. There must have been times when, fleeing from Daniel's violence and duplicity in the early years, or angry ex-husbands or boyfriends, or even the law, Mildred had learned to enjoy the art of deception.

But Mildred touched her hat and said, "This is ridiculous, isn't it? I found it upstairs in a church closet. It made me think of my old derby."

In that instant, I pictured it with such brilliant clarity—that derby snatched by the wind, outside of Muskellunge. In retrospect, that gesture by the elements seemed a warning to us both that whatever we had might be taken swiftly from us. And then, just as suddenly, I felt an eddy of uncertain happiness break loose into sheer relief at seeing Mildred safe before me.

When Mildred removed her hat, a long braid uncoiled down her back. I can say without reservation that even then, Joan of Arc would have killed for Mildred's profile. I had always assumed Mildred's life would bow her down, age her with the weight of a fugitive existence. But she did not look bowed down at all. She looked gleeful, and far younger than her forty years: strong and handsome, and more athletic than she had as a young woman, as though her life required her to be prepared to move quickly and nimbly at any moment. If her hair had turned completely gray, I could not tell, because it was dyed a terra cotta color.

Mildred did not lead me up the attic stairs to whatever person I had glimpsed leaning over the window sash. She sat down on the cool tile floor across from me. The bathroom had no window. It must have been the only room upstairs that would not throw a beacon of light into the outside darkness.

"You shouldn't have come to the church, Melanie," Mildred said. "You can't tell anyone you saw me here. People could get hurt. You have to keep this quiet."

I assured her I would. No other answer seemed right; I had brought myself to Mildred and the Railroad, uninvited. I had flown to her like a moth to a streetlight.

"I could pretend to be your lawyer," I joked, "and then I'd be forbidden by attorney-client privilege from repeating anything you said."

"Really?" Mildred asked. "I can protect us both by making you my lawyer?" She snickered and leaned forward when she said this. I found myself leaning away from her.

"No," I answered. "Not really. As a judge, I'm not permitted to represent clients. I was just making a joke out of nervousness."

Mildred looked a little disappointed. She sat back, tilting her chin toward me. In the dim light her silver eyes were like coins at the bottom of a murky pool. "Don't be nervous," she said. "I understand my father told you a little about the Railroad, but I wouldn't have chosen to involve you."

Now I leaned toward her, against the weight of alienation her words created, and I tried to gather as much information as I could. I asked Mildred how and where and how many places she and Ben had been living, whether their lives had been distorted by hardship or expanded by happiness, whether Helen Nobel and her daughter were in hiding with Mildred, where Ben was.

But Mildred had lost the candor of her early womanhood and she talked with circumspection. She evaded my questions and finally said, "Judge Ratleer, as an officer of the law, you really shouldn't want to know more than you already do." In that moment I worried Mildred was weighing how dangerous I might be to the Railroad—perhaps even contemplating locking me into the bathroom until something important had transpired. But this suspicion evaporated when she said, "I don't want to mess up your career. Christ, you just went right on going after Vogelsang, didn't you?"

The image of my life passed over me, a black bat with the wings of a judicial gown. I envisioned a different life, in which I passed my days at Aunt Mimi's house, devising plans for smuggling women along secret travel routes from one safehouse to another.

"I must be having a midlife crisis," I said. "When I think of going back to New York and occupying the bench, I feel like I'm returning to my own grave." I added, "I was glad, you know, that you got away. But I guess I didn't. After Daniel's custody suit, I turned around and went right back to wherever the hell I was. The whole thing shook me up for years."

Mildred repeated my words, only more sadly: "My case chased you back to wherever the hell you were?" The forty-watt bulb cast a sepia tone on the walls, on our hands and shoes and faces, so that I saw us as arrested within that light, as two women captured together in an old photograph.

"Do you remember," I asked Mildred, "telling me when you were twenty-five years old that you didn't believe in hell?"

"I still don't," Mildred said. "Just God. I just believe in God," she reaffirmed, self-mockingly, half defiantly.

"So where do you think Frederick Nobel will go when he's dead?"

"I don't know—maybe he'll be set right and made whole and forgiven. That's why I want to make sure he has a hard time while he's still on earth." Mildred laughed; her laugh hit the tile wall and returned to us. "Why? Mildred asked. "What do you think will happen to Fred Nobel?"

"I think he'll rot." We both chuckled.

There was a noise upstairs—a tree branch falling on the roof, a squirrel running between the walls, or a person moving something small—a chair, a toy, a pile of books.

I listened for the noise to repeat itself, but it did not.

"Judges are kind of above the law, aren't they?" Mildred asked me then, in a speculative tone, as if she had not heard the noise. "They read into the law what they want; they shape it and command it. You take the whole mess and mire of Hochwald's personality, his need to punish women, empower men, ignore children, and he gets to satisfy his weird personal cravings by interpreting the law any way he wants. Even though the law says his only concern should be the child's best interests."

Because I knew so intimately the experience Mildred had been through with Judge Bracken, I decided not to take her words personally. I had always striven to be a morally irreproachable judge, to apply the law as it had been intended, to temper justice with mercy.

"I sometimes ask myself," Mildred said, "if that was partly why you became a judge. Because you wanted to *be* the law."

"Recently, people seem to have been assuming just about everything about me. Even *I* don't know how I ended up where I am. Maybe I became a lawyer way back when because I thought if I didn't, some kind of terrible anger would get the better of me, I'd run amok or something. The law let me rein myself in, and rein the world in—"

There was another noise upstairs. Mildred held up her hand, at first to silence me, and then to pin me in place. She stood and slipped through the door. I did not hear her feet ascend the stairs, but a moment afterward, her voice was above me; no other voice responded. A minute later the bathroom door cracked again, and she folded herself into a cross-legged position opposite me.

"In any case," Mildred said, "whether you're the law or above the law or whatever, you need to be careful not to run amok before your nomination and all that." She did not allude to what had occurred upstairs.

"That's what John and Ottilie said," I answered. "But they should trust me to know the law well enough to keep out of trouble if I want to."

Mildred studied me and then grinned, as if considering what I had said in a way I had not intended. "Tell me, Judge Ratleer," she said, "whatever you know about this federal conspiracy law, this RICO act they use to put subversives in jail."

With that question Mildred again shifted our relationship: I saw that, despite my protest, she was asking for legal counsel. If I had been Mildred's lawyer, I might have protected myself with that rule that holds lawyers harmless for their clients' actions. But what I had told her was true: As a judge, I could not take clients.

"Theoretically," Mildred said, "if someone else committed an illegal act, and I joined that person afterward, would we make a conspiracy?"

"What other person?"

"Isn't the stuff about Nachtwey in the news yet?" Mildred asked. "It must be on the radio, at least. It's been on the Internet for more than an hour."

"Nachtwey?" I asked. "The man who used to work for Nobel?"

"Well, it's better you don't know, isn't it? Just tell me what you know about conspiracy."

"What's this about Nachtwey?"

"Melanie," Mildred said. "I promise you'll find out about Nachtwey soon enough. Can you answer my question or not?"

"All right," I said. "Under the federal RICO Act, and probably under this state's laws as well, you'd be guilty as a co-conspirator if they proved you had agreed with some other person—a criminal or terrorist or whatever—to engage in some unlawful act, and then took a single step toward that act. After that, you might be held accountable for any crime the other person committed in furtherance of the conspiracy." I spoke to Mildred at length, uncoiling a thread to lead her through the labyrinths of the law, and as I did so, my voice took on a conspiratorial tone.

"In other words," Mildred said when I had finished, "the greater the anarchy, the lesser the conspiracy, right?"

Mildred did not appear to think I had acted differently than any lawyer might have. Because after this bit of counseling and her response she sat back and asked me in a conversational tone, "So, what else have you been doing with yourself besides legal work? I hear you aren't married and you don't have kids?"

"No," I said, smiling at the conventionality of her questions. "I would never have expected you to ask that." I answered, a little sarcastically, "I haven't done anything except law. Life has passed me by."

"Really?" she asked, with what appeared to be genuine interest. "You think because you're unmarried that life has passed you by? I wouldn't have been able to accomplish what I have if I'd been tied up in a marriage."

I remembered Mildred telling me years before that some people are lost in life's turbulence, while some buoy up intact, above water, and swim to shore. I thought she must have made it to the shore long ago. "Mildred," I answered, "what you're doing, risking your neck for so many people, it's pretty amazing. Almost as amazing as Harriet Tubman herself."

When she answered me, Mildred's voice became so animated that she sounded like John Steck. "Harriet Tubman didn't just *escape* from the South. She returned on the Underground Railroad seventeen times, to free other people. Seventeen times! Just to run away once was almost a miracle. But the same thing that made Tubman's Railroad run, fuels ours. We didn't need a movement, we didn't need leaders. All we run on is the steam of the intolerable—the need to flee intolerable circumstances. Just by laying the first tracks, the Railroad has sparked a number of independent rebellions, and whether the women who rebel all join hands with one another, or just with one or two other people, really doesn't matter." With time I would come to understand that Mildred's Railroad was essentially anarchistic, a recalcitrant entity that existed in part for the sheer pleasure of savoring its own lively rebelliousness. It was a natural expression of Mildred's personality. In every instance where Mildred would be accused of leading the Railroad, she would deny it, not out of false modesty, but because she did not see herself in that role or desire it. She envisioned the Railroad as a spontaneous community of women and children and some men, just as her father envisioned a self-made community of madmen living in harmony with the sane world.

"You're your father's daughter," I told her.

She laughed, and I wondered if she was thinking, *And you're Ratleer's daughter.* Or she may have laughed because she loved her father and did not mind the comparison.

"Well, what are *we*?" she asked. "Are we stepsisters-in-common-law or something? Now that my dad and Ottilie have been hooked up for so long?" Before I could answer, Mildred leaned forward, eyed me with concern, and said, "You look a little depressed, Melanie. I figured it might be because your dad—"

"That's just my natural facial expression," I answered.

"Quiet!" she said.

Outside a police radio stuttered and fell silent.

Mildred stood, her finger to her lips. She opened the bathroom door, and I stood and followed her, down half a landing to a small window that overlooked the church's side yard. A police car idled outside, its blue light flickering. In the neighboring house a door opened, and a man dressed in his bathrobe came and spoke to a police officer, and gestured toward the church's basement stairs.

The officer flashed his light and approached the wall under us.

"Shit!" Mildred said. She grabbed my arm and pushed me up the stairs. "Remember Komar? At least they have a dumber sheriff now."

A door opened, and we heard the police radio again, followed by the voices of two men at the bottom of the stairs.

Mildred pulled me sideways and closed a door behind us. My foot kicked a pail, my elbow hit a long pole—a broom or mop. I could feel the tickle of Mildred's warm breath; it smelled like Timothy hay.

"The man in the next house must have seen me enter the church," I whispered.

"Shhh!"

Now we heard footsteps on the stairs. They climbed until they stopped just outside the closet. The beam from a flashlight slipped under the closet door and lapped our feet. A man shouted outside, and Mildred took my hand in the darkness. I grabbed her arm; my pulse beat as wildly as a heart in the throes of passion.

Heavy footsteps came up the stairs.

"Thank you for calling me." It was John. "It was probably just me Mr. Forrest saw. I was down here a little late this evening, checking on a leak I was worried about, and I broke that windowpane out of carelessness. It's nice to know the church has such good neighbors."

The men descended the stairs, and a door shut behind them.

"Wait," Mildred said, still holding my arm. We listened for the low grumble of the police car. The receding voice of its radio rose suddenly, and made a crazy, haughty sound, like a drunk woman tittering. I thought of how Matt heard independent will and intelligence in the voices of radios.

"I feel like I'm at a high school party, hiding from the adults," Mildred said.

We both giggled—strange, high-pitched giggles of relief, girlish and silly.

"Christ, I thought the authorities had finally caught us," Mildred said.

I had the sense not to ask who "us" might be—whether she meant the Railroad generally, or whomever she was keeping hidden in the church, or even herself and me. Mildred opened the closet door, took my shoulders, and gently steered me toward the stairs.

She let go, and my hand slid over the banister. I looked back, and she was gone; I missed her immediately. I wanted her to turn and call to me. I thought of Orpheus when he tried to lead his wife Eurydice from Hades, how he heard her stumble on her snake-bitten ankle, and lost her when he turned, failing to heed the gods' warning. She must have seen his face, his expression that said both *There you are* and *I've lost you*. Perhaps Mildred felt that if she turned on the stairs, whatever tenuous bond existed between us would break—she knew my obligations still pulled me away from her world. I almost choked on my own voice, holding it in; tears rushed to my eyes and waited there. Then I stepped outside into the dim morning.

6

BEFORE DAWN on June 28, the Nobel company's largest grain silo exploded, hurtling cement two hundred yards across an alfalfa field in Skelter, Wisconsin. Nachtwey, the disgruntled former employee of Nobel Grain, had left a tape recording on the steps of Skelter's police station in which he took credit for the explosion and revealed that he had locked Nobel Grain's board of directors in the company's central office during a late-night board meeting, before strapping enough plastic explosives to the office door to blow away all of Nobel Grain Industries.

In his recording Nachtwey said he would permit "the only newsperson who hasn't sold out to Rupert Murdoch and the multinationals, Mr. Richard Sparrow, to deliver a transmission unit down to the factory at six A.M. to pick up what I have to say. After that I'll blow up anybody who comes close, and the rest of you better keep three hundred yards back, because that's how far the Nobel company's going to fly."

Afterward Nachtwey returned inside the Nobel Grain factory, where he located a CEO's chair, black and decorated with a gold Ivy League insignia. He dragged the chair twenty yards outside of the plant's gates and deposited himself in it, directly in front of a white pickup truck containing a refrigerator-sized box on which he had written in block capitals: BOMB #3—TRUCK BOMB.

I learned of these events around noon on June 28. After leaving Mildred in the church I had returned home, carried John and Ottilie's radio to my room, and then listened to every station, switching back and forth from FM to AM, from one frequency of the tuning spectrum to another. But at this time there was nothing in the news that con-

firmed Mildred's intimations about Nachtwey. A news report discussed
the Olympics; an early morning radio personality counseled a caller not
to fall into the trap of self-pity; an evangelist preacher denounced fireworks. After I finally fell asleep, I slept until lunchtime.

When I awoke and slipped downstairs, I found John and Ottilie
sitting before a portable television in the kitchen, listening intently to
CNN. John had learned, without my telling him, of my meeting with
Mildred. He looked up when I entered and said, "You came close to
giving us away last night, Melanie." I tried to apologize, but he told me,
"Never mind," waving me into silence so that he could follow the television report. Ottilie poured me a cup of coffee, then also turned back
to the television. I pulled up a chair beside her, and we three huddled
in front of the television screen all day, as if it were a fire we warmed
ourselves by.

The news was all Nachtwey: I felt that I had conjured him in my
sleep. The television showed him seated in his black CEO's chair, facing
the camera. He was a wiry man in his fifties with thick gray hair and a
disconcerting resemblance to the portrait of Andrew Jackson found on
twenty-dollar bills, in which the former president's lean jaw and thin-
lipped grimace convey a mixture of consternation and bewilderment.

According to CNN's report, at five that morning, before television
networks began arriving, Nachtwey had run a cable out of the factory's
front gate, returned inside, and emerged carrying a small television and
a rifle case. From the case he pulled a microphone on a long stand, the
kind used by torch singers. He stationed it a few yards from his chair,
reentered the building, and re-emerged with a security monitor, connected by wire to the security guard's room where he had once worked.
The monitor now showed the inside door of the board of directors'
meeting room: a large metal box with a clock on it was connected to the
doorknob, and beside this was a television that had been turned on to
CNN, apparently for the benefit of Mr. Nobel and the board. On a
third trip to and from the factory, Nachtwey emerged with three more
monitors. These showed empty fields to the east, south, and west of the
factory, as if in anticipation of a SWAT team's sneak attack.

Government officials prevented the reporter Richard Sparrow from
responding immediately to Nachtwey's invitation to run a transmission
line to the factory. However, at about 12:30 P.M., Sparrow drove a van
equipped with a transmitter down the road to the Nobel Building, and
parked thirty feet from where Nachtwey sat. Sparrow, red-haired, with

a twisted leg and short as a child, limped toward Nachtwey and attempted to place a microphone on his shirt collar. Nachtwey shrank from this gesture of intimacy, and waved Sparrow away. Sparrow stepped back, conveying in a single look an attitude of cautious respect and even personal concern. Thereafter, he ran a cable to Nachtwey's microphone and placed a camera before it, and then did a brisk dog trot back to a group of television cameramen, who had watched from a wheatfield owned by Nobel Grain, about three hundred yards from the factory building.

At the conclusion of these preparations, while CNN repeated its report, John and Ottilie had a short disagreement. Ottilie commented on the events at the Nobel factory with the same breathless hilarity I had heard in her voice years before when she had called me to relate that a brazen young woman named Mildred Steck had helped Matt escape from a Chicago psychiatric hospital. Ottilie seemed tickled by Nachtwey, which baffled John, who found Nachtwey's actions objectionable because they embraced violence, and because he feared Nachtwey might endanger Mildred and the Railroad.

"It seems," John said angrily, "that Nachtwey intends to ride the wave of publicity generated by the Railroad about Frederick Nobel."

Ottilie answered, "Maybe Nachtwey will get the Nobel case the attention it needs. And it's not as if Mildred can ignore what's happened. Maybe she can put it to use."

"Put it to use? I didn't raise Mildred to put violence to use!" John answered. "It would have been better if she hadn't come forward at all. She could have continued for years without interference."

"Maybe she's tired of hiding!" Ottilie told him. "Or maybe she thinks Nachtwey's crime isn't much compared to the violence she sees on the Railroad."

This conversation ended when CNN announced that Nachtwey intended to issue a press release of some kind. The news that ensued confirmed that Nachtwey and the Railroad had begun to aid each other, however unplanned their alliance may or may not have been: Nachtwey kept the press focused on the Nobels, and Mildred gave Nachtwey focus.

Nachtwey positioned himself before the microphone and said, "Nachtwey here." He looked slightly to the left of the camera as he spoke, so that he seemed to be addressing someone behind the viewer's right shoulder. "First, I want to say that this"—Nachtwey held up a beige plastic rectangle—"is a detonator, set to go off if anyone tries to leave the board room. Second: I'm going to have to get up now and then to eat or use the facilities or whatever. Just because I do that, it doesn't mean anyone's safe."

He held up the detonator again.

"If I go inside to take a catnap, I just want to make clear that I've got security alarms rigged up to the roof and every building exit and the door to the board room. Third: I want my $600 that I'm owed in sick pay, and I want my job back." Nachtwey removed his cap when he said this, a gesture of politeness, and in doing so almost dropped the detonator. His left hand snaked forward and saved the detonator from hitting the ground. He returned his hat to his head.

After that, Nachtwey pulled a man's chain necklace from within his shirt, fastened the detonator to the chain with a wire, and dropped the necklace back inside his shirt. "That's to keep anyone from thinking of snipering me from behind or from the front," he said. "And if you shoot me in the head, you'll hit the truck." He leaned back in his black CEO's chair, framing himself before the white sign that read BOMB #3— TRUCK BOMB. Then he turned off the microphone and sat quietly, while CNN rebroadcast the same footage repeatedly.

During this period, other networks arrived outside Nobel Grain, along with police and federal agents who stationed their cars at a vast distance from the factory, along a dirt road that ran down the center of the wheatfield belonging to Nobel Grain. CBS and ABC interviewed various law enforcement officials. Officer Ross Donald, of the local police, was quoted as saying, "What's crucial in these stand-off situations is a heavy dose of the irrational."

Once toward late afternoon, Nachtwey got up from his chair, dragged two boxes from within the factory gate, and positioned them beside his black CEO's chair. The boxes were revealed to contain crates of tinned pineapple and sardines, which apparently were the essential staples of Nachtwey's diet, because the following mornings, when the sun rose over Nachtwey as he sat in his CEO's chair watching himself on television, he was eating the same foods for breakfast.

At 4:00 P.M., Nachtwey turned on his microphone and announced that he "hoped to be able to negotiate a realistic settlement." He then set forth his complaints again. He said that he had worked for Nobel Grain Industries for fifteen years without missing a day, and that he had been fired after being injured on the job, in fact "while doing work beyond the call of duty because killing rats was not in the job description, which included mainly security work, and some unloading of trucks on overtime." He had not received the money owed to him for the ten days' pay to which he was entitled as sick leave, and now that he was disabled he wanted to return to light work that would not strain his back. Nachtwey revealed that he had read the Railroad's proclamation, and agreed that it was also a good idea for all concerned if Mr. Nobel "gave up his job the way he made me give up mine," and left the state of Wisconsin. "I'm asking for that last thing because I told the truth already; I saw Mr. Nobel pick up his wife and throw her across the yard like a rag doll. No one listened to me when I said it before, but I guess they will now."

Nachtwey finished by describing for the press the interior of Nobel Grain's board room, which was paneled in mahogany, and which he had "been tickled pink to learn is equipped with a bathroom with brass faucet handles and a shower that will massage you." Accordingly, there was no need to fear that the board would lack for water or a bathroom. Nachtwey had also provided the board with several dozen boxes of hot dog buns. "So that if any of you out there have been suffering from compassion, you can stop now."

Nachtwey then repeated his grievances a third time, with little variation in his delivery, and reaffirmed that he wished to negotiate a settlement with Nobel industries and law enforcement officials. At the end of his speech, Nachtwey stated that he wished "to meet with the young lady who is also crusading against Mr. Nobel, on behalf of his wife." Nachtwey felt that they could forge a "joint settlement mutually beneficial to them both," which "could kill one bird with two stones."

THE FOLLOWING MORNING John's fears regarding Nachtwey doubled when Henry arrived at the house with the June 29 newspapers. The *Milwaukee Journal* and the *Chicago Tribune* had both reprinted a message they had received by e-mail from the Railroad:

> Steck, a spokesperson for the Railroad, offers to meet with Mr. Nachtwey in order to help negotiate a settlement of affairs. If her meeting with Mr. Nachtwey is used in any way that compromises the safety or anonymity of Helen Nobel, such assistance will terminate immediately.

This statement was met in the media with equal degrees of interest and antagonism. An editorial in the June 29 *Chicago Tribune* urged Wisconsin authorities to "take advantage of the Railroad's offer in order to avoid a loss of lives," and "to examine the Helen Nobel situation within the bounds of the law." A Wisconsin state legislator interviewed by the *Milwaukee Journal* condemned any governmental cooperation with "the militant leader of a radical and unlawful underground women's organization, whose apparent purpose is to further 'reverse discrimination' by helping women such as Helen Nobel abduct their children in blanket recognition of a superior feminine right to custody."

Mildred issued a brief response, which was repeated on the CNN late morning news:

> Steck is not the leader of a radical and unlawful underground women's organization. Women are tired of being told what to do, and don't need leaders. Nevertheless, Steck renews her offer to act as spokesperson for the Railroad and to meet with Mr. Nachtwey.

Mildred did not deny that the Railroad was a "radical and unlawful organization." Nor did government officials believe that the Railroad had no leader; perhaps nothing is more powerfully suspicious to authority than an overt relinquishment of authority, for within a week, government sources had begun to refer to the Railroad as "The Steck Railroad."

By the middle of the second day of the Nachtwey siege, the FBI had unearthed some facts regarding Nachtwey's past. Tabloid television shows and newspapers communicated FBI information that his full name was Clifford Nachtwey, and that he had been born in Atlas, Wisconsin, in 1935 to an unwed mother who abandoned him in infancy. Nachtwey had been raised in Burnett County's Catholic Home for Boys, located outside of Siren, Wisconsin. He had been an army volunteer between wars, in the late fifties and early sixties, and in fact had been discharged honorably, after he had developed hearing problems associated with a head wound, but not before he had received extensive training in handling explosives. According to one evening news report, the FBI was uncertain "whether Nachtwey was now acting alone, or was affiliated with the group calling itself the Railroad, which was responsible for engineering Mr. Nobel's false arrest, and Judge Hochwald's public humiliation." A demolitions expert examined fragments from the exploded silo and determined that Nachtwey's bomb had been manufactured from sophisticated plastic explosive devices.

CNN interviewed a Mrs. Barbara Frost, one of Nachtwey's neighbors in Skelter. She said that, as far as she knew, Nachtwey had never bothered anybody before. He had kept a nice garden behind his house, with a birdbath in it, and he seemed to like birds, because he had built several martin houses, which he stationed around his yard. He was not a joiner, but then, he wasn't unfriendly either. He sometimes spoke with Mrs. Frost over her hedge. He told her that he ate only once each day, and slept only a few hours at night, and she often saw him doing one-handed push-ups and leg lifts in the back yard at dawn. He bought seed packages from Mrs. Frost's son at Easter and raffle tickets from her daughter at Christmas, and was generous on Halloween, when he liked to dress up in a skeleton costume and have children take candy from a long cardboard box shaped like a coffin. Nachtwey had seemed upset after injuring himself and losing his job. His financial crisis had forced him to put his home up for sale. After it sold in late 1992, he disappeared, and Mrs. Frost thought of him as "a man who had lost what little he had, which maybe is what made him so dangerous, because he has nothing left to lose anymore." She had not seen him since he had sold the house. She added, "It doesn't surprise me that a man who does as he pleases with his wife also treats his employees just as badly as he wishes."

Another neighbor told reporters that she "did not want her name used, but it was common knowledge in Skelter that Mr. Nobel had once locked his wife out of their Skelter vacation house on New Year's, when the cold would have killed her if the Baptist minister's wife hadn't taken her in for the night." The neighbor recalled that Helen had returned to the Nobels' home in early morning of New Year's Day, "so that people wouldn't talk, and so her daughter wouldn't wake to find her gone."

Nachtwey could be seen watching these reports from his chair: He made a strange picture, for our television showed his lean, wiry figure watching itself on a television that showed Nachtwey watching himself on a television where a smaller Nachtwey appeared, on into the infinitesimal spirals of Nachtwey's eternity.

Shortly before dusk Nachtwey announced that he would be speaking again. He looked to the left of the camera and said, "I see that some people out there in television country are suggesting that I'm not normal. I'm as normal as you are." A laugh sputtered from him. "At least I'm American."

He opened a tin of pineapple expertly with a Swiss Army knife, and after eating all four slices in the can, he stood, pulled a clump of paper from his pocket, and unwadded it, revealing it to be a page of the *Milwaukee Journal*. He could be seen crossing out the headlines and printing larger letters over them with a red magic marker. When he had finished, he held up the page. Over the headline, he had written, "IT'S CLIFF NACHTWEY!" Underneath this was the three-day-old article by Richard Sparrow reporting on the mock hearing before Judge Hochwald. Paragraphs had been underlined with a red pen, and the name "Nobel," wherever it appeared, had been circled.

Nachtwey neither verified nor denied his affiliation with Helen Nobel's confederates. He folded the newspaper and told the camera, "I've worked for Nobel Industries for fifteen years, and I've met some dumb people. But I've never met people dumber than the FB of I. They make me scoff." Nachtwey made a scoffing noise. He proceeded to point out inaccuracies in the FBI's reports, which appeared to both amuse and irritate him. "Hell," he said, "they don't even have my name right. What's this 'Clifford'? What kind of dumb name is that? My name is *Cliff*. Cliff Taft Nachtwey.

"And I would guess," he added, "that the FBI is behind these reports that I'm 'mentally unstable.'" Nachtwey closed his eyes as if considering the information with a special intensity. Then he opened his eyes dramatically. "Compared to who? Mr. Nobel of Nobel Industries?" Nachtwey let out a single laugh, a pop of air, and then his mouth closed in a lipless smile. "I've done a lot of things, but I never hit a lady." He stared at a far point of horizon. "And I never tried to cheat someone out of ten days of sick pay, and then lied about his employment application." Nachtwey concluded by saying that he looked forward to meeting with representatives of the Railroad. He then turned off the microphone.

An hour later CNN announced that it would hold a panel discussion on the Nobel crisis the following evening, June 30, at 6:00 P.M. Speakers would include an expert on terrorism from the University of Chicago; a Princeton criminologist who specialized in the sociopathic mind; a prominent political commentator; and a former professor of domestic relations law from Harvard University. With some chagrin, I worried that we would miss the discussion and interim developments because we would be traveling to Spring Green to attend the Booths' memorial dinner and the service for my father.

AT 9:00 A.M. on June 30, John's van left for Spring Green. Before he departed I saw that John had renewed his disinclination to take me into his confidence. He told me that Sophie and Matt would travel to Spring Green in the van with Ottilie and him, but asked if I would ride in the Lincoln with Henry, who had promised to provide Matt moral support at the memorial service. John took Henry aside and talked briefly with him, pointing once in my direction. When Henry joined me, I told him I thought Mildred might be accompanying her father in the van. Henry did not answer. To this day I do not know where John drove first; the van arrived in Spring Green hours after Henry and me.

After we climbed into the Lincoln, I examined a road map and noted aloud that our drive would take us considerably closer to Nacht-wey, since Skelter was only sixty miles northwest of Spring Green. Henry frowned without responding.

I fiddled with the radio as the car left Muskellunge.

"It's broken," Henry told me. "Matt got everything in my car to work except the radio. He refused to touch it, because he dislikes radios so much." I was surprised by how disappointed I felt: the idea of passing three hours without a news report seemed intolerable.

The Lincoln passed Eklundville: it was almost gone—just a torn-down shack and a boarded-up blue building. I thought of the drive I had taken with Mildred into Muskellunge sixteen years before, and as the car sped on, I felt as if I were traveling backward into time. Over-grown cosmos swirled brightly around the house's front steps, as if Eklundville had been a pleasant and lively place, and not the icy location where I had waited after carrying a child to visit a dangerous man.

Henry and I talked about Nachtwey until we had nothing left to say that we had not already discussed, and we grew quiet with that jaded feeling that follows excessive news coverage. As we drove through fields of wheat and corn and soy, an overcast sky lowered itself. When I looked in the side-view mirror, the same unvarying landscape stretched out behind me and in front of me. It gave me a superstitious, uncomfort-able feeling that my life would repeat itself endlessly.

Henry slowed to read the road signs at an intersection. As we turned south, a monarch dropped down next to my window and flew alongside the car, its wings moving exactly like a swimmer's butterfly stroke. Its flight paralleled the Lincoln for what seemed an impossible distance; I speculated that it was taking advantage of a draft from the car.

"There's a butterfly racing us," I told Henry.

Without taking his left hand off the steering wheel Henry leaned over my lap and looked at the butterfly. The car veered dangerously toward the road shoulder before he returned to an upright position. "I love monarchs," Henry said. "I remember from my childhood that they're the hardest butterflies to catch. I used to go out in the fields with my father when he charted butterfly migrations. My father was an amateur naturalist. He was quite fond of Aunt Mimi's family, and they would all count butterflies together three times each year. They always took me with them because I loved the fact that it was possible to count every butterfly in a field."

"They would count every butterfly in a field? Why?"

"Oh, to verify migration patterns, measure environmental effects on species, that sort of thing. The cabbage butterflies flew so clumsily, you could kick them with your bare feet. And the morning cloaks looked like old rags with wings. But in warm weather you'd be standing in a field, and a monarch would race by, hell-bent for leather, looking as if it were made of something hard and unbreakable, and the next minute, he would be at the end of a field. My father had a great respect for monarchs.

"My father died a few years ago," Henry added so abruptly that I realized he had been trying all along, a little clumsily, to steer the conversation to the subject of fathers. "That's why I came back to Muskellunge, originally, after I got my accounting degree, to take care of my father when he got sick. He had Alzheimer's. He used to teach science and music at the high school. Even before he got Alzheimer's, when I was little, he used to play Mendelssohn on the violin, sitting in the high branch of a maple in the back yard. That's what killed the Nummelin family socially. Few people had ever done anything that strange before in Muskellunge. Of course, Mildred's family was a little peculiar as well. I didn't know Mildred then, because she was younger, but we attended John's church, and everyone knew Mrs. Steck. She once took off her shirt in the middle of a sermon. Male attendance at the Unitarian church soared for weeks."

"Your father must have embarrassed you, doing things in a small town that made your family stand out like that."

"Embarrassed me? Oh, no, I used to sit up in the tree with him. Sometimes we fiddled away together. That tree was where I absorbed several Mendelssohn pieces and a lot of math—that's where I learned that the sum of the digits of any number divisible by 3 is also divisible by 3. Either that's proof that God exists, or proof that the world doesn't need a God to operate. Or, what about this? To get the square of any number ending in 5, you take the digits to the left of the ones column, add 1 to one of them, multiply them by each other and then tack on the number 25. 'Take 45×45,' my father told me. 'Add 1 to 4—you get 5. Multiply 5 by 4—you get 20. Now tack 25 onto that—you get 2025— The square of 45!'" Henry thumped on the steering wheel. "The square of 75? 5625. The square of 105? 11,025. Magic. My father taught me the magic of numbers in that tree. We were a community of misfits, and I liked being a misfit. It was liberating. No one expected a thing of me."

I wondered if that was why Henry had been lured into Mildred's Railroad—he had always considered himself beyond the pale anyway.

I turned the conversation back in the direction Henry seemed to be avoiding. "Why," I asked him, "are you so involved in helping the Railroad?"

"Why wouldn't I want to help John's daughter and Helen Nobel? A lot of people would, wouldn't they? Not everyone shrinks away from everything, Melanie." Henry glanced at me and said, "I didn't mean that in an insulting way." It hadn't occurred to me that he had. "The fact is, I needed Mildred's help once, for a friend. An ex-girlfriend, whom I hadn't seen since college. She got tangled up with a bad husband. Now she lives a long way from here, writing articles on quantum physics in a country whose language I wouldn't even recognize if I heard it. That's sort of how I came to know Matt. Matt eggs me on, and I can't resist the challenge of it all. And then, I never acted with much thought to practicalities. My father was not a practical man, and I am not a practical man. What about yours?"

"My what?"

"Your father."

"I haven't seen my father since I graduated from high school," I said.

"That's what Matt told me. It's incredible," Henry answered. "Incredible that he wouldn't have looked out more for Matt."

"After Matt went crazy, we all went our separate ways." I readjusted my seat several times and leaned back, hoping the conversation was over.

"Maybe your father couldn't face the pain of it, so he didn't."

"Matt's the one in pain, isn't he? I wrote my father a few short notes, mostly about Matt, over the last ten years." I had gambled that age might mellow my father, alter him enough. "But he didn't reply. I called him when his wife died. The conversation was short and awkward. It was strange, as if Joel Ratleer had moved on to a new life that didn't implicate us." I thought of how my father had never reminisced about my own mother in my presence after her death.

Henry said, "Do you know Matt told me he wrote your father faithfully, the first of each month, for twenty years?"

"Matt did that?" I asked.

"Matt says he never got an answer. Not even once. Your father must have left the letters unopened."

"Christ," I said. I thought of Matt's abandonment by my father, not once, but over and over. "I'd like to kill him!"

"Melanie, I didn't mean to upset you. I'm very sorry. I was just trying to say that I have an inkling of who your father was, an inkling of what you might be feeling. We can talk about something else."

I felt embarrassed by my words, small and childish. And immediately afterward I thought that I could abandon the law just as easily as Mr. Ratleer had abandoned his son, and that in doing so I would be enacting a convoluted gesture of vengeance and rejection.

Henry interrupted my thoughts by saying, "Here's proof that numbers follow a different circuitry in the brain—you can count while thinking about anything else. Try it. Think, for example, about the route to Spring Green, or the news, and count to one hundred at the same time."

I could not resist trying: I reviewed the cities along our path on the road map, and when I was done, the numbers 32 and 33 walked through my head with the deliberateness of pack mules. I thought of Nachtwey's list of demands, of his detonator necklace, his sardonic scoffing at the authorities, and 64, 65, 66 followed, stubborn and friendly. When we turned onto the road to Spring Green, I was not thinking about my father, but instead about Matt's dislike of radios, of the numbers 98 and 99, of Matt's fear that radios could drown out his own voice with their tinny, rehearsed announcements.

I might have counted to one thousand or two thousand, but finally the numbers receded as the Lincoln approached Spring Green. There the land became hilly. Parallel green rows like the lines of a topographical map swirled up sloping fields and down into greener valleys. I wondered what would have happened to American architecture if Frank Lloyd Wright had been born in the flat countryside of central Wisconsin instead of the lush valleys of Spring Green. Raised in McCarthy or Muskellunge he might have designed buildings that warred against the landscape instead of trying to harmonize with it.

Henry followed small, tasteful signs for Taliesin. During his life Wright had surrounded Taliesin with a school and retreat for architectural students eager to worship him, and the first sign declared that Taliesin was "the world's most esteemed and influential architectural school." The second announced that it had been declared a National Historic Landmark in 1976.

However, these signs were overshadowed by gigantic billboards advertising Wisconsin's famous House on the Rock, which lies on a rocky promontory only a few miles away from Taliesin. Built by Alex Jordan, a renegade one-time student and self-styled rival of Wright's, the House on the Rock was advertised in progressively larger road signs as "mixing the fun of an amusement park with the awe of a museum and the beauty of art," and as including within its domain the infinity room, with walls constructed entirely of glass; the oriental statuary garden and the largest geranium display in the world; a showcase of life-size ethnic old-world Santas numbering over 6000; and the World's Largest Carousel.

Beside the House on the Rock is the Wright Hotel, an elegant building in the architect's style, with an angled sienna roof, bay windows, and a large satellite dish on the front lawn. Ottilie had left a telephone message at the desk saying that everyone would meet us later, around five. I unloaded our bags from Henry's car, leaving the white carton containing my father's ashes in the back of the trunk; I could not bring myself to keep them in my hotel room.

AFTER WE SETTLED in at the Wright Hotel, I turned on the television and invited Henry to watch with me. We sat together and caught up on reports of Nachtwey.

The Nachtwey siege had escalated to such a degree that I wondered whether the Railroad would consider retracting its offer to meet with him. According to CNN news, late that morning of June 30 Nachtwey had exploded another silo. Replayed news footage showed that by that time, a crowd numbering in the hundreds had collected behind police lines in the wheatfield owned by Nobel Grain. Many of the onlookers carried signs that showed support for Helen Nobel and the Railroad. Four women on stilts, dressed as giant sunflowers, handed out petitions to disperse throughout the state, requesting amnesty for Helen Nobel. Other spectators had arrived to watch for further explosions, as if in anticipation of a show of fireworks. In the dirt road dividing the yellow field, men sat atop a dozen vans and trucks, watching the factory, and drinking Pferd. Several wore T-shirts that said, REMEMBER WACO! and REMEMBER RANDY WEAVER.

The news rerun showed Nachtwey in the early light, the dawn blossoming pink over the factory and the white pickup that said TRUCK BOMB on it. Nachtwey evidently had rested well during the night, because he looked rejuvenated. He carried a heavy leather pouch, and after he seated himself in his black CEO's chair, he said, "It's paycheck time," and lifted an accountant's oversized checkbook from the pouch. He displayed blank checks and a list of employee names and salaries and said, "These checks need to be filled out to cover this week and next week. Mr. Nobel can sign them with this little gizmo." Nachtwey held up an inkpad and signature stamp. "I'm not letting Nobel Grain find an excuse to cheat anyone else out of their pay."

During this announcement, Nachtwey's detonator had been tied crudely to his arm with a piece of wire: Perhaps he had slept with it that way, so that he could act quickly if surprised in his sleep. He untwisted the wire and refastened the detonator to his chain necklace. He complained that during the night he had detected "moving figures slinking behind the factory grounds" so that he had had to keep on the floodlights, and he cautioned that "as a security man, there's not an inch of Nobel property I don't know better than any FBI Rambo would-be. And I'll tell you now," Nachtwey continued, holding in a smile and bending forward slightly until it passed, "that the only blueprints to the building are in the security room, because that's how Mr. Nobel tried to keep things. So I know where everything is, but you don't. And if anyone tries to tamper with the electric current that runs to the floodlights or any part of the factory, tell him to cover his head, because three seconds later Nobel Grain will be a shower of dirt."

Nachtwey turned off his microphone. He rotated his chair ninety degrees, and surveyed the horizon east of the factory. Behind him, a football field's length away, a stone silo lifted from the ground as if, all along, it had hidden a nuclear missile waiting to learn the name of its target. The silo turned red below, and then crumbled neatly and silently. A ball of fire rose into the sky above it, fell, and flattened. The effect of watching the explosion without sound was eerie. It seemed to be happening and not happening at the same time.

Nachtwey turned the microphone back on, and announced that over the last six months, he had "mined every silo on Nobel property." He planned to blow them up, one by one, starting with the farthest and working his way toward the Nobel company, if his demands were not met, until he finally "would have no choice but to set off the factory itself." There were two silos between the ones he already had exploded and the factory. Nachtwey said he hoped to get a response soon, because he knew that the town counted on the factory and he did not want to put people out of work.

CNN thereafter reported that the majority of the silos that spiraled around the Nobel Building were of no commercial value. They were of some historic value, however, since they dated from the mid-1800s. Nobel Grain's factory tour included stops inside three of the silos, during which spectators could look upward into inverted wells of darkness.

7

JOHN'S VAN ARRIVED at the Wright Hotel a little before five. Matt stayed in Henry's room, and Sophie moved in with me. Before the Booths' dinner she bathed for an hour and then emerged from the bathroom smelling of bath powder. She leaned toward the dresser mirror to evaluate herself and applied circles of coral rouge to the hollows in her cheeks. She tied back her hair with a green rubber band and then slipped into a magenta satin dress with low shoulders. She did not seem troubled that everyone else wore informal clothes.

John looked exhausted when we knocked on his door.

"Maybe you should stay here," Ottilie told him. "You don't have to come to the Booths."

"No, of course I'll go with you," John answered.

At 6:30 we all rode together in the van, up the Booths' sloping driveway toward a brick house with a screened-in porch. Blue jays screeched "Steve! Steve!" in the trees. Mrs. Booth looked a little taken aback by the gathering. Only three out of the six of us had any direct relationship to my father. I remembered that Mrs. Booth's invitation had been for family only; I had never apprised her how many people would be coming.

Ottilie greeted Mrs. Booth by saying, "What a mob of blue jays you have! There must be a predator nearby for them to be so nervous and noisy." Unlike John, Ottilie seemed animated, even ebullient. "I've always been mystified by the way blue jays go after birds of prey. Just like crows and ravens do. Jays belong to the same family as crows, you know." As we entered the house, Ottilie began explaining to Mrs. Booth that crows were among the only birds who can count. "They can count to six," Ottilie told her. Mrs. Booth smiled, uncertain how to answer. Her dress was a subdued lavender gray, her neck roped in pearls.

"Why do they stop at six?" Henry asked. "Why not five or seven?"

Mr. Booth rose from the living room couch as we entered and turned off the television. He shook hands with John and made a remark about Henry, John, and Sophie being "support staff for Joel's service." Mrs. Booth frowned.

She had laid a supper, buffet style, onto tables in the back yard. There was enough for a flock of people, so that I had to conclude that Mrs. Booth's expression of dismay at the size of the gathering did not arise from any anxiety about a paucity of food, but instead reflected pure disapproval of my social ineptness in having failed to notify her of our party's number. A whole sliced ham wearing a necklace of pineapple sat at the center of the table before a stainless steel knife with a well-worn handle. Beside these were a salad plate of pale sliced cucumbers and radishes cut into miters; a pink aspic, which quivered languidly whenever anyone jarred the table; two long loaves of dark pumpernickel; and a narrow jar of mustard. White wrought-iron furniture circled the table. A rolling green hill descended behind the house into the valley, and Taliesin spread magnificently in the background.

Ottilie engaged Mrs. Booth in polite conversation, pussyfooting around any mention of my father. Henry sat with Matt, the computer on both their laps as they bent over, oblivious of Mrs. Booth's stare. Henry held a printer the size of a box of tin foil.

Sophie sat down before her portable easel several yards away, putting a finishing touch on a purplish oval with spidery legs and a sinister smile. A photograph marked PLEASING FUNGUS BEETLE, which she was copying, was clipped to the easel. Her dress rustled when she moved her brush even slightly. She leaned forward to gaze, irrelevantly, at the landscape that had inspired Frank Lloyd Wright, and she remained poised there, so motionless that she appeared to be made of marble. Matt wandered over to her, placed his hand on her shoulder, said something that made her chortle, and then returned to Henry's side.

Mr. Booth and John sat together on a white wrought-iron settee, drinking whiskey sours. About forty minutes into the supper Mr. Booth leaned toward John and said, "So what do you think about this Nobel thing? The governor's really got himself into a pickle, having to decide whether to give in to the radical contingent, and let them meet with

Mr. Nachtwey. After all, isn't that Railroad organization responsible for Nobel getting falsely arrested? And now, here he is, confined again." Mr. Booth laughed a cynical old lawyer's laugh. "What a great opportunity for the Railroad, that a nut like Nachtwey would create such a drama! I wouldn't mind catching the eight o'clock news report, but I suppose that wouldn't be proper, would it?"

John asked, "What eight o'clock report?"

"They announced it during the CNN panel discussion ten minutes after the panelists started, right as they got dull. The radical representative of the Underground, this Steck person, is expected to arrive at the Nobel factory at eight."

"Arrive in person at the factory? That's too dangerous!" John said this so emphatically that Mr. Booth looked at him with a puzzled expression before continuing. He had never made the connection between John and Mildred; like his wife, Mr. Booth called John "Reverend Crail," and John never set them straight.

"I'd like to see the eight o'clock report," I said without thinking. I felt Mrs. Booth eyeing me and I did not turn toward her.

Mr. Booth answered, "They've been going back and forth all day at the governor's office, trying to determine the politics of the thing. Now they're craving it. At least they're not going to prevent this Steck person's meeting with Nachtwey. How would they stop her anyway, shoot her?"

Mrs. Booth hovered over Matt and Henry and told them, pointedly, "I know you must not have much of an appetite at a time like this."

Henry snapped the computer closed.

"Don't you feel we should talk about Joel a little?" Mrs. Booth asked Ottilie.

"Why don't we do that tomorrow?" Ottilie answered. "We could save up our thoughts and think them all at once."

Mr. Booth smiled darkly, and Matt looked relieved.

At seven-thirty clouds of gnats spread over the food, and the high sighing of mosquitoes filled the air. All of us moved to the screened-in porch to watch the darkness fall. Sophie drifted toward the porch steps, Matt prodding her from behind so that she appeared to travel according to a strict observance of the laws of inertia, floating forward until some resistance stopped her. When Matt reached the porch's screen door, he took Sophie's elbow, guided her onto a porch swing, and sat down with her.

John said under his breath, to Ottilie, "Maybe I should return to the hotel and catch the eight o'clock report," but Ottilie answered, "They'll repeat it later. They always do. She'll be all right."

Henry sat down beside me on a wicker couch. Mrs. Booth asked, "Are you and Mr. Nummelin significant others?"

"Oh—" I said. "Oh no, we've just met."

Mrs. Booth clutched one hand with another, and then looked at me, with an expression of terror, as if I were a phantom. She appeared panicked—she frantically examined the wedding ring on her left hand, so that I wondered, illogically, whether her horror at my uncoupled state had possessed her completely.

"My diamond is gone!" she said. "I've lost the diamond to my wedding ring! I must have dropped it on the lawn!"

Everyone but Sophie gathered around her. We looked at the gold setting on Mrs. Booth's finger, the pointy teeth biting a pocket of air.

"It's gone for good," Mr. Booth said. "A needle in a haystack."

We all gazed over the dark lawn spreading toward the evening sky.

"Gone forever!" Mrs. Booth said.

Henry asked for a flashlight.

Mr. Booth answered, "Well, if you just want to make her feel better."

Henry and I followed Mr. Booth into the kitchen. He stumbled slightly before he looked under the kitchen sink. When Mr. Booth straightened, a small black flashlight in his hand, his boozy breath brushed my cheek, and I realized that he was slightly tipsy.

"I'm sorry about your father," he said kindly. "But Joel lived his life fully, didn't he? If only Molly had outlived him and were here now—" Mr. Booth caught himself, and his words hung oddly in the air. Did he mean, if only Molly had had a little time to herself after my father's death? Or that she would have shown her grief better than we did?

"She was a nice woman, Molly," he said.

We returned to the back porch. Henry wandered with the flashlight into the darkness saying, "We just have to divide the lawn into twenty-four quadrants and then . . ." Several yards away the flashlight flickered on, and I joined him, a little curious.

Henry lay on the ground with his head on the lawn, one eye closed, his soot-black hair mingling with the dark grass blades, the flashlight's beam cutting a low semicircle in the night. "I've always liked this viewpoint," he said. "The beam catches on everything if you lay a flashlight parallel to the ground. Dust motes look like boulders." Without lifting his head from the grass he extended a long arm and waved me toward him. "You've got to see."

I folded down onto the lawn, the top of my head knocking his, and I looked along the flashlight's beam. It moved across the ground like the finger of an angel. A pebble glinted gold and threw a shadow twenty feet long. Grass blades were craggy tors. A mountain ridge of dandelion leaves blocked the eastern sky. Grass tickled my ear, and I imagined myself walking through a world so infinitesimal that it knew no boundaries.

Mrs. Booth's voice rose a little behind us, and the voices of others—a note of concern, an embarrassed voice, a comforting, unintelligible male tone. I stood, and Henry continued to search, saying, "I've often wished I were a virus, or even smaller. If people were suddenly made small, what would it matter that most of the country is cut-down forests and malls and car dealerships? The distance between one end of a back yard and another would be enough to contain an entire perfect world. A cemetery would be like a continent. The rain forests would grow unmolested, and our new oil spills would be the size of bathtubs. It would cure all our problems if mankind was suddenly shrunk down to the size of ants. *That's* what the government should be concentrating on, shrinking us all down. Then we couldn't wreak such havoc. Mr. Nobel could be reduced to the size of a quark."

As Henry moved methodically forward over the grass, his voice trailed behind him: "Of course, the ants would have to be shrunk down too—who'd want to meet an ant bigger than a person—but the trees could stay the same size and . . ." Henry was no longer talking to me, just musing to himself. He laughed, and I heard him say, "They better shrink down the anteaters, too! I read somewhere that they suck up 30,000 ants a day."

When I returned to the house, Mrs. Booth was standing under the porch light, saying, "It was priceless, you know, the only real thing of value I've ever had."

Mr. Booth frowned.

I stepped into the house looking for a bathroom and surprised two people in a dark hallway. It was my brother and Sophie, pressing against each other and kissing. I felt myself blush—I was sure that even in the darkness, they could see my embarrassment.

"Sorry," I said. I fumbled for a doorknob, entered the bathroom, and splashed cold water over my face. (Did Sophie and Matt know the law made it a felony for either of them to sleep with the other, to love any person incapable of consent by reason of mental illness?)

When I emerged, Sophie and Matt were no longer in the hallway. I walked back onto the porch. People were talking quietly, and Mrs. Booth perched on a chair, staring tragically in front of her, her hand cupped in Ottilie's. Moths flared in the darkness along the porch light's edge. I closed my eyes and listened to the singsong of voices.

John told Mr. Booth, "Ottilie's Aunt Mimi says that in Madagascar, they eat zebu brains."

"Found it!" Henry's voice sailed over the lawn. "Come see!"

Mrs. Booth stood uncertainly as if she believed a trick were being played on her. The look on her face was one of pure wanting to believe—as if she had been told she was about to witness a miracle she should have known was a work of charlatanry.

Over the flashlight Henry's long arm rose again in the air, and he waved the memorial party toward him. "It's worth looking at before we pick it up."

One by one every member of our memorial party knelt and pressed his or her head to the grass to look along Henry's beam. Mrs. Booth went first. She bent down next to Henry and said, "I don't see anything!" Then she lowered her head to the ground and exclaimed, "Oh my, yes, there it is! Oh my, yes!" She stood up and told us, "I'm sure he's found it!"

Ottilie and John looked together. John said, "It reminds me of the Virgin of Guadalupe," and Ottilie laughed.

Matt bent Sophie's head beside his. She said, "You should just leave it there. Don't ever move it." And then, "It's just like you, Matt. That's how you are to me."

Mr. Booth put his eye to the grass and pronounced, "Pretty damn good, Nummelin. You should congratulate yourself."

I went last. I let my head rest again on the grass, and I saw, in front of the flashlight, a bright yellow dandelion, a great ball of power and pleasure, petals flaring like sunspots. Henry said, "No, over there," and shifted the beam. Only a yard away a sparkle of light jumped into the air like fireworks and disappeared into a dark iridescence. And then the beam shifted back: It was the first time in my life I understood why women thought diamonds beautiful. That jewel caught the light and scattered it in a blossom of fire. Green and yellow and white gleams prickled the darkness, as impressive as a rainbow or the aurora borealis. I felt as if I were looking at a spectacular natural phenomenon that had no name yet. I allowed myself to believe that that vision meant joy would triumph over gloom, liveliness over numbness. My head jostled Henry's, I felt our skulls tap each other, and I hoped unreasoningly that he would not retrieve the diamond, but that everyone would agree to keep it where we could always gaze on it. I thought Henry lay there just a few moments longer than he needed to. Then he pulled me up, walked three paces forward, and picked up the glitter in his flashlight beam. He told Mrs. Booth, "There you go," as if he were doing something as simple as giving her change at a dime store counter.

"My," Mrs. Booth said in a voice of exquisite pleasure.

"Well, there's nothing to do now but go in and watch the news," Mr. Booth announced. He slipped toward the porch while his wife stood in the darkness, rapt, her hand clasped over the diamond.

We all followed Mr. Booth into the house. Mrs. Booth ignored us and walked into an alcove adjoining the living room. She pulled a purple cloth from a drawer, wrapped the diamond inside, and carried the cloth upstairs.

"I'll be right back down," she said, although afterward, she remained upstairs for some time.

Mr. Booth snapped on the television, saying, "It's exactly eight-o-five." I sat down hurriedly with the others before Mrs. Booth's anticipated return. We had missed a preliminary CNN report, but not the live broadcast: The screen showed Nachtwey seated in his black CEO's chair, before Nobel Grain.

Walking along a dirt road that ran toward the factory from the west was Mildred Steck. Later, people suggested that she had chosen not to mask her face for strategic purposes—that by presenting herself openly she humanized the Railroad and drew support from other women. But I think Mildred's reasons must have been more private, simply true to her personally. She had been bound by silence and anonymity and self-effacement for so long that the act of unveiling herself must have been a pleasure as pure as disrobing before the mirroring eyes of a lover.

She wore jeans and a man's white shirt, and a fairly outrageous maroon velvet hat of a style popular then, a dented stovepipe shape that made me think of the Cat in the Hat. The hat hid her hair and made it appear cropped. Had I not seen and spoken to her days before, I might not have recognized her in her televised image until she turned and revealed that breathtaking profile. That turning affected me as it had over a decade before: She seemed like two people, an ordinary one and someone else entirely unordinary.

Ottilie placed her hand on John's shoulder and said, "She'll be all right," but John did not look convinced. He tugged at his ponytail, his face creased with worry.

When Mildred reached Nachtwey, she squatted down and bent her head toward him. Nachtwey must have felt less lonely, and reassured to have Mildred there. He gazed at her handsome profile with exaggerated reverence. He whispered something into Mildred's ear, and afterward, the look on that lean, Andrew Jackson face was a combination of sheepishness and pride.

If the authorities had agreed not to prevent Mildred's meeting with Nachtwey, they must have bargained on the chance that her mission was diplomatic, that she would urge Nachtwey to a more reasonable position. (They would not have known that her special skill was her ease of discourse with mental instability.) If this was so, her response to whatever Nachtwey said to her could not have been reassuring. She doubled over laughing.

When she finished, she spoke to Nachtwey for about ten minutes, after which he stood and disappeared into the factory. He returned a few minutes later with a folding chair for Mildred. He also carried a scroll of papers, which he handed to her. When she unrolled them, the camera revealed them to be copies of blueprints with the word SECURITY in square capitals at the top of each.

Matt leaned forward on the sofa, trying to see the blueprints.

Nachtwey nodded at something Mildred said. She rolled up the blueprints, and then they talked together for about an hour, while the coverage alternated between commentator's reports and repetitions of earlier broadcasts. An anchorman speculated whether "the young woman calling herself Ms. Steck personally helped to engineer Frederick Nobel's false arrest and incarceration on murder charges," or was simply a spokesperson. CNN then ran a taped interview with a former FBI "psychological profiler," Dr. Eely, who offered an analysis of Nachtwey that I was glad Nachtwey did not hear.

Mrs. Booth came downstairs during this part of the news, and began to clear away dishes from the back yard. She traveled restlessly between the kitchen and outside dishes, and repeatedly let the screen door slam behind her.

After an hour, CNN returned to the front of the Nobel factory. Dusk had fallen over Nachtwey and Mildred as they sat talking. Nachtwey rose and turned on the floodlights outside the building, while Mildred entered the factory. When she returned outside twenty minutes later, Nachtwey rose and took the microphone. As he had done consistently until now, he looked slightly to the left of the camera, again giving the impression that he was addressing someone standing behind the viewer.

"Miss Steck has told me," Nachtwey announced, "that her Railroad doesn't hold with violence." He paused and stared at the night horizon. "Despite our differing philosophies, she has not attempted to force her point of view on me, and I respect her for that." He again repeated all of his demands, after which he handed the microphone to Mildred.

Without removing her velvet hat, Mildred looked directly into the camera and said, "I have verified that the Nobel company's board of directors is safe. Mr. Nachtwey and I will continue talking, in order to reach some kind of compromise. I have impressed upon Mr. Nachtwey the importance of nonviolence and told him that we can't condone the use of explosives."

Nachtwey nodded. Mrs. Booth entered the living room, vigorously drying a dish, looked at us all, and returned to the kitchen.

"We can't condone the use of violence," Mildred continued, "although Helen Nobel has lived under the shadow of violence for years, far longer than Mr. Nobel, feeling the very dread he must feel now. And of course, all over the country, there are women and children living in the same kind of terror. And although we don't condone taking hostages, the law held Helen Nobel's child hostage in Milwaukee, to force Helen to return to this state, where she lived in danger, and we don't approve of that either."

Now Nachtwey seemed moved to speak, for he stepped up behind Mildred, politely keeping his hands in his pockets. Mildred concluded, "I have appeared on behalf of the Railroad, but Mrs. Helen Nobel has not been asked to condone or agree with the Railroad's participation in this matter. This decision has been made independently of Helen Nobel. Her sole concern at this time is the safety of herself and her child." I realized then that Mildred had not questioned me about the law of conspiracy in order to insulate herself from liability for Nachtwey's actions. She had done it to protect Helen Nobel.

Mildred returned the microphone to Nachtwey. He stared at the ground for a few seconds, as if in silent prayer. "I don't see," he began, "why something can't be done for Mr. Nobel's wife while Mr. Nobel's waiting out this crisis. This Railroad isn't asking for much. Just a look into Mr. Nobel's past. And that Wisconsin declare itself a free state, which Mr. Nobel can't live in anymore." Nachtwey looked toward the wheatfield where the police and media and spectators were assembled. "The Railroad says it is fighting the devil and the devil is the law—but the law is a devil that makes Satan looks like snakeshit, if you ask me. The law never did anything when Mr. Nobel fired me without cause, and the law is hunkered up there in that field waiting to shoot my head off." Nachtwey seemed to reach for the next word, looked a little baffled, and then issued a tired, heartfelt sigh. "That's all I have to say. You can see there's a lot of disjustice here."

Nachtwey conferred briefly with Mildred. Afterward he lifted the microphone and added, "While you're investigating Mr. Nobel's life, you can start by questioning all those people in this town who have kept their mouths nailed shut, like Minnie Horsvelt and Olen Foil, and Joseph Krupp."

After this both Mildred and Nachtwey entered the factory. Nachtwey appeared a moment later, and removed his monitor, microphone, and boxes to just within the front doorway of Nobel Grain.

Then he ducked back inside. After thirty minutes nothing more had happened. Mrs. Booth clattered some dishes, filled a bucket with a blast of water, and banged the floor with a mop. We heard it lap the tiles with a repeated motion.

We said good-bye to Mr. Booth around eleven. As soon as we arrived back at the Wright Hotel, we turned on our televisions: It seemed from then on as if we journeyed from one television to the next, as if those bright screens were oases. We watched them from the time we unlocked our rooms until we fell asleep, and then we rose early, and turned them back on.

ON THE MORNING of July 1, the fourth day of the Nachtwey siege, there was a violent hailstorm. Stones the size of dice bounced on the asphalt around the Wright Hotel, and misfortune thickened the air for local farmers, who feared crop damage. Mrs. Booth called at 6:00 A.M. to tell me that thunderstorms had been predicted for all that day. Evidently she had been listening to a different newscast than the rest of us.

She suggested that even if the sky cleared by evening, we postpone the service to the following morning; she felt we should honor my father's intent that the memorial service be held at dawn. Neither John nor Ottilie acted inconvenienced by the change in plans. He told her, "It would give us more time to do things from close by. No one could possibly know we're here." At 7:00 A.M. John and Ottilie put on their raincoats and sallied forth into the hail, to look, John claimed, for motor oil. He seemed very ill at ease.

I watched television in Matt and Henry's room, while Sophie slept late. Matt and Henry played chess against the computer as the news reviewed the night's events repeatedly. Television cameras periodically panned the empty front gateway of the Nobel factory.

At around eleven the hail turned to rain, and then a light drizzle. Ottilie called; Henry picked up the phone, talked briefly with her, and after hanging up, said, "John and Ottilie won't be back until early to-morrow morning." Before I could ask what they were doing, Henry said, "Ottilie didn't tell me where they are. She just said when they'd be back."

Sophie awoke at noon, hungry, and Matt took her to the hotel restaurant.

Henry stayed in the room, bent over the laptop computer. "Bring me back a hot dog," he told Matt. "And bring your sister something healthy."

After they had left, Henry asked me, "Are you as upset as John about Mildred's meeting with Nachtwey? The Railroad never employs violence. Except in self-defense. Mildred believed she could defuse the situation, and so she went. And she thought she might help Helen and the Railroad by making use of the press's attention to Frederick Nobel."

But I didn't believe it was that simple at all. I thought of my meeting with Mildred, and her questions about Nachtwey, and I allowed myself to imagine that she had known him all along, that they had forged an alliance months or even years before the Nobel factory crisis. And then I slipped into a daydream in which I planted explosives in Nobel Grain's silos. I laughed maniacally as I shut the board members in the confer-ence room; I winked at Frederick Nobel as I wired a bomb to the board-room's doorknob. I felt a surge of righteous vindication as I strolled proprietarily through Nobel Grain's empty offices. Perhaps, I thought, Nachtwey had suffered violence as a child in Burnett County's Catholic Home for Boys, and so he sympathized with the Railroad's cause. Perhaps he was dying of cancer, had only three months to live, and truly had nothing to lose by sacrificing everything for this final gesture.

"What are you thinking?" Henry asked.

"I was imagining I was Nachtwey," I said.

Henry snorted. He hit a function key on the computer, and then snapped it closed and drummed his hands on top.

"I know that what Nachtwey's doing is crazy," I said, "and I'm worried about Mildred and the men inside the factory. But I still hope the authorities don't end up killing Nachtwey."

"Mildred doesn't think he's as dangerous as he might appear."

"That's kind of a risky assumption to make."

Henry answered, "Did Mildred tell you that the first time she met Helen Nobel, Helen came close to shooting her?"

"Shooting Mildred?"

"Yes, Mildred knocked on Helen's door late at night, and Helen thought it was her husband. Mildred said that when Helen opened the front door, she was pointing a pistol right at Mildred's heart. You see, Helen had decided she couldn't go on any longer. She had decided that if her husband threatened her one more time, it was better for her to defend herself by shooting him, and then to go to jail and have her daughter's grandmother raise her. What I'm trying to say is that Mildred's life is pretty risky anyway. She's been taking risks for years and years. Sometimes she's had to escort women and children from under the noses of their homicidal husbands or boyfriends: Once she had a gun pointed at her heart. Once a man doused her with gasoline and threatened to set her and his family on fire. Once she impersonated a policewoman, handcuffed a man, and led him into a police precinct. Then she left him there while another member of the Railroad whisked away his girlfriend to a hospital where she could be treated for a stab wound under an assumed name, without worrying that he would attack her again in her hospital bed. What's a deranged employee after dealing with domestic violence?" I realized that by giving me such details, Henry was opening the door to the Railroad a little wider—almost wide enough for me to slip through.

Matt and Sophie returned, bearing a hot dog for Henry. Sophie handed me a round tin containing liver and bacon and fried onions. "This is very healthy," she said.

Mildred and Nachtwey appeared a little while later at the mouth of the factory. Mildred no longer carried the scrolled blueprints. She

looked tired. She turned on the microphone and announced that Nachtwey had agreed to release Nobel Grain's board of directors. All except
for Frederick Nobel.

Nachtwey looked relieved; maybe he had dug himself too deeply
into the pit of his rage, and now that he was there, he did not know
how to climb back out. He may have worried that he would become as
much a prisoner of the Nachtwey Crisis as Nobel Grain's board, and
had been glad to be able to negotiate a partial compromise.

Mildred handed Nachtwey the microphone, and he set forth his
settlement with a notable and single-minded attention to detail. "After
talking with Miss Steck," he announced, "I have come to reconsider my
position, and I am willing to backtrack insofar as I no longer wish to
work for this company. However, I require the $600 in sick pay owed
me, and I want Mr. Nobel to give up his job and leave the state of
Wisconsin. I'll let the board go, but I'm requesting at this time that Mr.
Nobel first sign everyone's paychecks. These paychecks have already
been made out in the correct amounts and you can check them against
this employee salary list, which shows how little everyone here makes.
And I want Mr. Nobel to send along with the checks $600 from petty
cash for Cliff Nachtwey. This money is already owed to me and is mine
and I am not attempting to commit any act of robbery by forcing anyone
to pay me anything that is theirs. If Mr. Nobel does not have access to
petty cash, I suggest the board members raise the money among themselves and have Mr. Nobel provide them with some kind of IOU. Then
the board members can file out one by one, with their hands raised. But
if Mr. Nobel goes anywhere near the boardroom door, I will blow everyone of us up," Nachtwey warned, suddenly, and then paused, as if trying
to regather the thread of his thought.

"It's a bank holiday Monday," he continued, "so I'll make sure that
the checks Mr. Nobel signs clear the Tuesday after July 4, and if they
don't, I'll blow up the next silo, on Wednesday, July 7." Nachtwey added
that the next silo would be "the blue silo east of the factory, which is not
historical. It's a new commercial grain storage bin valued at $800,000.
And if arrangements aren't made for Mr. Nobel to leave the state,"
Nachtwey concluded, "then on July 8, I'll blow up Nobel Grain."

After this speech Nachtwey unplugged the monitor showing the
boardroom's interior and disappeared into the factory. The board members might have made a rush for Nachtwey when he came upstairs to
fetch them, carrying the leather pouch containing the unsigned pay-

checks. They might have refused to leave without Nobel, or tried to enable him to slip past Nachtwey. But the board members did not; they were obedient, the dozen of them. Thirty minutes later they emerged behind Nachtwey, in single file like a ghostly mule train, their heads lowered as they walked into the drizzling rain.

The first man held the brown leather pouch containing the paychecks. He and the men who followed him looked sleepless and hungry and hot. All but one had removed his necktie. Mildred paused to speak to him, and he waited while Nachtwey examined the checks and counted a small stack of bills. He nodded at Mildred. The board member continued on and joined the others. They moved like men in a dream, past Mildred and up the drive toward the field where the cameramen waited, half-hoping for an explosion.

Matt said, "Now, Mildred, get out of there!"

Nachtwey plugged the monitor back in. It showed the same picture of the boardroom as before: a bomb wired to a doorknob. Mildred rose, whispered to Nachtwey, and shook his hand. The camera showed him gripping her arm with sincere feeling, his eyes watering. Then Mildred walked away toward the back of the factory. Nachtwey looked grateful that his solitude had been broken, if only for a couple of hours, and sorry that he had to take up its burden again.

8

BY THE FOURTH DAY of the Nachtwey siege the newspapers still characterized the FBI's plan to rescue Frederick Nobel as "unavailable." The plan, revealed only after the resolution of the siege, was that the government would send a special team through an old underground shaft that ran from the first blown-up silo to the interior of the Nobel factory. Once there, the team would cut a hole in the boardroom floor and rescue Frederick Nobel. He would be escorted back down the tunnel while a second team surprised Nachtwey from behind, from inside the factory, and took him by force.

On July 1, after seeing Nachtwey and Mildred on television viewing the factory's blueprints, the FBI had employed a computer expert to access Nobel Grain's computer system. He discovered a file containing computer-aided design diagrams of the Nobel company. The file, apparently commissioned by Nobel in a moment of grandiosity, was headed with a paragraph worthy of Frank Lloyd Wright, which explained that "The unique construction and design of Nobel Grain Industries render it one of the Titans of Wisconsin architecture." Diagrams showed the architectural oddities of the factory, including interiors of the silos and boardroom, and a tunnel that ran from the first exploded silo toward the second, and then angled off into a passageway terminating in Nobel's office, which was situated under the boardroom.

The FBI's discovery of the computer file must have elated them, because they had not been able to locate the original blueprints to the Nobel Building, just as Nachtwey had promised. I learned years later, when I obtained FBI documents under the Freedom of Information

Act, that an attempt had been made to track Mildred after her televised meeting with Nachtwey, but that she had been lost after she disappeared "into an underground access to the factory grounds, a possibility anticipated by previous FBI inability to obtain diagrams of the building site." From the day after Matt's televised meeting with Nachtwey until almost a week later, a special government team tunneled its way underground toward the place where they believed they could enter the room under the one where their hostage waited.

On the night of July 1, the FBI's team began excavating a caved-in area near the first exploded silo, and discovered cement piping, collapsed in places and still filled with rubble, but large enough to stand up in. The piping headed for the second exploded silo, where it was assumed the passageway again collapsed, before turning toward the factory. The FBI's rescue efforts were complicated by the heavy rains that recommenced around two that afternoon and continued through the following day.

At 2:00 P.M. on July 1, Nachtwey sat within the front doors of Nobel Grain, eating tinned sardines and pineapple. It was a strange afternoon, with the CNN report repeating itself tirelessly, while it aired footage of spectators and police huddling together under umbrellas and inside vehicles. Despite the storm, by early afternoon, the collection of vehicles behind police lines had swelled. Onlookers sat in their cars and vans and trucks, some of them displaying banners behind their windshields that said FREE HELEN NOBEL! and ONE WACO IS ENOUGH. According to CNN, T-shirts embossed with a state map and the slogan, I'M FROM THE FREE STATE OF WISCONSIN! were being sold in downtown Milwaukee and Madison. In Skelter, bumper stickers were distributed that read simply, I WAS IN SKELTER, WISCONSIN, ON JULY 8, 1993, WHEN THE FACTORY BLEW UP.

At this time there were conflicting assessments of Mildred's role in the Nachtwey siege. Immediately after the release of most of Nachtwey's hostages, a news commentator speculated that "Steck's Railroad" had communicated with authorities and secured their noninterference during the meeting with Nachtwey. Another theorized that Nachtwey was part of the "Steck Railroad conspiracy" and asked whether Mildred would be indicted with him under the federal RICO act as his co-conspirator. A secretary interviewed during her lunch break by a Chicago reporter said, "I bet they didn't even discuss Mr. Nobel. I'll bet the Steck Railroad decided from the beginning that they might as well just keep him where he is. They probably figured, it's kill or be killed. Hell, let's *Steck* him."

Mildred's name seemed to have permanently fixed itself to the underground. The head of a prominent women's rights organization praised "Ms. Steck's courage and ingenuity" and advocated that the Wisconsin governor pass "Stecking measures" that would insure Helen Nobel's safety once Frederick Nobel was released. Later, women's groups that rallied around Helen Nobel's cause advocated a "Stecking bill" in the Wisconsin state legislature that would grant temporary amnesty, state residence, and the right to file custody proceedings in Wisconsin to women who could show by clear and convincing evidence that they had fled other jurisdictions to escape domestic violence. A month later a member of the Minnesota legislature would propose a draft of a thirty-page "Stecking Law," arguing that Minnesota should step in where its sister state had failed.

At the time of the Nachtwey siege tabloids were unable to unearth information on any Ms. Steck. I discovered long afterward, when I obtained FBI documents, that Mildred's 1977 FBI file on the Pferd storeroom incident involving Judge Hochwald had been listed under the name Mildred Munk. Her divorce action had been docketed as *Munk* v. *Munk,* so that in 1993, she was not immediately linked to her true identity. Moreover, the FBI's search was frustrated by the existence of several hundred Stecks in the Midwest. Not until six weeks after the Nobel Crisis would the FBI send agents to Muskellunge to investigate "facts relating to the Steck uprising and the family history of Mildred Steck, who engineered the false imprisonment of a Wisconsin judge in 1977, and the false arrest of Frederick Nobel in 1993. Her complicity in the Nobel Crisis is suspected." Federal agents would knock on the door to Aunt Mimi's house, and visit Muskellunge Unitarian, and sniff around the insect garden. FBI files for 1993 indicate that a neighbor informed federal agents that she had seen Henry vacuuming wasps from a hornet's nest behind John Steck's residence, an event which she found "disturbingly odd," and she recalled the period, a decade and a half earlier, when Reverend Steck had dispensed "Arab lunches" while delivering left-wing sermons from the Unitarian pulpit.

BY LATE AFTERNOON of July 1, Richard Sparrow had found Minnie Horsvelt and Olen Foil and Joseph Krupp, the residents of Skelter

named by Nachtwey. They all lived in the neighborhood behind the
Nobel family estate, although in considerably less elegant circumstances:
Foil and Krupp occupied opposite sides of a duplex behind the Nobels,
and Minnie Horsvelt lived with her aging father in a small home cater-
corner to the duplex. Foil worked as a packer at Skelter Industries, and
he refused to be interviewed. Sparrow accosted Minnie Horsvelt as she
walked to the Skelter grocery store. She said she had "nothing of note
to tell anyone," although she was willing to confirm: "I believe Cliff
when he says that Mr. Nobel threw his wife across their back yard."
Upon further prompting, she noted that "On one occasion we could
hear Mr. Nobel yelling at his wife from a block away."

What she omitted to tell Sparrow was supplied by Joseph Krupp,
who was home in bed with a bad sprain when Sparrow knocked on his
door. Krupp had missed all but the first television news coverage, because his entertainment center was located downstairs, and he had been
confined to his upstairs bed for a week, "condemned full-time to his
wife's care." He was in a talking mood. He described himself as a man
who "by habit, did not read the newspapers," and he asked Sparrow to
fill him in on goings-on at the Nobel factory.

Thereafter Krupp told Sparrow a story that seemed credible because
of the peculiarity of its details. He related that two years before, he and
Minnie Horsvelt and Olen Foil had been outside on their lawns doing
summer yardwork, not together, and not talking to each other, when
they had heard Mr. Nobel shouting "like a crazy person. We all ran
down to his yard. I got there first. Mr. Nobel was kneeling on the hood
of his European car, yelling and banging on the windshield, and then
pressing his face against the glass and shouting again. His wife and little
girl were in the front seat, with the car locks down. He was so angry
that foam was coming out of his mouth, as if he was a dog."

When Minnie Horsvelt arrived beside Krupp, she immediately
stepped back, "looking away and turning red, and then heading home
to let the men solve things." The reason for this, Krupp divulged, was
that Mr. Nobel was "stark naked from his shirttails down. He was a big
man, and he was terrifying those two in the car. Whenever he pressed
his face against the glass, the little girl screamed the way only animals
do, that kind of shriek a caught rabbit makes when it's so terrified it
can kill itself from fright. It made me feel sick."

Krupp and Olen Foil approached the car. Olen "had the presence
of mind to pull a sheet off the clothesline, and then he kind of crept up

behind Mr. Nobel, like he was going to net him, and pulled the sheet gently up over his back and said, "Is there anything I can do for you, Mr. Nobel? Is something bothering you?" According to Krupp, Mr. Nobel "just stepped down off the car, graceful, as if nothing had happened and not much was on his mind, and walked back into the house, leaving the sheet on the ground."

Olen Foil and Joseph Krupp asked Mrs. Nobel to unlock the front car door, which she did, and they helped her and her daughter out. "Mrs. Nobel's head was all black and blue in front and under the hair, and her glasses were smashed, and her nose was cut where they'd pressed into her when her husband hit her. But the worst thing was the girl, because the little girl crawled under the car when Olen moved to help her around the door. She didn't look hit or hurt; she just crawled under the middle of the car, whimpering. Her mother ducked down and called and called to her but she wouldn't come out, and so her mother crawled under there with her, and just held her, and then we couldn't get to either of them."

After that, Krupp said, someone called out that Nobel would get shot if he stuck his head out of the house. Then Krupp went and got Minnie Horsvelt, and it took her forty-five minutes to talk Helen and her daughter from under the car, and then she took them home. Afterward, someone threw a rake through the car's windshield.

By the time Sparrow's interview with Krupp was published in the morning papers of July 2, the jurors who had acquitted Nobel of battery in the Cook County criminal proceeding received envelopes on their doorsteps. The envelopes contained copies of Sparrow's interview with Krupp; Skelter police blotters, inadmissible at the criminal trial, which showed that during the first year of her marriage, Helen Nobel had called the police four times, and that they had responded by talking to Mr. Nobel over the telephone; medical records from four years later, indicating that Helen Nobel had been treated for broken ribs following a miscarriage; and finally, an affidavit from Lucy Barksdale, a Milwaukee woman who had an affair with Nobel during the middle five years of his marriage. The affidavit attested that she had "been compelled to terminate their relationship because of Frederick Nobel's violent temper and following an incident in which while attempting to choke me, he broke my jaw so that it had to be wired shut for several weeks." She averred in addition, "I did not dare to file charges because I believed this would inflame him, and I knew that Frederick Nobel could afford lawyers who would make me appear to be lying or crazy, and I thought I would find it additionally humiliating to be cast that way."

Afterward four of the Cook County jurors polled by a Chicago news station reported that they wished they had convicted Frederick Nobel. One of them said that she "formally rescinded her vote of acquittal." A second said that after he "walked out of the courtroom, it was like a spell lifted and I knew something wasn't right but I couldn't put my finger on what it was." The forewoman refused to comment, other than to say that "she would stand by the verdict to her dying day."

THE MORNING of July 2 commenced with lightning and a downpour, and the weather forecast promised continued rain through evening. Mrs. Booth again called to cancel the service. This time she seemed almost tearful, apologized for the expense and inconvenience to us of staying an extra day in the hotel, and proposed that, if the rain continued through Saturday morning of July 3, as predicted, we move the service to Saturday evening.

"I'm sure that would be fine," I told her. However, I could not help thinking that my father must have plotted his own rebirth when he arrived on the symbolism of a dawn memorial service held on the first day of the month—and here we would be, consecrating him to the twilight on an undistinguished day. In any case, I felt relieved by Mrs. Booth's call, because Ottilie and John had not returned by early morning, as they had predicted.

I felt apprehensive for them as I turned on Henry and Matt's television to catch the morning news. At 8:30 on July 2, Richard Sparrow interviewed a line of people standing with umbrellas outside Skelter National Bank, waiting to deposit their paychecks. One man joked that if the checks cleared on Tuesday, it would be the first paid vacation he'd ever received from Nobel Grain. Sparrow commented that Nachtwey's effective display of concern for Nobel's employees, "whether it was of his own design, or thought up by the secretive Railroad, was a stroke of political genius." The crowd huddled in cars and vans in the wheatfield was now estimated at fifteen hundred people. One newcomer announced that he had brought fireworks, "so that no one would miss July 4." Skelter's Officer Ross Donald confiscated them, saying that "a loud noise might set off an unbalanced mind."

As I watched television, Matt and Henry played Matt's old version of checkers, discussing all the while how they would devise a computer program that captured the game's nuances. When Sophie awoke at noon, she sat next to me, ignoring the news, and drawing a series of tiny midnight-blue butterflies with eerie, human faces. She paused in her drawing only to eat lunch.

At 3:30 P.M. Richard Sparrow appeared on CNN, as a guest correspondent. The regular anchor revealed that "the leader of the secret society called the Railroad" had agreed to answer questions by telephone if Mr. Richard Sparrow conducted the interview. Apparently to avoid being tracked, Mildred had specified that the interview could not last more than a few minutes.

Sparrow fiddled with his headphones and leaned forward on his chair. Beside the handsome anchorman Sparrow looked almost simian, out of place, with his shock of red hair and slight, twisted body. He wore the look of intense personal interest that had attended his reportage on Judge Hochwald and Nachtwey. When Sparrow questioned Mildred, he spoke in an intimate tone, as if he believed he would be deeply and permanently affected if she erred in the course of her dealings.

By contrast, when Mildred answered Sparrow's questions, she spoke with that irony characteristic of her expressions of political conviction fifteen years earlier. All of her answers seemed to convey a mockery of the truth itself, as if she found what she was forced to tell absurd but believed it absolutely nevertheless:

SPARROW: You preach nonviolence, and yet some say you've used Mr. Nachtwey's violence to further your own political message. You contend that Mr. Nachtwey has transgressed the limits of what is reasonable. Just where do you draw the line?

STECK: I've never criticized Mr. Nachtwey. I've said we don't agree. Of course, it's pleasant to be able to act reasonably. To be removed from a sense of rage. And despair. And vengeance. And hatred. That must feel really nice. Unfortunately, not everyone is in that position.

SPARROW: The Railroad claims that Frederick Nobel is dangerous to his wife and child. Is the Railroad a better judge than a legal tribunal, which can carefully weigh and test evidence?

STECK: Who really cares about evidence, Mr. Sparrow? I could tell Judge Hochwald that Mr. Nobel once threw his wife from a moving car while his daughter sat in the back seat, and Hochwald wouldn't let it bother him. And I could tell that forelady in Cook County that a week before Helen disappeared, she answered the door to receive her daughter from visitation, and instead, Mr. Nobel stood alone in her hallway and peed on her wall and told her he'd never let her see her daughter again if Helen did not accept him for a visit that night. I could tell that forelady that Mr. Nobel sat in Helen's apartment for an hour, on her bed, and threatened to kill her while he sat there, and that he refused to let her leave the house, and that he was able to do this because she weighs 120 pounds and he weighs 250. But it wouldn't matter to the forelady. For all of these reasons, we've stopped worrying about evidence, and instead we just try to focus on keeping people from being killed.

SPARROW: You aren't troubled by the idea of a secret society taking the law into its own hands?

STECK: We're not taking the law into our own hands. We're working around it. And we're not a secret society: Any person scared enough can join the Railroad. We persist because our sympathizers are legion, but you don't have to belong to us to be in the Railroad. Anyone listening out there, you can start your own railroad tracks. Run away or help someone else escape. Then we'll have a whole national underground Amtrak.

SPARROW: Mrs. Nobel stated during her call-in to her husband on an earlier radio show that you had "asked people not to turn you in." Can you explain that a little bit?

STECK: Have you ever read that science fiction book by Ray Bradbury, *Fahrenheit 451*? At the end the hero is running from the government in this world where everyone has huge television screens that cover entire walls. The government comes on television and says, "Everyone open your back door at the same time," and in that world people are so obedient, that everyone opens his or her door, and that's how they spot the fugitive. Well, we don't live in that world. What I'm trying to say to you is: *Don't open your back door. And if you do, don't see us.*

SPARROW: You have proclaimed that women have no effective means of protesting as a group. Is the Railroad principally a woman's organization?

STECK: The Railroad is not an organization. It's an escape route. It may be that one effect of the Railroad is to even the score in the so-called Gender War. But our principal aim is to protect children. And we try to prevent needless homicide.

SPARROW: How do you answer criticism that the Railroad practices "reverse discrimination" against men?

STECK: If a man comes to us, in flight from violence in his home, we take him in. But that happens once in a blue moon. We didn't make the world. The people who ask for us are mostly women with children. Men have a monopoly on sheer physical terror, and a lot of the men we deal with control the money. You have to think of what it's like for a woman with children to get away, when the man who's terrorizing her is the person she has to go to for escape money. It's harder for a woman to leave a bad situation. There's a whole nation of women out there, Mr. Sparrow, who live in terror, trapped and dependent, with and without children, and the law won't free them.

SPARROW: Why did the Railroad's meeting with Mr. Nachtwey fail to secure Frederick Nobel's release?

Mildred indicated that the interview should terminate. Her decision not to answer Sparrow's question left us all contemplating a taunting silence. You figure it, she seemed to say. Sparrow concluded by asking whether she wished to volunteer any statement before hanging up.

Mildred answered, "I'm speaking to whoever wants to hear. How can you help the Railroad? Don't let your whole life pass without doing one thing, just one thing, big or small, to assist someone like Helen Nobel. All of us know or will know a woman in her particular kind of danger. When you do, be prepared to take some risks. Help her with money. Watch her kids while she gets a job or finds a place to stay. Take her to a shelter, or take her in yourself, or buy her a ticket to go somewhere far away. Everyone can do something. Don't turn your back on what you see. And don't trust the law to do it in your place."

Mildred paused briefly, and said, "If you want to show your support for Helen Nobel at this time without condoning the use of violence, the Railroad would be grateful if all you sympathizers out there could just buy Helen a little time and let her know you care what happens to her. It would help the Railroad a lot if you would make it hard for law enforcement authorities to locate her by phoning anonymous tips to your local police, saying that you've seen Helen Nobel even though you haven't."

The broadcast appeared to have concluded, when Mildred's voice returned, and she added what seemed to be an extemporaneous statement: "It's four o'clock, so I have to assume most of you sitting in front of the TV out there are women. Now, it's Friday of July Fourth weekend, and you don't want to be left without cash." Mildred snickered, and her snicker was just like the one of fifteen years before, when she plotted to take me up Muskellunge's hill to the Pferd factory. "What's it like for a woman in a home where someone else controls the cash? If every woman watching out there who happens to have an automatic teller card would get up right this very minute and go to your nearest ATM money machine and withdraw the maximum amount, there would be a lot of men out there walking around without cash in their pockets for a three-day weekend. You know how those machines are; they run out of money on Fridays. You might make the only moment in the history of man where men who can afford bank accounts experience what it's like not to control the cash. So, that's what I'd like to ask you to do now, if you want to show support and cast your vote for Helen Nobel. Just go to the bank if you have an ATM card, and take out the maximum amount."

After this statement the telephone conversation terminated. The *Chicago Tribune* would report later that the FBI had traced the call: it led to a phone booth in Raleigh, North Carolina. By then, I assumed, the Railroad used a remote device to obscure Mildred's tracks.

AT THE TIME of the Steck-Sparrow interview, the government's special agents were crawling like moles through an underground maze behind Nobel Grain. By evening they had shifted debris to a muddy pile on the west edge of the first silo's bomb crater, and moved seventeen feet within the tunnel adjoining it.

By late afternoon of July 2, police in Chicago, Detroit, Minnesota, and throughout Wisconsin were inundated with calls reporting sightings of Helen Nobel. Helen had been seen lunching with her daughter in a family eatery in Warren, Illinois; touring the Ripon Good Cookie factory in Ripon, Wisconsin; canoeing in Kewaunee County; and dining with an older man, who sported a toupee, in a four-star restaurant in Chicago. She had boarded a ferry on Lake Michigan, crossed the Canadian border in a Greyhound, and caught a plane at O'Hare bound for Iceland. She had held up a liquor store in Oshkosh. There were also hundreds of calls in which people claimed to have seen "Ms. Steck." These calls continued over a period of weeks and must have added to the FBI's difficulty in tracking Mildred to Muskellunge.

By six that evening local networks were reporting that money machines had been tied up from Skelter to Milwaukee, and in Minneapolis, Detroit, parts of Chicago, and Buffalo. Reporters interviewed people outside banks: Some were festive, some were irate. One man in line outside a Chicago bank said, "I don't know the name for this crime, but I'm sure it's a crime." A woman in front of him answered, "What crime? What crime are they committing? Is it a crime to make you think?" The man responded, "I'll tell you what the crime is. Interference with interstate commerce! That's the crime." A woman behind him said, "I work. I didn't hear the report. And now I'm going to be left without cash for the weekend. I don't see how this helps anybody." "I'll tell you how it helps," the first woman answered. "If Helen Nobel comes to my door, I'm not turning her in. And if she doesn't, maybe I'll start my own goddamn Railroad."

If it was fair to characterize the response to Mildred Steck's provocative plea as a show of support, the results were formidable. Of course, it was just as likely that the directness of her command, or the merry subversiveness of it, or the fear that others would rush to withdraw cash and leave latecomers moneyless, motivated much of the response. "But the heart of the matter," Richard Sparrow concluded, as he stood outside the Skelter National Bank, "is that for one day, events in Skelter, Wisconsin, controlled America's heartland."

At 4:30 I myself borrowed Henry's car keys and drove to the center of Spring Green, waited in line in the pounding rain, and took $500 from the bank. I felt almost intoxicated with relief when the twenty-dollar bills poured into my hand. I returned to the Lincoln feeling capable of anything, and for the first time that I now recall, I had a clear picture of myself writing a letter of resignation in which I forfeited my federal judgeship.

As I pulled out of the bank parking lot, I thought of how Mildred had avoided portraying the Railroad as a movement of the downtrodden. It had probably never occurred to her to wear her victimhood as a badge. Instead, the Railroad had mocked and upended the world of its adversaries so that they suddenly had to see themselves from the bottom up. I drove the Lincoln to the parking lot of the House on the Rock and sat for an hour behind the steering wheel with a pile of twenties in my lap and a red pen in my hand, writing in the pale green strip above Andrew Jackson, "Support Helen Nobel!" and "I'm from the free state of Wisconsin," and even, "Remember Nachtwey!"

AROUND MIDNIGHT on July 2, John's van pulled into the parking lot, and three people got out. I was so relieved, that I ran into the hotel hallway wearing my nightgown. I allowed myself to hope that Mildred had returned with Ottilie and John, smuggled through the rainy night into the Wright Hotel. However, when John approached the hotel's overhang, I saw that the person accompanying him and Ottilie was a young man, broad-shouldered as John Steck, a little taller, with darker hair.

As they entered the hallway, I stepped back into my room. Ottilie said, "It's all right—that's Melanie." She stopped in front of my door. The eyes of the young man behind her were silver-gray, but his face was lean and angular and handsome, like his father's.

"Ben," I said.

He answered, "I'm used to being called Jake."

I followed them all into Ottilie and John's room. "Jake?" I asked, wondering how I could be wrong. Up close, Jake looked like Daniel peering out of Mildred's face, or Mildred hooded in Daniel.

"I chose that name when I was three. Our first next-door neighbor had a Labrador retriever named Jake, and I named myself after him." He said this in a half-humorous, mocking tone that jogged my memory and kicked loose from nowhere the image of Mildred teaching Ben to shave with peanut butter.

Of course, I thought, he would have had to use pseudonyms, too.

"Jake Brown," he said. "But I'm trying to get used to 'Ben' again."

"He's a fine young man, isn't he?" John said, beaming. "Strong, and—big! He wants to study oceanography. Oceanography!" John looked as he had the day of my arrival in Muskellunge—as if he were a man ready to die of joy.

I asked him, "Is Mildred coming, too?"

"She's—no," John said, reconsidering his answer in the middle, suddenly recollecting who I was. "But thank God she's safe now."

Ottilie slipped off Ben's raincoat, and he sat down on the bed.

"Stay here," John told him. "I'll get your things from the trunk."

"I can do it," Ben said, but I did not want him to leave: I wanted to stare at the bright jewel of him long enough to believe he was really here among us.

"It would be better if you didn't go back out tonight," John told him.

"I'll come with you," Ottilie said.

"Don't do that—it's not necessary," John answered, but she followed him anyway, hooking her arm in his. They ran across the parking lot, still hooked together.

"I remember you," Ben said to me. "You once told me this story that scared me to death—you were a spider who would sit on my bed in a spider dress and crawl under my pillow while I slept."

"You remember that? I can't recall anything that far back in my childhood." I laughed. "I was trying to put you at ease, Ben."

"I never guessed."

I thought that I would cry, watching him joke like that. But I could not say whether the tears I held back were tears of joy, from seeing Ben there, whole and a man, or whether they were for my brother. I imagined Matt at eighteen, on the brink of manhood, whole, unhurt.

"Do you remember my brother?" I asked. "Matthew?"

"Matt? He sends me e-mail all the time, and we talk on the Internet. We already met up—" Ben caught himself, reddened, and looked unsure whether he should continue.

I did not want to press him. "How is Mildred—your mother?" I asked.

The look that passed over Ben's face made my blood stop in my veins: it was Daniel's look, alluring and opaque. But then Ben smiled, and said, "I'm going to miss feeling like I'm living in the middle of a whirlwind. Everything around here is so quiet. People are friendly, but sort of keep their distance, you know? Too polite. They don't fight in public and yell hello to each other across the street."

Evidently, he had not grown up in the Midwest.

"Back in Brazil and New Or—" he began, but before he could continue, John entered and said, "Jake—Ben, someone's on the phone for you in Henry's room." Ben jumped up from the couch and whirled into the hallway, and his grandfather followed him.

ALL NIGHT, as the rain continued, I tried to gather as much information from John and Ottilie as I could. I wanted to know whether Helen Nobel and her daughter were in hiding with Mildred, whether Ben would stay with John now, whether Mildred's sending us her son meant she would relinquish any future closeness with him, and whether, now that Mildred and Ben were both in the open, they felt threatened by Daniel.

But John still acted as uncomfortable with my questions as he had in Muskellunge, and he only answered one. When I asked him about Daniel, John said that Ben had tracked his father down a few months before, and "did not intend to visit him again for some time." For the last two years, Daniel had been living bigamously in Indiana with the daughter of the president of the college that now employed him. Apparently his new wife knew nothing about his marriage to Mildred, or Ben's very existence. Sources informed Mildred that Daniel had been denied tenure at the Ohio college where he had formerly worked, after a faculty member charged him with maintaining inappropriate liaisons with students. Daniel did not wish to endanger his current position or ostensible marriage by coming forward with facts about his past. John doubted very much that Daniel would risk entering the limelight by identifying Mildred.

"We may have a little time," John said, "before someone knowledgeable reports recognizing Mildred from her televised meeting with Nachtwey, and she's traced back to Muskellunge."

I related to John the substance of Mildred's interview, concluding with her ATM scheme.

"I know." He smiled. "My daughter caught me without a penny in my pocket."

"I have enough to pay for our meals and the hotel."

I heard talking in Henry's adjoining room. Raising his voice, John told me, "There have been reports from people claiming to see Mildred everywhere, Melanie. In Atlanta. Manhattan. Alaska." He shook his head.

"John, if there's something I can do in the Railroad, why don't you tell me? I have a lot of savings. If Helen Nobel or anyone else needs help in the way of travel money, I'd be glad to—"

"That wasn't what I had in mind, although we do need to buy a reserve of antidote for hornet stings, for Helen's daughter."

"For Helen's daughter?"

"Well, money is always a help, and you wouldn't have to make a more tangible commitment."

I must have looked disappointed, because John said, "We have to be careful, Melanie."

Later, almost apologetically, John asked me to wait for him and entered the adjoining room. As John opened the connecting door, I heard Henry say, "There it is, under the west field."

"What a paranoid," Matt told him.

Henry answered, "He's probably got a subterranean chamber full of canned food and unfluoridated water where he and the other board members plan to wait out the nuclear war."

Matt said, "If you position this part of the tunnel, then it comes up right there under the bunker."

"Cool!" Ben said. "How does that work?"

"Where did you learn to do that, Matt?" Ottilie asked.

"It's logarithmic," Henry said. "*Life* is logarithmic, if you think about it. Beginnings always seem dense with experience, and then life stretches out clear and fast."

"There it is," Matt announced. "The real tunnel."

"Mark down the coordinates!" Henry exclaimed.

"We left that part in the dark, where the FBI will stumble right over it," Matt said.

"Man, oh, man," Ben answered.

John returned, closing the door behind him. He gave me a packet of letters, secured with a rubber band in a tattered envelope. Under a post box address, someone had scrawled the message: "Keep these—we need to start a permanent archive, and type them into the Internet."

After John returned to Henry's room, leaving me alone, I read all the letters. I felt so much rage accumulating in the spaces between their words that, for a moment, I wanted to believe and believed that Mildred had engineered the Nachtwey siege from the beginning. The letters came from every part of the country, every walk of life, every stage of grief and terror:

Dear Railroad,

    After ten years I come to understand that my wife is a dangerous person, without a sense of right and wrong. And who can I possibly tell? When I ask her why she hurts the children, she says, mind your business. Who are you to tell me what's right and wrong? I say, when I want to know in my heart what's right, I ask, "What would God think of this?" And if the answer is, He'd think it's wrong, then I try not to do it. She burned our four-year-old daughter's stomach with an iron. And that's when I finally embarrassed myself before all, and went to the town court and asked for an order to keep her away. But no one pays attention or even believes me, no one. The court has appointed this guardian lawyer who's supposed to watch out for my children, but when we keep coming to court, the guardian just can't deal with the ugly facts. I tell him: talk to the kids, will you, talk to the kids! But he never has once, not in 11 months. He couldn't pick any one of my kids out of a two-kid lineup. The judge won't protect my babies. He says: A woman would have to be a monster to do that, to attack her own baby. He can't believe these things happen, and sometimes I can't either. My children's life is a nightmare. If I give up my job and run, who will support them, what will I do? Meanwhile, they are worse and worse, scared, wetting their beds, doing bad in school, looking dirty. And when I leave them at her house, they grapple onto me like I have to tear my arms off to get away. Is anyone out there suffering like this? What do I do for my kids, they are changing before my eyes.

Dear Railroad,

I was curious to hear about this Helen Nobel not being allowed to live with her mother in Chicago. Let me tell you about Kings County Family Court, every day that sea of tired faces waiting in line, mostly black mostly women. Go inside the court, there's a white lady judge looking at you. Where does she get off telling my husband I never should have left the state? And threatening to take my children from me because I moved back in with my mother in Maryland? That judge makes us all take a bus every week from Maryland to New York for so-called visitation and her court dates. 1200 miles a month or more, she's breaking my health and my children's, taking food from our mouths for travel money. She thinks she'll wear us down, and force us back to New York City before the hearing we're supposed to have ever happens. You may think this is crazy, but a lot of judges up in Brooklyn are doing this to women who have run away. Talk to the women in line. Who are we to stop those crazy judges? The poorer you are, the crazier they act. They sit up there with their rustly robes, loving pushing us around. It's me who loves my kids, not them. My judge saw my boys on a dark street, she'd probably run. Here's three things she needs to know. One: I'm sick to death of hearing I have to keep the kids near their father, when he once held a knife to my throat and never gave us a penny. Why do you give him power over where I live, power to take away my freedom? Does he own me? Two: Don't tell me I can't live with my own mother, who watches after us and gives us a home. That's just plain stupid. How else would I and my children be able to leave him? What's wrong with you? Three: Are you blind not to see I can't leave my husband and stay alone with my boys around all the city drugs and violence, that I have to take them back to where they can get some moral upbringing and not be shot? I'll tell you what, Judge, you give me your fancy house in Long Island, let my kids go to your kids' schools, and you come out and live in the projects with my husband, send your boys to my boys' so-called school, and we'll see how long you last.

Dear Railroad,

When will someone listen to us? I told the judge the last time my husband came to the house he held my head down in the sink with the water running. While my sons were hiding under the table, he was yelling that he'd drown me, and then he kicked me from behind across the floor. He's going to kill me. I went to the judge for what they call a protective order, but what does he do? Does he order my husband to stay away? No, the judge says, your house is his house too, and I won't tell him he can't go there. I swear if he comes in our home one more time and touches me one more time, my oldest son will kill him.

Dear Railroad,

I write you from jail. I am here for shooting my husband. He beat me until I thought he would kill me. He would not let me leave the house, not even for church, unless he was with me. The public defender made me take a plea bargain, Bargain For Your Life, he said. And so I went to court and never got to say a thing except twice, when I was told to answer Yes to the judge's questions. I believe I will die in here.

There were dozens of letters, all written in a single month, June of 1993. I felt such admiration for Mildred when I thought of her taking on the weight of so much sorrow and carrying it for so long. The letters spiralled on and on, the same story retold with variations, until their redundancy formed a dense, hard obsidian ball of pain, meaningless and terrifying. After half an hour, I felt so overwhelmed that I set the stack down.

Under the last letter in the packet was a small folded note that said:

Hey Judge Ratleer, how are you holding up? What do you think of Ben? Didn't he turn out smart and handsome? Keep an eye on him for me. You're the only legal person I trust.

Mrs. Hatch

I placed the note with the others; it belonged there, in that community of letters. And then, I picked the stack back up and read on, until those voices rose in chorus, penetrating as the multitudinous song of cicadas on a hot day—until the very air in the room around me felt electrified by the noise.

9

THE RAIN WITHDREW by early afternoon on July 3, the day of my father's postponed memorial service. Evening sifted toward Taliesin, and a sluggish, pale powdery heat fell over our memorial party. We rode together in the van, passing a shadowed green field, and a gold one darkened to mustard in the unglittering twilight.

The House on the Rock had posted signs all the way to the entrance to Taliesin, advertising a special fireworks exhibit to be held that night.

"Maybe you could visit that later, Melanie," Henry said. "No, I'm sorry. Of course, you won't feel up to it. I just thought you might want to get out a little."

"I'd like to go," Sophie said.

When we arrived at the Booths', a silver three-quarter moon stared at us from above the treeline. We met the Booths in their driveway. Carrying unlit flashlights, we walked up a slope along the edge of Taliesin, with Mr. Booth leading the way, and Sophie drifting off to the side. Mrs. Booth looked questioningly at Ben, and Ottilie told her, "He's our grandson." After that Mrs. Booth's gaze measured Ben and then Sophie and Matt, as she searched for a resemblance.

John walked beside Ottilie, his thoughts elsewhere. I assumed Mildred had sent us Ben to clear him of my implication of involvement in the Nobel Crisis. John must have been afraid to leave Ben alone in the hotel, where the law or anything might snatch him away so soon after his grandfather had regained him.

John bent his head toward Ottilie and said something. She murmured a reply that contained the name "Nachtwey," and that is why, as

I walked toward the small summit where my father's ashes would be released, I was reflecting on Nachtwey instead of him. I wondered if Nachtwey felt cut off and solitary, as he stared across the carpet of fields that extended to the ragged horizon. What desolation, I thought, to be abandoned there, left in charge of the factory and man that had cast him out, just as the night descended, threatening to pull up another day. Perhaps Nachtwey derived comfort from his contact with the Railroad, felt its arms circling the country in that darkness, its whispers of reassurance spoken through back doors where fugitives were ushered with their children into the night's safety. How comforting conspiracy must be, I thought: it consoles the conspirator in equal proportion to the discomfort of those conspired against.

When our memorial party stopped at the top of the hill, we looked down on Taliesin, a shadowy rectangle perched on the border of the nocturnal world. Evening had not yet stolen all of the colors from things: The trees were a black-green and the buildings a bronze-black, and our faces luminous in the way faces are only in darkness.

Mr. Booth eyed the carton of ashes in my hand and said, "There's not much wind. We'll have to wait for a little breeze, or they won't scatter."

Henry, Matt, and Sophie stepped back in an uncomfortable circle. None of them was dressed quite right for a service. Matt and Henry wore khakis and short-sleeved shirts, and Sophie wore her pink sundress. The rest of us were in dark clothes, but only Mrs. Booth seemed to be in mourning. Her veil descended from her pillbox hat like a navy-blue ocean wave.

"Maybe you could say a prayer, Reverend Crail," Mrs. Booth told John.

"He's semidefrocked," Henry answered.

"Oh."

Ben smiled.

"Joel wasn't religious," Ottilie volunteered.

"It would be appropriate for someone to speak about Joel," Mrs. Booth answered.

I looked at the faces around me; they were quickly growing dim. I thought of my father's indifference to us all, his failure to respond to Matt's letters, month after month, for twenty years, and a dark voice rose in me, black-humored, antic, sleek, and caught in the trap of my throat.

"I'll say this," Mr. Booth volunteered. "Joel was a damn fine attorney. If I'd ever murdered someone, Joel Ratleer is the man I would have hired to represent me."

A little bark of a laugh escaped me. Mrs. Booth looked at me sternly. "I'm sorry," I said. "It's the nervous strain."

Ottilie intervened. "It's been a long time. A lifetime, really." She paused, drew a deep breath, and said, "I always admired the fact that Joel had such relentless energy. He had more energy than any man I've ever known."

I looked at Mrs. Booth, as if she were our community's repository for small truths. Again, I felt a tickle of hilarity, and suppressed it. "All right," I announced. "I have something to say." My voice sounded off-kilter, out of control. "Maybe we should consider that Joel Ratleer has been as good as dead to us for a lifetime, and that he left a lot of bodies in his wake."

Mr. Booth laughed. John rested his hand gently on my shoulder, and Ben watched me from the semidarkness, with what I imagined was a quizzical expression. Henry's long fingers fumbled for my hand and did not let go.

Sophie announced in a flat, formal voice that she would like to read a poem.

"Ah, good idea," Mr. Booth answered.

Looking directly at Matt, Sophie held a piece of paper before her. Its letters were barely visible in the twilight. Matt lifted his flashlight over the paper.

Sophie said, "Matt wrote this. It's called 'Lake Michigan, July 4th, Early Morning.'" She remained silent for longer than a minute, until it seemed that she had revised her plans and intended only to share the title. Mr. Booth coughed. A breeze tickled Sophie's paper. She stepped forward and intoned:

> *The far shore catches fire,*
> *stretches its arms to me.*
> *I feel my shade loosening*
> *from my hip, suddenly, like a slip.*

Sophie told Mrs. Booth, "I know just what he means."

Ottilie answered, "Of course you do."

Mrs. Booth looked now at Matt, waiting for him to speak. But Matt shook his head and turned away from her. Mrs. Booth then stepped forward in our circle with a suddenly apparent impatience, as if only politeness had moved her to prod us each to speak before she finally uttered what she had wanted to say all evening.

Looking at no one, she held her head high and pronounced: "Joel was so *alive*." This statement struck me as peculiar; it made me wonder whether my father had ever seduced her. I thought next that she had not simply been impatient to speak: she had wanted the last word.

"There's the breeze," Mr. Booth said. "There's the breeze. Take advantage of it."

Henry let go of my hand. While Matt pointed the flashlight at the carton, I opened its top and peered at the ashes inside. Ottilie leaned forward and something about her lighted face—a look of anticipation—made me feel as if she were checking to make sure that Joel Ratleer was really dead.

Matt stepped back and made a choking noise. He looked at me, his eyes shining with tears. I stepped forward to embrace him and leaned my head on his chest: Matt's sobbing repeated itself beside his heart, and grief for him overcame me. Mrs. Booth handed me a handkerchief. I held it wonderingly—it had been ages since I'd met someone who still used handkerchiefs—and then I realized she had given it to me because I was crying. I felt shocked: a sudden sense of absence, as if a cloak of ice had slipped from my shoulders, and I stepped back.

"Now, there's the first good wind," Mr. Booth said. A gust grabbed Mrs. Booth's veil and twisted off her hat. She bent to retrieve it.

I opened the carton and upturned it. The ashes rose thickly, like white coal dust, and blew back in our faces.

AFTER THE CEREMONY we strolled for half an hour along the border of Taliesin's grounds, as Mr. Booth, who called the great architect "Frank Lloyd Wrong," loving the joke, pointed out Taliesin's barely visible features against the backdrop of purple sky. When Mr. Booth had finished, Sophie said that she wanted to visit the special fireworks exhibit at the House on the Rock. Despite his wife's protests Mr. Booth offered to drive Matt and Sophie there. John and Ottilie said they had to return to the hotel with Ben, but Sophie climbed into the Booths' car, and Matt slid in beside her. Mrs. Booth remained where she was, watching, while Mr. Booth took the wheel.

"Are you coming?" he asked me and Henry.

But Henry had changed his mind, despite his earlier recommendation to attend the fireworks exhibit. He said, "I think I'll try to admire Frank Lloyd Wrong by moonlight, and walk the .7 miles back to the hotel. I need to burn off some jittery energy."

Ottilie leaned toward me and whispered, "Walk back with him, Melanie, what will it hurt?"

"Hurt?" I asked before I grasped her intentions. As she climbed into the van, I felt that gradual unfurling of feeling that is peculiar to me, that moment when I suddenly sense the muffled world. I was glad Mrs. Booth did not overhear our conversation.

"Henry!" Ottilie called. "Wait for Melanie."

I stepped back and watched the van drive off before I joined Henry. The moon hung crookedly over us, a tilted silver eye, and wet grass shimmered under the security lights. A vein of water plunged down a hill into darkness.

"We'll cut across Frank Lloyd Wrong's estate," Henry said. "It'll be a lot shorter." He moved down a slope with the exhilaration of a trespasser. I felt as if I were entering a black glittering mine from which I would never return. In the trees overhead the insects shrilled, "katydid! katydid!"

"Henry," I said, catching up with him. "If you and Matt would just let me in on—just tell me some work I could do for the Railroad. I want to help Mildred somehow."

"How would you manage that, Melanie? Acting as a judge, and working for the Railroad at the same time? Would you uphold the law by day, undermine it by night? It certainly has its possibilities from the Railroad's perspective, but that kind of double life might drive you a little crazy. Do you know there's a late-night program now about a judge who's a vigilante motorcycle rider at night? He hunts down the criminals he can't sentence to death during the day. Apparently it's very popular."

"I'm going to refuse my appointment," I said.

Henry stopped walking. "Refuse it?"

I was glad for the darkness, because I could feel my voice tighten; tears threaten to fall. I waited to steady myself, and instead, I felt a shifting in my blood, a loosening, that made it impossible to hold back words or tears. "I hate my work. My life feels like a prison, a trap. I hate my life!"

Henry reached for me; I felt his arm brush empty air near my ear. I stepped away from him and whispered, "Let me into the Railroad! Tell me what I can do!" I wiped my eyes.

Henry took so long to answer, I thought that, in his preoccupation with something else, he had not heard me. Finally, however, he answered, "There's plenty you can do. The Railroad can always use help." Then he sank into silence again.

"Tell me!"

"I'll talk to Mildred." Henry continued walking through the darkness, and I followed him. "John said you offered money, but what we really need right now is vital statistics. Almost everyone we can come up with on short notice has loaned theirs out already."

"Vital statistics?"

"We need Social Security numbers, passport numbers, birth certificates. . . ." Henry seemed to be talking to himself.

"That wouldn't place me at much risk, Henry," I said. "I could always deny knowledge of misuse of my Social Security number." But the truth was, I almost hoped to get caught.

"It's a start, Melanie. Maybe you should take a little while, to be sure of your decision. After all, this is an emotional time, right after your father's service, and—"

"Whooah!" I said, slipping down a wet hill. I reached to where I thought Henry stood, but found only darkness.

"Here," he said.

"Where?" I groped toward his voice, unbalanced him, and crashed down on him like a pile of dry sticks.

"Melanie?" Henry asked.

"Please," I said, pulling myself to a sitting position. Henry's sinewy arm felt like a net of ropes. "Please tell me what's going on with you and Matt and the computer."

"All right, Melanie." Henry sighed, a deep, heartfelt sigh like Nachtwey's. I felt the warmth of his breath, and then a quick sensation in my stomach, a leaping.

Henry revealed to me what my brother had done, and with that confidence, Henry must have known that he bound me permanently to the Railroad. Matt, Henry told me, had downloaded from the Internet a distorted "computer-aided reality" program into the Nobel company's computer system. He had designed the program's data file from the factory's blueprints and headed it with the invented paragraph worthy of Frank Lloyd Wright. Matt privately had titled his file, "The Alekhine Diversion Maneuver," as if it were a chess play. Matt's program, seized on by the FBI after they viewed Nachtwey examining the company's blueprints on television news, inaccurately represented a key aspect of Nobel Grain's property: the tunnel the FBI team was excavating led not to the factory, but to a bomb cellar of the kind popular in the fifties, forty feet south of the factory and unconnected to it by any passageway.

"It was all Matt's idea," Henry said, "to ask Mildred if she could get Nobel Grain's security department blueprints. The night Mildred spent with Nachtwey in the factory, she sent a hundred faxes to different locations to cause a little confusion, and then she faxed the blueprints to an untraceable receiver where the Railroad picked them up.

"Matt said that Nachtwey would be easier to reason with if he knew he was safe. Isn't everyone? And then, I think Matt just liked the idea of befuddling the authorities." Henry's voice lowered in admiration, so that I had to lean toward him. "It took him less than half a night to make a computer-aided design of Nobel Grain. I felt exuberant from the moment Matt suggested it. I wish I had thought of it." Henry's words tickled my face. "So there it is, a lone halfway house resident thwarting the law and a powerful, violent man. It's Matt's moment."

I remembered how, over twenty years before, Matt had told me that the FBI was sending him insidious messages through the *New York Times* chess page. I pictured the FBI agents now, tunneling through the earth like badgers, lost in their own computer-aided reality. When I thought of Matt decoying and tricking them all, I felt a black happiness, boundless and airy as night, twinkling and beautiful. And then I felt myself pulled into a vortex in which I sensed only the coolness of my own skin and the prickle of Henry's voice.

"Melanie?" Henry grasped my arm tightly. His hands were warm. I thought of the olive color of his skin under his shirt sleeves, under his collar. The moon glowed behind him like a tunnel opening.

"Henry, I can't even see you," I told him. But I could see him well enough in my mind: his oxblood eyes, his long limbs, his soot-black hair.

He leaned toward me, so that his cheekbone brushed mine. "We're two bodies in the night," he whispered into the whorls of my ear.

I laughed. "Try to imagine me," I told him. "I have violet eyes and long chestnut braids and a fish tail."

"No, I see your minky hair," he said. He kissed me, and when I kissed him back, I felt a drop inside me, one of those little deaths.

"Such long bones," Henry murmured. "Such long, bony bones."

He was already sinking into a unselfconscious swoon. I did not lose time: I reached for his zipper.

Henry counted my parts out loud: "This is how I used to lull myself to sleep as a boy," he said. "1: the numeral one looks like a fire hydrant. 2: a cobra standing on his tail." His hands felt like dark loam. "3: a bird flying sideways. 4: a boat sailing off."

I felt myself tumbling through blackness. Henry searched for the dark hard center of me that could blossom into fire. I pulled my dress over my head, and we met like two miners in blind darkness.

ON SUNDAY, JULY 4, and the bank holiday of July 5, Nachtwey made no broadcasts, as if in deference to the holidays or to emphasize the seriousness of his demand for proof that Nobel Grain's paychecks would be honored on Tuesday. The sun blazed yellow as a dandelion in the sky, and over the weekend, the crowds burgeoned. Police lines were moved far back in the event of an explosion on July 7.

At nine on Tuesday morning of July 6, five Nobel Grain employees exited the Skelter National Bank and told reporters that Nobel's salary checks had cleared. Later that morning the vice president of Nobel Grain's board of directors issued a short press release saying that by vote of the board, Frederick Nobel had been removed from his position and would be heading the company's northeastern division in New York. Under no circumstances would the board acknowledge Nachtwey's demands. Such a move had been planned, irrespective of the Nobel Crisis and the Steck Uprising.

The press greeted this report with predictable skepticism, since no mention had been made before of Nobel's anticipated transfer, and because Frederick Nobel's decision to counterclaim for divorce in Milwaukee suggested an intent to remain in Wisconsin for the long period a matrimonial case requires to wend its sluggish way through the legal process. Instead, it seemed more likely that the gathering publicity regarding Frederick Nobel's personal life had created a severe public relations crisis for Nobel Grain. The chairwoman of a prominent national women's rights organization had advocated a boycott of Nobel products, and Nobel stocks had been depressed since the company's destruction by explosives had become an imminent possibility. A secretary of one of the board members leaked to the media that "Over the several-day period the board was locked in with Mr. Nobel, it seems he proved a little trying," although she did not go into details.

Helen Nobel's lawyer announced that he would file for divorce in Chicago on her behalf, and that, with Frederick Nobel's departure from the state of Wisconsin, residency requirements would prevent him from continuing his action in Milwaukee. The attorney announced that "Judge Hochwald has now become moot, although his resignation remains necessary for the safety of all Milwaukee women and children."

Nachtwey smirked when this information was released on the July 6 morning news, as he sat in his black CEO's chair eating tinned pineapple. All that day he was eerily quiet, as if he had spent what he had to say, and now needed only to prepare mentally for what came next. On the evening following the announcement of the board's decision, Nachtwey adjusted the camera so that it centered on the front door of the factory. Then he disappeared inside and turned off the floodlights illuminating Nobel Grain's exterior.

On July 4 and 5, the FBI's rescue team had continued digging through Nobel Grain's back field, and cleared rubble from the piping that approached the second collapsed silo. On July 6, the ninth day of Nachtwey's siege, the agents finally surfaced in a hot gray rectangle of building. They shone their flashlights inside the windowless structure, and when they called out to one another, their voices thudded heavily, as if echoing off lead. They had found Nobel's bomb cellar, equipped with a full bar, CD player, and shortwave radio; a library of videotapes, which included everything from *Rocky III* to *The Story of O*; a thirty-year supply of canned meats and vegetables; an arsenal of weapons and ammunition; the original blueprints of the Nobel Grain Company, rolled in moisture-proof metal tubes; five hundred bags of flour fermenting with a heavy smell, and infested with weevils; a large wine cellar; and enough pharmaceuticals to last a dozen men a lifetime, and several medical manuals.

This private Hades did not appear in the Nobel Grain computer-aided design program. FBI documents later noted that there was evidence someone had tampered with the company's computer files "to create a three-dimensional world that corresponded with nothing in known reality." Thus, by the evening of July 6, no concrete progress had been made in FBI efforts to rescue Frederick Nobel.

AFTER OUR DEPARTURE from Spring Green, I stayed in Muskellunge at Henry's, watching CNN in the brown darkness of Henry's
bedroom while he and Matt worked at Pferd. I began then, in the hours
when the morning news became too repetitious, to enter the Railroad's
letters into a computer file that Henry christened *The Ratleer Chronicles*.
I arranged the letters by date or topic or degree of desperation, annotated them with footnotes on the state of the law, and recorded in an
encrypted history what I knew about the Railroad. I would work until
fresh evening news of Nachtwey lured me from the computer monitor
to the television's screen. In the evenings I would turn from Nachtwey
and see Henry watching me, his arms and legs brown, his middle a
glimmering olive suit of man draping from a tanned neckline. During
those nights we planned nonsense: We would turn the insect garden
into an enormous insect zoo with indoor terrariums. The halfway
house's residents would run it. Busloads of children would arrive in
winter to see Dr. Eatman's Insect Paradise.

"It will put Muskellunge on the map," Henry pronounced. "When
the FBI finally arrives here looking for Mildred, all they'll find is a jar
of bugs."

That week I tendered my letter refusing the federal judicial appointment. The excitement I felt at letting go of the musty, mildewed book
of the law, the exhilarating risk of watching it fall into a coal-dark abyss,
was almost more than I could bear. Henry, his long legs wrapped
around my middle, asked me if I would act as a lawyer for the Railroad,
but I wanted complete metamorphosis; I could not leap into a new life
with the old one still encasing me like a husk.

"Mildred might need a good lawyer soon," Henry said. "John wants
her to think about coming forward and taking her chances at criminal
prosecution. He thinks there will never be a safer time."

"Is that what Mildred wants?" I asked.

"She hasn't decided. She says she won't do anything until Helen
Nobel's custody suit is resolved. But the Railroad has contacted women's
rights groups asking them to lobby for amnesty for Mildred as well as
Helen. Mildred will need a lawyer's advice about seeking amnesty, and
then, she may need a defense attorney."

"I'll have to help in some other way," I said.

"Fine," Henry answered. "There are quite a few attorneys out there
who are willing to take this on for publicity."

"My father would have gobbled it up—" I began, but Henry cut me off.

"You can help *me* with something. I'm going to travel soon. Ottilie says you want to travel, and I have 21.6 vacation days due from Pferd. If they don't give them to me, I'm taking over the factory. I'll blow up the bottling machine, and then I'll drink all the Red Hoof and eat the Pferd Percherons, one by one."

I could not help but laugh, although I felt an edginess, a sympathetic anxiety for Nachtwey. At that time, four days after we returned to Muskellunge, he still had not emerged from Nobel Grain. CNN reporters kept a restless vigil in the company's wheatfield.

Frederick Nobel would not be rescued until two days later, on July 9. On that day Richard Sparrow made a second run down the road from the wheatfield to the Nobel factory. When he came to Nachtwey's black CEO chair, Sparrow stopped, and picked up a letter. The letter, later aired repeatedly on the news, said:

WARNING FROM CLIFF NACHTWEY:
I will be watching you all.

Apparently, Nachtwey had slipped away in the dead of night as early as July 6, perhaps through a passageway revealed only in the original blueprints. After the letter fell into Sparrow's hands, a special bomb squad, comprised of a half-dozen men, entered the Nobel factory and dismantled the metal box on the boardroom door, which they found empty.

A second bomb squad descended on Nachtwey's white pickup and revealed that the refrigerator-sized box labeled TRUCK BOMB contained nothing but one-hundred-pound sacks of flour: in a press statement, the FBI labeled this a "decoy bomb" or "hoax bomb." The newspapers enjoyed this, and speculated that even the bomb attached to the boardroom door had been imaginary from the beginning. I pictured Mildred doubled over with laughter, and wondered if Nachtwey had confided during their meeting that he had decided not to tempt himself with the potential for such destructive violence. Or perhaps there really had been an active bomb on the boardroom door, and Mildred had persuaded Nachtwey to take it with him when he departed, to destroy evidence hazardous to him and possibly to the Railroad. The bombs in the silos had been real enough.

After examining the flour in Nachtwey's truck, the agents led Frederick Nobel through the factory's front gates: He looked gray and pasty and angry.

By the third week in July popular and media support for Helen Nobel had swelled to such a degree that the company's board of directors opposed pressing criminal charges against her for any complicity she may have had in engineering Nobel's false arrest. In addition, it was said that the board pressured Nobel unsuccessfully to withdraw his Milwaukee divorce action. Despite Helen Nobel's attorney's strategy of filing for divorce in Illinois, Judge Hochwald had refused to relinquish the case, proclaiming that "Venue lies where parties reside at the initiation of an action, and that's in Hochwald's territory." This would begin a jurisdictional conflict between the Wisconsin and Illinois courts that would endure another two years before its resolution by the federal judiciary.

Helen Nobel's attorney declared that if she did not prevail in transferring venue to Chicago, the Milwaukee court would hold the first custody proceeding in Wisconsin history in which a parent petitioning for relief was in absentia: Helen Nobel would remain hidden while a string of witnesses testified to Frederick Nobel's violence. This was necessary because "Judge Hochwald's lack of common sense would render Helen Nobel's personal appearance in his court too perilous." She would not surface until her right to custody was secure, or until the state of Wisconsin passed its own Stecking law, or until Judge Hochwald left the bench. While this threat remained in the air, a group of matrimonial attorneys and their clients who had appeared in the past before Hochwald met, compared notes, and drew up a list of grievances against him and a petition for his impeachment. By late 1993, an amnesty movement on behalf of Mildred and the Railroad's users had gained wide popularity. Mildred remained underground while Helen Nobel's case continued and the amnesty movement gathered broader backing.

My active role in the Railroad during those early years began four days after Nachtwey's disappearance, when Ottilie came to Henry's carrying a pile of documents.

"Melanie?" she asked, slipping through the front door, and waiting while I closed the front of my pajamas. They were Henry's, pale green with orange stripes. "You need to take Helen's daughter out of the country. Helen will have to leave separately with Henry, because someone will be more likely to recognize her if she and her daughter travel together. They're not safe in the United States until Helen's right to custody is established."

Ottilie pulled three passports from an envelope and handed them to me. "You've never applied for a passport before—they had no record of a Melanie Ratleer."

I examined the passports. The first belonged to "Melanie Ratleer," and contained a cropped version of a photograph I had sent Ottilie two years before. The second was identical, except that beside my face, the name "Melanie Klonecki" appeared. The third passport held a child's photograph: Helen Nobel's daughter, now called "Mary Klonecki."

"You need to travel on the Melanie Klonecki passport, as the girl's mother," Ottilie said. "Later that passport will be altered and your picture replaced with Helen's. You can return to the United States as Melanie Ratleer. John will have the Ratleer passport stamped with a Brazilian entry visa for you." Ottilie smiled and added, "You could stay there and travel, you know. It would give you time to think about your decision to give up legal work. If you want, when you get back, you can help John out at the co-op until you find something else." I imagined moving into the women's halfway house with Sophie; I would let my mind go helter-skelter and spend my days planting summer squash and kale. "You're always welcome to stay with us," Ottilie said, "unless of course, you remain at Henry's."

My own face looked back at me from my two passports with a single repeated expression, as if giving me an extra chance to claim myself. And underneath, dressed in a tartan jumper, Helen's daughter looked up, her dark eyes old in her chiseled, oval face, her straight eyebrows level, her barrette pinned carefully on her dark hair.

IN EARLY EVENING on July 17 John waited for me beside the church, on the edge of the garden. Behind him dogbane beetles were everywhere, shimmering like sapphires on the silver-green leaves. John led me into Muskellunge Unitarian, and we ascended the stairs to the church attic. Every step of our passage seemed to increase the temperature by ten degrees, as if hell had been relocated in the heavens.

"Once Mildred's traced to Muskellunge," John said, "we won't be able to use the church any longer as a hideaway. But there are other churches and synagogues."

A startling blast of air-conditioned cold greeted us as John opened the attic door. In the upstairs room the air was dark and cool, brown umber. A child with brown hair sat on two stacked suitcases. When we entered, she cried out and ran into an adjoining room. In a moment, she emerged, clinging to the arm of a middle-aged woman. I barely recognized the woman: She wore a stylish dress and had bangles on her arms, and a long black braid.

"Helen," John said, "we should leave now." The girl, small for her age, peered at me, from that dark-eyed face. "Helen, this is Melanie, my common-law stepdaughter." John laughed. His instructions revealed that as a protective measure, the Railroad gave no detailed information to its passengers until the final hour: "Melanie will drive you to St. Louis, Helen. O'Hare might be watched too closely. From there, Melanie will drive on to Dallas with your daughter. Someone will meet you on the other end and take you to the location where you'll rejoin Melanie. I'm sorry we have to separate you and your daughter even for a few hours, but it's safer this way."

John opened a thermos and tilted it toward me. I looked into its mouth: A small vial, the color of amber and packed in ice, rested in the mirrored chamber. "There's antidote for hornet stings in here," John said. "The dosages are written on the prescription, and the prescription is in your name—if Nobel had any sense, he'd have airport officials looking for a little girl with allergy medicine for stings. Don't forget to give the thermos to Helen when you meet up with her in São Paulo." He sealed the thermos and placed it in my hand.

John ushered us downstairs to where a rented van waited behind the church. The voices of locusts shrilled in concert from the tree branches above us. Henry sat in the van's front passenger seat, almost as unrecognizable as Helen: He wore the tailored suit of an American businessman and a gold wristwatch. When Helen and her daughter were settled in the back of the van, John told me, "Drive in four-hour shifts, well within the speed limit. Don't stop anywhere except for the safehouses, and limit as much of your driving as possible to after dark. When you get to St. Louis, Helen and Henry should catch a taxi downtown, and go on without you to the airport. When you arrive in Dallas, leave the van in the terminal's parking lot. Your contact in São Paulo will identify herself by showing you this." I leaned forward to see the sign: it was a private joke that made me smile—a Pferd beer bottlecap, black with a red horse head.

I steered the Lincoln onto the road, turned on the van's radio, and took us out of Muskellunge toward a turbulent sky. Blackbirds flocked over yellow fields, and the road reached to the edge of the flat world. I rejoiced that this was the end of my life as I had lived it. My letter of resignation was somewhere between Wisconsin and Washington: I had given as my reason, "serious health problems related to the cancer that afflicted me in my early adulthood." An old lie.

Henry and I had plotted thousands of miles of travel. Ben had recommended the Iguaçú water falls in the south, more immense than Niagara's, and the interior's swamplands where lily pads with ten-foot diameters scattered like planets across boundless dark water, and a red-clay road that ran to a small stucco house in which eight Brazilian women lived in hiding together, exchanging stories and ideas as outrageous as our own. After that, I contemplated nothing—just a vastness, spreading out before me with limitless possibilities. I would dedicate myself to the underground, I would turn into a minky animal and hole up with Henry, I would never marry, I would lead school tours through Dr. Eatman's Insect Paradise by day, and write *The Ratleer Chronicles* at night. I would play poker until early morning with Mildred and other escaped women in unlikely cities.

The radio was full of news of her. After the police and reporters and spectators dispersed, an uncaught person, described as a "derelict," returned in the dead of night to Nobel Grain's wheatfield where the crowds had once gathered. The derelict set the field on fire from three directions and slipped away. The flames crackled and swirled and crested. They sank deep into the soil so that for a while, the wheat knew the sensuality of the fire, like a woman combing her hair with it. The wheat felt what it was to burn fervently, to know an anger that turned into exhilaration and joy. The field rose in wave after wave of fire, swaying between its horizons, and that flat land lit up, orange at the bottom like a flaming sea, and black as a sea bottom above, a mirror universe, in which silences were uttered and noises hushed, the published biographies erased and all the names of the lost drowned revealed. The fire multiplied through the wheat, covering everything, as the heartland's oceans once must have.

Paula Sharp is the author of *Lost in Jersey City*, a New York Times Book Review Notable Book of 1993; *The Woman Who Was Not All There*, a Book-of-the-Month Club selection and winner of the Quality Paperback Book Club New Voice Award; and the critically acclaimed short story collection, *The Imposter*, which received the Wisconsin Library Association Banta Award. She is a translator of Latin American contemporary fiction, including Antonio Skármeta's novel, *The Insurrection*. Her short stories have been anthologized in *New Stories from the South: the Year's Best*, and she has received the New Jersey State Council Distinguished Artist Award, and a National Endowment for the Arts fellowship. A graduate of Columbia University Law School, she practices in New York.